NANCY BILYEAU, a Michigan native, has worked as an editor on the staffs of *InStyle*, *Rolling Stone*, and *Good Housekeeping*. Passionate about history and art, she wrote an award-winning trilogy set in Tudor England before creating a heroine, Genevieve Planché, who holds personal significance. Nancy is descended from a Huguenot settler who came to America in 1661 and draws on her fascination with French Protestant refugees when writing the character of Genevieve Planché, a Huguenot artist. Today Nancy lives in upstate New York with her husband and two children.

PRAISE FOR NANCY BILYEAU'S *THE BLUE*:

'Nancy Bilyeau's passion for history infuses her books' – *Alison Weir*

'Fascinating' – *Ian Rankin*

'Definitely a winner!' – *Kate Quinn*

PRAISE FOR NANCY BILYEAU'S *DREAMLAND*:

'Achingly believable' – *Publishers Weekly*

'Fast paced, engrossing' – *Library Journal*

Also by Nancy Bilyeau

The Blue
Dreamland
The Crown
The Chalice
The Tapestry
The Ghost of Madison Avenue

THE

FUGITIVE

COLOURS

A Genevieve Planché Novel

NANCY BILYEAU

LUME BOOKS

LUME BOOKS

Published in 2022 by Lume Books

ISBN 978-1-83901-466-6

Typeset using Atomik ePublisher from Easypress Technologies

www.lumebooks.co.uk

To the Woodstock Byrdcliffe Guild

Prologue

"Long live the knife!"

It's been at least an hour since I was dragged through Covent Garden and pushed into this long, dark room in the magistrate's courthouse, but the chanting on the street has not died down. The crowd is still enraptured by the singing of Giovanni Manzouli, the Italian castrato. It's bitterly cold on Bow Street, and a swelling army of thieves and lawless creatures prowls the darkest shadows, hungry for spoils. Yet, this group of operagoers simply refuses to disperse long after the curtain descended. I don't have the slightest idea what Manzouli sounded like, what thrilling notes he reached tonight. At the same time that he was acting out a story of love and hate on the stage of the Theatre Royal, I found myself in a far different type of establishment in Covent Garden, standing in a room filled with mahogany furniture, gleaming oil portraits and gold-and-pink wallpaper matching the colours of the porcelain vase.

1

And sitting behind that exquisite Chippendale desk was a dead man, a knife driven deep into the lapel of his embroidered coat. It was the end to a real story of hate – and only the most twisted and empty kinds of love.

The knife in that expensive coat was mine, and I told them as much. That's why I am here, in the courthouse up the street from the opera house, slumped on a bench, a rough blanket flung around my shoulders.

A weak fire hisses. Sitting on this hard bench, I can smell the lingering odours of those who waited their turn at justice today: damp wool clothing and dirt-caked boots and sour winter sweat. A whiff of mutton from someone's dinner turns my stomach. The only other person in the room at present is the implacable young man who brought me here and stands guard. I know the others will follow soon with their questions. I must decide what to tell them, how much to admit to and how much to conceal.

I haven't killed anyone, I want to scream. More than anything, I long to be home in Spitalfields. My family, my friends, are they asleep now? If it goes badly for me in the next few hours, my loved ones will wake to find me missing. Yet every time I form a rational sentence, I hear, "Long live the knife," the cry honouring the sacrifice of the castrato. It reaches through the wall in dreadful mockery, and my explanation dissolves.

Is that the key turning to the door onto Bow Street? My throat closes in panic. I don't know what to say yet. I know I must fight as hard as I've ever fought in my life to save myself. It's just that there are so many secrets to protect...

2

One Month Earlier

Chapter One

It might come as a surprise to learn that a conversation about the shade of a particular flower that grows on an island four thousand miles away could bring work to a halt in Spitalfields on a cold October morning.

But such is the delicate state of my business, a silk design workshop that I run from the third floor of my Fournier Street house, that when the clock chimes nine, the musical notes are drowned out by an argument between the two young artists I employ. They growl at each other as if they were a pair of truculent terriers, and as usual, I can't seem to find the words to calm them.

"Jean, you are so easy to predict," says Caroline Mowbray, my head artist, clutching her paintbrush so tightly, her fingertips whiten. "But tell me, why is it this important to dim a scarlet to dullness?"

My assistant artist, Jean Orgier, shakes his head. "You are the predictable one, set on indulging yourself when you know it's the customer to be pleased, not yourself."

I have to put an end to this, or I'll never finish the new designs for delivery to Monsieur Nicolas Carteret in two days' time.

"Come now," I say, using the firm-but-fair tone of voice I've cultivated for exactly these moments. "Absolutely no need to quarrel. Let's examine the book. It always helps to return to the source."

To reach this book, I ease past our work table, dotted with paintbrushes, specially ordered grid paper, dishes of water and the different colour cakes. Spread open on the table is the chart created by naturalist Richard Waller that displays all one hundred and nineteen known colours. It's difficult to match some of them in watercolour, but I always urge Caroline and Jean to try.

On the bookshelf, beside the French and English pattern books to be found in every design shop, stands a slim, unbound volume obtained for me by none other than my husband, Thomas Sturbridge. He secured it from a friend who is a fellow at the Royal Society. *The Flora and Fauna of Le Grenade* offers twenty detailed colour plates of its native flowers. When England won the West Indies isle of Le Grenade from France in the peace treaty, we became privy to its exotic delights. Resources such as this volume give my workshop an advantage over competitors, who copy designs from boring pattern books or must haunt London's gardens and greenhouses for ideas.

With a flourish, I open the volume to the intended page, propping it on the table as I nudge the candle closer. Our painting table is set perhaps five feet from a wide lattice window facing Fournier Street in the middle of Spitalfields, but the sun, as usual, sulks behind low-hanging greyish-brown clouds. There is not enough natural light. Our artistic efforts demand candles all day long.

The particular flower we scrutinise takes up a whole page. We ignore its tiny Latin name. It doesn't matter what it is, only how it looks, and such a beauty. Its lush scarlet petals burst from a black pistil and hang down in a gorgeous carousel of long spikes. Our challenge is capturing the character of the flower in a design pattern that can be woven into silk fabric, intended for the gown of a customer of discriminating taste. This may sound like a speculative, even fanciful, idea for a business. But be assured, if there's one thing to count on in 1764, it's that there are many, many wealthy English women who are mad for gowns of flowered silk.

My eyes drift from the flower to the young faces studying the page with near frightening intensity. My irritation melts. How dedicated they are, my two protégés. It's all that unites them, for they are such opposites.

Jean is the younger at twenty-one, his face round, his lips rosy, his brown eyes fringed with long lashes. One might say he has the look of an innocent boy were it not for the jagged scar running down the left side of his face. Jean was injured while rioting last spring, aflame with ideas of liberty. Just the sort of bellowed ideas sure to bring a constable's truncheon down on his skull. Or perhaps, it was a blow from a drunk jostled on the street. Jean himself doesn't know. His brothers discovered him senseless and carried him to the hospital.

As for Caroline, she'd no sooner take to the street to cry for freedom than storm a stage to play Polly Peachum. Art is her passion, her sole passion so far as I know. Twenty-three years of age, she is a woman with no family, no husband. While Jean's garments are coffee-stained and reeking of tobacco, Caroline is immaculately dressed under her work smock. Tall and slender, she has a pale complexion. Her thin lips press together as if holding in a storm. Only her green eyes betray what she's feeling, and at present, they meet mine with puzzlement.

"You have a question, Caroline?"

"Mrs. Sturbridge, you have often said you support free discussion of our designs, that we should never feel pressed to keep silent."

"Very true," I say.

What rich irony.

I was once an eager protégée, employed in the workshop of

Spitalfields' leading silk designer, Ana Maria Garthwaite. In the most obvious way, I have modelled my little business on hers. But I've also copied the standards of the workshop at Derby Porcelain Factory, where I worked for nearly six months. The head of the porcelain painters, a capable Quaker named Joshua Holcroft, earned my respect. However, I did chafe against his rule of silence. That could never be the way I would rule a workshop, I'd vowed. Art requires an open airing of ideas.

Now, much too late, I see the wisdom in Mr. Holcroft's rule.

I say, "This flower is certainly unique enough to be a huge success on silk. It's a matter of how we distil its special quality to the medium of fabric and—"

"But the colour is what makes it special," Caroline interrupts. "Without that, it's just like any other flower."

"Oh, really?" counters Jean. "The shape of the petals, the size of the petals? It's different in a dozen ways."

"But why ignore such a rich, splendid red?" asks Caroline, her voice rising again. "It's compelling!"

Jean folds his arms and says, "Because it will do nothing but jar the eye if it were woven into silk in a repeating pattern. Yes – of course – the shade is beautiful, but it's not the correct red for a rich Mayfair wife, it's not correct for a Virginia colonist's wife, either."

I say, "Slightly muted shades may be the very latest fashion, Jean, but remember, it's the originality of our colour choices that sets us apart. I believe there may be a market for a vivid red."

"In a brothel, perhaps?" jokes Jean. "It would nicely suit some well-fixed harlots."

"Now, Jean, that's enough of that," I say sharply.

"*No.*" Caroline rises from her stool, so distressed, she cannot say another word.

"Enough of this!" I declare. "I'm going downstairs for tea. During this time, I don't want to hear a word from either of you – and trust me, if one is uttered, I will be close by enough to know about it."

I march to the door, pausing to look over my shoulder and deliver a stare meant as the severest reproof. Caroline doesn't even notice because she's staring out the window. The foul air outside is a match for her mood.

As for Jean, slouched on his stool, he says, completely unintimidated, "But, Mrs. Sturbridge, what is it that *you* want?"

My hand on the doorknob, I say, "When I return, we will discuss it."

I descend the stairs, my head throbbing. I am equal parts angry with Caroline and Jean and with myself for such weakness as a workshop mistress. What do I want? A quiet, well-ordered room, occupied by artists committed to keeping to schedule. If we were to lose Monsieur Carteret's business, within a month, I'd be pressed to pay Jean's and Caroline's wages *and* the butcher bill. Oh, but how I loathe thinking about money in the morning. It is bad enough that such worries robbed me of a restful sleep last night.

My steps quicken. This escape from workshop squabbling will not only fortify me with tea and sugar but also give me a few minutes with Pierre. Where is he? I don't hear my son chattering within the second-floor room we share. He must be downstairs, watched over by Sophie, our maid. He'd be playing with toys in the parlour now.

Once I reach the first floor of the townhouse, the sweet, high voice of my three-year-old meets me, but faintly. Not coming from the sitting room but from the ground floor, the kitchen, which is, happily, where I intend to take tea.

How can I blame Pierre for liking it here? I was drawn to the kitchen when I was a child. It was and is the domain of Daphne, our housekeeper, and exudes the spirit of her lost home in the South of France.

9

In this tiny corner of Spitalfields, the district of Huguenot emigres that hugs the east end of damp, murky London, she re-creates a kitchen of the dry and sunny Languedoc. There's nothing as comforting as one of her biscuit pastries, soaked with blackberry jam.

"Mama!" shouts Pierre. I scoop up my child, named for my beloved grandfather, and laugh at the force of his arms flung around my neck.

He's getting so strong.

I plant a noisy kiss on Pierre's cheek and luxuriate in the mop of his silky red hair.

"I could hear her causing you trouble all the way down here – I expected you'd be stopping for a bit, Madame Genevieve," says Daphne, shaking flour from a sack into a large wooden bowl. Her tongue could not easily take on "Mrs. Sturbridge", so we'd settled on this. "A cup of chocolate?"

Ah, she never will change.

"You know it's tea I want, Daphne."

"*Comme vous voulez.*"

My housekeeper is a woman of such stubborn preferences. Tea was not popular in the Languedoc. And here, among the Huguenots, it wasn't a common choice when I was a child, either. I faintly remember my grandfather calling for the "Chinese drink" for his ailments. But just about everyone drinks it these days. It is expensive. But without my Bohea black tea and sugar, I'd not be equal to the day.

I say mildly, "You know, Jean was causing me just as much trouble as Caroline." Daphne shrugs. She has never taken to Caroline. I assume it's because Jean, springing from the enormous Orgier family, first among Huguenots, would earn her trust over English Caroline without his even trying.

Pierre returns to pushing his toy across the floor under Daphne's table. It has wheels, but I can barely make out its shape, as the kitchen, with a single narrow window, is a bit dim. My son shouldn't play here all morning.

"Where is Sophie?" I ask.

Daphne is silent for a bit, her mouth twisting.

"Sophie is not here – she was feeling unwell yesterday," Daphne finally says. "George helped her home."

"Again?"

Yes, that sounds unkind. But Sophie is often ailing. And George Harris, our manservant and her husband of a year, must see to her when illness strikes. Which means they are within their home in Whitechapel rather than here, in my home, performing the duties for which I pay their wages.

Thinking back, I realise that Sophie and George most likely left before sunset yesterday, and I hadn't even noticed. I took some pudding for supper upstairs with Pierre and then, while he played on the bed, I went over the monthly household accounts, which is akin to having a tooth pulled.

"I hope Sophie recovers and we see them here soon," I murmur, and Daphne nods, relieved that no fury will descend on the couple she adores.

Anyone not privy to the history of my household might judge me London's most pitiful dupe, a weaker mistress to the servants downstairs than I am to my artist protégés upstairs. But it all traces back to a pledge I made to my grandfather two years ago, the day before he died.

His voice a whisper, Grandfather asked me to take care of Daphne for the rest of her life. Of course I said yes. I was – and am – devoted to Daphne. What's important to know is how different she is from the rest of the Huguenots, families bound together by one, two, even three generations of English exile. Daphne fled French persecution when she was older than thirty. The severe beatings in a French prison have left her with a permanent limp, and now that she is approaching sixty, her arms are strong, but she cannot climb stairs. This made hiring another maid necessary. We found Sophie, a meek young woman who somehow managed to marry George within three months. George's truckle bed and tiny alcove weren't fit for a married couple, thus the renting of two rooms in Whitechapel, thanks to an increase in wages I felt I had no choice but to grant. And so, here we all are.

Daphne is busy heating the water and measuring black tea leaves, but knowing her as I do, I can tell she is troubled about something besides Sophie's health.

I put my hand on her shoulder. "What is amiss?"

"The post came yesterday afternoon, you do know that, Madame Genevieve? George gave you the letters? I think there were two."

My stomach lurches.

"George gave me nothing."

"That was wrong of him." Daphne winces. "But he was so worried about his little wife, poor man."

I search the sitting room and the kitchen, even my bedroom, but can find no letters. George never comes up to the workshop, but he does trudge up and down from cellar to kitchen, and it's there, in the cellar, sticking out from under a dirty sack of onions, that I spot the corner of a letter.

Blast you, George.

I am going to have a serious talk with my married servants – I *will* put a little fear into these two – but first, I must attend to the letters. I brush off the onion dust. Even in the dank semi-darkness of the cellar, I detect that they are both of heavy paper, bearing seals. Just holding the letters, feeling their weight in my fingers, sends a cold dread through my veins. What important and possibly urgent messages have I missed?

In the light of the sitting room, I examine them. The light-grey letter is folded with a black seal I don't recognise, just the initials "*JR*", but the cream-coloured letter bears a burgundy seal imprinted with the name "*Carteret*".

I break the seal, read the letter and, within seconds, I'm charging up the stairs, shouting over my shoulder to forget about tea.

"Caroline – Jean – I have correspondence from Monsieur Carteret. He expects the book of new designs today and no later than noon," I say, gasping for want of breath.

"But we're not finished," protests Caroline. "It was expected in two days' time, Thursday, not today. We have his order document."

Jean shakes his head. "Everyone knows Nicolas Carteret won't be held to any original order document, even if it came from his own quill, should he change his mind. If he wants the work today, he must have it or else…"

"Or else he will cancel all future commissions," I say flatly.

Jean nods. He is familiar with the character of Monsieur Carteret. The two men are deeply opposed on politics, and the master weaver tolerates Jean – just barely – because Carteret's mother is an Orgier.

A strange silence fills the room. It's as if the two of them hold their breath while waiting to hear my decision. More and more, I feel this burden, the expectation that I will come up with the wisest solution to any problem.

I say, "We will prepare the designs that are finished already – the red flower will wait for the next order or another client. He won't miss what he doesn't know about."

"But it's the most beautiful plant on the island," laments Caroline. "It's the *piece de resistance*."

"I know – it's a shame, but we haven't a choice. Help me with the book bindings, Caroline."

"Yes, Mrs. Sturbridge."

Thankfully, she ceases arguing and helps me insert pages into the book.

Jean asks, "What's the import of this other letter?"

"Heaven knows, I haven't opened it. I don't know who sent it. Would you mind doing so, Jean? You might need a knife for the seal."

I am concentrating on writing notations on the dimensions of our watercolour rendering of a spiky, light-green plant when I hear Jean's whisper.

"*Merde.*"

Jean, who I know well is no angel, rarely curses in the workshop. For him to slip, it means he has been badly jolted.

"What does the letter say?" I ask, my stomach churning.

Blinking and half-smiling, he says, "Joshua Reynolds invites you to his home for an evening affair."

Caroline snaps, "That's not funny, Jean. We are rushed for time."

"I'm not joking."

I put out my hand for the letter.

"*The presence of Mr. and Mrs. Thomas Sturbridge is requested on the 6th of November at the home of Mr. Joshua Reynolds, Number Forty-Seven Leicester Fields, at the hour of seven o'clock to commemorate the life of the sadly departed Mr. William Hogarth alongside those who most greatly respected his art and genius. Respectfully, Mr. Joshua Reynolds.*"

Caroline, who has read the letter alongside me, whispers, "Joshua Reynolds? The leading artist in all of England… He is sending for you? He knows who you are, Mrs. Sturbridge?"

"Yes," I say. "He does."

I put the letter down on the table, gently, carefully, as if I were handling a fanged snake.

"We don't have much time left," I announce. "If this design book doesn't find its way to White Lion Street within the next hour, we will be in danger of losing business forever."

"But what about the evening at Joshua Reynolds' home?" asks Jean. "What an opportunity! You will accept his invitation, won't you?"

A sound fills the workshop, something harsh and ugly.

It is a laugh – my laugh.

"No, Jean. No. I don't intend to make the same mistake twice."

Chapter Two

I shouldn't have said so much.

I feel as if I lead two lives. One is that of a Huguenot painter, raised by her grandfather, married to a loving husband and blessed with a child, now endeavouring to run a silk design business. Then there is the other life, kept carefully hidden from everyone in Spitalfields, known only by a few people on this earth, principally my husband. It's a shadow life, one that was pushed firmly into the past when Thomas and I returned to England more than three years ago. And it must stay in the past.

To Caroline and Jean, a letter from Joshua Reynolds is akin to a royal summons from our new king, young George III. Reynolds is the most sought-after portrait painter in England, using his superb technique to capture the likenesses of an array of subjects, from princes and admirals to debutantes and actresses. Who will he paint next? That's the question. The newspapers carry stories offering glimpses into his world: the exhibitions, the lectures, the private clubs, the parties. There are few in London who would not leap at the chance to become part of his circle.

My fierce refusal of just such an offer silences Jean and Caroline.

They help assemble the book of designs for Monsieur Carteret. I've won a reprieve from their questions about Reynolds, but knowing the natural curiosity of my two artists, it won't last long. For my own part, I struggle to put the invitation out of my mind, but it torments me like a scab to be picked. Why would the celebrated Joshua Reynolds single me out – me and my husband, Thomas – for an evening at his home paying tribute to Hogarth? Reynolds and I met on one occasion six years ago, and I made anything but a good impression. How does he know I am married and where I live?

The old feeling is back: frustration over being blocked from pursuing my dream of becoming a true artist and resentment toward those who refused to help solely because I am a woman. The last thing I need is to plunge back into that angry turmoil. There is no possibility of Joshua Reynolds suddenly deciding to help me. To believe anything other than that is half-witted.

I force myself to the task at hand, avoiding the sidelong glances of Jean and Caroline. When we've finished the book of designs, I see the time is just past eleven. I hurry downstairs to give the delivery to George. A brisk walk to White Lion Street is well within his capability.

But George is still missing.

"Sophie must be ill indeed," says Daphne, wringing her bony hands. "If only he would send word, some message to us."

"Who is there to bring a message but George himself?" I snap.

I stalk to the parlour to find my cloak.

"You shouldn't walk across Spitalfields without someone to protect you, Madame Genevieve," says Daphne.

"Well, George isn't here, and Jean cannot set foot in Carteret's home. That *would* be a disaster. And I need Jean at the work table."

"Please wait a few minutes more for George."

Daphne follows me to the front of the house. Her limp is very bad. Behind her, I spot Pierre, a smile dawning because he thinks today is shaping up into one of our adventures outside the house.

As he scrambles up the corridor, Pierre reminds me so much of his father. A pair of inquisitive eyes sparkling beneath a mop of red hair. I miss Thomas terribly, his work has kept him from us for two months now.

My steps falter. Couldn't I stay home, drink that cup of tea, chat with Daphne, play with my son?

With a hard shove, I push up the latch on the door.

No one, absolutely no one, shall prevent me from delivering the book by the noon hour.

On Fournier Street, it's colder than the last time I was out. I take a few steps. My eyes sting, and an itch crawls up my throat. A sulphurous cloud, the colour of ash, has enveloped me. The smoky air of London is like an old, grim companion, but this morning is particularly ominous. Not only is the sun invisible, I can't even see the details on the row of townhouses across the narrow street. The solid red brick buildings are but an outline through the sea-coal haze.

Turning onto the wider Brick Lane, I can at least make out the two most imposing buildings of Spitalfields: Christ Church with its two-hundred-foot-tall, graceful spire and, squatting off Brick Lane like a small city, the Black Eagle Brewery.

There are plenty of carriages and carts rumbling along the streets and a fair number of people on foot, though their presence doesn't reassure me. I tighten my grip on the book. No thief in his right mind is after watercolour flowers, but these days, the footpads seize anything. The rich grow richer now that the war is over. Those lurking in the shadows of the city intend to share in the prosperity.

I've heard that the miscreants drag their victims off well-travelled streets to narrow, twisting, rubbish-strewn lanes, cracking open the heads of the luckless after stealing their goods.

I try not to stare with suspicion at the passers-by on the street. Daphne is right. I see men, or women accompanied by men. I'm the only woman walking alone.

A quote from Voltaire, unbidden, seems all too fitting: "*I don't know where I am going, but I am on my way.*"

I fight down the impulse to break into a fast trot. That, too, would bring attention. As I pass, a tavern-keeper throws open the front doors, pausing to leer at me. Not only am I vulnerable to theft out here but likely to be confused with a harlot.

This all strikes me as wrong. Shouldn't England winning the long war make people's lives better? The streets of Spitalfields seem more dangerous than my memory of what they were like before the war with France began. Desperation hangs in the air as heavy as the smoky mantle.

The wretched of London. They were once fodder for the art of William Hogarth, who sought to bring attention to the cruelties of society. Loveless marriages arranged for financial gain, lives ruined by a dependence on gin, innocent girls tricked into becoming prostitutes. He forced everyone to face it.

I didn't need Reynolds' invitation to deliver the news of Hogarth's death. I had read about it in the newspaper a few days ago. For hours, I had been at war with myself, sadness over the loss of a great man fighting with anger and shame over his rejection. Hogarth had refused to consider taking me on as an apprentice, and he had done so within the hearing of Joshua Reynolds. I was nothing but an embarrassment, at best a curiosity, the female pleading to be one of them. I managed to conquer the pain associated with those memories and take comfort in my family and my business. Reynolds' letter arriving today brings it all up again.

A large figure looms, blocking my path.

I freeze, my arms wrapped tightly around the book. I won't give it up without a fight, nor do I intend to be dragged off to some twisting lane. If it's my fate to have my head cracked open, so be it, but I refuse to be flung onto rubbish.

"Mrs. Sturbridge, isn't it? What brings you out alone?"

My shoulders sag with relief. Before me is the warden of the district, assistant to the constable, or is it the beadle? I don't remember the man's name, but his trademark heavy coat and thick stick are welcome sights indeed.

"I have urgent business on White Lion Street."

"I can take you as far as the market, ma'am."

We walk together, the warden nodding or barking greetings to those he recognises. Some are coming back from the market. That, too, is a place not as enjoyable as it used to be, what with food prices steadily rising.

After this length of time in the warden's company, I realise that his imposing size is due to a mountain of fat. And his breath reeks of ale. How valuable would he be in a fight with hardened thieves?

When I reach White Lion Street, I say, "I can see the Carteret house from here. I shall be fine, thank you. There are other people about."

The warden scowls at me and bangs his stick against the corner of the nearest smoke-blackened wall.

"Remember. It's not the ones in front of you to fear, Mrs. Sturbridge. It's the people you don't see. Until it is too late."

With this cheering bit of wisdom, the warden lumbers off, and I continue on to my destination, an imposing brick townhouse that stretches five windows wide and five storeys high.

Everyone knows the master weavers of Spitalfields – ambitious, proud, stiff-necked and righteous men of the Protestant faith. Within this group, Nicolas Carteret is the one the others keep watch over. It's not because of his demanding nature and exacting standards, which are the reasons we scrambled to meet his deadline. Huguenots are famously hard-headed business people; no one would ever condemn a master weaver for that. Nicolas Carteret has a reputation for going his own way, and for that reason, I deduce he is not completely trusted by his peers. He follows independent ideas. For instance, he maintains his weavers – some fifty journeymen and apprentices – in a separate factory, rather than in the upper floors of his house, as do the other masters. I've only spoken to him at his factory, but the place is on a bleaker street. I decided from the beginning to drop off my book at his house, which lies under the protective shadow of Christ Church.

My knock on the front door brings a bearded manservant who listens gravely to my explanation, my words tumbling out. What must he think of this nervous female showing up without an appointment or card to offer?

After conferring with unseen people deeper within the house, the manservant declines to take the book I'm trying to hand to him but gestures for me to step inside. Monsieur Carteret wishes to speak with me. He is engaged at the moment, however. The manservant leads me up a grand set of stairs to a small room to wait.

I take a seat, feeling far from comfortable. I am not sure how best to explain bringing the book personally. I don't think it will do me any good in his eyes to admit I own no carriage nor had time to hire one, that I have come on foot because my manservant is missing. For the first time, I wonder if he will think I have shown up to angle for more commissions. Although, would that be such a bad thing to do? We would benefit from a steadier flow of work.

The room where I sit is furnished in quiet good taste – a side table and chairs made of walnut with a fine fringed carpet covering half the floor. I wonder if Madame Carteret, who I've met only twice, will make an appearance. But there's no sign of her or the children, only the murmur of men's voices from the other side of the door.

I notice something strange about a framed print. At first, I think it merely shows a plaza filled with people. But closer scrutiny reveals the plaza overflows with people in Renaissance dress being stabbed, throttled and beaten by men dressed as soldiers. It's not just men but women and children who are being brutally killed. This could only be the St. Bartholomew's Day Massacre.

The massacre is something all Huguenots think about their entire lives – the day that the Catholics murdered twenty-five thousand Protestants. It was a turning point for us, two hundred years ago. Afterward, many more terrible things were done to the Huguenots, persecutions that spurred us to flee France. We sought refuge in such large numbers in England that they created a word to describe us: *refugee*.

Still, it's not the sort of turning point that most of us would want to frame for a wall.

The sound of men in conversation rumbles on. I can't distinguish any words. I'm fairly sure there are just two of them. One voice is low and calm, the other man's is pitched higher and growing less calm.

"You'll regret it. You'll see. Don't expect a damn thing from us then!"

The higher-pitched voice has exploded.

A door in the far wall flies open, and a man appears, filling the frame like a conjured dark cloud before hurtling through the room. In those seconds, I take in the appearance of someone unlike any being I've seen in Spitalfields. He's unusually tall, well over six feet, and broad-shouldered. He's dressed completely in black, his coat so

22

filthy with spilt food or drink (or heaven knows what) that the material gleams on those patches. His face is long with a knobby chin, and his thick, dark hair is pulled back and fastened. A few strands of grey signal that he is not a young man. Most incredibly, his left eye is covered by a patch, held tightly with strings around his head.

The man streaks past me without even taking note of my presence and thunders out of the room, his feet stomping so hard on the stairs, I wonder the wood doesn't crack.

"Ah, Mrs. Sturbridge, I am delighted to see you today."

Nicolas Carteret appears in the same open doorway. He's half the size of the last person to stand there. A neat, compact, fine-featured blonde man in his forties, the master weaver seems completely unperturbed by the fact that a huge creature as terrifying as a highwayman threatened him seconds ago.

"Won't you join me?" he asks. "I have something particular to discuss."

Chapter Three

Monsieur Carteret ushers me into a room warmed by a brisk fire, lit to a golden lustre by a half dozen candles. An entire wall is covered by three towering bookshelves, packed with volumes. It's an awe-inspiring library, though another saying of Voltaire's dances maliciously in my mind: "*The more I read, the more I acquire, the more certain I am that I know nothing.*"

The room's other walls are papered with a design invoking the columns and temples of the ancient world, a decorating choice I know to be costly. But without a doubt, the most impressive piece of furniture in the room is the desk, heavy and gilded, polished to a gleam. It looks more fitting for a Whig grandee than a Spitalfields weaver. I wonder that the dishevelled man who made such a furious exit dared to breathe upon its regal surface.

Nicolas Carteret takes a seat behind the desk, but not before I hand him my book of designs. I perch on a settee opposite.

Watching his eyes flick over the pages, I cannot tell if he is pleased with our efforts. Perhaps the flowers of Le Grenade are too exotic for him? I curse myself for my misguided idea. What was I trying to prove? I should have stuck with English fruit and flowers.

Nicolas Carteret closes the book, expressionless. A frantic apology bubbles up in my throat.

But then he smiles across the desk. Everything about the man's face is symmetrical, eyes, nose, mouth. Only his frizzy blonde hair escapes his control. And now, his smile, a wee bit crooked, transforms his features into something approaching human warmth. He says, "Perfect, Mrs. Sturbridge. I shall do very well with such creative designs."

It is something indeed, to win such praise. The sour taste of bitterness that Reynolds' letter brought me is gone. A watercolour design for silk may strike some as not nearly as artistic as an oil painting. And yes, I once railed against using my talent to decorate the belongings of wealthy aristocrats. But my business makes genuine use of artistic effort, and I'm proud of how far we've come.

I thank him and rise. I'm eager to share the news on Fournier Street.

Monsieur Carteret stretches out his hand and, his fingers extended, lowers it several inches as if we were connected by invisible string. "I would like you to take tea with me," he says. "I have a new proposal to discuss."

I sit down again, forcing a smile as he rings a desk bell. This *should* be a welcome development. I have no idea why it might not be. More work is exactly what we need – not filling custom orders here and there that the other master weavers toss our way, but another commissioning of a book of designs following a theme.

His manservant sticks his head into the room.

"Please inform Madame Carteret that I'll be having tea with Mrs. Sturbridge," he says.

I brace myself for awkward questions about why I've come personally to deliver the book, but they are not voiced. Monsieur Carteret instead turns to what seems, at first, a very benign topic – the dire air outside his lattice window.

"Now that it's growing colder at night, I'm afraid we will see the smoke render the streets particularly unbreathable," he says.

"Is there such a direct connection?"

"Of course." He looks surprised, as if he expected me to possess more knowledge. "People burn Newcastle coal to keep warm, and now that England is the victor of Europe and London its biggest city by far, many more can pay for coal. That's only part of it, I think. The breweries, the tanneries, the glasshouses, there are more of them on the east side of London than the west. It's all worsened by the fact that the wind blows west to east. But you know all this."

"Yes, Monsieur."

In fact, I don't, but it seems best to let him ruminate until we can get to business.

"Why do you think Spitalfields was open to the first hundreds of Huguenot families getting off the boat from France?" he asks. "It has the worst air – and more."

With care, Monsieur Carteret picks up an object from the corner of his desk that had been propped on a wooden stand. It is dark green, or rather it was. Now, it's faded, slightly cracked. A small container of some sort, round at the bottom with a narrow neck.

"Do you know where this came from?" he asks.

"I'm afraid I don't know what it is," I admit.

"My dear Mrs. Sturbridge, it is a flask made of glass, and it came from the grave of a Roman soldier. I estimate it at fifteen centuries old."

I can't help but recoil. Monsieur Carteret keeps grave goods on his desk?

"It was found before the time of the Great Plague," he says, staring at the flask as if it were hypnotising him. "When they were scavenging the grounds of the monastery that King Henry the Eighth demolished, looking for monks' gold, they found hundreds of graves. The ghouls must have been excited, but they then learned it wasn't monks buried there. The monastery was built on part of an ancient Roman cemetery. If you look out of this window, you'll see a corner of the ground they dug up. I think many of our houses are built on Roman graves. We live beyond the wall here, the land east of the city, beyond the jurisdiction of the guilds. This is where they've always put that which they don't want."

I nod uneasily. Spitalfields is no paradise. But I have a different perspective. When my husband and I finally obtained permission to return to England after the perils of our misadventure – we were near destitute, my belly swollen with child – and we reached Fournier Street, my fingers faint with exhaustion as I knocked on my grandfather's door, I wept with joy as the door swung open, to be reunited with him and all of Spitalfields.

At this moment, Madame Carteret walks into the room, carrying a tray of tea things. I'm surprised she brings it herself. She's as trim and fine-featured as her husband and wearing a dress of light grey damask silk. This is not the best idea, though. Should a drop of tea land on silk, it could be stained forever. Washing a silk dress is a perilous enterprise.

Madame Carteret says nothing in response to my greeting. She pours the tea, first for her husband, hands it to him and then pours another cup. Her face is screwed up in concentration; perhaps she fears a spill too. Doing so makes evident the wrinkles around her eyes and mouth.

I wait for her to pour a third cup, but instead, she turns, and with a decisive swish of her damask skirts, she leaves. Clearly, she will not be joining us.

Monsieur Carteret's eyes follow her out of the room. He doesn't seem at all surprised, but neither does he seem pleased. How daunting it would be to have such a sphinx for a husband.

"Milk, Mrs. Sturbridge? Sugar?"

The master weaver waits on my response, all attentive politeness in contrast to his wife's curtness. When he hands me my saucer and cup, our fingers brush very slightly. It's all I can do not to shudder. I dislike being close to him for a sustained period.

I try to appear perfectly nonchalant as I sip bracing hot tea from the porcelain cup. The underlying bitter acidity of this black-tea strain is complemented by the dollop of sugar and then mellowed to a point of delicate richness by milk. Sugar is expensive, and I can't help but thrill to the generous amount. This tastes nothing short of superb.

Monsieur Carteret sips his own tea with undisguised relish. At least we have this in common – a love of the China drink.

"You were an artist in the employ of Ana Maria Garthwaite for how long?" he asks.

"Four years," I answer.

When will we get to the proposal for new business?

"At her Princelet Street workshop, where she taught you how to design pretty little geraniums, roses and delphiniums, did she not?"

There is a condescending tone to his question. Mrs. Garthwaite was my mentor, unfailingly kind, and I was saddened by her death last year. With strong tea humming in my veins, I respond with more vigour than I would have been able to call upon twenty minutes ago. "It wasn't just the ordinary florals we painted. She encouraged ambitious designs for silk as well. I worked on a series of pomegranates and pineapples."

Monsieur Carteret leans across his desk. "But you must admit you have travelled far, far beyond your former mistress in scope. I used to hear that Madame Garthwaite received ideas and inspiration from walking through the Spitalfields market. The market!" His lip curls with disdain. "The ladies I cater to in my business are quite sophisticated. They appreciate the flowers and the plants and curiosities from faraway places, from wherever the British navy can take one. India, Africa, the Americas, the West Indies, the Far East."

He taps my book. "These look authentic. May I ask how you were able to obtain detailed botanical sketches of Le Grenade to copy from?"

I shift on the settee. There is nothing improper about it, but I hesitate to disclose my methods. I finally say, "My husband is acquainted with someone whose connections to the Royal Society were helpful."

Monsieur Carteret brightens. "Was it through Cambridge University? I have to tell you, we still talk about your husband's two lectures at the Spitalfields Mathematical Society. He was able to make us understand some of the most significant developments in electricity."

"I'm so glad," I say. Yes, Thomas' talk on electricity was a sensation. The master weavers are all obsessed with science and the new inventions.

Monsieur Carteret cocks his head, studying me. Whatever question comes next, I have a feeling I won't welcome it.

"How did you and Mr. Sturbridge ever meet?"

The most dangerous question of all. I look him straight in the eye and say, as calmly and simply as I can, "My father's cousin made an introduction possible, Monsieur."

"Ah. How nice. I'm afraid I never knew your father or any of his Planché relations."

It is the response that Thomas and I devised years ago to keep our secret. It bears a very loose relationship to the truth and benefits from my father, a silversmith, being scarcely known in Spitalfields before he died of typhus when I was a baby.

I can't help but imagine Nicolas Carteret's reaction should I tell him what really happened: *My father's cousin, Andrew Planché, arranged for me a position at the Derby Porcelain Factory, but I only took it because a ruthless spy, Sir Gabriel Courtenay, was trying to obtain the formula for a new shade of the colour blue that Derby was developing in secret. If I stole the formula for him, he'd give me sufficient money that I could live as a real artist in Venice. But everything went awry when I finally found the man who was developing the formula, a brilliant chemist named Thomas Sturbridge, and fell in love with him.*

Monsieur Carteret asks, "Is your husband continuing to lecture? How is he employing his scientific talents?"

I don't want to answer these questions, but I can't think of a reason to refuse to do so without seeming rude.

"Mr. Sturbridge is employed as a tutor by the Earl of Sandwich, teaching science to one of his sons," I say. "His lordship attended the same college, Trinity College, as Thomas, and he turned to Mr. Sturbridge for his expertise."

Monsieur Carteret's eyebrows meet in puzzlement. But then he nods and says, "Well, that explains it."

I stiffen.

"Explains what?"

"A woman running a business is rare. Ana Maria Garthwaite was a spinster and not a Huguenot. But you – married, a mother, the grand-daughter of Pierre Billiou? Now, I perceive your husband's humble position, I see why it's possible and even necessary."

Angry hot tears prick the corner of my eyes. I hate that he called Thomas *humble*. How could Nicolas Carteret understand our situation? It's difficult for a man who studied chemistry to earn money in a profession. A chemist must either work alongside apothecaries in druggist shops, mixing medicines or, at the other end of the spectrum, call himself a natural philosopher and conduct grand experiments. But someone must pay for such experiments. There are others like Thomas, highly educated people, earning money to teach members of aristocratic families. This is becoming more and more common. I heard of a duchess who hired a trained artist to give her daily lessons on botanical drawing.

But this is only part of it. There are other reasons why a tutoring position is the only sort of thing Thomas could take, reasons that must be kept secret.

I clutch my hands deep in my skirts. Why should our private life be subjected to scrutiny from this arrogant Huguenot? I ache to storm out of the room, shouting threats as serious as those voiced by my predecessor.

The face of my son floats in front of me and not just his. I see Jean and Caroline, Daphne, even George and Sophie. They depend on me.

And so I fight back tears and force myself to say nothing. Throughout my inward turmoil, Monsieur Carteret is still talking. He seems oblivious.

"Do you know in France there is no serious employment of women in the arts or sciences? Here in England, I welcome this opportunity to employ you and your little band of artists, even though one of them is Jean Orgier. Mrs. Sturbridge, I'm prepared to triple the amount of work I commission over the next six months."

Triple it?

No more agonising over the grocer bills. Much better-quality paint brushes and paper for the workshop. New clothes for Pierre. Perhaps I can even contemplate hiring a nurse for him, as Sophie is not the most reliable person.

Monsieur Carteret then names his figure, how much he will pay for triple the work. And after a surge of pleasure, I freeze, for I realise that it is no more than double what he's already been paying.

Summoning up my courage, I ask, "Are you certain that is the correct sum, Monsieur?"

"Quite certain. I take on a significant risk when I allow it to be known that I'm investing Carteret money in a workshop business operated by a woman. There are those who don't approve."

"Such as your wife."

After all the efforts I'd been making to hold my temper, keep my perspective fixed on what's best for my family and my workshop, it simply flew out of my mouth.

Monsieur Carteret doesn't deny it. He sits back in his chair and studies me as if I am another piece of excavated glass.

"Is my proposal not acceptable to you, Mrs. Sturbridge?"

What a calm voice. I recall how the earlier conversation in this room had progressed, how that visitor had grown more and more agitated before he exploded, while Monsieur Carteret never lost his composure.

"It is acceptable," I say.

"Very good. Yes. Very good."

That crooked smile appears, though this time, I perceive no warmth. The master weaver has a heart colder than that of the floor of the most subterranean ice house in London.

Minutes later, I am back on White Lion Street. A new wind nips at my face and hands. A part of me feels light with relief – I submitted the book of drawings and won a hefty new commission. But I went through such an ordeal. Must all dealings in business be this way?

I am particularly stung by his comments about my husband. How would Thomas himself have reacted to it? I plan to never tell him. We rarely talk about money in any case. It is a sore subject.

Thanks to the rising wind, the smoky air is dissipating. I can see the buildings lining the street more clearly, the faces of the passers-by come into focus. This clarity extends to other aspects of the conversation with Monsieur Carteret.

Have I just been taken advantage of?

It had taken quite a long time before the master weaver voiced his proposal. I wonder if those preceding topics had been anything but idle. Has Nicolas Carteret manoeuvred me, learning what he needed to about my personal circumstances so he could set a less-generous fee for his proposal? I've just agreed to a sharp increase in the amount of work we create. I should be earning enough money to compensate me fairly. But I didn't press for that. I'm not even sure if the three of us are equal to this commission in the time I have agreed to.

As the Spitalfields Market comes into view, I realise that Nicolas Carteret has succeeded in making me feel fortunate to even have him for a client. I wonder if his wife's snub had been worked out in advance. She does not seem like the sort of female to risk offending her husband's guest unless instructed to do so.

I've not always possessed a suspicious nature. For me, conversations once took place on the surface of the pond, no dark and dangerous currents underneath. When did I become the sort of person who took apart an encounter like this?

My face flushes as the answer comes. It was my tutelage under Sir Gabriel Courtenay, who recruited me to obtain the formula for the colour blue, that altered my character. His every word and gesture was calculated. The spymaster urged me to not only behave with greater cunning but to recognise it in others.

I've not laid eyes on Sir Gabriel since the night he walked into the darkness outside Sèvres Porcelain five years ago. Nor have I heard a word of his existence. For all I know, he is dead. To my horror, I learned partway through my spy mission that he was far more dangerous than a spy hired to achieve financial gain. Sir Gabriel was one of a small circle of spies who reported to King Louis XV himself. I was caught in a struggle between France and England for supremacy in art as well as military prowess.

Unfortunately, both Thomas and I were tarnished by Sir Gabriel Courtenay's espionage. It is a miracle that we were ever allowed to set foot on British soil without being arrested.

I met Sir Gabriel on the very same night that I entered the sphere of William Hogarth and Joshua Reynolds. There was never any criminal connection between English painters and the spy for King Louis. They enjoyed the same rarefied air at the top of London society. But it's not safe for me there. I must stay clear.

And yet.

"What is it that you want, Mrs. Sturbridge?"

Jean's question from this morning torments me. In the most private part of my soul, I want what I've always wanted. I thought I'd stamped out this ambition, but why else would Joshua Reynolds' unexpected letter trouble me so? Here, on this cold and dreary Spitalfields street, I must face the truth that my dream of success as a true artist still lives.

Chapter Four

When I let myself into the house, I can hear the hum of conversation both above and below. Back in the kitchen, it's quite a cacophony, with George and Sophie's voices standing out. They sound cheerful enough.

I hurry to the third floor. It's my workshop artists I wish to see first. I tell them of Monsieur Carteret's commission, a bit fearful that they will baulk at this tripling of the number of designs expected. But to object to the work is the furthest thing from their minds.

"How splendid," says Caroline, clapping her hands.

"That is quite an offer from a master weaver like Carteret," says an impressed Jean. "He doesn't take any risks without being sure it will line his pockets. Nothing frightens him except a drop in his profits."

"Well, I must agree that he doesn't seem easily frightened," I say. "Even of something – or someone – who would put fear into me."

I've said too much not to explain it now. I describe the man with a patched eye who left Monsieur Carteret's parlour in a fury.

To my surprise, Jean says that he has a good idea who the man is.

"I know only his first name – Guillaume – but he's part of a new group of agitators calling themselves 'The Bold Defiance'," Jean says.

I laugh at the pretension of the name. "What do they agitate for?"

"Wages for the journeymen weavers keep dropping, and they claim they're close to starving. They want to set some fixed rates of payment for their work and force the masters to follow them. The Bold Defiance are the ones trying to get money out of everyone to support their cause. I heard they deliver letters saying, 'Send your tax to us, care of the Dolphin Tavern on Cock Lane, or pay the consequences.'"

The man on White Lion Street delivered his menacing message in person but received no satisfaction. So Carteret is under pressure from the silk weavers themselves. Now I'm surprised he was prepared to pay me more for the designs.

Caroline says scornfully, "The Bold Defiance probably drink up their 'tax' at the tavern."

"I'm not sure they should be taken so lightly," I say. "Look what happened during the Spitalfields riots last year. A great many people got hurt."

Jean says, with a chuckle, stroking the side of his face, "You don't have to tell me what can happen during a riot!" He grows serious again and says, "But I don't take to the street over weaver wages – the rights of all mankind are my concern."

Caroline rolls her eyes at that, but her face is turned away from him so only I can see her. Jean can be pompous about his politics, but I have a tender place in my heart for such passion. I was once someone who raged loudly over the inequalities of life. Why should people accept poverty and suffering as their due while others are born to privilege? Like Jean, I have drunk in the writings of Voltaire, Rousseau and other philosophers. "*Mankind is born free, but everywhere is in chains,*" wrote Rousseau, and I can't help but agree.

After the workshop business of the day ends, I find my way to Pierre, who is being looked after by Sophie. I soon discover that my maid has some important news.

"I'm going to have a baby, Madame Genevieve," says Sophie, a quivering smile stretching across her face.

I congratulate her while wishing she wouldn't call me "Madame Genevieve". That is for Daphne and George.

"God is good – God is good!" exclaims Daphne, who joins us. Her reddened eyes and puffy cheeks tell the story of Daphne's reaction to the news. George is like a son to her, so this must be akin to becoming a grandmother.

I also bestow my best wishes for a healthy baby on George. He beams with pride, his shoulders thrown back. Life has never been easy for him. Though he is young, tall and physically strong, George often stoops, his gaze sidelong and wary. He is marked by terrors from childhood. Daphne rescued him, and he's been with us ever since.

"I'll do my very best to carry out all my duties," says Sophie.

I should be grateful that she is calling attention to a sensitive dilemma. How will a woman of flailing health, who is pregnant, take care of a lively three-year-old? Her absence from the house until midday could be a harbinger of what's to come. I feel a trifle cornered. But with Daphne's worried gaze bearing down on me, I reassure Sophie. I was horribly sick the first two months of pregnancy – how could I not offer kindness to a fellow mother?

"I know that you will, Sophie," I say. "We will find accommodations to your condition."

She bobs a curtsey. As far as I'm concerned, curtseying is *never* necessary. I turn toward Pierre, but as my son has just scrambled to the other side of the chair, I turn back. In that instant, I catch sight of Sophie's expression. No longer the wan supplicant, she's pulsing with a particular energy I've never seen before. Her cheeks plump, and her light blue eyes flash. She is smiling at George. No, she is *gloating*.

I freeze, and in the next second, it changes. Sophie's smile vanishes.

She asks Daphne what will be needed to prepare supper. George stoops to pick up something Pierre dropped. George did not smile back at Sophie; his face is blank. But as Daphne hums one of her wordless French tunes and everyone goes through the expected motions of their duties in the house, I am convinced that in those fleeting seconds, I saw something. I just wish I could understand it.

I don't sleep well. Bits and pieces of what I've seen and heard throughout the day keep spinning around in my head. A dusty green flask poised above a grave. The shocked and disapproving cries of those who came upon tragedy on Princelet Street. A letter with the portentous seal, "*JR*". And swirling through it all, a trail of grey smoke.

I wake up determined. A tiny bit of me may be curious about this invitation, but there is no time to be wasted on fantasies about joining the glamorous world of Joshua Reynolds. As of this morning, I will turn all my attention to the commissioned designs for Nicolas Carteret. Even though the additional money he quoted is not as much as I would wish, it should be enough to address some urgent matters, such as hiring a nursemaid for Pierre.

I wish I could solve the problem by keeping my son with me during the day. That had been my plan when I launched my design workshop. Pierre would play or nap by my side wherever I went. Unfortunately, energetic little children and silk-design conception do not mix.

One thing is indisputable, we will all need to work hard. Shortly after Jean and Caroline arrive, I present them with a book I purchased from a shop on The Strand, that I hope will inspire our ideas for an entirely new set of designs: *The Beauty of the Mughal Empire*.

They fall on it with enthusiasm, studying the flowers, plants, insects and animals of India, more exotic than those of the West Indies. Just as I'd expected, it's the colours that captivate my artists the most. A trailing flower of deep violet has great potential for our designs, and Caroline notices it immediately as well.

Naturally, the discussions turn to bickering, and I must intervene to be sure tempers don't get too hot. However, it occurs to me, as I smooth out one sticking point, that some of the best designs emerging from this workshop have resulted from the most fevered arguing in the early stages. Perhaps we've reached some ideal combination of talents in this messy room on Fournier Street. That would be highly amusing since neither Caroline nor Jean shone like bright stars at their previous employers' workshops.

Caroline was my first employee. To be the boss of another person was a difficult step for me. When I was looking to earn money for the family by falling back on my silk design skills, I didn't imagine there would be more commissions than I could manage myself. It was my mentor, Ana Maria Garthwaite, who had asked me to take Caroline on. Miss Garthwaite gave me those first much-needed assignments. When I went to her workshop one morning, she took me aside and said that she'd throw me more sub-commissions if I would do her a favour and hire Caroline.

"The other artists have never taken to her," said Ana Maria with a sigh. "An artists' workshop must be delicately balanced in temperament. Caroline makes them uncomfortable."

Taken aback, I said, "I don't know that I would like to be in close quarters with someone who is unpleasant."

Ana Maria hastened to assure me that Caroline's character contained no distasteful flaws. She faltered when trying to explain the other artists' aversion to the young woman. Finally, Ana Maria opened the door a crack between her atelier and the workshop to allow me to see for myself.

That is when I had first set eyes on Caroline, sitting at a middle spot on the long table, surrounded by others yet an island unto herself. Her ferocious concentration was on display, back ramrod straight, mouth set in a grim line, unblinking eyes on her draft paper, her long fingers clenching a paintbrush as if her existence depended on it.

Oh, to care so deeply! How could I reject a spirit such as hers? I hired Caroline, who came willingly – perhaps she'd been more aware of the other artists' dislike than Ana Maria realised – and I never for a second regretted my decision.

The only aspect of her character that has puzzled me is a steady aversion to talking about her past, to the extent that I have no idea where she learned her admirable drawing technique, acquired before she was hired by Ana Maria Garthwaite. Much of Caroline's life is a blank. Seeing that I've drawn a veil across several years of my life, I do not feel in a position to demand explanations. What matters is her work, and it is excellent. I sometimes have to pull the brush from her hand at the end of the day and coax her to leave.

When it comes to Jean, there are fewer mysteries. He is part of the same community as me and vulnerable to the same quirks of character. Huguenots are famously pragmatic, devout and industrious, consumed with success – but there's another side too. Some of us fall victim to drink, others to the lure of radical politics. In the grip of either, extortion and violence can seem solutions. All Huguenots feel ashamed of the Calico Riots, when young weavers, enraged by the popularity of cheap calico that was putting silks in jeopardy, ran wild across London, abusing women wearing calico. The apprentices snipped at the dresses with scissors or tossed soil, ink and even bottled acid on fabric. It was a miracle no women were killed.

Last year, Francois Orgier tapped me on the shoulder on my way out of church, and although I didn't know him very well, I could see he was distraught.

"My son Jean is a wonderful worker, but he keeps losing apprenticeships because he won't stop talking about politics," said Orgier. "Because of your past activities, Genevieve, would you be the one able to handle him? I promise you, he's as bright a boy as Spitalfields ever produced. And he has a knack for drawing!"

When Francois Orgier made mention of my "past activities", he was not referring to my spying or flight to France. No one in Spitalfields had an inkling. I accrued a questionable reputation when I was younger still and briefly engaged to a journeyman weaver named Denis Arsenault, so handsome but also so wild and reckless. He led a "cutting" rampage against a master weaver, destroying his looms and robbing him. Denis then disappeared from London. Ah, my neighbours have long memories.

With Jean, my reservations lay not in his politics but whether he was capable of putting all of his effort into my wholly female enterprise. To my relief, and I admit my surprise, he showed nothing but enthusiasm. There could not be many headstrong young men in England who would submit to the dictates of a woman. I found one in Jean Orgier. What he lacks in artistic training, he makes up for in shrewd instincts on taste and the market. I especially value his technical side. Finding new ideas and rendering them in watercolour is only part of what we do. The draw loom and weaving process have strict requirements. Our designs must accommodate the process, laid out precisely on grids drawn on ruled paper at the end. Jean can even match a design's proportions to the movement of loom threads.

So here I stand, candles lit to compensate for another murky, smoky East London morning, watching over Caroline and Jean as they study the Mughal empire book and make their notes and first rough drawings. I'm preparing to sketch out my own first try at a representation of the violet flower when my eyes meet Caroline's. She seems sad, which is unusual for the first day of a new project.

"Is something wrong?" I ask.

"Oh, no, Mrs. Sturbridge," she says quickly, looking down.

I say, "I hope you feel enough comfort and support here to speak your mind, Caroline."

"I've never felt more of that anywhere in my life," she says quietly.

"Then speak, please."

Caroline swallows as if to gather her courage and says, "Are you not proud of the work we do here?"

"Of course! Why would you think otherwise?"

She nibbles on her lower lip.

"Caroline?" I am close to pleading. "You must tell me what concerns you."

"Why else would you decline the invitation from Joshua Reynolds, unless you don't wish to speak of this business and the art we produce?" she says. "I am well aware we don't paint oil portraits or history paintings here, but aren't our designs good enough to own up to?"

Caroline's theory is so wrong and so completely unexpected that I'm struck dumb.

Jean looks over, eyebrows raised, but he does not seem surprised by her question, which makes me suspect he feels the same way. Perhaps they've even discussed it.

I manage to find my voice. "I can assure you I feel nothing but pride in our work here."

"Then why not attend the gathering at Mr. Reynolds' home?" she says, perplexed. "You've spoken of your admiration for Hogarth. What would be wrong in honouring him? It is not as if you were seeking some sort of favour from Joshua Reynolds."

And with that, I laugh a little. Not the harsh, bitter laugh that escaped me when I read the letter from Leicester Fields. No, it's a rueful chuckle that comes from the realisation that, though the path taken to it was wildly wrong, Caroline has led me to something true. I have looked upon this invitation as if it were yet another opportunity for me to feel slighted and rejected. I've grown accustomed to a hateful role, that of the inferior woman who must seek advancement opportunities from a male.

But I need nothing from Joshua Reynolds. England's leading artist is most unlikely to grant me any favours, and I accept that. How fortunate that I have none to request!

There *is* something that Reynolds can do that would make me happy.

"I will accept this invitation to Leicester Fields," I say. "But I have a condition that you must meet, Caroline."

"I must, Mrs. Sturbridge? What can I do?"

"You can accompany me to the house of Mr. Joshua Reynolds."

Chapter Five

And so I find myself, once again, in a hackney coach, riding across London from east to west. My destination is a gathering of artists, as it was on that night, six years ago. But so much is different now. Then, I had snatched a Christmas party invitation not intended for me and wormed my way in, desperate for a chance to plead my case in person to Hogarth. Tonight, I hold an invitation in my name, extended by Joshua Reynolds, whose star was ascending six years ago and is the brightest light now.

Sitting next to me in a flimsy hired carriage that rattles and leaps whenever its wheels hit a bump is Caroline, but she is a woman transformed.

Shortly after I persuaded her to accompany me – the invitation was for two after all, but my husband couldn't leave his duties in Huntingdonshire for a social occasion in London – I realised that dress could be a problem. One of the many painful lessons of Hogarth's Christmas party was that a woman must wear proper clothes when out in society or risk being ignored or even ridiculed. As I suspected, Caroline owned nothing but plain dresses. I have but one gown that is fashionable myself, featuring a square bodice strung with ribbons and layered, hanging sleeves.

We didn't have enough time to order a new gown for her and have it fitted. That was when I remembered another dress in my keeping, a beautiful silk one that Madame de Pompadour had given me so that I could properly attend a social occasion at Sèvres Porcelain. I wore it once and afterward stored the shimmering French gown in a box. When I extracted it from the layers of tissue, I felt a rush of memories of King Louis' manipulative mistress. This dress was part of her campaign to keep Thomas in France as the new chief chemist of Sèvres Porcelain. Her only motivation to please me was to please my lover – and later, husband – Thomas Sturbridge, and her campaign for securing the loyalty of Thomas and producing the most beautiful colours in the world was coldly plotted. Yet my resentment is softened by the fact that Madame de Pompadour no longer lives. The news of the favourite's death filtered out of France this past spring. King George II... my grandfather... Ana Maria Garthwaite... Madame de Pompadour... William Hogarth. It has seemed like a parade of death, the last two years.

I shook off the melancholy while I made a practical assessment of the dress. It was of a cut and fabric still fashionable. Oh, but look at its tiny waist and tight bodice! Motherhood has bestowed a thicker waist and larger bosom, which Thomas insists makes me more attractive than ever.

The dress fitted Caroline perfectly, though it took some coaxing for her to wear it. In the end, curiosity about Joshua Reynolds triumphed over her deep shyness.

Daphne and Sophie helped us with our gowns and dressed our hair. My housekeeper did her best to overcome her dislike of Caroline while I struggled with my antipathy for Sophie. To my surprise, Sophie possessed some expertise in powdering hair. My thick chestnut locks were piled high and lightened to a pale Titian red.

As we stood in the parlour, readying ourselves to go, Daphne cried, "You are so beautiful, Madame Genevieve!"

I kissed her cheek – carefully, since my face was creamed and rouged – and thanked her. Daphne's praise was an expression of love and loyalty more than any sort of objective assessment. I turned thirty years old this summer, which does not trouble me at all. I'm content to be a wife and mother in Spitalfields. I've certainly no wish to entice anyone tonight. My only wish is for us to blend into the company.

Gazing at Caroline, though, I wouldn't wonder if she drew admirers. Her wavy blonde hair, usually hidden under a cap or tightly braided, is on full display, towering above her smooth forehead and powdered to a dazzling white gold. It took only the lightest smearing of rouge to turn her complexion from pale to luminous. Caroline's reserve works to seal her beauty tonight. She's like an impossibly aloof Greek goddess.

"Caroline, do you see marriage in your future?" I ask as the coach recovers from a particularly sickening lurch.

"I never think about it," she answers. She's not offended by my question, which is of a prying nature, but her tone is firm enough to end the enquiry. She has a way of doing that.

As far as I know, Caroline has no family to settle a dowry on her. She has never spoken of any romantic attachment, nor a desire for one. Neither does she seem keen on acquiring a comfortable home or raising children. A female earning her living as a silk designer might seem a lonely existence, but it is what she wants. She has both talent and training. Many genteel young ladies dabble in paints, chalk or etching. There's a vast chasm between art as leisure and art as profession. How did she bridge it?

I have a more immediate problem than the mysteries of Caroline. Our hired coach barely moves. The timepiece I've brought shows it's fifteen minutes to seven, when the gathering begins, but we've a fair distance to go until we reach Leicester Fields. Reynolds' house is in the middle of London, not too far west, but the streets are thronged with coaches, larger carriages, sedan chairs, men on horseback and a multitude of people hurrying along on foot.

I bang on the door until the driver leans over far enough that I can see the corner of his face.

"Is it possible to go any faster?" I shout at him through the small opening in the window.

"Not 'less we grow wings!" he shouts back.

"Zounds," I mutter. I'm more angry with myself than him. I haven't allowed enough time. I have forgotten that November signals the beginning of the London season and its exhaustive round of operas, theatre, balls, concerts, dinner parties, salons and outdoor gardens. The nobles and merchants and members of parliament depart their country houses and grand estates for places in town. In Spitalfields, there is no "season". Everyone lives and works there all year round. But from autumn to spring, the city of London from The Strand to Hyde Park thickens like a snake that's swallowed a brace of rabbits.

I had been so unprepared for the people of society – the beau monde – when I went to Hogarth's house, charmless, badly dressed, my face unpainted. What has happened to me since has at least helped me to know how to look the part. But shall I be equal to the evening in my sensibility and taste? I'm not at all sure of that. Of course, it would help matters if we managed to arrive at all.

To help distract me from my fretting over being late, Caroline asks what makes Joshua Reynolds a celebrated artist.

I think about it for a minute.

"I suppose it has to do with the vast number of people he paints," I say. "I heard that the number went higher than one hundred subjects a year. To me, that seems impossible. But it's more than the numbers. I read about a young woman he painted who is to be the bride of some grand Scottish earl. Reynolds painted her as a shepherdess in a pale blue frock. She looked very… ethereal. All the newspapers wrote about it."

As I contemplate how prolific Reynolds is, another aspect occurs.

"I believe he's a moving force behind all these public exhibitions of paintings," I say. "It used to be that a portrait was ordered, the artist finished it, it went up on the wall of the person who paid for it, and that was it. In other cases, a history painting or a landscape could be commissioned for a specific building. But now, for the first time, there are showings of art by different painters, gathered and hung all in the same room, to be exhibited at one time. It's really changing how people see the work."

Caroline says, "So it's the artists that the public talk about, not just the art."

I smile at her shrewd insight. "Yes, that could be so."

We continue chattering until the hired coach jerks to a halt. Peering outside, I recognise Leicester Fields and even the house we've paused at. It is that of William Hogarth, but not blazing with candelabras and brimming with people tonight. A single candle in an upstairs window illuminates the profile of a woman, her shoulders sagging and head bowed. Is that Hogarth's widow? I would think she'd be one of Joshua Reynolds' guests. Perhaps it's a servant.

Our carriage rumbles forward again, we are not at our destination quite yet. Reynolds lives in another part of this square. A moment later, we come to a complete stop. Yanking the coach door open, the driver says, "So ye're goin' to Mr. Joshua Reynolds' house?"

Even the hack drivers know him!

"You're familiar with Mr. Reynolds?" I ask, dumbfounded.

"Not him. His carriage. We all of us know that carriage."

As Caroline and I make our way toward the front door of the elegant brick townhouse at number forty-seven, the carriage standing in front comes into full view. Even at night, under the street lamps, it is something to behold. Huge and incredibly ornate, the carriage boasts panels painted with bright figures that seem to represent the four seasons, for heaven's sake. Its wheels are gilded and encrusted with some sort of ornamented foliage. A coachman in silver-laced livery sits atop it, his eyes slits of boredom.

It's like a coach crossed with a chariot, grand enough for a king. In fact, one ruler is not enough. Throw in three kings, a sultan and a cardinal, and then it's ready to embark.

Caroline's eyes are as round as mine. What awaits us this evening? Anyone who reads the newspapers knows that Joshua Reynolds is a success, but I didn't know that a painter could be this wealthy. I recall, unwillingly, the icy reception given me by Hogarth's ancient servant when I tried to blabber my way through the door. What kind of welcome can I expect here?

I shoot Caroline a smile. My nerves must not get the better of me, not when I've gone to such lengths to attend, and talked Caroline into it as well.

Forty-seven Leicester Fields exudes elegance and good taste. The brick townhouse has three storeys above the ground floor, with candle-light flickering behind most of the curtained windows. I've heard that Joshua Reynolds' studio is located somewhere inside the house. I would dearly love to see it.

My firm knock on the door brings a servant, a youngish one, harried, wearing the same silver-laced livery as the coachman, but his coat is missing a button. He beckons us inside without hesitation.

"I'll take you to Miss Reynolds," he says.

I haven't the slightest idea who that may be. I didn't think our host would be old enough to have a daughter to meet.

Caroline and I follow the man down a corridor leading to the back of the house. The further we walk, the louder the voices ahead. Laughter. Even shouting. My expectation of a solemn evening filled with remembrances of Hogarth couldn't be more wrong. This is a party.

Reynolds' servant hurries us into a long gallery, lit by candles and a roaring fire halfway down the length of the room. Large, framed paintings are hung on the walls, but I can't make them out because at least two dozen people gather in the room, standing in small groups. It has the air of happy intimacy. Which makes me wonder again why I was invited, for I'm at best an acquaintance of the man. I'm relieved to spot some women among the guests. Hogarth's Christmas party had been overwhelmingly male.

"Mrs. Sturbridge?"

A woman of about my age walks toward us. Dark-haired and a trifle plump, she has plain features – a blunt nose and mud-brown eyes – and a smile of sincerity. Instead of a curtsey greeting, she squeezes my hands. Her palms are very moist.

"I'm so happy you're here, we were beginning to give up hope," she says. "I'm Frances Reynolds, I keep house for my brother and act as hostess for his evenings, though I'm sure he would prefer a more sparkling female." She laughs ruefully. "I was overjoyed when Ralph came with word of your arrival. I'm sorry you missed Joshua's eulogy about William Hogarth. Everyone was very moved. But now you've come – you've come. I know that Joshua was hopeful of conversation with you and your husband."

Her eyes drift to Caroline, standing silently at my side.

"I'm afraid Mr. Sturbridge is away from London until later this month," I say. "I took the opportunity to bring with me Miss

Caroline Mowbray, my fellow artist in my business endeavour. We are silk designers."

Frances gasps and lets go of my hands. "Oh – oh – women artists, how incredible! And you are both so *handsome*. I must hear every detail of your endeavour, I must!" She turns frantically, her eyes searching the room. "Where is Joshua? Still in the studio with Mr. Johnson, oh dear. I understand the poor man needs cheering up, but really. All these guests. Ralph! Ralph!"

The Reynolds' servant reappears.

"I'll try to extricate Joshua. He can't neglect the room, what can he expect of me? Do you like our gallery, Mrs. Sturbridge? Joshua had it especially built, adding it to the structure of the original house, this was once a garden where we stand. Oh, but you ladies must have libations. See to it, won't you, Ralph? Everyone else in the room has had libations aplenty, heaven knows. Ralph, won't you help me see to Mrs. Sturbridge and Miss Mowbray?"

"I can't organise that if I don't know what they're having," says Ralph irritably.

She turns to us again. "What would you like, ladies? Joshua is partial to negus this week, it's a fine concoction for the cold weather. Wasn't it cold yesterday? Today's a bit milder. I admit I like the taste of nutmeg, you wouldn't think it'd mix well with lemon, would you? I made sure the nutmeg was fresh, that's the trick to it. We have a pot of it kept warm in the kitchen. But we can offer you any sort of libation, Mrs. Sturbridge. We have champagne, burgundy, sherry, madeira, port. Oh, I suppose port is a man's drink. But you're artists, so I make the suggestion."

I say yes to a negus, more to calm the excitable Frances Reynolds than because I desire it.

"And you, Miss Mowbray?"

"I shall have nothing," says Caroline.

"Oh, you must, you *must* permit us to wait on you, Miss," says Frances Reynolds, growing more flustered.

"I never drink spirits," responds Caroline.

Too late, I realise that in my eagerness for Caroline to enjoy an evening in the company of leading artists, I'd not taken into account her rigid ways. I am well used to it after employing her for a year and a half, but hers is a character that can put people off. In the gallery of Joshua Reynolds, Caroline is presenting a charm of appearance, but she is simply not a woman who possesses a charm of manner.

"A glass of sherry – would that be acceptable?" asks Frances, nearly reduced to pleading.

"It would be *very* acceptable to Miss Mowbray," I leap in to say. "Thank you."

Frances Reynolds backs away from us, saying Ralph will fetch the negus and the sherry while she finds her brother to alert him of our arrival. With a last nervous glance at Caroline, she disappears.

We are left alone now at the perimeter of the group of guests. Two things occur to me as I stand there. The first is that Caroline and I might be overdressed. Frances Reynolds is wearing a gown of expensive fabric but simply cut. I also note that a red-haired woman talking quietly to a man near the fireplace, her hand resting on his arm, is neither powdered nor rouged.

The second thing, and this could be connected to the first, is that Caroline and I are attracting attention. I feel the warmth of curious stares. I am doing my best to not return their gazes. Frances Reynolds left our side before making introductions, so we have no choice but to stand here, marooned among strangers, until either Joshua Reynolds appears or someone else approaches us.

Of course, if my husband were here by my side, or accompanying both of us, there would be no sense of unease. A man's presence solves everything, I think with considerable resentment. The amusing aspect of Thomas being here, smoothing things over, is that he has fewer social graces than me. He's a considerate man but one who speaks his mind at all times.

After a few more awkward moments crawl by, I see out of the corner of my eye just such an approach. The couple standing by the fire, the red-haired woman and her companion, are making their way over. They smile at us with true warmth.

"I am Jane Burke, and this is my husband, Edmund," says the woman. She has an Irish accent. Her dress is presentable while not at all fashionable, her husband's suitcoat has a patched pocket. How I wish I had chosen more ordinary clothes for this evening!

"I hope you do not mind that we've come to speak to you," says Jane Burke. "I am not from London, and when we came here to live, I at first found gatherings like these rather trying if Edmund left my side. A woman could feel at sea, and I would not wish that on anyone. So I told Edmund that it's time to cross the room."

"I'm glad you did, and I'm very glad to speak to you," I say, dipping a curtsey. "I'm Mrs. Sturbridge, and this is Miss Mowbray."

As I'm introducing myself and Caroline, I'm aware of two more guests, both men, heading over.

A tall, barrel-chested man with a long moustache claps Edmund Burke on the back with one hand, his other gripping a glass of wine, and says, "Good for you, Edmund." He laughs, though I don't find this amusing. "You've found a path to these ravishing ladies. No need for the acquaintanceship yourself, eh? Sam and I are grateful."

I don't like the man's familiar tone one bit, and neither does Caroline, who frowns. I notice that his friend – it must be the "Sam" he refers to – is shaking his head, as if to discourage such clumsy banter. He's tall as well, but thinner, sombrely dressed, with a high forehead and unpowdered coal-black hair spilling onto his shoulders.

Oblivious, the man continues, "I only came tonight to have some news to carry back to Gainsborough. I've no burning wish to honour Hogarth. I'm a bit muddled on why Reynolds has convened the group. But the evening is looking up, by God."

He makes a clumsy bow, a bit of wine sloshing out of his glass in the process. "Henry Hoppinger, at your service, ladies," he says.

Caroline looks to me, her face a silent plea.

"I am Mrs. Sturbridge," I say icily.

He laughs loudly, spraying my face with wine-soaked spittle. "Of course, there is no Mr. Sturbridge at your side. I'd wager there's never been a *Mr.* Sturbridge! Or if there is, he won't mind you making your own friends."

How dare he say such a thing?

Edmund Burke says, "You're making a bad mistake, Henry."

"I don't believe so," the man crows. "I'm rarely wrong about the ladies, am I, Sam?"

His friend winces and says, "For God's sake, shut up."

Would that he took his friend's advice. Instead, he leers at me, his eyes lingering on my bosom.

"Yes, Joshua has made a new discovery." He suddenly lurches toward Caroline. "Or discoveries, I should say. By Jove, this one is delectable."

Caroline takes a step back and then another. I've never seen her look so horrified.

I move in front to shield Caroline. Henry Hoppinger seems to think we are artist models and not from a respectable level of society. I will set him straight.

"We are guests here, sir," I snap. "Mr. Reynolds sent me an invitation. I suggest you adopt a more seemly tone."

"I've never laid eyes on you two before tonight, nor has anyone else here, and this is an evening for Reynolds' friends," he sneers. "This must be a game of his."

"I met Mr. Reynolds in the company of Mr. Hogarth in Mr. Hogarth's home if you must know," I say between clenched teeth. "I am an artist."

"You, an artist? A woman artist? Now that's the most amusing thing I've heard tonight. As if women had the sensibility to create art."

And with that, I lose grip on my temper.

"If I were only a man, I would call you out for these insults," I say. My voice is thick, not with wine – as is the case with this belligerent fool – but with rage. "It would give me the greatest pleasure to shoot you, but I will have to make do with the weapons close at hand."

I snatch the glass out of Henry Hoppinger's hand and throw his wine smack into his face.

Chapter Six

"What do you think of our two sisters, Mrs. Sturbridge?" Edmund Burke asks.

We're standing in front of a large full-length portrait of two young women in filmy white gowns, their arms draped around each other. They are apparently sisters.

Less than five minutes earlier, I'd doused a guest of Joshua Reynolds with wine. In the uproar that followed, the stupefied man was dragged away by his friend, Sam, while Mr. and Mrs. Burke decided to lead Caroline and me on a tour of the paintings on the other side of the room, not making mention of the crisis.

I appreciate the Burkes' efforts to calm my temper and look after Caroline, who was close to tears. This cannot be what she expected from an evening with artists. I can only imagine what the other guests think of me. Henry Hoppinger treats me like some sort of bawd, and in response, I fall to brawling. I haven't covered myself with dignity. How my temper plagued my grandfather, who tried so hard while raising me to teach me temperance. Worse than that, I remember how Sir Gabriel Courtenay once marvelled at my "wild streak", and my cheeks burn with furious embarrassment.

"I say 'our' because Elizabeth and Maria Gunning are Irish," Burke continues, determined to distract me. "The luck of the Gunning, they say. I'm not completely sure why."

"Because of their marriages, of course!" chimes in his wife. "One of them married a duke, the other an earl. Do you know that when they were young girls, their father couldn't pay for new dresses for a ball? They had to borrow costumes from the local theatre. They were so beautiful. A few times, the girls were mobbed in London because everyone wanted to see them up close. Ten thousand went to Maria's funeral."

"Oh, my dear, was it that many? I thought perhaps two thousand."

"It was ten thousand," his wife says firmly.

Ralph appears with our negus and sherry at long last. He carries them on a tray, crowded with other glasses and mugs. Someone calls out to him, "Have pity, Ralph, I'm parched."

Ralph shoves the drink in my hand before hurrying away. He shows no sign of being aware of the drama that has just taken place in this room. I hope that Joshua Reynolds and his sister, who are both still absent, are likewise ignorant.

Now that the short, thick-rimmed glass, warmed by the negus, is in my hand, I've little desire for it. This is an evening entirely too tilted toward spirits as far as I'm concerned.

"Mrs. Sturbridge, you should at least try it," says Edmund Burke. "Somehow, amid all the mayhem, the drinks are always good in Joshua Reynolds' house."

More to please the kindly Burkes than from any craving for alcohol, I take a sip. It is sugary, tart and spicy all at once, rather overwhelming, but its sweet warmth does its job. I feel the tension between my shoulder blades ease, and my temples no longer throb. Now that I am more relaxed, I can properly focus on Reynolds' painting.

Here are the man's artistic trademarks – the fluidity, the expert use of light and shadow and the range of colours. Deep green leaves above and grey sky above that, and the women, two ivory faces with red-gold hair. The Gunning girls' faces are a showcase for Reynolds' exceptional control of colour. Their lips are painted a rosy coral – were the shade a touch stronger, it would be too dominant, a touch weaker, it would lose its allure. But there is more to this painting than sublime technique. A certain feeling leaps off the canvas. The look in their eyes, their tender smiles, the languorous poses and glowing skin, the sisters convey not just desirability but an acceptance of their desirability. Their lure is one of equanimity.

The next Reynolds portrait shows a triumph of a very different kind. A commander of the British army – a general, I suppose – stands triumphant astride a rock, unsmiling and wigged, his finger pointed. He wears the brilliant scarlet uniform and long sword of a warrior of the British Isles. Behind him stretches a barren, rocky plain with a deep blue sky arching overhead, as if this were plucked from a dream. I wonder if the commander in the portrait is shown on a plain he conquered in North America. The destruction of "New France".

"Ah, at last," says Edmund Burke. "Joshua has returned."

Yes, I recognise the host of tonight's gathering from Hogarth's Christmas party. Dark-haired and rather short, Joshua Reynolds could not be called handsome with the same stout frame, puffy cheeks and stubby nose as his sister. But he is an attractive man nonetheless. He moves with confidence and seems in the best of moods, smiling and joking with his guests.

Soon enough, he reaches me. I am nervous, but more than anything else, I am curious. Will Reynolds share with me the reason for my presence?

"Mrs. Sturbridge, I am so happy to see you again," he says, after executing a graceful bow. "I understand from my sister that Mr. Sturbridge is not in town? That is a shame, I was looking forward to meeting him."

I take this as a courtesy on Reynolds' part and say, "I am certain he would enjoy meeting you as well. My husband does not return to London for another two weeks. Then, I am happy to say, he will reside in London at least a month."

"At least a month?" Reynolds says. "How nice. Yes, how nice."

I introduce him to Caroline, who cannot control her nerves. A stricken smile stretches across her face. Reynolds takes a few minutes to ask her about her silk design pursuits – Frances must have told him of our business – and listens to her halting responses with keen interest. I begin to see how Joshua Reynolds is able to put his subjects at ease when they pose for portraits. This close to him, I see nature has not blessed him. His round cheeks bear faint smallpox scars and his upper lip is scarred. But there is something so engaging about him.

Turning to me, Reynolds says, "I applaud you on the success of your business, Mrs. Sturbridge. I do recall that when I met you in the company of Mr. Hogarth, you expressed a strong interest in a career in art."

So that night is going to be mentioned.

"Yes, I did," I say as steadily as possible. At least he's recounting what happened in a way that puts me in a favourable light. Reynolds could accurately say that he met me when I begged Hogarth for his attention and was spurned.

"Of course my thoughts turn to Hogarth," says Reynolds. "Our late esteemed friend was not receiving company the past few years, his health was sinking, and well, his brush was not busy." He smiles sadly and shrugs. "That Christmas party was one of our only meetings, Mrs. Sturbridge."

I am taken aback. Wasn't their acquaintanceship closer?

Reynolds continues, "But also, I had a letter from my good friend, James Boswell, in Naples. He's met the most remarkable young woman, a Swiss paintress named Angelica Kaufmann, travelling with her father, who is an artist. They paint in Venice and Rome. She has the highest goals for herself, to be a portrait painter of the first calibre. She managed to persuade David Garrick to sit for her in Naples. Boswell says she has developed excellent draftsmanship and can convey facial expression. And she is only twenty-three! She reminded me of you, Mrs. Sturbridge. Reading this letter made me want to see you again."

My heart is pounding, fast and quick, as hope, so long suppressed, flutters. My hope for a career of canvas and oil paint. Joshua Reynolds is speaking of such a possibility, not with mockery but approval. It flits through my mind that he knows nothing first-hand of my draftsmanship or talent. But I have no further opportunity to mull over the difference between Angelica Kaufmann and me. Reynolds has linked his arm with mine to introduce me to his guests, leading me from group to group. He's acting as if I am his guest of honour. Caroline follows close behind, trying her best to conquer her shyness as she too is introduced.

We meet Mr. Samuel Johnson, an author and bibliophile, a tall, heavy-set man with a fierce expression that softens into attentive politeness at our introduction. He was the friend that Joshua Reynolds sought to cheer up in his studio, according to Frances Reynolds. We meet more authors, a playwright, two actors and another lawyer besides Edmund Burke.

Joshua Reynolds could not be more personable or more

high-spirited. These people seem to be all good friends of his. But a different side to my host emerges as we approach a trio standing near the fireplace. I've not noticed them before now, though they are certainly striking. They are more elaborately dressed than the other guests, sporting white wigs and layers of face paint.

One of the two women has the face of an angel. She smiles sweetly as we approach and gives a fluttering wave.

I can feel Joshua's arm tense as he says in a low voice, "Mrs. Sturbridge, I'd like you to meet Miss Kitty Fisher."

"I'm pleased to make your acquaintance," says Miss Fisher. Now that I am closer to her, I wouldn't call her an angel exactly. While young, no more than twenty-four, I'd wager, she has the air of a worldly woman. Her smile is practised, her eyes are cool. Or perhaps, it is due to their unusual colour, a shade somewhere between blue and green. Her silk gown is the height of sophistication, a round, laced neckline, a tight waist and billowing sleeves hanging over a bell-shaped skirt. Such a dress is costly, and so is the diamond necklace resting on her creamy bosom. Although her greeting is polite enough, Miss Fisher follows it by looking away and biting her lip as if she were trying to keep from laughing. I'm not sure what to make of her.

Joshua gestures toward the man at Miss Fisher's side.

"May I present Hervé Gaynard."

Just as she is the best-dressed woman at Reynolds' gathering, he is the best-dressed man. Certainly, he presents a different picture than the slightly dishevelled writers and lawyers I've met so far. He wears a neatly coiled white wig and embroidered silver jacket and waistcoat. Jewelled shoes sparkle on his feet. Lacy white cuffs hang at least three inches from his sleeves. His brown eyes, deep set in a long, lightly lined face, spark with interest while he looks me up and down. A smile deepens. He and Miss Fisher exchange a glance. It is a flicker, but I take note of it. Something definitely amuses them.

The man steps forward and takes my hand. To my dismay, he then pulls my hand to his lips for a courtly kiss. I inhale violet powder, a scent I last encountered at a reception for Sèvres Porcelain.

He says, "How delightful to meet you, Mrs. Sturbridge." There is no mistaking his origin now.

"You are French, sir?" I blurt.

He says, "I claim that honour, yes."

Miss Fisher says, "Now that the tiresome war is over, our friends from France can come and visit us in London again."

I can't help but wonder how these "friends" feel about the portrait on the gallery wall not far from where we stand, showing the British commander who helped rip New France away from the French.

Joshua Reynolds interjects, "But this is more than a visit to London, isn't it, Hervé? I thought you had a stake in the Drury Theatre?"

"I do," he replies. "The theatre is one of my business interests. I must look after them. My stay in London began in February of this year and could continue… indefinitely."

My host pivots to the third member of the trio. "May I present Mademoiselle Duvall." The woman, rail-thin and wearing a rather severe deep-grey dress and a dark gold necklace, is closer to Hervé Gaynard's age than Miss Fisher's. Her snow-white wig makes an arresting contrast with her large dark eyes and thick black eyelashes. Those eyes are now fixed on me in a stare even cooler than Miss Fisher's.

"You hold a grudge against the French?" asks Mademoiselle Duvall in a voice not much louder than a whisper.

"That would be impossible," I say. "I am from a Huguenot family. My mother's family left France for London seventy-five years ago."

"And what of your father's family?" asks Mademoiselle Duvall haughtily.

"They left France when my father was a child," I say.

"So, it seems you are one of us," says Hervé Gaynard.

How would I respond if Joshua Reynolds weren't standing next to me? *One of us?* I am not one of them, and they know it. Yet the last thing I want is to cause another scene. I doubt that Reynolds would understand the two centuries of division between Catholics and Protestants in France. And now, after England defeats France in war, the Catholics trickle over here? I'd not expected that.

I wish we could move on, but Joshua Reynolds has his feet planted firmly before Miss Kitty Fisher. Which I suppose is none too surprising. But it is Hervé Gaynard who dominates the conversation.

"I've been to Spitalfields, what a thriving little neighbourhood," says Gaynard patronisingly. "The silk business has been good to the Huguenots."

Miss Fisher says, "I adore silk," and runs her finger down her billowing sleeve in a slow caress.

Joshua's eyes follow that finger.

Gaynard says, "Most people have no idea what goes into the making of silk. Mrs. Sturbridge is the exception, I am sure." He inclines his wigged head in my direction. "I've seen the creation of it, the genesis. My father was from Paris, but Mama was a Piedmontese. It's one of the few places in the world they raise silkworms outside of China. Mama took me to one of those special farms. It's not anyone who can see the secret of the silkworm, who is allowed the privilege of seeing it with their own eyes. But I was permitted. Mama was a charming woman."

Smiling to himself, Gaynard removes a small round box from his upper coat pocket, taps the lid, opens it and takes a pinch of tobacco between two fingers, sniffing it quickly.

"Oh, Hervé, please," pouts Miss Fisher. "Tell us the secret. You know I hate something being kept from me."

"Yes, do tell, I'm most interested," says Joshua, genuinely curious.

Gaynard hands the snuffbox to Mademoiselle Duvall. He must intend for her to hold it while he speaks, an unchivalrous act, but I suspect that despite his show of manners, he's not the most chivalrous man. To my shock, Mademoiselle Duvall takes a pinch of tobacco and sniffs it herself. Her necklace resting on her flat bosom quivers from the quick, controlled snort. I recognise the jewellery from books as a very old design. A family heirloom, no doubt. For a split second, I imagine the Spitalfields church fathers witnessing all this, it would confirm all their worst opinions of the depraved French.

Gaynard, with a hand lightly resting on his right hip, begins his story. "The worm does not know its future is to adorn the bodies of human beings. It knows only one thing, that it wants to become a moth. It is blind, it can do only one thing. It eats the leaves of the mulberry to prepare itself, as the worms have known how to do for many, many centuries. It spins and spins and spins a tiny cocoon of beautiful threads – a precious house for it to, to…" He pauses, turning to Mademoiselle Duvall. "What is the word, to change into something else completely?"

"Transform," his companion says in a louder voice, her black eyes glowing as if the word holds special meaning.

"Yes. The worm means to transform within its house of threads once all is ready. After days of spinning, maybe three, maybe ten, it rests to prepare for the final moment when it will turn into a moth.

64

And that is when the farmworkers, who have been watching closely the whole time, they pick up the sleeping moth in its house of threads and drop it in the boiling hot water with the other sleeping worms. They keep the threads that will be silk, that is all that matters. I saw the cauldrons of water the workers dropped the worms in. All those little worms they boil alive before they are able to transform. After the workers brought out the threads, my mother let me climb a ladder so I could look in the cauldron to see for myself. All those fat, white, dead worms, floating in the water."

I suppress a shudder, not at the story itself but at Monsieur Gaynard's evident glee at the fate of the worms: boiled alive. Joshua Reynolds and Kitty Fisher both look aghast, while Mademoiselle Duvall merely raises an eyebrow. The teller of the tale, Hervé Gaynard, is watching for my reaction, not theirs.

"I was right about Mrs. Sturbridge, she knew the details of the life and death of the silkworm before I opened my mouth," he says.

"People have tried to raise the worms in Spitalfields and Chelsea," I say. "If we could have a go at it first-hand, I'm sure we'd find a way to prevent the creatures' suffering. But we haven't succeeded, the worms don't thrive. Perhaps it's the white mulberry trees here, or else England is simply too cold. So, we must import and accept the tradition of silk cultivation. No choice."

"Ah, yes," says Gaynard. "You Huguenots are so very… practical."

To my relief, Joshua Reynolds changes the subject to David Garrick, recently returned from Italy but unable to join tonight's gathering. Reynolds and Gaynard share a joke about the actor. Miss Kitty Fisher laughs in delight, while Mademoiselle Duvall eyes me thoughtfully.

At last, Reynolds gestures that we must move on. Gaynard bows again, this time flourishing with his hand as he rises and takes a step backward. Why is he behaving as if this Leicester Fields gallery were the receiving room of Versailles? I must fight to hide my irritation, for he is a guest here, as am I.

Joshua ushers me toward his next cluster of guests, Caroline in our wake. What a strange trio of people. They seem strongly connected to one another, but I can't fathom the nature of their ties. Gaynard is old enough to be Miss Fisher's father, but there isn't anything paternal about him. Perhaps she is an actress – he has interests in the theatre. Her name is familiar, though I can't place it. As for Mademoiselle Duvall, she and Gaynard clearly have a rapport. But what is an unmarried Frenchwoman of noble family even doing in London? I can't fathom it.

I glance over my shoulder and catch Miss Fisher whispering excitedly in Gaynard's ear while she stares at me and Caroline with those aquamarine eyes.

Fortunately, the next group of guests is blandly polite without mysterious undercurrents. The wife of a pamphlet publisher has a soft voice, and Joshua takes a silver trumpet from his pocket and holds it to his ear, leaning toward her. Despite his being somewhere in his thirties, Joshua has a hearing deficiency. I note that he didn't use his trumpet while listening to Gaynard's long story. Could it be vanity? He wouldn't want to appear decrepit in front of the delectable Miss Fisher. It makes me feel more warmly toward him. Joshua Reynolds, despite his famous accomplishments, is a human with flaws, like the rest of us.

The last guests whom Joshua Reynolds wishes to introduce me to are none other than Henry Hoppinger, skulking in a corner of the gallery, and his friend, Sam.

"Henry, you shall be pleased to meet Mrs. Sturbridge and Miss Mowbray, for they are artists, just like you and Sam," says Joshua.

What a relief. I'm fairly sure he doesn't know I threw wine in the face of a fellow guest.

His face wiped dry, Hoppinger says something of bare courtesy through clenched teeth. But Joshua Reynolds isn't really listening to him anyway. Our host regards me with a new energy, a smile playing, and pulls me away for a private conversation.

"Your grandfather, Pierre Billiou, he was an artist, wasn't he? Quite a good portraitist, and I had heard he was a source for Hogarth on Spitalfields when Hogarth was working on his series about the apprentices, *Industry and Idleness*."

"Yes," I say, pleased that he knows of my grandfather. "It was a long time ago, and I did not have an opportunity to meet Mr. Hogarth at that time, but Grandfather told me all about it later. He made some introductions in Spitalfields and took Mr. Hogarth to see a master weaver's workshop so he could witness the apprentices up close."

"And I'm told that your grandfather painted the people of the silk weaving industry as well, made his own studies?" asks Joshua.

How astounding that Joshua even knows this. "Yes, Grandfather did a series at the same time. I think he found his contact with Mr. Hogarth inspiring."

"Do you have the series in your possession? I'd like very much to see it."

I can't speak for a moment, I'm too overcome.

"Of course, Mr. Reynolds," I finally manage to choke out. "For you to take an interest, well, my grandfather would be honoured. It's just eight paintings, but yes, I have them in my keeping."

"I do not know when I can come to your house, for I have many appointments," he says. "But may I look into a time and communicate with you further?"

I assure him nothing would please me more.

"Fine art must be seen and supported, no matter whose brush it comes from," says Joshua Reynolds with a meaningful press of my hand. And then he begs my forgiveness but says he must attend to his other guests and slips away.

I'm left reeling as I absorb this latest turn of events. Joshua Reynolds is interested in my grandfather's work? And could be interested in *my* work?

Jane Burke strikes up a new conversation with Caroline, and I'm glad of the moment it provides to gather myself. I no longer feel the pressure to exchange pleasantries as I consider what the patronage of Joshua Reynolds could mean.

"Mrs. Sturbridge, if I may?"

A man's voice behind me interrupts my excited train of thought, and I turn reluctantly to find the friend of Henry Hoppinger, who I know only as "Sam". He is alone.

"Yes?" I say warily.

"I pray you will allow me to apologise for what happened earlier this evening," he says vehemently. "The fact that Mr. Hoppinger had had too much wine is no excuse for his rudeness. You were invited here, you have as much right to respect as anyone present. More, perhaps, because as Mr. Reynolds says, you have a special connection to Mr. Hogarth. I entirely blame myself, I should have stopped him from insulting you, throwing him down, sitting on him and stuffing his mouth with a handkerchief if necessary."

I cannot even take in all the aspects of his apology, for the picture he creates in my mind makes me laugh. "That would have been quite a sight to see," I say.

His face crinkles into a smile, and his brown eyes radiate relief. It's only then that I learn his full name, Sam Baldwin. It is a simple name, and the truth is, I had at first taken him for plain and unprepossessing. Up close, he offers more detail to his appearance than the other guests. He wears a long, deep-grey waistcoat under a jacket, the waistcoat subtly embroidered with swirling waves and ivory buttons. I catch a glint of a metal circle peeping out of the top of his waistcoat pocket. I've heard of this. Men have begun carrying small timepieces around. They're called pocket watches.

I say, "I appreciate you conveying regrets over what were not even your words, Mr. Baldwin, but I confess to being at a loss as to why your friend should make such a serious error of judgement. I gave him no cause, definitely no encouragement. Even wine cannot account for it."

He freely agrees with me. "Henry's not fit for company such as this, he spends too much time in Covent Garden and not enough in a church pew. I can only say that not every man in England is a gentleman. Those who show the most scrupulous conduct in society are officers in His Majesty's army or nobles at court. Artists belong in neither of those groups."

I find Sam Baldwin's analysis provocative – and perhaps correct.

"But what of our host, Mr. Reynolds?" I ask.

"Oh, Mr. Reynolds is much closer in manners to the people he paints than to the swarm of painters below him," says Sam Baldwin. "A house like this, a carriage, a bevy of servants and studio assistants. All made possible by the rates he charges. One hundred and thirty guineas for a single full-length portrait."

My face must show my shock at learning exactly how much money Joshua Reynolds earns. I pay Caroline – and Jean – less than that for a year's work!

With a chuckle, Sam Baldwin says, "May I fetch you something to drink, Mrs. Sturbridge? You look as if you might need it."

"I've no wish for another drink, but you are remarkably well informed, Mr. Baldwin. I'll pose a question, if I may? I'd be interested in your opinion on something."

He makes a mock bow. "At your service."

"If this is an evening devoted to Mr. Hogarth, why are there so few artists present besides Mr. Reynolds? I've met lawyers, writers, publishers, people in the theatre business. But the only artists are Mr. Hoppinger and yourself."

He folds his arms. "I have formed an opinion on just this topic, but it's one that I'd prefer not to be spread far and wide."

"I'm not a gossip, Mr. Baldwin."

"So you say, Mrs. Sturbridge. But previous to two hours ago, I did not, to my tremendous regret, know of your existence. And yet we are to trust each other with private opinions?"

"When you offered your apology, you said you wished there was a way to make amends, Mr. Baldwin. I believe I have found it."

He rubs his chin, grinning. "Very well."

Sam Baldwin peers around him to be sure no one is within earshot. "I think the reason there are so few artists here is that Joshua Reynolds hates any painter who he thinks could pose a threat to him."

"Hate?" I say incredulously. "A strong word, sir."

"Over and above all others, Reynolds loathes Allan Ramsey, whom the king selected as court painter instead of him. To my knowledge, Reynolds has never had much good to say about Hogarth, but he's dead now, so it seems he can afford to be magnanimous. George Romney and Thomas Gainsborough are very much alive and younger than our esteemed host and gaining notice, so they are in his sights."

I've heard of Ramsey but not Romney or Gainsborough. I peer across the room at Joshua Reynolds, smiling and laughing.

"His temperament is anything but malignant," I say. "I can't share your view."

Sam smiles, and I ask him, "If you have such a low opinion of Mr. Reynolds, why are you here?"

"Oh, I respect him, Mrs. Sturbridge. I respect his self-made success more than you can possibly imagine. I confess that I was hoping he would open his studio to guests. I've heard all sorts of interesting things about how he works. But no such luck."

I share his curiosity about Reynold's methods, I can't deny that.

"Mr. Baldwin, I doubt he invited you only because he thinks you unworthy of his hatred, on that I insist you're mistaken."

He shrugs. "Perhaps I've done him a favour, made an introduction, and this is my repayment. That is how it works, Mrs. Sturbridge. Favours are made and repaid all day long across London. It's a more reliable currency than gold."

I say, "I paint almost every day, I see exhibitions, I read about artists' doings in the newspapers, but what you are describing? That world is new to me."

Sam Baldwin says, "And Joshua Reynolds is the main force shaping the world of art in England. There is no better way to gain fame quickly than to pose for Reynolds." He pointed at the portrait of the gorgeous Gunning sisters. "How do you think they achieved their status – their celebrity? Through sitting for portraits like that one. They become more famous, and so does he. And his sitting fee goes up another notch."

I look at the gallery walls once more, the dukes, actresses, officers, countesses and ministers, interspersed with several paintings by the Great Masters of Renaissance Italy who Reynolds so admires. "I think that, for the first time, English artists might be in a position to exert some real influence in our own country," I say.

"Oh, there's no question they are gaining power. You could learn more about all that if you wish. There's an exhibition a week from tonight sponsored by The Society of Artists. I heard there's going to be a chance to see a Hogarth painting that the owner agreed to lend. The exhibition opens officially next Monday. I'll be there, and so will others, including," his eyes twinkle, "at least one of the artists who Mr. Reynolds heartily despises."

"A second glittering gathering in a week?" I say. "You have entirely the wrong idea of my sociability if you think I'm equal to it, Mr. Baldwin. But thank you."

A hand gently tugs on my sleeve. "Mrs. Sturbridge, I think that others are beginning to leave," says Caroline, who clearly would like to be among them.

Later, when we've found our hackney carriage and climbed inside its cold cab, I try to discover whether there was any part of the evening that Caroline enjoyed.

"Mr. Reynolds was all kindness," she says softly.

"Yes, very much so."

"He seems intent on seeing your grandfather's paintings. What a patron for your family. I don't suppose there could be anyone better situated in London to take an interest."

Caroline is correct. Yet I find myself questioning why he wants to help. When I'm in the presence of Joshua Reynolds, his warm and attentive focus fixed on me, I feel like the only person in the room. All is well. Now, as I think back on the evening – the excitable sister, the kind Burkes, the mocking trio with thickly painted faces, the artist who insulted me and the artist who shared fascinating insights with me – it all seems strange, like an orchestra told to play the same piece of music but each musician was given a different key.

One thing is for certain – the departed William Hogarth played the smallest of roles. I remember with a pang, the silhouette of the grieving older woman in the window. Reynolds' gathering had had little to do with Hogarth's memory.

And as I continue to analyse the evening, I come upon something not just discordant but wrong.

When Frances Reynolds said her goodbyes to us, she was still aflutter over our being there in the first place.

"Women artists – I'm so thrilled that you could be here, Mrs. Sturbridge! I only wish I'd had more time to speak to you. Serving as hostess, it's not easy for me. Ah, maybe there will be more evenings, another chance. I remember so clearly the day that Joshua received the letter from Mr. Boswell in Italy. I went to church that morning for the All Souls' Day service. I wanted Joshua to go with me. But he never agrees – never. But I sat down to dinner with him that afternoon, and he read aloud the entire letter. Mr. Boswell writes such a fine letter. And a young Swiss paintress, bold enough to paint David Garrick, imagine that. It was such a fascinating letter that I almost forgave Joshua not going with me on All Souls' Day."

I don't recognise the problem immediately. But at some point between passing through the stately door of the Reynolds house and locating our humble hired carriage on the cold street, it dawns on me.

Joshua Reynolds said he learned about the existence of this Angelica Kaufmann in a letter, and his sister says the letter in question arrived on All Souls' Day, which was November 2nd. But I received my invitation to his house on October 30th, three days previous to that.

Mr. Reynolds quite clearly said that he wanted to seek me out after learning of my Swiss counterpart. But he is mistaken. Or else he's not being truthful.

But why on earth would he lie?

Chapter Seven

The next morning, I am faced with a contrast in the workshop, a subdued Caroline and an agitated Jean. He wants to know everything that was said and done at Joshua Reynolds' house, but his priority is not the art.

"You were in the same room with Edmund Burke and Samuel Johnson – that's such a privilege," he cries. "They are both important writers. Did Burke say anything about Parliament or John Wilkes? About the rights of the common man?"

"Not that I recall."

Caroline responds to all of Jean's entreaties for conversation details with a frown, a shrug or a clipped response. She is pale, with violet rings under her eyes that suggest a night of little rest.

My sleep was broken too – how could it be otherwise after an evening of such intensity? But I am brimming with nervous energy. It is difficult to concentrate my thoughts on the selection of subjects for the next book of designs for Nicolas Carteret.

"*Hot oatcakes – hot!*"

The shouts of the man selling his wares on Fournier Street and Brick Lane float up to our third-floor workshop and vibrate through the glass. A moment later, he's joined by the refrain of another street vendor, "*Small coals for sale!*"

I pause at my sketches, looking out the window as memory hits of a much younger Genevieve Planché, who hated the sound of Spitalfields, of men shouting their wares. How I'd longed to join the ranks of true artists, who I imagined lived a far different and more glamourous life.

Last night, I brushed elbows with a true artist and his circle, and yes, in Leicester Fields, their lives *are* quite different to mine.

I force my attention back to my sketching paper. When that doesn't work, I refill a dish of water for dipping our brushes.

If I've learned nothing from my past mistakes, then I am a lamentable fool. I once had a tendency to let my imagination flare into rash hope, and before I knew it, I would imagine highly detailed scenarios of artistic success and personal adventure, all scenarios revolving around myself. As pleasurable as such fantasies could be, the pain of their never coming true would outweigh it.

I may never see Joshua Reynolds again. In fact, I probably won't. His desire to include me in an evening inspired by William Hogarth's demise was some sort of whim, no matter the truth of its genesis. Reynolds is the busiest artist in London. He's most likely forgotten about his expressed interest in seeing my grandfather's series. If Reynolds does contact me, it won't be for a long time. Yes, it would be best to put that offer firmly out of my mind.

About two hours later, there's a tentative knock on the door of the workshop.

"Excuse me, Madame, but a letter just came, delivered by a special messenger," says Sophie, her narrow face avid with curiosity.

I take the letter bearing the crest "*JR*", my fingers too numb on the paper to open it at first. Once I manage to pull it open, I see a hurried, friendly scrawl of ink:

76

"Mrs. Sturbridge, I hope it won't be an inconvenience to your plans of the day if I come to your house tomorrow evening at six o'clock to see Pierre Billiou's paintings. My confirmed appointments in the studio don't permit me to come at an earlier time. If you could send word today telling me if this is possible, I would be grateful. Your friend, Joshua Reynolds."

I sit there, stunned, before I tell my workers what the note says.

"Mr. Joshua Reynolds is coming to Spitalfields?" asks Jean. "I'd never have thought that likely!"

"It turns out it is likely," I say wonderingly.

After I've written a note welcoming the visit and given it to George to deliver, I make my way to the fourth floor of our house, where my grandfather's paintings are kept, along with mine. It was once my studio, the place where I tried my hand at expressing what I felt about the world through canvas, brush and paint. I rarely go up there now. Between having a child and starting a business, there's been no time.

As I ease myself into the corner where Grandfather's work is kept, a sickening doubt rushes through me.

Are his paintings any good?

My devotion to Grandfather could have caused me to exaggerate the work's merits. If the paintings are not up to an accepted standard, tomorrow could be an awkward disaster. I curse myself for not examining the paintings *before* I sent George on a westward mission to confirm Reynolds' coming to the house tomorrow.

My knees weak with worry, I pull out the paintings from Grandfather's series on Spitalfields weavers, done in concurrence with William Hogarth's famed *Industry and Idleness*. I prop them up in a line on the floor, resting against boxes and crates. To better see them, I push open the old curtains hanging in front of the street-facing window. The light pours into the room, but the dust shaken loose from the curtains sends me on a coughing fit.

My throat burns, and my eyes water, but at last, I can get a proper look at the eight paintings. Relief moves through me, replacing the worry. These are well-rendered figures, each of them playing a different part in the community of Spitalfields. Most, but not all, work in silk weaving in some capacity, dyers, throwers and all the others.

Although there's much work to be done to prepare them for display, I have no choice but to return to the workshop. We must meet the schedule for Monsieur Carteret. The rest of the day streaks by quickly.

I wake with the dawn and select a dress to wear. Of course, I can't pick a silk gown or anything ornate. But I don't want to look like a poor refugee either. A dark green plain cotton dress will do.

I've barely finished my bread and tea when Caroline and Jean arrive. We agree to spend the morning focused on our usual work and only then use part of the afternoon to tidy the workshop and decide where to display Grandfather's work for Mr. Reynolds. If we stay on course for the rest of the week and the weeks to come, we should make our all-important deadline for Carteret.

Ah, but Voltaire never said it better: "*On the day that everything seems well, you are looking at an illusion.*"

In the late morning, George brings me a message delivered. It comes in a packet marked "*11 Downing Street*". This is not a communique that I can read in front of others. I excuse myself and tear open the packet in a corner of my bedroom. Inside is another sealed paper, this one scented. I slit open the seal, my breath coming quicker.

"*Genevieve, there is something important for us to discuss. I will be at the Tower of London Menagerie at two o'clock today with Diana. Please meet me there. Lady Evelyn Willoughby.*"

Short and to the point, as always with Evelyn.

Today is the worst possible day for me to leave the workshop for hours, not that it would ever be convenient. Yet I must go. This is a summons impossible to deny. It's as if George Grenville himself had issued it. The Prime Minister does, after all, live at 10 Downing Street.

Although puzzled by my needing to leave, Caroline and Jean promise to tidy the workplace and ready my grandfather's paintings for display before Joshua Reynolds. I assure everyone I will be back in the house well before six o'clock.

"I trust you to make all the right decisions regarding Mr. Reynolds," I say to Caroline.

It's not the first time I've expressed confidence in her abilities. Still, Caroline seems especially moved and says, "You can always trust me, Mrs. Sturbridge."

The Tower of London is but a mile from my house in Spitalfields, yet the route to William the Conqueror's ancient fortress is indirect, and one must pass through neighbourhoods that are not the best. I prise George loose from the house so that he can accompany me.

When I was a girl, I shivered at the Tower's ghoulish stories of tortured prisoners and unfaithful queens. Approaching the grim stone wall running along its perimeter, I wonder if Evelyn chose the Tower for a reason apart from its animal collection. She and her husband, Sir Humphrey Willoughby, have their ways of making points understood.

I met Evelyn Devlin, as she was known then, at Derby Porcelain Factory. Evelyn and I became close friends, a connection that was weakened but not destroyed when I confessed to her that I had only taken the position to learn the formula for its colour blue.

Sir Humphrey Willoughby, who was on the trail of my spymaster, Sir Gabriel Courtenay, came to Derby to turn me against him. Sir

Humphrey reports to important people at the ministries, as he struggles to root out foreign spies or Englishmen who have turned spies. Sir Gabriel was the latter. I agreed to Sir Humphrey's plan. But then I fled to Thomas' side without permission, giving Sir Gabriel a chance to abduct us and force us both to go to France. There, Thomas was made to create blue and other beautiful colours for Sèvres Porcelain, and I was imprisoned in a nearby house to put pressure on him.

I learned later that while all this was happening, Sir Humphrey and Evelyn, thrown together while he followed his assignment in Derby, fell in love and were married. When Louis XV finally released Thomas from Sèvres, the two of us set out for England, eager to return to our family and friends, Evelyn among them.

If only it had been that simple!

When we managed to alert the English authorities that we were homeward bound, the two countries were still very much at war. Thomas and I found ourselves stuck at the Hague in Holland, a neutral country, where the ambassador to France opened negotiations with the ambassador to England on our behalf. Those negotiations dragged on for months and months and months. It was obvious our fate was a priority to no one. Thomas and I married, I worked on a series of paintings, and I became pregnant. Only then did we receive permission to set foot on English soil. However, there were severe restrictions on what Thomas could do or where he could go, imposed by none other than Sir Humphrey Willoughby.

I'll never forget the shock on Thomas' face as he read the letter listing those restrictions. "I think they'd very much like to find an excuse to send me to prison," he said. It was a rare admission of fear – and resentment. Most of the time, Thomas reassured me that all would be well. I always pretended that I was convinced. But fear nagged deep inside me, and alongside it, guilt.

George and I reach the public entrance to the Tower of London, very near the river. The Thames is crowded with masts, ships eagerly arriving from all over the globe to convey their goods, tea, silk, sugar, coffee, spices, furs, timber. Watching all this booty arrive is the Tower, squatting on the north bank.

My manservant grimaces. George holds superstitions about places with violent pasts. I can't really blame him for his unease, especially not today. It's anything but a cheerful afternoon. The sky is leaden grey. The river mist, which can be impenetrable at dawn, still clings to the Tower walls and gates, mingling with the coal smoke. It creates a fitting atmosphere for what one suspects took place on the other side of the wall.

He might not care to accompany me inside, but I couldn't very well have George standing outside the Tower walls for heaven knows how long. "George, there's a row of shops and a coffee house over there," I point to a cluster of small establishments on a shallow hill northwest of the Tower. "If I give you sixpence, could you wait there, find a place inside if it gets too cold? I hope to not be within the Tower for too long, but I don't know exactly how long, I'm afraid."

George agrees at once and scrambles toward the shops. I take a deep breath and find a place on the line of people waiting to be let inside. There are three things to see inside the Tower: the Crown Jewels, the Armoury and the Menagerie. Different attractions for different people.

I don't see Evelyn anywhere, but knowing her character as well as I do, I'm certain she would purchase her pass to the Menagerie and make her way there with her daughter, Diana, expecting to meet me inside. I shuffle along in the line. In front of me, a group of people talk about a favourite topic no matter where one goes in London, the burdensome taxes we pay. New ones are being added with painful frequency. The newspapers claim it is to pay our war debt, the cost of seven punishing years.

"So now, I have a tax for the soap I use to wash, a separate tax on my tea and my sugar, a tax on the salt for my food and one on the beer that I drink," wails the man in front of me. "What's next – a tax on the air I breathe? You have to be a Bristol sugar baron to survive!"

I hate all the taxes too. It's one of the main reasons I've so little money saved, but the loud and repetitive complaints set my teeth on edge. After what seems like an endless wait, I reach the front of the line. On my printed pass, it says, "*The Lion Tower*".

I spot Evelyn, not among the lions but the monkeys that are leaping about in the smaller building. She and her daughter and a third person, most likely a nurse, are laughing and pointing at the frenzied creatures on the other side of the iron gate. Despite my cauldron of warring feelings for Evelyn, I am glad to see her in the flesh. She's wearing a long, grey cape that must provide superb warmth during such a cold, damp afternoon. Her black hair shines likes a tight helmet on her finely moulded head.

"Oh, Genevieve, there you are," she says, all friendliness.

"Lady Willoughby," I answer with a curtsey. Since she married the son of an earl, she is entitled to certain gestures of respect from everyone, even old friends. One might think it astounding that she, the stepdaughter of a Derbyshire banker, captured a member of the nobility. But there are advantages on both sides. Humphrey is a youngest son, without land to inherit, and Evelyn brought a large dowry settlement to the marriage.

"Diana wants to see the polar bear, but there is no sign of him anywhere," she says. "Say hello to Mrs. Sturbridge, Diana."

The girl turns from the monkeys to favour me with a bright smile.

Diana is a winning combination of her parents' physical traits, Evelyn's black hair and Humphrey's light blue eyes.

"I was hoping you'd bring Pierre to the menagerie so that he and Diana could play together," Evelyn says. "The children are so close in age."

"I thought you had something important to discuss, something of an urgent nature," I blurt. "That is why I'm here."

She regards me coolly. Or does sadness pull at the corners of her mouth? I can't always tell.

"Is it so unpleasant to see me again, Genevieve?" she asks wistfully. So it's sadness. And I've just been rude.

"Of course not," I say. "But I've taken an important new commission for my silk weaving design workshop. There is a certain amount of pressure regarding when we finish."

Evelyn expresses interest in my design business, posing all sorts of questions. In the back of my mind, I know this is not why she asked to see me. But I'm happy to keep this thread of conversation going for two reasons. The first is that I am dreading the true cause of her summons. The second is Evelyn has one of the quickest, most perceptive minds of anyone I know, man or woman, and I always benefit from her insights.

"It is quite impressive how you've built up this workshop," she says. "And it has not gone unnoticed how, ever since you returned to England, you've kept clear of any… controversy. You live very quietly."

The evening I spent at Joshua Reynolds' house was hardly quiet. But for some reason, I don't want to tell Evelyn anything about that.

"As has Thomas," I point out. "He lives quietly. Don't you agree?"

The friendly light in her eyes dies, and her lips harden as if she must push herself forward now to complete a dreaded but necessary task.

Evelyn says, "Let's have a spin around the lion house, shall we? It might not be so crowded now."

My stomach clenching, I nod and follow Evelyn, her child and her maid into the lion house.

Chapter Eight

If Evelyn had hoped for thinner crowds milling around the cages holding the Menagerie's largest beasts, she was mistaken. Simply opening the door and making our way inside is difficult. But Diana is jumping up and down with excitement at the prospect of seeing a live lion, so we push forward.

The story goes that the Menagerie had its start when the kings and queens of England conveyed to the Tower the inconveniently large beasts they had been given as gifts by rulers around the world. They were in possession of lions, leopards, tigers, monkeys, bears, ostriches and even an elephant who arrived courtesy of the Spanish king. As entertaining as the exotic beasts could be, caring for them was difficult. The animals ended up at the Tower. The Menagerie grew out of those intermittent attempts to shelter the beasts, and then, due to the public's persistent interest, to display them.

I do know something about uncertain fates. The animals have my sympathy.

Evelyn instructs her maid to take Diana closer to the lion cages but to hold her hand tightly at all times and to keep hold of her money purse as well, since pickpockets favour the Tower attractions.

"Do you think there are criminals among us here, pretending to take an interest in animals?" I ask.

"Humphrey says there have never been more criminals in London than now," she says very seriously.

Humphrey hasn't been good for her sense of humour.

Evelyn leads me away from the animals and toward a corner without a good view into any of the cages and so less crowded. The smell manages to reach us here, different than that of any London street or stable. It's the smell of wretched and uncomprehending captivity. Outside a narrow, filthy window, I see the sky is turning a deeper grey. Either a rainstorm is imminent or it's beginning to get dark.

"Genevieve, have you heard of the Comte de Guerchy?" she asks in a low voice.

"Never," I say. "Did you think I would know him? Is he a Huguenot?"

"Hardly that. De Guerchy is Louis the Fifteenth's ambassador to the English court."

"I didn't expect that King George was receptive to French ambassadors," I say.

"Well, the treaty ending the war was signed early last year. So our two countries are supposedly friends and should trust each other."

The sarcastic way Evelyn said *friends*, I knew that she – and by extension, her husband, Sir Humphrey – felt no friendship for the French. Thinking of the strange French couple I met at Joshua Reynolds' house, I have to admit I share her antipathy.

Lowering her voice even further, Evelyn says, "A means was found for Humphrey and his colleagues to intercept letters passing back and forth between the Comte de Guerchy in London and the Duc de Choiseul in Paris, read them surreptitiously and allow them to pass along. De Choiseul is the chief minister of King Louis, as I'm sure you know."

I can't pretend to be surprised. Years ago, Sir Gabriel Courtenay told me that the British government's idea of spying was to open other people's mail.

"But what has any of this to do with me?" I ask.

"Nothing to do with you. It's Thomas. His name was mentioned in de Guerchy's letter posted to Paris last month."

I recoil. "No, I can't believe it. Why would this ambassador mention Thomas? What did he say?"

"Not very much." Her lips clamp shut.

"Evelyn, please tell me. You must. Why do the French even care about him now? It's been years since we came back to England. Unless they're still angry about what happened, that he didn't want to remain at Sèvres and serve as its chemist? Oh, if Thomas is in danger—"

Evelyn says, "You are becoming overwrought. Please, Genevieve. We must not attract attention."

I force myself to say, more calmly, "Is there anything you can tell me about this letter?"

She answers my question with another question: "Have you heard of the Chevalier Charles d'Eon?"

"Now, who on earth is that?"

"An aristocrat, a dragoon in their army, decorated for bravery during the war." She pauses. "He is the subject of the letter. It seems he is causing them no end of trouble. He was sent to London last year as the Plenipotentiary Minister, ostensibly to perform certain diplomatic duties, such as final prisoner-of-war exchanges."

"Why do you say 'ostensibly'?"

"Because at Westminster, they're fairly certain that Chevalier Charles d'Eon is one of the Secret du Roi, just as Sir Gabriel Courtenay was."

Now I have to truly fight to stay calm. The Secret du Roi is an elite group of spies, most of them aristocrats, who answer only to King Louis XV.

"If that is the case, what's d'Eon doing in London?" I ask. "The war is over."

"Oh, you can't be so naïve, Genevieve. The French despise us as much as ever. They'd do anything to cause our country pain. Now, what Chevalier d'Eon is doing here specifically, I'm afraid Humphrey hasn't been able to learn his spying instructions. It's not something one can ask of anyone and get an honest answer. For most of this year, d'Eon has been causing King Louis grief, not our government. He was recalled but refused to leave England. The Chevalier d'Eon is threatening to publish letters with details of the king's private life unless he receives a huge pension. In Paris, they're so angry that they're writing about kidnapping d'Eon and forcing him back to France."

I know exactly how terrifying that sort of kidnapping can be. As does Thomas. Which brings me back to my most pressing question.

"How is Thomas mixed up in the misdeeds of the Chevalier d'Eon?"

"It's not clear."

"Evelyn, why are you telling me these things, frightening me to death, if you can't be explicit?" I demand.

She takes a deep breath. "The content of the letter is about the Chevalier d'Eon and progress made in trying to find him, as he seems to have gone into hiding. But in between the written lines of the letter, in invisible ink, is a short message about Thomas."

Sir Gabriel instructed me both how to write in invisible ink and how to convert its hidden messages back to visibility. Its use in this letter means that, to the French, Thomas is a matter of urgent importance, perhaps more so even than tracking down their blackmailing spy.

Over Evelyn's shoulder, I can see the nearest cage, and when a group of people shuffle along, the lion himself comes into view.

Large and of a dark gold colour, with his famed long mane, he sits on a pile of straw in the middle of the cage. Even from here, I can feel his furious misery.

"What is the short message?" I ask.

"It's a few sentences, phrases really, saying that Thomas Sturbridge, presently in the household of the Earl of Sandwich, is of the highest calibre of all the chemists in England, and he trained under Jean Hellot, the head chemist at Sèvres and chief chemist of France. That's all."

"Why does Thomas' ability interest the French ambassador?"

"That's what Humphrey doesn't know. It could be that they are preparing to approach him, trying to involve him in some enterprise. Humphrey doesn't know what. It could all be detailed in a different letter he wasn't able to get his hands on."

"I have to tell you, Thomas would not be any good at finding a French spy who has gone into hiding."

"Thomas could be wholly unconnected to the Chevalier d'Eon. But I wanted to see you, Genevieve, to say that it's never been more important for Thomas to avoid contact with questionable people and to stay away from anything remotely connected to what he did at Sèvres."

I say slowly, "But Evelyn, you know very well that Thomas agreed, in writing, never to create blue or any other shades of colour for the rest of his career. He's a tutor now. He teaches and he lectures on things like electricity. His work has nothing to do with art, it has little to do even with chemistry. If Thomas gives his word on a matter, that is final."

Evelyn is unmoved by my speech. "In his letters to you, Thomas has not mentioned anything about a particular visit, a message, an approach?" she presses me.

Did her husband instruct her on what to say to me today, the exact questions to ask?

"No," I say.

An awkward tension fills the air.

"How would the French find their way to Thomas, when he's at the country house of the Earl of Sandwich?" I say. "Unless the earl himself is under suspicion?"

She shakes her head. "Oh, heavens, no. The Fourth Earl of Sandwich has held the highest responsibility in His Majesty's government. He was First Lord of the Admiralty. He is guilty of being overfond of the gambling table – and other dissolute pursuits – but nothing more threatening than that. He's a Montagu, after all."

Now I am completely certain that Evelyn is of one mind with her husband. She'd never describe a man in those words. And I have a horrible feeling that her requests of me are about to get worse.

"Genevieve, when is Thomas returning to London to spend his nights with you in Spitalfields?"

My heart sinks.

"At the end of next week or the week following."

She purses her lips. "Why isn't he in London already? The season has begun, Parliament is in session. The Earl of Sandwich is here."

"But his son isn't, not the younger son whom Thomas teaches. I don't suppose there is a pressing need for the son, who is twelve, to be here at the moment Parliament opens."

She looks distinctly unconvinced.

The lion in the nearest cage roars. It's nothing like the rattling growls that have sounded through the room since we stepped inside the lion house. It is louder, angrier, far more savage. The fury of the beast makes something stir inside me.

"Evelyn, it's wrong and it's unfair for you to question Thomas' actions," I say. "He is loyal to England – he shouldn't be blamed because his name appears in a letter he had nothing to do with."

My taking offence only pushes Evelyn to take a harder tone.

"Genevieve, this is an unofficial line of enquiry, based on our friendship. It could be otherwise. Do you want to have Thomas summoned to Westminster to appear before my husband and his colleagues, answer for his name being written in invisible ink by the French ambassador? I don't think that the Earl of Sandwich would be pleased by such a development either."

"No," I say, much more quietly. "No one wants that."

"I'm sorry," she says, touching my arm tentatively. "This is difficult for me too. But nonetheless, we need you to speak with Thomas when he returns to London, ask if he's been approached, and then…" her voice trails away. "Genevieve, just keep your eyes and ears open."

Before I can say anything to that, Diana runs to her mother, crying, the nurse behind her.

"My darling, what is it?" exclaims Evelyn, sweeping down to embrace her daughter.

"He's dead, he's dead!" her daughter wails.

"Who? Tell me!"

"The… polar… bear," she chokes out.

The nurse says, "The man who cleans the cages says the polar bear died of disease last week. The children kept asking him where it was, and he shouted it at them."

"You'd think the man could choose his words better when talking to children," says Evelyn furiously, as she tries to soothe her inconsolable child. After a few minutes of this, she tells me there's no choice but to leave. The nurse is sent ahead to arrange for the carriage driver to pick them up at the main gate.

"It's a long carriage ride from here to Kensington at any time – but this one is sure to feel endless," she says with a sigh.

You'd never think that we are anything but old friends parting after a shared visit to the Tower Menagerie. It isn't as though she's just told me to spy on my husband, who is suspected of committing treachery with French agents. No, never that.

She hugs me, surprisingly tightly, and whispers in my ear, "Don't make any mistakes, Genevieve."

And with a final brisk wave at the gate, Lady Willoughby and child scramble into their waiting carriage.

As for me, I must find George. While walking up the hill to the line of shops, raindrops spatter my face and arms.

I peer into each shop and coffee house on the street. No sign of my manservant. The raindrops turn into a steady drizzle. I think long-ingly of Evelyn's long, hooded cloak. And her permanent carriage.

When I ask one of the shopkeepers the hour, I'm horrified to learn that it is half-past four. Joshua Reynolds will be on my doorstep in fewer than two hours. I'm prepared to abandon my search for George and hurry to Spitalfields by myself when at last he comes around the corner.

"I wasn't off this street for more than a minute," he whines when I demand to know why he didn't stay and wait where he agreed.

I don't have time to debate falsehoods. The goal has to be getting home. I'm not convinced when George says he should be able to swiftly find a hackney coach to hire. But walking a mile in the rain is a daunting prospect. The mud of November creates veritable quick-sand of the London streets. I would look like a drowned rat, with little time to change.

I keep dry now by waiting under the eaves of a small coffee house. Peering inside, I see a long table, filled with young men passing around newspapers. As with so many societies, clubs and drinking establishments in London, women are discouraged, if not forbidden, from entering.

I've weightier things on my mind than the rules of the coffee houses. Evelyn's revelations have left me shaken. The more I think about it, I'm frightened for Thomas. What could the French want with my husband? And what will the English do to him if they think he's disloyal?

Thomas was never someone personally interested in the grandiose ambitions of artists or the policies of kings and counsellors. He is a man of science. Years ago, he discovered a cobalt mineral in the caverns of Saxony that, when processed, could produce the new, transcendent shade of blue. Converting it to pigment for porcelain had been extremely difficult. Only Thomas, through painful trial and error, had been able to control its stability. Derby Porcelain Factory had paid him to produce the colour for its china, but in secret, so that they could have a great commercial triumph. When the French heard rumours that a revolutionary shade of blue was being developed in England, they set out to steal it.

My husband ceased working on developing blue, or any other colour, after we left Sèvres. But in doing so, he gave up a great deal. Science and art – and philosophy – intermingle when it comes to the world of colour. For chemists, using their investigative rigour and laboratories to find new colours or improve methods for producing known ones is a prestigious career. Not only does Thomas possess a wealth of knowledge, he worked closely for months with Jean Hellot, the venerated chief chemist of Sèvres and leading man of science in France.

Nonetheless, Thomas turned away from the sphere of colour forever. He'd had no choice.

Standing, pressed up against a coffee house, the rain coming down in sheets, I realise with a sickening lurch that that's not correct. There *was* one other time, after we left France but before we returned to

England, that Thomas' fingers touched paint to improve colours. And I was the one who encouraged him to do it.

When we were at The Hague, waiting permission to enter England, every day seemed like a month and every month a year. I turned to painting, it was how I hoped to quiet my nervousness. On the one hand, it seemed an obvious pursuit. We were, after all, living in the Dutch Republic, home to the most magnificent painters of the last two hundred years. There were no artists living in England who came anywhere near Rembrandt and Vermeer. And now, here I was in the shadow of greatness. If there had ever been a time to try my hand at a still life, this was it. So, inspired by the ghosts of resident geniuses, I painted a bowl of pears and a vase of wilting flowers, both resting on a wooden table below a thrown-open window.

Thomas was delighted with my efforts, so much so that one day, I invited him to join me. He's not someone who can draw anything but stick figures, but Thomas is always game to help me in anything.

I was struggling with capturing the natural light streaming in through the window. The light of the Netherlands is famously beautiful – and famously difficult to capture on canvas. One day, Thomas disappeared. I thought he was buying food, but my husband had gathered some chemical supplies to assist in colour experiments on my behalf.

He brought back to our small rooms a minuscule amount of some special element with a long, undecipherable name that he mixed with other chemicals to produce *fond jaune*, the golden colour of Sèvres. I tried to mix it in the tiniest quantity with my yellow paint. But it was so dazzling that it turned the faint haze of day into something shimmering and bold. I used a few of his specially mixed colours after that, quietly giving up on my try at realism, because it gave me such pleasure to see Thomas swell with pride. He'd stretch out on our bed, his hand propping up his head, and watch me paint, biting his lip to keep from speaking so he'd not distract me. More often than not, he *would* distract me just the same. Thomas was so handsome and brilliant, I could never get over my surprise that he had strong feelings for me, and I desired him intensely.

Oh, how I loved Thomas.

I hastily amend that. I love Thomas still – I love him *now*. That is why it's so important to protect him. That still-life painting will be removed from the corner of the fourth-floor studio where it's propped up, and boxed, sealed away. Technically, he did not break any of the rules imposed on us, for he mixed the colours after we left France but before we touched English soil again. But we can't take any chances.

Just thinking of the fourth floor makes me ache with impatience to return home.

The rain slows, and even though dusk approaches, making the streets significantly more dangerous, I am tempted to walk to Fournier Street by myself. I've only taken a few steps north of the coffee house when I hear George shouting, "Mrs. Sturbridge! Mrs. Sturbridge!"

He's secured a shabby carriage, but it's better than nothing, and I leap inside. Its floor is covered with straw, and it stinks of sweat, but at least I'm dry.

I tap my hand against the door, unable to control my impatience as the carriage stops and starts on the crowded streets. I want to open the door and scream, "Get out of the way!" I resist, not out of propriety's sake but because it would be useless. There is already plenty of screaming in London.

We are but five streets from my house when my small hackney carriage rumbles ahead of a far wider conveyance forced to proceed very slowly. My heart lurches. Did I glimpse painted foliage bristling on the wheels of the carriage I just passed?

I am neck and neck with Joshua Reynolds, heading for Fournier Street.

With all my strength, I pound on the roof of the carriage cab, urging the driver forward faster. When the horses slow about five minutes later, I push open the door before the carriage has stopped. I hurl the payment at George to award the driver, pick up my skirts and run as fast as possible to my front door. A fearful look over my shoulder confirms that the Reynolds' coach hasn't turned onto Fournier Street. But it can only be minutes away.

"Daphne – Sophie – help!" I cry when I've tumbled inside.

They do their best to help me look more presentable. Daphne pats my head dry, and Sophie finds a shawl to throw over my shoulders. Jean calls downstairs, "Mrs. Sturbridge, are you back?" just as a sharp rapping thunders at the front door. I take a few steps deeper into the parlour and breathe deeply.

It's Sophie who opens the door. I can hear the voice of not only Joshua Reynolds but also other men. A stab of panic jolts through me – did he say he was bringing others and I forgot? – but I force a smile. No matter what, I must appear calm and gracious.

What an incongruous sight, the celebrated Joshua Reynolds stepping into my sitting room.

"Ah, Mrs. Sturbridge, I'm overjoyed to see you again so soon," says Reynolds with the same solicitous warmth he showed me at Leicester Fields.

However, his friendly greeting is diminished by the expressions on the faces of the two men who've accompanied him. Neither appears older than twenty-one years of age. The pale, delicate young man on Reynolds' left looks around my sitting room, his nose curling in scorn.

The young man on Reynolds' right looks not at my admittedly plain and worn furniture but at me. His hooded dark eyes radiate curiosity mingled with confusion. He finds something about me baffling. I have always appreciated frank countenances, but I am less appreciative when the people in question show disdain for me.

Joshua Reynolds doesn't introduce these two men or even acknowledge their presence.

I take the cue from him and behave as if all is normal. After exchanging pleasantries for a few minutes, during which Reynolds informs me he has never been to Spitalfields before in his life, I suggest we go upstairs to see my grandfather's paintings.

We pass a watchful Daphne on the way to the staircase as well as Sophie, bright-eyed with interest. George is proving himself useful by playing with Pierre in the kitchen.

As I lead the three men up to the workshop, a reluctance to go through with it seizes me. I even wonder what words I could use to deter Reynolds from examining my grandfather's work. But of course, the time has passed for that. After an eternity of stomping and creaking on the wooden steps, we reach my workshop.

Inside, Jean and Caroline stand at attention next to our long work table. The room is tidy, well ordered and bright with freshly lit candles. I am, as always, grateful for their dedication. Grandfather's eight paintings are mounted throughout the room on easels or propped against the floor.

I make my way to what I consider the best of the portraits, prepared to share with Mr. Reynolds some background on Grandfather's work. On my way across the room, I stumble against a stool and nearly fall.

"Are you all right, Mrs. Sturbridge?" asks Jean.

"Yes – I'm sorry about that," I murmur.

Jean pushes the stool against the wall as if it were a dangerous object capable of causing more harm. But it isn't the fault of the stool. I stumbled because of the shock of seeing one of my own paintings mounted for display among my grandfather's. It is the still life completed in The Hague, revealing the colours hand-created by my husband, Thomas.

Chapter Nine

With a hum, Joshua Reynolds begins his survey of my grandfather's work. It's a faint hum, but I can make it out because no one else utters a sound as the artist scrutinises each painting.

All the time, I'm wondering why the devil three of my paintings, all oils, are strewn among Grandfather's. Admittedly, they are my best. The still life is not a painting of remarkable composition or detail. What makes it exceptional is its use of colour.

Jean is watching Joshua Reynolds respond, as are the two young men accompanying Reynolds. But Caroline's eyes are on me, and she's worried. I deduce what has happened. While sorting through my grandfather's eight paintings assembled on the fourth floor, Caroline came up with the idea to display my work too. Only someone with an artist's discernment would have selected these three. No doubt, she thought she was helping me take a step forward with my career.

Now I can only pray that London's leading artist doesn't take note of it and press me with questions.

"This one is very interesting," says the fair young man, pointing right at the still life. "But by a different artist, I think?"

My heart pounding so hard it's like a drum in my ears, I say, "It is mine."

I wait in agony for more questions. But Reynolds shakes his head at the younger man as if to discourage further enquiries. He himself takes in the still life with his back to me, so I can't read his face.

The humming stops.

If he asks any questions, I won't mention Thomas. I'll come up with a lie to explain the presence of such vivid and unusual colours – but what?

Reynolds' humming resumes. He continues to the next painting, another one of Grandfather's. He finishes his tour of the room and heads over to me, that smile radiating his special storehouse of energy.

"It's just as I'd hoped, Mrs. Sturbridge," he says. "I have an idea of how your grandfather's paintings can be seen to best advantage. Are you interested?"

I nod.

"There are two challenges," he says. "The first is that the eight of them should be seen together, not broken up and shown with other artists' paintings. And I don't think you'd enjoy being part of the jumble of exhibitions sponsored by either The Society of Arts or The Society of Artists?"

I nod again.

He continues, "The second challenge is the paintings' connection to *Industry and Idleness*, which I believe Hogarth put forth in 1747. Those morality tales of his aren't the new thing in town, and everyone in London is obsessed with what's new. You'd have trouble with either of the societies, talking them into an individual exhibit. Here's my idea. Everyone knows William Hogarth had a long and fruitful connection to the Foundling Hospital. That was the place to have an art exhibition before The Society of Art four years ago. I believe the hospital has excellent copies of the engravings of *Industry and Idleness*. Now, if we were to intersperse the two artists' work, to complement each other—"

Joshua Reynolds starts speaking and moving more rapidly, sketching out for me his vision of the exhibition. Witnessing how his mind works is a privilege. I am, of course, delighted to hear that he has developed these plans for my grandfather's paintings, but I feel dazed. The shock and fear I experienced when I saw displayed the very painting I most wished to hide – it has taken its toll on me. Another distraction quivers across the room, where Jean seems to be having a testy exchange with the two men who came with Reynolds.

"So, with your permission, I will put the proposal to the Foundling Hospital?" asks Joshua Reynolds.

"Of course, of course," I say, with as much enthusiasm as possible. "Thank you, sir."

He takes a step closer to me and lowers his voice, saying, "This is just the beginning of our collaborations, Mrs. Sturbridge. There is more to discuss. Much more."

And with that, Joshua Reynolds makes his apologies, "But·time is flying by. I've tickets to Drury Lane Theatre tonight – I must see what Garrick has cooked up for the launch of the season."

In what seems like the blink of an eye, Joshua Reynolds is gone, along with the two young companions whom he never introduced. My house is mine again, containing the small number of people who live and work within its walls every day. Yet things are changed. There should be exhilaration in the air, but instead, I sense an uncomfortable sourness.

"What happened between you and those two young men?" I ask Jean.

He makes a face.

"I asked them their names and their business with Mr. Reynolds. You would have thought I was a stableboy asking to share their golden throne! One of them twitched his nose like a mouse and deigned to say he was the assistant in the studio to Joshua Reynolds. The other – looked like he ate a side of rotten beef this morning – said he was a student. All I did was ask if he was the assistant to the assistant. Seemed a fair question."

I should scold Jean, but I haven't the stomach for it. The two of them *were* unbearable.

But it's otherwise with Caroline.

"My paintings were not meant to be displayed today," I tell her.

She bows her head, stricken. "I'm sorry. They are just so beautiful, Mrs. Sturbridge, and he did express interest in you as well, the evening in Leicester Fields…"

Her voice trails away.

I think the matter settled when she looks up, her eyes fiery.

"For women to advance, we must be bold," Caroline announces.

I can't scold her for saying such a thing. But there are special reasons for hiding my still-life painting, reasons I can never share with her. I take the still life away and hide it in the corner of my bedroom.

What I'm learning about Mr. Joshua Reynolds is that when business is being advanced, matters proceed rapidly. And sure enough, the notes with "*JR*" seals begin arriving the next afternoon with scrawled requests and instructions. The Foundling Hospital is making available a date, one that comes far quicker than I thought. In two weeks' time, Grandfather's paintings will be shown alongside prints of William Hogarth's *Industry and Idleness*.

I'm grateful, I'm filled with anticipation. But there is another feeling, not suspicion precisely but an uneasiness with the situation.

The more I think about it, the more attending the opening of The Society of Artists seems a wise idea. I want to know more about this world.

The next days are demanding. I give Jean and Caroline Saturday and Sunday off, but I work steadily on both the silk designs and the plans for Grandfather's exhibit. When the day arrives for the society's show, I dismiss my two artists early and prepare for another evening outing. I will go alone this time.

I select a simple dark blue dress. What any Huguenot woman might wear. My face will be unpainted, my hair coiled up in a bun but without elaborate dressing, powder or ribbons. I have learned the lessons of Joshua Reynolds' gathering.

I ask George to escort me to a hackney carriage, which he does reluctantly, for Sophie is feeling poorly, and he wants to take her home.

Once again, my carriage is caught in the evening frenzy of London society. I watch the city slowly move past as I sit back – the red brick and grey sooty smoke and white torch fires. I am not at all nervous this time. The fitful starts and stops of the carriage, slowed down by sedan chairs, grand coaches and other hackneys, don't trouble me. As no one is expecting me, it doesn't matter when I arrive.

The Society of Artists holds its exhibitions at the Great Room on number ten, Spring Gardens, near Charing Cross. I know the building is not terribly far from Leicester Fields, but more important to me, it's close to Soho. If Spitalfields is home to the largest community of Huguenots, Soho is home to the second largest. Hundreds, perhaps thousands, of French Protestant families live on or around Threadneedle Street. Very few work in the silk industry. This is where the French silversmiths, furniture makers, barber-surgeons, eyeglass makers and dentists cluster. I've met more than a few Huguenots from these fine families and liked them very much.

My carriage draws near Charing Cross, the place of travelling inns and other big, bustling buildings. There's no sign of the Huguenots' quiet existence. The November night belongs to the carousers. How loud and exultant these crowds are. The nights of early curfew and furtive after-dark entertainment during the war are truly forgotten.

I reach the street where The Society of Artists holds exhibitions. I arrange for the carriage driver to return for me in an hour's time. As soon as I step out, I am caught in the pull of the crowd to a large, square building with doors thrown open. Londoners are mad for theatres and pleasure gardens, but this is neither, it's the hall holding the art exhibition. I am amazed to see so many people being drawn here – and from all walks of life. A wigged man in silk brocade escorts a female wearing *robe a la Francaise*, not unlike the dress Caroline had worn. Moving toward the same entrance, right behind the grand couple, is a trio of ordinary fellows, all wool caps and worn cotton shirts and breeches.

I'd never thought to see this, an enthusiastic crowd gathered to see the work of English painters collected in one space.

I'm waiting in an outer lobby, standing in line to pay my shilling, when I hear my name called.

"Mrs. Sturbridge, this is wonderful – delightful," cries Sam Baldwin, pushing through the crowd to reach me. Wearing a finely embroidered, short waistcoat under a long coat as he had the previous week, Sam stares down at me as if the sight were too good to be true.

"Yes, Mr. Baldwin, I thought I'd attend after all," I say, pleased, if a trifle embarrassed by the fervour of his greeting. "I must thank you for telling me about the exhibition."

"And did you choose this sombre attire in order to come incognito?" Sam asks.

I laugh, thinking this is a joke.

"Why would I need to conceal my identity? I am beyond obscurity."

"You're being modest, how refreshing," he says.

Sam insists on sponsoring my shilling and escorting me into the main room. As this is being organised, he tells me some background. Four years ago, The Society of Arts was founded for the purpose on display tonight, to show paintings to the public, as was already happening in Paris and other parts of Europe. But some artists felt excluded or disagreed with the group's ideas and formed a rival, The Society of Artists, Joshua Reynolds being one of the leaders. Now, the second group has the upper hand.

"Is Mr. Reynolds here tonight?" I ask.

"I haven't seen him. I heard he'd sent over a painting to be shown, but there's no sign of it yet."

In the doorway to the main room, I'm overcome. My eyes burn, my ears ring, yet my heart sings. What an orchestra of bright colours! In a high-ceilinged room, lit with dozens of candles, paintings cover the walls, closer together than I've ever seen before. People flock in front of them, pointing, arguing, laughing, shouting.

I'm longing to get closer to the paintings and concentrate on them, but being in the company of Sam Baldwin delays this. He seems to know most of the people here, and not surprisingly, when these people greet him, he introduces me. Some seem strangely enthusiastic to gain my acquaintance. I cannot account for it.

One man, sporting a short, square black beard, brings me closer to understanding my situation. "*You* are Mrs. Sturbridge?" he says, his face lighting up. "I'm so happy to meet you. I've heard much about you."

"What have you heard, sir?" I ask.

He says, "I only know what everyone else knows, Madame."

At this point, I tell Sam Baldwin I am in need of an explanation.

"Well, your being a new favourite of Joshua Reynolds is a topic all over town," he says.

I am a favourite?

"He's pulled strings to arrange the show for your grandfather's paintings connected to Hogarth at the Foundling Hospital, hasn't he?"

Shocked, I say, "People have heard of the hospital show? But I've told no one."

"Well, it would seem Joshua Reynolds has told others." Sam hesitates, biting his lip. "And then there's the incident with Henry Hoppinger."

"Oh, no, *no*. I don't want that. People have heard of the quarrel? That I threw wine?"

"Yes, well, Henry is quite a gossip," Sam says. "But after telling the story a few times, he stopped because no one took his part. You became the heroine. Now he's gone into hiding. He's probably gone off to be with Thomas Gainsborough in Bath."

Detecting my embarrassment, Sam says, tactfully, "Perhaps it's a good time for viewing that Hogarth. It's a portrait made from one of his engravings, I'm told."

On our way to viewing the Hogarth, among all the people jostling for a view of this painting or that, we pass a remarkable woman. She holds forth to a tight group of admirers, her every gesture imbued with confidence. Somewhere between thirty and forty years old, she is tall and shapely, her wig stretching so high above her head that if I were trying to wear it, I'd be in danger of collapsing. Just as eye-catching is her dress, *robe a la Francaise* of green silk satin, a row of thick ruffles down the centre. Her ensemble is completed by earrings, heavy with rubies.

Unable to contain my curiosity, I ask Sam who she is.

"Her name is Mrs. Teresa Cornelys. She was once an Italian opera singer, and now she's London's leading hostess. She took the lease on Carlisle House in Soho square, and everyone lives for her evenings."

"What happens there?"

"Music, dancing, gaming tables, dining. Everything you can think of and probably a few things you can't. At some of her balls, men must come dressed as women and women as men. She calls herself the 'Empress of Magnificent Taste and Pleasure'."

"How humble of her."

I am standing too far away for Mrs. Cornelys to hear me, but she looks over as if she has. Her eyes rake over my plain dress and hair, my jewel-less state and the celebrated hostess tosses her head in scorn.

Her contempt amuses me. And to think that I chose my dress carefully for the evening. I keep missing the mark.

We reach the painting in question. It's a portrait of a man in his middle years, kneeling under a tree and wearing a monk's brown robes, though he doesn't look too monastic, with a full head of hair and a white shirt peeping out from beneath the robes, his lips curving in a slight smile. The man kneels before a small table crowded with objects, a book that could be the Bible propped open, a masquerader's masque, a crucifix hanging from a set of beads and a small statue of a figure.

Scrutinising it closely, I realise the figure is that of a naked woman on her back, her legs spread wide.

Well, Hogarth was known for his earthiness. He employs his salty spirit in his fearless depictions of women and men, always to make a point. The painting I look on satirises the man in the portrait, no doubt, but I'm not familiar with the subject, so I'm at a loss over what Hogarth is trying to say.

"Stand back, could you stand back, please?"

The request is directed at Sam and me as well as a half dozen others positioned directly in front of the portrait. A haughty young man, short in stature, is asking us to move away so that someone in particular may see. Without questioning him, we do so.

Only then do two men approach, who by their bearing, their wigs and their expensive dress, must be members of the nobility. One is in his late fifties, fat, with heavy jowls. The other is taller, about ten years younger and much slimmer. Everything about him is angular, his long nose, his sharp chin.

"There you kneel, my lord, how very amusing," drawls the taller man.

So, the brown-robed man in the portrait is a depiction of the fat man standing in the room this evening. Yes, I recognise him, but my, it must have been painted a long time ago.

"What did I tell you, John?" says the older, larger man. "You're in my halo."

It's true. There's a long, narrow circle hovering above the man's head, like a halo or a mirror. The face reflected has a narrow, pointed chin and a pair of beady eyes.

Sam whispers to me, "My God, this is an occasion. It's Sir Francis Dashwood, and he's brought the Earl of Sandwich with him to see the painting."

So that is John Montagu, the fourth Earl of Sandwich.

I've never seen Thomas' employer in the flesh before. The earl has lived in the country for months, I believe he hired Thomas to tutor his son through a series of letters. But this imperious, cold-eyed figure doesn't seem the kind of father who'd go to so much trouble to ensure his son is instructed in the sciences. He makes me feel uncomfortable.

When they are a safe distance away, I take a closer look at the Hogarth painting. Its title, printed at the bottom of the frame, is *The Worship of Venus*. That's who the statue of the naked woman is supposed to be. And a closer scrutiny of the book proves it's certainly not the Bible.

I'm having difficulty getting the sound of their lecherous snickering out of my head. What appalling men. It drives home the sad fact that this exhibition is a victory, but only for the men. What I see around me are men painting subjects to be appreciated by other men. How could it be otherwise? The London academies do not give lessons in art to women. And as I can attest, the leading artists do not take women as apprentices.

Sam, still by my side, says, "I suppose Sir Francis Dashwood was attempting to shock everyone by wearing the habit of a Franciscan monk while worshipping Venus."

"I am more than a little surprised that Mr. Hogarth would take the time to depict such nonsense."

"Dashwood has, I believe, set up a private, exclusive club for those who share his beliefs. William Hogarth might have been part of their circle." He brightens with a new idea. "Mrs. Sturbridge, I'd like you to meet a friend of mine. I do think you'll like him. His paintings are the most interesting on display tonight."

"Please lead the way."

We thread a path through the increasingly crowded room. Is the entire beau monde of London here tonight? In trying to cross over to the far wall, Sam and I nearly bump into Sir Francis Dashwood and the Earl of Sandwich. They're deep into conversation with a third man. When I see who it is, I stiffen.

Hervé Gaynard, dressed in a dark gold ensemble, is holding forth on a musical performance he witnessed in this same room months earlier.

"You should try to hear them play, Sir Francis, before they leave London," Gaynard is saying. "You cannot believe that such young children could play the harpsichord like that. The girl is twelve, and her brother is only eight."

"I would rather hear the Italian castrato sing, what's his name? The one visiting London this season?"

The Earl of Sandwich says, "His name is Giovanni Manzouli, and oh, what a soprano!"

"Long live the knife!" cries out another man in their circle.

The earl says, "Long live the knife indeed. Yes, the Magnificent Manzouli is much more worth your time this season than the Mozart children. I heard they were not real children. The boy's a dwarf."

Hervé Gaynard says, "Your taste in music is superb, my lord. But to speak to their authenticity, I have seen them up close, and the Mozarts are real children. Prodigies from Salzberg. I admit the father is unpleasant. He thought as I am not English, he could complain to me about London. The food without taste. The high cost of every-thing. The criminals who rule the street and holes in the road so big one may break a leg." He pauses dramatically. "Not that he is wrong about any of that."

The two noblemen laugh as well as the sycophantic group that hovers around them. As for Gaynard, with a self-satisfied smile, he surveys the group beyond the Earl of Sandwich and Dashwood. When his gaze alights on me, interest leaps in those dark eyes. His eyes flick to Sam, standing next to me, and then to me again.

His mouth opens, and I twirl around, quickly, and push my way through an opening in the crowd. I don't want to hear from Hervé Gaynard.

But the room is so full, I end up being blocked by a group of five men, considerably younger and less aristocratic than the Earl of Sandwich and Sir Francis Dashwood. They don't notice me. Laughing and sneering, they swarm around two young ladies, sisters by the look of them. One of the men twirls a curl of hair belonging to the taller lady, and red-faced, she knocks his hand away. With considerable difficulty, the distraught pair push their way out of the circle of men and flee.

The entire episode upsets me. I clench my fists in the folds of my dress. So, women who come to see art without male protection become prey to insults.

"What swine," I say between gritted teeth.

"Yes, they are."

Sam has caught up with me, and he looks as pained as he did when trying to stop Henry Hoppinger from insulting me.

"Are these men also artists?" I demand.

"Two painters, two engravers and an illustrator, actually. I'm sorry they are behaving so abominably. As I told you at Mr. Reynolds', artists are… well, they're not gentlemen."

"But *you* are an artist and a gentleman," I point out. "Is your improved conduct due to the influence of your wife?"

Sam's eyes widen, and I realise I've asked too personal a question.

"I am not married," he says, a smile playing on his lips, and looks away.

Should I apologise for my forwardness?

111

"Here is my friend at last," he says. "Let me introduce you to George Romney."

It almost looks as if this artist is hiding from the crowds. An incredible attitude to take, seeing that Romney has more art hanging on the walls tonight than anyone else. I remember that at Joshua Reynolds' house, Sam said that our host disliked Romney as a younger artist on the rise. I'm curious to speak to him.

The man himself is crouching low within his tight circle of companions. He is tall, so such crouching is not easy. He is handsome, or would be if his features were not twisted into a nervous scowl.

"Ah, there you are, George," says Sam, in a manner both friendly and soothing. "I'd like you to meet a friend of mine."

George Romney bows to me and, with a visible struggle, forces himself to enquire as to whether I am enjoying the exhibition.

"I confess I've not seen enough of the paintings, there are so many enthusiastic patrons swarming in front of them," I say.

"George has already sold three portraits, enquiries are coming fast and furious," another friend tells Sam.

"Yes, I shall be shackled to portraiture for the rest of my days," says Romney gloomily.

"Nonsense, my good man," says Sam. "The *Rizzio* painting is the talk of the evening."

Hearing that, a smile lightens Romney's funereal features. "It's kind of you to say so," he says.

"I would very much like to see this particular painting," I say, warming to the tormented George Romney.

Sam and I wait our turn to take position in front of Romney's celebrated painting. During that time, I learn about his interesting life. The son of a cabinet-maker, George Romney had no personal connections to London or any successful painters. His obsession with art drove him forward. He managed to find an apprenticeship and then gain portrait commissions. While in training, he was too poor to tour Italy to study the Great Masters, as Joshua Reynolds and others have done. Yet since moving to London, Romney set himself a high ambition. History painters are the most illustrious of all artists. They recreate dramatic scenes from the Bible or from Greek or Roman antiquity. Romney's inspiration was to paint scenes of high drama in the style of a history painting that occurred in modern times. Last year, he painted *The Death of General Wolfe at Quebec*, with the men not in togas or classical dress but in contemporary clothes. It caused a sensation.

The painting he shows tonight, *The Death of David Rizzio*, features a famous moment in Scottish history. A young Mary, Queen of Scots is throwing herself in front of David Rizzio, to protect her male secretary, as rough Scottish lords brandish swords and knives. In its classical light and colour and its composition, the painting is simply beautiful.

My concentration dissolves. It would have to be something momentous to seize the attention of everyone in this exhibition room. Yet that's what is happening. The loud voices surrounding me have grown hushed.

"What is happening?" I ask Sam.

"I've no idea."

Two men are busy with something across the room. I see one of them reaching up to move a painting to the left.

"Are they hanging something now?" says Sam, wonderingly. "All of the paintings for the exhibition were to be submitted by yesterday at the latest."

But that seems to be exactly what is happening. And I recognise one of the men, he is presently taking a framed painting out of its paper wrapping to hang.

"That's Ralph, Mr. Reynolds' servant," I whisper to Sam.

In the next second, I recognise the other man as Reynolds' assistant who came to my house.

By the *oohs* and *aahs* that emanate as people crowd in front of the newly revealed painting, I can assume this work is exceptional. And it can only be a Joshua Reynolds. I shamelessly push my way forward.

When I reach a gap large enough to see the painting, I slip through, look up, and see…

The pretty face of Kitty Fisher.

The young woman I met one week ago looks down on me. In the portrait, she wears a dazzling light lavender dress and no wig at all, so her natural hair colour is on display, a rich chestnut brown. There is a certain look in her aquamarine eyes, difficult to put into words, but it's as if she is glorifying in some secret. It is not necessarily a nice secret. I remember that quality of hers when we met. In a subtle yet unmistakable way, Joshua has conveyed Kitty Fisher's character.

"Can you believe Reynolds painted her a fourth time?" someone murmurs behind me.

Sam Baldwin finds his way to me again, and I ask why this portrait is causing such fuss.

"Didn't you meet Miss Fisher at Mr. Reynolds' house?" he asks.

"Yes, but I know nothing about her. Is she an actress?"

"No," he says and hesitates. "I think one way it's phrased is that Miss Fisher is a lady well known around town."

"That doesn't tell me anything. You seem to me to be a man known around town."

Sam runs his hand through his thick black hair and laughs uncomfortably. "Ah, yes, but Mrs. Sturbridge, I am not a courtesan."

The revelation leaves me speechless. So this is why her name seemed familiar. Courtesans are kept women, adept at extracting jewels, dresses, houses, carriages and even pensions from their besotted lovers. Yes, their exploits are favourite fodder for certain newspapers, and I can understand why Joshua Reynolds paints her. But to invite her to his home to mingle with guests gathered to honour the memory of William Hogarth? Then I remember that Hogarth painted Dashwood while praying before a statue of a naked woman. London's sophisticated set have different morals than the Huguenots of Spitalfields.

"She might be the most famous woman in London at this moment," Sam says. "And Reynolds is part of the reason. He once painted her as Cleopatra with a pearl and a goblet. He bestowed her with this celebrity."

"On behalf of my sex, I wish the fame would come from different reasons."

"Oh, no," groans Sam. "George is not taking this well."

Romney is shouting at one of his friends, his face splotchy red, as another man tries to pat him on the back. I hear him blurt, "I'm not a child!" Across the room, heads turn.

Sam hurries over and pulls Romney aside. It looks as if he's succeeding in calming the volatile artist until Romney shouts, "But Sam, you see what he does. You see!"

George Romney charges out of the reception room, muttering curses as he goes. Everyone watches. As for Sam, he is stricken. He tells me, "This is the latest strike against him, that's what he says. Before you judge George to be unsound of mind, there was an incident earlier this year. He submitted his painting *The Death of General Wolfe* to The Society of Arts competition. Everyone was impressed by his talent."

"Then why is Mr. Romney so disheartened?"

"The word is that the society was supposed to give him the second-place award in the important competition. It would have carried a prize of fifty guineas, which he could badly use. And it would have made his career. But then the prize was reduced to twenty-five guineas, and the award itself was nearly withdrawn."

"That's a shame, but how is Mr. Reynolds to blame?"

"The gossips say he intervened with members of the society to criticise the painting and oppose the award," says Sam. "He applied pressure to cancel it or reduce it."

I take a step back. "Is there proof of it?"

"There's one thing everyone agrees on, and it is that Mr. Joshua Reynolds is a clever man," says Sam. "So no, there is no statement for the public, no proof."

I sigh and, looking around me, notice that the crowd is beginning to thin. "I suppose I should see about leaving. But wait, Mr. Baldwin, I have monopolised you at this exhibition and not even seen your work. I can't believe I've been so rude. Please forgive me, and lead the way."

Sam looks more flustered than at any other time that evening. "I don't have anything up. I'm working on something new, and it's not ready. I would very much like to see one of your paintings, Mrs. Sturbridge. Portraits, are they?"

"Oh, no. My grandfather painted portraits, but that's never been my interest."

He looks confused. "Since Reynolds is your patron, I assumed... well, no matter. Are you a painter of landscapes then, like Gainsborough?"

I bite my lip. "I fear it's hard for me to explain. I know that history painters are ranked the highest among all the artists in esteem, with portraitists next and landscape painters coming below that, but my aim is to try to paint moments of everyday life in London. By doing that, I want to show the truth of their existence in difficult times." My face flushes. "I realise that might sound strange."

His reaction is anything but what I expected.

Sam steps forward and takes me by the hand. "But Mrs. Sturbridge, that's exactly my vision of what art should be. We must discuss this further! There's a group that convenes at Old Slaughter's Coffee House. I am sure you would find the conversation lively."

"You dare tempt me with a coffee house that permits a woman to enter?" I tease.

"I swear you would be made welcome," he promises.

But the hour is late, and I tell him it's impossible.

Sam conquers his disappointment and makes it his business to help me to the hackney carriage I'd hired. The driver has had to wait far longer than I told him to expect, and I fear he has left.

At first, it's difficult to tell the hackneys apart. But as other people climb into carriages and they rumble off, it becomes clear that my driver is not in the vicinity. We agree to search for a while longer.

Sam pushes several yards ahead of me and turns off the bright, noisy street and onto a dark and narrow one. "Your man could be down here," he calls out.

"Wait," I say. "We should stay on the main street."

He doesn't hear me. I pick up my skirts and hurry to reach him. Sam may know a lot about the rules of the art world, but he doesn't seem as familiar with the laws of the streets.

He has not walked ten strides into the lane when they're upon him, like bees drawn to nectar.

"Good evenin', luv," coos one young woman.

Another woman grabs him by the arm, laughing. A torch flickering from its fixed place on the slick building wall reveals her breasts are almost completely exposed. An echoing laugh bounces off the far wall, and a third woman emerges from the shadows to lay her hand on Sam's other arm.

He pulls away from their clinging grasps, but one boldly sticks her hand into his waistcoat pocket, tugging on his pocket watch. He refuses to let her have it, and a tug of war ensues.

I am not sure what to do. Although he is a tall, fit man, there are three women. They could rob him, they could have associates waiting in the shadows. Relieving him of his pocket watch is the least painful possibility.

I start toward him. Sam, spotting me, wrenches his watch from her and shouts, "Be off with you," and tries to back up toward me.

A low, gravelly voice, one that could be a man or a woman's, emits from a dark doorway to my left, "Ye think ye're too good fer us?"

I shouldn't have looked that way, but my curiosity overcame my sense. The person who spoke *is* a woman. Even in the shadows, I can make out a dark violet, tattered dress. She holds a white masquerader's mask to her face.

The woman steps forward, just far enough to enter the circle thrown out by torchlight, and lowers her mask. Her nose is a decayed, bloody hole in a gaunt face. Above it, two eyes brim with hatred, yes, but also with pain. If Kitty Fisher is at the pinnacle of the profession, this female, riddled with the pox, is at the bottom.

With a crash, a door swings open in the circle of the torchlight. A trio of young men appears, laughing over something. The women pawing at Sam spring back; the diseased harlot melts back into the darkness.

Sam sweeps me along and out of the lane. The women's harsh laughter follows our hurried steps into the brighter street.

"What a foul group of bunters," says Sam angrily. "The constables are a useless lot. It's unbelievable, those women's boldness. How dare they put hands on me?"

Sam's voice sounds different. Under stress, a different accent emerges, one like Joshua Reynolds' West Country voice. I felt unnerved by the women and frightened too. His reaction veers to outrage, and I'm a little uncomfortable.

I spot my hackney carriage a few minutes later and bid Sam Baldwin a quick goodbye.

On the journey home to Spitalfields, I think back on everything I have seen and heard since I walked into the exhibition. What a jumble of bright colours and sharp words. Even after the carriage reaches the boundary of the East End, my heart beats faster than normal. I like this feeling. I would have enjoyed continuing the conversation – the analysis, the debate and the gossip – at a coffee house, to be honest. If only such a thing were possible. And the more I reflect, Sam Baldwin's anger was understandable. He probably felt embarrassed that he was ensnared by the women and only freed by the propitious arrival of three males.

I let myself into my dark and quiet house. Pierre always sleeps with Daphne on the rare occasions when I am out at night and cannot put him to bed myself. I fumble in the darkness to light a candle and make my way to Daphne's tiny room next to the kitchen.

Daphne is snoring steadily – and she is alone.

Where is my son?

I don't want to wake Daphne if I don't have to. First, I'll check my bedroom; perhaps he made his way up there alone? I race up the steps.

There, in my bed, two forms are visible under the blanket.

Mystified, I hold my candle higher. Now I can distinguish their two heads on the pillows. One is my son, and the other, longer form, is my husband, Thomas.

Chapter Ten

Tickling Pierre in our bed the next morning, Thomas says, over our son's delighted laughter, "You've no idea how I've missed this."

My head propped up as I lie beside them, I drink in the sight of the two beings I love best in the world.

"I just wish I had been here last night when you arrived," I say for the fifth time.

"You know I've always been terrible at surprises," Thomas says. "And the exhibition sounds worth seeing. I am glad you were able to go, Gen."

In a few whispered sentences last night, I told him where I had been. I soon learned Daphne had already shared this when he came through the front door. Thomas told me that the Earl of Sandwich's son arrived in town yesterday, earlier than planned. The Montagu family encouraged Thomas to see his own family. He is to return to his tutoring the following week.

No more was said. We didn't want to wake Pierre, and Thomas seemed completely exhausted.

Even now, after a night in our bed, Thomas' face is pale. I fear it is not just the rigours of travel down from Huntingdonshire but his return to the foul air of London.

I tell Thomas about the new commission from Nicolas Carteret and the exhibition of Grandfather's paintings at the Foundling Hospital. "How pleased your grandfather would be," is his response. Which is true, of course, but the significance of Joshua Reynolds being the one to sponsor the exhibition is a trifle lost on him.

I have not yet told him the news most significant to our lives, that my old friend, Evelyn, Lady Willoughby, says that Thomas' name was written in invisible ink in a French ambassador's letter. I recoil from that conversation.

"You should rest today," I say, running my hand up his back. My concern deepens as my fingers brush the sharpness of his shoulder blades through his nightshirt.

But of course, Thomas will have none of rest.

"This little man is in need of an adventure with his papa," he declares. "We will go for a walk to the market and push on to other sites. Perhaps you could join us this afternoon, Gen?"

"If only I could, Tom. We have much to accomplish today in the workshop, or else we'll fall behind."

"But you had the time to see the art of Hogarth and Reynolds yesterday?"

A defensive rush of words swirl until I see his eyes crinkling with amusement. He is teasing me. I've lost the rhythm we have of easy banter, of challenging each other. Not *lost* it of course. It's just that he has been away for a few months. The strange tentativeness I feel, the edge of irritation, will surely be over soon.

Breakfast is loud and cheerful, thanks to Pierre and Thomas singing a song between bites. Daphne is all smiles, and when Caroline and Jean arrive, the happiness only increases. My fiery Huguenot radical immediately pelts Thomas with passages he read of Montesquieu, as if their discussion of the most outrageous French philosophers lapsed but a few hours ago. Even more impressive is Caroline's pleased demeanour when she spots Thomas Sturbridge. Watching Caroline as she talks to Thomas, the absence of wariness, I realise how uncomfortable she is around most men she meets. Thomas is definitely the exception, with his gentle manners and respect for others' views.

As much as I hate to do it, I say goodbye to my husband and son and usher Jean and Caroline to the third floor. As we set up our watercolour stations and fresh paper for the day, I can hear Thomas and Pierre calling to each other downstairs and laughing at the door. Once it slams, I am both free of their distraction and relieved that Pierre has somewhere to go. George and Sophie are late arriving, as is the case one day out of three.

We make good progress in our sketching and painting. Perhaps it was the pleasure of speaking to my husband, but both Caroline and Jean seem less prone to rivalrous quarrels. I, in turn, feel less drained. I'm not being forced to calm down and smooth over conflicts. Before long, I hear the noises of Thomas and Pierre's return and the delicious smells of Daphne's cassoulet drifting all the way to the third floor.

"I'm so fortunate to sit at the table with dishes prepared by the best cook in England!" declares Thomas when we sit down to eat.

Daphne, putting out a platter of bread for dipping in the cassoulet's rich sauce, allows the compliment with a dignified nod. Praise usually makes her uneasy. This drives home to me how much everyone who knows him adores Thomas Sturbridge. I only wish that I, who love him most of all, did not have to bring up something so ominous during our first evening together – his being dragged into another dark spying scheme of the French. How could I justify keeping this knowledge from him after tonight, though? The cassoulet's sausages, laced with garlic and rosemary, form a lump in my stomach.

My husband says he encountered Nicolas Carteret just off White Lion Street.

"He remembered my talk on electricity at the Spitalfields Mathematical Society. He was with a small group of other weavers and came across the street to speak with me. He even coaxed me into giving another speech next week."

"Yes, Monsieur Carteret can be most persuasive," I say dryly.

"There was something odd that happened after I agreed," says Thomas. He takes a sip of wine and then begins the story.

"A group of six or seven young men came up the street. They started calling out to the weavers across from us. Shouting about the rates of work being too low, making threats. I pulled Pierre in closer to me. I didn't think we were in immediate danger, but it wasn't a good situation for Pierre. So he and I backed toward the house on the corner, but that left Carteret alone where he stood. He could have drawn away with us, but no, he began to chastise the young men who were calling insults at his colleagues. He spoke rather contemptuously."

"I'm aware of that side of him," I say. "But I did not think he would be so foolish as to pit himself against a group. He is not young, nor is he imposing in size. Was he carrying any sort of weapon?"

"None that I saw."

"What happened when he captured the attention of the ruffians?"

"The largest and most frightening of them all, a man with a patch over one eye, said to Carteret, 'You've been warned.' The men were muttering together as if they were deciding what to do. I admit that I thought the man might be attacked in front of me and Pierre. Who would stop them? I had Pierre to protect, and there was no warden or constable anywhere. I don't think I saw one all day long."

I tell Thomas that the man with the patch was doubtless Guillaume, one of the group calling themselves The Bold Defiance. "How on earth did Monsieur Carteret escape their violence?" I ask.

"They did not take a single step toward him. As I watched and prepared to put my hand in front of Pierre's eyes, one of them threw a stone at Carteret. It landed at his feet. It was a single stone, grey and round. Like a large pebble. It held some significance for Carteret. He looked down at the stone, and then he turned around and walked up the street, away from them. He seemed to forget I was there."

"And the men? Were they emboldened by his retreat?"

"Not at all. They just went about their way. It's as if the throwing of the stone held significance that all parties understood completely."

Now I find myself drawing deep on a glass of wine. The story leaves me unsettled. There is a meaning beneath the words and actions. And with my connection to not only Monsieur Carteret but the entire silk weaving industry of Spitalfields, I wonder if this will all affect me. Perhaps not tomorrow, but soon. How distant they seem at this minute, the gay, rivalrous crowd of The Society of Artists.

Thomas says, "The Bold Defiance," his tongue wrapping around each syllable. "I suppose that it is just the beginning."

"The beginning of what?" I ask.

"The reckoning of England. What must now be suffered because of the victory over France."

"What do you mean, Tom?"

"The debts. The expectations. The strain on honest industry like silk weaving. Most of all, the burden of being the victorious country over all of Europe. How to pay for the war just won, how to keep hold of all the territories all over the world. Will the people of Great Britain and all its colonies prosper through the coming turmoil? I think not."

When Thomas discusses the fate of England like this, so coolly and dispassionately, it makes me nervous. As a man of science, he regards politics and even war from a certain remove. But wars have a way of bringing harm close, very close.

I must tell my husband about the letter that concerns him.

Although Sophie looks to be preparing to leave with George for the night, I tell her I need her to take care of Pierre for one hour more. She pouts, which I pretend not to notice.

Thomas smiles expectantly as I lead him to our bedroom. It crushes me to disappoint him. I only chose this room so as not to be overheard, not to sink into each other's arms.

In a low voice, I relay the entire conversation to Thomas as we sit next to each other on our bed.

He does not interrupt. But from the vein pulsing on the side of his forehead, his leg tapping at the floor, I know how this displeases him.

Shaking his head, he says, "How very excitable Sir Willoughby is."

"Yes. It's so ridiculous."

I wait for further response, for him to roar with outrage, but that terse comment is all he offers. Silence stretches between us, I can faintly hear Sophie talking to Pierre, telling him a story perhaps.

"Thomas, no one from France has written to you or come to see you at the Earl of Sandwich's house, have they?"

As the words tumble out, I realise, too late, that it sounds as if I am interrogating him.

"I'm sorry, I'm sorry," I say.

Looking straight ahead, he says, "Genevieve, do you ask me this because Evelyn told you to do so and you dare not refuse her or because you yourself do not trust me to act with integrity if approached by a French agent?"

I am aghast. Neither of those choices is acceptable, although the first is uncomfortably closer to the truth.

"No, Tom. I am just worried."

"What use could I even be to anyone who wishes to experiment with colour?" he asks. "Haven't I been reduced to low enough status?"

"Oh, my love," I put my arms around him. It is so painful to hear bitterness from him. The feel of his warm skin under his shirt stirs my blood. When we first came together, and into our marriage for quite a long time, I felt it was the two of us against the world. We would seal our devotion to each other with ecstatic lovemaking.

Grabbing his hand, I feel something rough above his wrist.

"What's this?" I whisper.

Thomas doesn't answer me, and when I pull up his sleeve I see a nasty red scab running up his arm.

"It's nothing, nothing," he says dismissively.

"That looks like a *burn,* how on earth—?"

"Shhhhh," he whispers, his attention elsewhere. He rises and beckons for me to follow. As he moves, he puts his finger to his lips, indicating I should stay silent.

Thomas walks carefully out of the room, trying not to make the floorboards creak. Now, I realise what's happening. He hears something amiss and wants to investigate without betraying his presence. Following his lead, I make my way out of the bedroom.

Coming down the stairs, I hear only one thing: Sophie's voice. She is still telling some sort of story to Pierre.

"Everyone thought this was it for Honest Jack, that he didn't stand no chance of breaking free," she is saying. "But do you think that could hold Jack in?"

"No, no, no," says Pierre, thrilled.

"It might've been his third time behind bars, but they didn't know what he were made of."

127

I recognise her story, it's of the infamous Jack Sheppard.

Thomas strides into the parlour and says, "Sophie, that's enough for this evening."

Pierre cries, "Papa!" He runs to his father and throws his little arms around Thomas' legs.

"Pierre, Mama will take you upstairs," he says. "I need to speak to Sophie."

I catch sight of Sophie's expression – she is batting her eyes in a show of demure innocence. She cannot be in doubt, though, that Thomas is unhappy with her.

I've just begun to get Pierre ready for bed when Thomas joins me. His mouth is set in a firm line as if he were still in the middle of a quarrel.

Once Pierre is settled, he tells me that he informed Sophie that the life of Jack Sheppard, renowned for his string of prison escapes, is not fit for his son's ears.

"She should not have done it," I agree. "Jack Sheppard is a legend in East London. I heard about his feats when I was very young, but my mother certainly never told it as a bedtime tale."

"Do you know, when I suggested she read him a proper nursery story, she replied, 'That's all well and good, Mr. Sturbridge, but I can't read.'"

"What? She told me she could when I hired her."

I am mortified that Sophie was able to fool me. What a terrible household manager I've turned out to be.

Thomas does not chide me, it is not his nature. "I suppose she felt it best to keep that fact hidden. I know I should have sympathy for Sophie – I suspect she's had a terrible life up to coming here – but all I can think is that my son is spending his days with an illiterate maid who holds admiration for a criminal hung at Tyburn."

This time, when I embrace him, he takes my hand and squeezes it. The truth is, I feel just as badly as he does.

"When I take Pierre outside, the air is so bad, one can barely breathe, and we're dodging street fights," Thomas says. "Inside the house, he's looked after by Sophie."

"I should be the one to look after him," I say, my voice thick.

"Or I should," says Thomas. "I'm not criticising you, Gen. You must run the workshop." He pauses. "The path we are meant to follow is sending him out of London to a proper school as soon as possible – and hardly lay eyes on him after that. That's *not* what I want for us. Those are not the teachings of Jean Jacques Rousseau. Remember what he wrote about the importance of nature in a child's development?"

"But what are we to do?" I ask.

He doesn't answer. My feelings are in great turmoil. Our life here is not fulfilling many of our family's needs. Yet the house on Fournier Street, left to me by Grandfather, is all we own. Where else would we go, and what could we do? I could not run a silk design business anywhere but Spitalfields.

We ready ourselves for bed in silence. I know that Thomas wants to leave London. An angry voice inside me says, *"Well then he should find a way to pay for it."*

He's in his nightshirt and pulling back the covers when a coughing fit strikes. It is the sort I especially fear. Each round of deep coughs leaves Thomas wheezing and gasping. I hurry to the kitchen, light a candle and go down into the cellar to pour cold water into a tall cup.

Thomas was injured in an explosion in Saxony years ago while he was underground in the caves, securing the cobalt and running tests. That same rock would yield the component creating the colour blue he hoped would make his name. He has suffered from debilitating coughing fits ever since. Although I hate to admit it, his health

129

improved while he lived in France. Since returning to England, it has worsened again.

He drinks the water gratefully, and the coughing subsides.

We pull the covers up to our chins, for it's a cold night, and I've let the fire nearly go out in our room. I think Thomas has fallen asleep when he says, "You asked what are we to do, Gen, and the answer is, a way must be found out of our present circumstances. Going along as we have done will not do."

He kisses me on the cheek and says, "Good night, sweetheart." There is to be no discussion tonight on what this "way out" should be.

In what seems like less than a minute, Thomas' breathing turns into those long sighs that signify sleep.

I, however, have rarely felt more alert. I stare up at the ceiling, going over each word Thomas said and every gesture he made. For it has not escaped me that Thomas never actually denied being approached by someone. It might be a French spy, it might not, but I feel certain that something is amiss. It could be his pursuit of the way out he spoke of. But whatever it is, Thomas, my great love and the father of my child, has decided not to tell me.

Chapter Eleven

I attended two very different events in the second half of November, the first being Thomas' lecture sponsored by the Spitalfields Mathematical Society, the second, the exhibition of my grandfather's paintings at the Foundling Hospital.

Each time, the presence of an unwelcome visitor would have far-reaching consequences.

When Thomas and I step inside the room holding the Spitalfields lecture, the first man we see is Nicolas Carteret, hurrying over to greet us. "Every chair is filled tonight," he says, greatly pleased. I've not seen Carteret since our meeting on White Lion Street and am relieved to find the mercurial master weaver so cheerful.

Thomas says, "Oh, it is not the prospect of listening to me, the subject of tonight's discussion – Newton's theories on motion and gravity – it would draw interest no matter who gives the lecture."

"It is the speaker, sir, as much as the subject," insists Carteret, who ushers him to the plain wooden podium. I take my seat in the front row of the assembly room, brightly lit by rows of candles but not too warm. Keeping my coat fastened, I look around to see if I recognise anyone. What a nice surprise, there are other women in attendance. Science should not be the preserve of men. One young woman seated to my right is not just gazing at Thomas, she is staring, unblinkingly, a smile curving her lips. I have to fight back my own smile. Yes, my husband, with his coppery red hair pulled back and fastened, his high cheekbones and lean frame, wearing his best coat and silk stockings, is a far more attractive speaker than most who are scheduled by the Mathematical Society.

Thomas launches into his talk on Sir Isaac Newton, and everyone sitting on the hard chairs and stools, men and women, listens attentively. Thomas is an excellent speaker. He makes his scientific subjects comprehensible but never patronises his audience.

I must confess though, that after a while, my thoughts stray to an unpleasant outburst in the workshop yesterday.

For days, Caroline has reacted to the slightest whiff of criticism with anguish. I've had to choose each word with tremendous care. But of course, Jean, even when he means to be helpful, has not chosen so judiciously.

I'm not sure what precipitated it, as I had not been following their conversation, but Caroline's angry voice suddenly filled the room.

"I can no longer bear your recitations of the violated rights of men, the disadvantages and inequities you face," she'd said shrilly. "Voltaire says this, Montesquieu says that, and then there's the great Rousseau. But men have everything, and women have nothing – no rights and not any degree of safety!"

"Good God, Caroline, what did I say?"

"Oh, you're hopeless. You are completely hopeless."

She no longer shouted. Caroline was in despair, shielding her eyes with her hand. She asked for a few minutes to compose herself and fled the room.

"I swear, Mrs. Sturbridge, I did not say or do anything to upset her," Jean had said, not a little upset himself.

My sympathies would have rested with Caroline ordinarily. I have felt the same resentments as her many times. But I also know Jean's character, that he was being truthful when he'd said he did not think that he'd made an insulting remark. He can be thoughtless, but Jean is not malicious. I fear that Caroline is becoming too sensitive. How are we to increase our work commissions in such an atmosphere?

I am jolted back to the Mathematical Society, with applause erupting. Thomas has made a point so well that the audience is beside itself.

When the clapping subsides to satisfied murmurs, one loud voice rings out:

"But what do you say, Mr. Sturbridge, to the report that Sir Isaac Newton was always hiding his true interest?"

Thomas, still smiling at the applause he received a moment ago, says, lightly, "And what would that true interest be?"

"Alchemy, sir."

"Absurd," mutters the man sitting to my left. The man to my right turns around to see who started this dialogue.

I am curious about his identity too, but my attention is fixed on Thomas. His smile fades. He looks down and up again as he purses his lips, a sign that he is considering his next words carefully.

"Alchemy is a pursuit from the past," Thomas says. "Because of the revolutionary thinking of Newton, we now have new systems of mathematics and accepted laws of physics."

Again comes the voice from the back, "I take note, Mr. Sturbridge, that you have not denied Newton's obsession with alchemy."

Why is this man being so persistent?

I can't resist the urge to turn around in my seat to take a measure of Thomas' interrogator. A fair number of other people are craning to scrutinise him too, and following their stares, I alight on a blonde man with smooth, shiny skin, sitting casually in his chair in the back row, as if it were no concern of his that he's attracting so much disapproval.

Nicolas Carteret has risen to his feet, his face tense with anger. Looking back at the persistent questioner, he says, with a dramatic point of the finger, "You are argumentative, sir. Alchemists were charlatans! They promised to turn base metals into gold by use of a philosopher's stone! Sir Isaac Newton was a genius. He was no alchemist."

Thomas taps his fingers on the podium, shifting from one foot to the other. I suspect he disagrees with one of the points Carteret just made.

My husband says, "Some alchemists in the thirteenth, fourteenth and fifteenth centuries were charlatans, but others were in pursuit of essential truths, of perfection, which is what we also seek today, although now we use the scientific method. The word 'chemistry' even comes from the word 'alchemy', and that, in turn, derives from an ancient Egyptian word that means the transmutation of the fertile earth."

"Transmutations?" The stranger from the back of the room seizes on the word eagerly. "So, Mr. Sturbridge, if you don't care to discuss Newton in this regard, what do you think of the *transmutations* of Dr. Johann Konrad Dippel? He is the one who conducted experiments in Germany in order to bring the dead back to life. And fifty years ago, he invented a new colour as well. The perfect alchemist, wouldn't you say?"

A startled gasp escapes me. This is the first time anyone has spoken about colours being invented in Thomas' presence in public. It is what he dedicated years of his life to, but the condition of his return to

England was that he cease such work himself and never write about his experiences or refer to them in public settings. To be compared to Dippel comes dangerously close. I've heard about this German doctor. His shade Prussian Blue – created by the oxidising of certain chemical compounds – is considered the first synthetic colour.

I've never heard that Dippel strove to bring the dead back to life. It is stomach-turning.

But no one is looking at me to gauge my reaction. The eyes of the audience are on Thomas. His face is wiped clean of expression. Only I, who know him so well, realise how much of an effort that requires. Then I spot his hands, gripping the sides of the podium so tightly his knuckles whiten.

My neighbour on the left is nothing less than outraged over the direction of the lecture. "I didn't come here to listen to someone prattle about alchemy," he announces. "Trafficking in the dead. It sounds more like necromancy. What twaddle!"

Thomas rallies, and says with a rare sternness, "I believe we are here to discuss Sir Isaac Newton, not to debate the accomplishments of Dippel or any other alchemist from the texts. If you insist on this topic, sir, we can make a private arrangement after the lecture."

To my relief, the blonde man in the back row falls silent. I find myself mystified by the exchange. What possessed the man to try to turn the lecture into a discussion of alchemy?

I look over my shoulder again. But the chair he'd sat in is empty. Perhaps he'd grown too self-conscious to stay. No one had appreciated his questions.

It isn't until we walk home that I ask Thomas what he thinks about the strange questioner.

"Oh, it sometimes happens," he says. "A fellow in love with his own voice will attempt to dominate a discussion."

"But to insist that Sir Isaac Newton was an alchemist?"

Thomas says, "That's not so fantastical as you assume, Gen. There is still a lot of talk about Newton at Trinity College. His scholarly papers are well known, very much in the public sphere. But he kept secret journals too. I was told that he wrote extensively on his studies of alchemy. Perhaps one hundred separate journals. I couldn't find anyone who had read them. They were locked away. I think the college was worried about how the public would react."

"Why would Newton even be interested in twaddle?" I ask, borrowing the description of my irate neighbour.

Thomas says, "You want to know how the man who invented calculus and wrote *Principia* could give credence to the Philosopher's Stone?"

"Yes, I do."

"I don't know that we will ever find out for certain. He was very private. But there was also an... observation."

Intrigued, I tighten my grip on his arm. "What?"

"Newton heated certain metals in a cauldron hanging over his fire. He went without sleep for days to keep the cauldron heated at a specific temperature. Newton allowed no one else into the room. But someone peered in the window and said that the colour of the metals bubbling in the pot was like nothing ever seen in this world."

I shiver but not because of the November wind clawing at my skirts. This does seem to put the great Newton in the same category as Dippel, Flamel, Bacon and all the other alchemists whose quests fell into the category of the occult. In past centuries, these men could be imprisoned, tortured or burnt at the stake for their pursuits.

A few minutes later, we reach Fournier Street. Daphne, thank goodness, has just stoked the fire. She lays out a late supper of cold meats and fruit, which I dive into, finding myself ravenous. Thomas, I note, has less appetite. But it's not that he is ready for his bed either. In the sitting room, he opens a newspaper. After a few minutes, with Daphne gone to bed and our son already fast asleep upstairs, I ask the question that's been nagging at me for hours.

"Do you think, Tom, that that man's mention of Johann Dippel and the fact that he invented a new colour has some special meaning?"

He lowers his newspaper. "Such as what?"

"First, there's the letter from the French ambassador saying you're a master of colour and then this man brings up Dippel."

To my astonishment, Thomas bursts into laughter. "If a French agent schemed to approach me to develop a new colour or conduct an experiment, I hardly think it would take the form of shouting questions from the back of a crowded room."

Put like that, it does sound ludicrous.

"What of Dippel's meddling with the dead?" I ask.

"We know he was a doctor. I've heard that he was a scholar of anatomy, an avid dissector. He cut up the bodies of the dead as part of his obsession with transferring a soul from one body to another."

"That is beyond blasphemy," I say. "So incredibly *gruesome*."

Thomas only nods.

"Why, when so many artists and writers and philosophers – and chemists, of course – are seeking enlightenment, would this man pursue darkness?" I say. "It's unfathomable."

At that moment, something chilling happens. He is sitting right across from me, not moving, but I feel as if Thomas is pulling away. He has rendered his face expressionless. Can my husband be treating me as he did the audience earlier tonight? His true feelings must be hidden? I am on the verge of saying something more when he picks up his newspaper and resumes reading. And a quarter of an hour after that, Thomas says he is going up to bed. I say nothing in reply.

There was a time when we kept nothing from each other. When did it change?

I keep hoping for a return of the effortless harmony that existed between us for years. I hate the watchful silences, the feeling of being sealed off from my husband's thoughts. Circumstances do change in the next few days. Though it raises still more questions.

Despite the entire Montagu family coming down from Hinchingbrooke House to reside in town, Thomas has not been released from his teaching duties. The Earl of Sandwich and his family stay in their house in Chiswick, which is on the other side of London. This means Thomas must leave quite early and secure a carriage. He returns to Spitalfields very late, needing to, once again, organise transport for the following day. This cannot be sustained. It seems the only solution is for Thomas to stay in the family's house at Chiswick instead of with his own family. But a solution presents itself, or I should say presents himself, in the form of a driver by the name of Lawrence and his carriage.

"Very pleased to make your acquaintance, Mrs. Sturbridge," says the broad-shouldered, dark-eyed man with a broken front tooth and a brash London accent, who stands before me in dark blue livery, clothing that fits him much better than that of the servants of Joshua Reynolds.

I learn that the Earl of Sandwich is lending a carriage and driver to Thomas for the winter, which I can scarcely believe. His second son's tutor is to enjoy this privilege?

"It is to everyone's advantage, you see," explains Lawrence, who insists on being called by his first name while we are "Mr." and "Mrs.".

"I'm first coachman of the house, but we have a new man who would benefit from driving his lordship," he says. "He needs the practice. The oldest son is away with his regiment. So I shall have Mr. Sturbridge to drive in the second carriage."

"But for you to have to lodge in Spitalfields?" I say wonderingly. "If only we could put you up in the house, but we sadly do not have a room."

"Isn't it nice of you to fuss over me! The East End suits me well. Fine stabling for the horses, clean rooms to let and plenty of chop houses and taverns."

"You are quite the agreeable person, Lawrence," I say. This all seems so unlikely, but I can tell these easy answers are all I'll get from the coachman.

"Mr. Sturbridge's wellbeing is important," he says firmly.

Lawrence's presence in our lives alters everyone's bearings after just a couple of days. We see more of Thomas, and he is less exhausted, which is welcome. But it's more than that. It would be hard for me to say who is more thrilled by the good-tempered Lawrence and his carriage, my son Pierre, obsessed with the horses, or my manservant, George. Lawrence, shrewdly perceiving the importance of Daphne's good opinion, takes the time to speak to her and manages to overcome her distrust of anyone who's not a Huguenot. One night, after delivering Thomas, he lingers at the house long after I assumed he had left. I can hear Daphne laughing in the kitchen, and later, I spy two cups of chocolate drunk on the table.

He even manages to find the good side of Jean, who is deeply sceptical of any man who chooses to dedicate his life to serving aristocrats.

I witness this first-hand on Fournier Street. Lawrence, with a rag and a bit of oil, is cleaning the Montagu family coat of arms, carved into the side of the carriage. Jean stands by, shaking his head.

Pointing at the outline of a knight's helmet in the centre, Jean says, "Yes, I suppose you'll tell me, 'Oh, they came over with William the Conqueror.' But what has the family contributed to the good of the country in the last hundred years?"

Lawrence says, "It was a Montagu who came up with the Bank of England."

"Ah, excellent," crows Jean. "Now I know who should be blamed!"

After several more days of driving back and forth, Thomas tells me something genuinely amusing: I am the one who most impresses Lawrence.

"He wants to know how he can secure such a superior wife," Thomas says.

"Better be good to me," I tease. "Or else I'll abandon you for him."

My husband laughs and hope leaps within me. Perhaps we have pushed through our strange and baffling disharmony.

Lawrence agrees at once to convey us to the exhibition of my grandfather's work. The Foundling Hospital in Bloomsbury is well known to me. Ever since my love of art bloomed and I could persuade Grandfather to take me, this was the place where I would drink in the details of the paintings hung on the walls. I spent joyful afternoons studying the work of many artists, committing to memory their choices of composition and colour.

I cannot pretend to be perfectly calm, though, as Lawrence speeds us efficiently to Bloomsbury. Caroline and Jean continue to be at odds, slowing down the progress of our work. We cannot seem to settle on the first set of plants from India to be painted for Monsieur Carteret. No matter what Jean says or does, Caroline is offended. I even wonder if the true reason that Caroline says she cannot attend the exhibition is that Jean is determined to be here. At least I won't need to pull my two artists apart in the middle of an important evening.

And make no mistake, the exhibition *is* important to me. Ever since I received the letter from Joshua Reynolds inviting me to his house, I've found myself on the edges of the London art world. I'm grateful that people will have this opportunity to see my grandfather's work and learn about him. I'd be less than honest if I didn't admit to hoping that my own fortunes could rise too. Perhaps the deep prejudices against female artists will be eased. I could devote more time to my work, my paintings could be seen and appreciated.

Tonight could be the beginning of a new life.

Who would have thought this hunger for a new life could rage so strong? Ambition was a force driving me when I was younger, but the disaster of spying and then marrying and having a child, the daily necessities of life, banked those fires. Or so I thought.

"This is not what I expected of a foundling hospital," comments Thomas. It is approaching dusk when our carriage arrives at the front gate, and we continue through to the long, sweeping gravel drive. There's just enough light to take in the two majestic brick wings – one for the boys and one for the girls – and the chapel resting in the middle, its windows glowing with white-orange light. About twenty years ago, a grand sea captain named Thomas Coram, childless himself and worried about destitute orphans, came up with the idea.

"Before it was built, children without parents had no means to keep themselves alive beyond the charity of their parish," I point out.

"It's very commendable," says Thomas, but in that new way of his, polite and a bit distant. How I hate it. So much for our becoming close again.

The person we see first is Jean Orgier, standing just inside the main doors. He has come early, wearing his Sunday best. I'm touched by his personal support for my family.

"To think I might meet Edmund Burke or Samuel Johnson in person tonight, what an opportunity," Jean exults, bounding after us.

Of course. *This* is why he was so eager to attend. I can't hold it against him, knowing his passion for justice and his eagerness to hear the ideas of the foremost intellectuals of England. I hope that Reynolds' friends will accompany him or join him here. I think I made a favourable enough impression on Edmund and Jane Burke that they will want to be here. I look forward to seeing them.

Reminding myself that what matters most is my grandfather's paintings, I push on to the room where the exhibition is being held. I've been here twice in the last three weeks, bringing the paintings over and then viewing where they hang. On the latter trip, I was joined by the fair-haired assistant of Joshua Reynolds. He was much more agreeable that day compared to the evening when he followed Mr. Reynolds up the stairs to my workshop. He discreetly advised me how much to charge for the paintings, doubtless after discussing it with Mr. Reynolds.

The room, to the left of the main entrance, is lit with fine candles for the occasion, and with a surge of pleasure, I take in my grandfather's portraits of the people of the silk-weaving industry. Sprinkled among them are paintings adapted from the twelve engravings of Hogarth's *Industry and Idleness*, the story of what happens to an apprentice who works hard as opposed to an apprentice who becomes a criminal. The different works are not crammed next to one another as they were at Charing Cross. There's more space allowed. It seems fitting to the spirit of the occasion.

I hurry to greet Mrs. Tensington, the Foundling Hospital person assigned to this event. I've had the pleasure of meeting her during my earlier visits. She assures me that all is going smoothly. She will be present to answer questions, arrange any sales, should someone express interest, and oversee things during the fortnight that the exhibition is up.

It's been advertised in a few newspapers that tonight is the first night it opens to the public, a two-hour viewing. I know from my experience at The Society of Artists event how crowded these rooms can get. I happily brace myself for the throng.

During the first half-hour, though, only a trickle of people appear. I watch one handsome couple as they make their way around the room. My stomach clenches as they skip over Grandfather's portraits to focus on the adaptations of Hogarth's engravings.

Thomas slips his hand around my waist and says quietly, "William Hogarth was famous for a long time. His name will draw people here."

"Oh, it's fine – I am happy with how it is going," I insist, pulling away from him. "This is the most fortunate thing that could happen to my family."

As I finish speaking, Joshua Reynolds walks into the room, accompanied by his sister, Frances. Everyone stops to stare. Reynolds gives no sign of being aware that he is an object of fascination as he surveys the works on the wall. He had sent word to me yesterday confirming that he planned to be here. Still, to think that he did not attend the first night of The Society of Artists exhibition, but he appears at the Foundling Hospital? I am greatly moved. It's impossible to believe Sam Baldwin's story, that Joshua Reynolds moved behind the scenes to demolish the fragile George Romney. He's thoughtful and supportive, not cruel.

Once he's made a quick turn around the room, Reynolds approaches us. "All seems as it should be, Mrs. Sturbridge."

"I cannot tell you how grateful I am for your proposing this exhibit and all of your attention to it," I say, smiling, turning to Thomas. "I would like to introduce you to my husband."

Joshua leaps forward to take Thomas' hand and shake it with vigour. "I am glad to make your acquaintance, Mr. Sturbridge."

Thomas says with courtesy, "And I yours, Mr. Reynolds."

Frances Reynolds is in full flutter, expressing her delight over seeing me again. "I would like to discuss the path to women becoming recognised artists with you, Mrs. Sturbridge," she says with a conspiratorial wink, drawing me away from her brother and my husband.

This is welcome, though unexpected. Joshua's sister will lay out the first steps toward my finding a foothold in a more serious art career?

Her face flushed, Frances Reynolds plunges forward. "Everyone keeps talking about the Swiss paintress Angelika Kaufmann and how promising she is. There's even been discussion of sending letters encouraging her to come to England. Imagine that, forsaking Rome for London, just for the sake of your art career? Joshua is always saying that his studies in Italy were the making of him."

I say, "Miss Reynolds, I believe one can pursue art anywhere."

"Oh, I'm so glad to hear you voice that opinion – oh, yes. Because, you see, I am a painter too. I tell practically no one. I have focused on miniature portraits, Mrs. Sturbridge, and have done so for some time. It isn't easy. Mr. Samuel Johnson – you met him at our house, didn't you? He's not just Joshua's friend, he's my friend too. He really is. But Mr. Johnson says that portrait painting is improper employment for women because it requires them to stare at the faces of men for long periods of time, and that is unseemly. Do you agree with him?"

"No, I most definitely do not," I say. How disappointing that the man who produced something as wonderfully modern as a dictionary would hold these antiquated views.

"Thank you for that," she says. "I was delighted to hear Joshua talk about Miss Kaufmann favourably to you and to other friends since. But my worry, my lingering worry, is that she is twenty-three years old and said to be very beautiful. Are youth and beauty prerequisites for advancement in art if you are a female?"

I am not sure what to say. I know nothing of Angelika Kaufmann.

"Mrs. Sturbridge, I was hoping you might have an informed opinion on how we should respond to the challenge," she presses.

We? My breath tightens. Does Frances Reynolds put herself in the same artistic category as myself with her secret miniatures? And she thinks we are both thrust into the shadow by a lovely twenty-three-year-old? Anger claws my already taut nerves.

Across the room, I spot Abraham Bougeous, one of my grandfather's friends, inching his way into the exhibition room, a cane supporting his trembling progress. Beside him, to my surprise, stands Nicolas Carteret. I had no idea that he planned to come.

"I'm sorry, I must greet some people who just arrived," I inform Frances. "Let me think upon your question."

She smiles tentatively as I hurry away from her.

"Pierre would be pleased," warbles Monsieur Bougeous once I reach him. "You've done well here, Genevieve."

I thank him and offer to guide both of them around the room. Monsieur Carteret says, "I wanted to have a brief word with your husband first. Is that possible?"

145

With a wave of his cane, Monsieur Bourgeous says, "Yes, go and talk to him, go – I'm not so old I can't take in a single room on my own."

Thomas stands by himself. Joshua Reynolds has moved on to converse with someone else. I beckon for my husband to join us. I assume this has something to do with the Mathematical Society of Spitalfields.

Without preliminaries, Carteret says, "Mr. Sturbridge, you are employed by the Earl of Sandwich, is that correct?"

"I am," Thomas replies, glancing at me. I try to signal that I'm as surprised as he is by the question.

"I have been told that a bill is being debated in Parliament that would restrict the importing of French and Italian silks to England, which is what Spitalfields weavers need more than anything else on this earth," says Carteret. "The government must put a limit on such imports, to have those foreign silks flooding the British market now, it would be a disaster."

Thomas' confusion deepens.

"The Earl of Sandwich opposes the protection bill along with the Duke of Bedford," continues Monsieur Carteret. "It would be most helpful if you could have a word with him and explain the importance of the bill's passing, help him change his mind."

Thomas opens his mouth, shuts it and then opens it to say, "I am a tutor to one of his sons. We do not discuss bills before Parliament."

"But surely, you could find an opportune moment to do so?" presses Monsieur Carteret.

"Politics is outside my role," Thomas says simply.

Nicolas Carteret's lips tighten. "Come now, His Lordship has given you a carriage, I hear. You can hardly expect me to believe that you're a servant of no account."

What Monsieur Carteret has not yet managed to grasp, but I have realised immediately, is that Thomas won't intervene on behalf of this bill because he doesn't wish to do so, not because he lacks the status to do it.

"My husband has never cared for politics," I say, struggling to explain.

Nicolas Carteret takes his measure of us both before speaking again.

"You make clear your distaste over me mentioning the matter, but the welfare of a great many families hangs in the balance with this bill, not least of all your own," he says icily and walks away.

This evening is not turning out the way I would wish.

A fresh group of gentlemen stride into the room. Among them is Hervé Gaynard.

I shake my head in wonder. Of all the people who attended Joshua Reynolds' gathering, he is the one I would least wish to see. Yet here he is!

Naturally, Monsieur Gaynard makes a beeline for Joshua Reynolds. He is accompanied by another man, one several years younger than himself and a good four inches taller, with olive skin and a long nose. He wears the same ornate clothes and elaborate wig as Gaynard. I would wager every shilling I have that his companion is not English.

"May I present the Chevalier de Seingalt, who is visiting England," says Gaynard to our small group. "He has come from Paris, though his homeland is Italy. Venice, to be specific. But he has found much to amuse him here." Gaynard bares his teeth. "Not enough to persuade him to learn English," he continues, indicating that his friend has not understood the introduction.

I am alarmed to hear the word "chevalier". Evelyn Willoughby told me about a French spy who went into hiding in London carrying that title, but I recall his full name was the Chevalier d'Eon.

"You have been in London long, Monsieur?" asks Joshua Reynolds in mediocre French.

"Since last year," the Venetian replies.

Monsieur Gaynard says, "The chevalier had an audience with the king and queen. King George wanted to meet him."

"How did you find them?" someone asked, also in French. It seems everyone in our group can speak the language to some degree.

The Venetian chevalier replies, "Your Queen Charlotte was charming, we conversed for a little while. I tried to converse with King George, but he spoke so quietly, I could not understand what he was saying, so by way of reply, I bowed wherever he paused. I hope it sufficed."

Everyone laughs politely, and the Venetian chevalier smiles. It softens his hard countenance. He continues, "I've seen the king and queen once more since my audience at court. It was at the Drury Lane Theatre. They were in the royal box." He shakes his head. "It was an extraordinary evening."

"How so?"

"There was a change in which play was to be performed, and the audience took it badly. The actor, your country's most famous actor, David Garrick, stood onstage and pleaded with them for order to be restored. This just made the people angrier. Garrick left, and the royal couple was forced to leave the theatre. All the better people departed. This pitched the mob into action. They ran out to the taverns and then returned to tear apart the building itself. Drury Lane Theatre was wrecked."

"It cost a fortune to refit, a fortune," sighs Hervé Gaynard.

Two thoughts run through my mind. One is that although he was considered important enough to receive a royal audience and has attended the theatre at least once, the Chevalier de Seingalt does not possess much money. I spot an old brownish stain – sauce or soup – on the edge of his embroidered sleeve. The coat is no longer presentable due to such stains, but if it were cleaned, it could fall apart entirely. His stockings are not of the best quality either. In sum, I would say the chevalier looked grander – and younger – at a bit of a distance.

My other thought is that this story about the king and queen was practised between the two of them ahead of time. The tale of the tumult in the theatre too. But who are they trying to impress?

"The mob is not to be controlled here in London," says Gaynard. "There is, quite simply, no one to do it."

"Those most at risk are your English nobles," observes the Chevalier de Seingalt. "If you wear court clothes in the street and have no armed guards surrounding you, you could be stripped of the clothes and valuables where you stand."

Annoyed with their complaints about England, I say, "You are unused to rough manners, I take it."

Gaynard says, "I would say that we are used to roughness with a little more... finesse."

This makes Joshua Reynolds laugh, and Gaynard flicks a triumphant glance my way. Also drifting in my direction is his signature scent, the cloying powdered violet.

The Chevalier de Seingalt says, "I hear about Joshua Reynolds everywhere I go, and I've had the privilege of seeing your paintings with my own eyes. They are superb, Monsieur."

Joshua Reynolds inclines his head and smiles. I'm sure he hears this praise wherever he goes, although a malicious little voice inside me says he likes to hear it all the same. Nonetheless, Reynolds says, "Tonight is not about me, but about the art of William Hogarth and a Huguenot painter named Pierre Billiou, the late grandfather of Mrs. Genevieve Sturbridge."

Gaynard says, "I have had the distinct pleasure of meeting Mrs. Sturbridge in Leicester Fields." His gaze shifts to Thomas. "Am I fortunate enough to make the acquaintance tonight of the esteemed Mr. Sturbridge?"

Thomas is courteous to Gaynard and his friend, the Chevalier de Seingalt, but I perceive my husband's discomfort. Even if the French were not a source of trouble for us, he would recoil from a man like Gaynard, who oozes insincerity. His supercilious Venetian friend seems no better.

At that moment, Joshua Reynolds says he must leave. He has not been here for very long, it is barely seven o'clock, but I imagine his social diary is full. Turning to me, he says, "We have important matters to discuss. Would you and Mr. Sturbridge care to dine with me and my sister at home? Is the day after tomorrow convenient?"

So soon! I'd understood that Joshua Reynolds' social commitments were fixed weeks ahead. Glancing at Thomas for confirmation, I tell him that we would be happy to dine with him.

"Good. Good. Walk with me to the door, Mrs. Sturbridge?" he asks quietly.

Apparently, some confidential matter cannot wait until the day after tomorrow. I accompany Joshua and his sister across the room. Frances is trying to catch my attention, her eyes pleading. But at the door, he pauses and says, abruptly, "Frances, go on ahead to the carriage. I'll be with you in a few minutes."

With a martyrish sag of her shoulders, Frances Reynolds does as she's told.

As he removes his small ear trumpet from his pocket, Joshua Reynolds says, "Mrs. Sturbridge, I must ask you something."

I assume the question to be private, and I am to answer him discreetly, necessitating his trumpet.

"Yes, of course," I say, taking a step closer to him.

"Is Mr. Sturbridge in poor health?"

Startled, I say, "My husband is well. Why do you ask me this, sir?"

"Mr. Sturbridge's cough," he says. "It seems serious. I wondered...?"

I know what he wonders. I had thought it myself when I first met Thomas, lean and pale with a persistent cough. "He does not have consumption, should that be your concern," I say. "The cough... has another cause."

Joshua looks relieved but doesn't leave it at that. "I have a physician, a very good man. One of the best in London. I can give you his name should you wish it. Your husband's health is no small matter."

His question and following offer seem intrusive. I thank him without asking for the doctor's name, and then I bid him goodnight, for he has nothing more to say to me alone, I think.

On this, I am, once more, mistaken.

Joshua says, "I fear that my sister is trying to draw you into conversation about her ambitions to paint. I must ask you, as a personal favour, do not encourage her in any way."

He puts his trumpet away, assuming my stunned silence is acquiescence and leaves the Foundling Hospital.

I stand in that hallway, deeply baffled. So he doesn't support the creative dreams of his younger sister. My grandfather had, at least, encouraged me and taught me what he knew, supplied me with materials. Does Joshua agree with his friend, Samuel Johnson, that women have no place in trying to make a living as serious artists? Is his support of Angelica Kaufmann tied to her youth and beauty as Frances speculates?

I have to admit I really have no idea what he thinks of my work. He saw three of my paintings in Spitalfields. It troubled me then, and it troubles me now, that he said nothing specifically about them. It seems unlikely that the day after tomorrow, he will put forward his plan to champion my career as an artist. But then, why else are we dining together?

Returning to the main room, I note that others are leaving in Joshua Reynolds' wake. Perhaps twenty people remain. Edmund and Jane Burke and Samuel Johnson? They never made an appearance.

At the far end of the room, Nicolas Carteret stands next to Abraham Bougeous, who is inspecting one of Grandfather's paintings, his face no more than two feet from the canvas. Carteret's hands are linked behind his back. I note Jean has maintained a careful distance from Carteret all evening. Well, that is for the best.

And then there's my husband. Thomas stands alone. He looks as if he's concentrating on something, not a painting but some problem miles away. That sensitive, handsome face I fell in love with? It could be the shadows thrown by all the tallow candles, but he looks gaunt and ghostly pale. Yes, no matter how much I hate to admit it, Thomas looks ill. It isn't a surprise that Joshua Reynolds should wonder about the state of his health.

"Mrs. Sturbridge?"

The voice is familiar. It is Sam Baldwin, just arriving. The candle-light gleams off his tall forehead, above those eyes crinkling with warmth and sympathy.

"Mr. Baldwin, I am so very, very glad that you've come," I say.

Heads turn to see who I'm greeting.

Smiling down at me, he says, "Of course. I wouldn't miss this for the world."

"You've missed Mr. Reynolds, I'm afraid. He and his sister came, but they left a short time ago."

"Did they?" he says with a shrug. Sam takes in my grandfather's painting of a master weaver. "This is interesting," he says. "He has a proud look but is fairly guarded. Keeping a secret, maybe." He glances around the room. "You must be very happy with the exhibit."

"I'd be happier if more people had come to see it," I blurt.

It feels good to be able to confess my disappointment. Still, it doesn't put me in a favourable light. I hasten to add, "I didn't mean to sound unappreciative. I suppose I thought that since this was Mr. Reynolds' idea…"

My voice trails away.

"He'd produce a crowd for you?" finishes Sam with a laugh, but it's a kind one. He scans the room quickly. "I see Hervé Gaynard is here, he is sure to tell his friends about the exhibit, the man knows half of London."

"Hmmmm."

I'd like to say I would happily trade all of Monsieur Gaynard's friends for his absence, such is my distaste for the man. But I don't have a good reason for my antipathy, or at least, not one I can share.

Sam explains, "Most of Joshua Reynolds' friends are from the publishing world or the theatre. He's tricky with other artists. He is determined to be first, with any second perched on a very, very distant horizon."

I smile. "And how is Mr. Romney?"

"Oh, nursing the darkest of suspicions."

Consumed by curiosity, I ask, "What could that be?"

"That Joshua Reynolds was able to ferret out that Romney had several paintings up and *David Rizzio* could attract serious acclaim, become the painting of the night. So he hatched his plan to unveil the new portrait of Kitty Fisher, London's reigning tart, after everyone already was in the room, to dominate the evening."

A voice raised in anger disrupts this engaging gossip of Sam's.

"I tell you, your insults cannot be allowed to pass!"

I whip around to see what's happening. It's Jean Orgier. His face contorted with rage, he is lunging toward Hervé Gaynard as if he means to tear him to pieces.

Chapter Twelve

Before I can make it across the room, Thomas reaches Jean. He pulls my art assistant away from Hervé Gaynard, who, amazingly, shows little discomfort with the attack. In fact, he is laughing.

"What is it that you think you heard?" Gaynard says, his fingers moving inside his coat as if groping for something. With a lurch of my stomach, I wonder if it is a weapon. He's the sort of man who might carry a dagger.

His Venetian companion speaks rapidly to Gaynard in what I assume is Italian. He seems more alarmed than Gaynard.

"Jean – Jean – what is happening?" I demand.

"You are acquainted with this excitable young man, Mrs. Sturbridge?" asks Gaynard, still groping for something in his coat.

"Jean works for my silk design business, Monsieur," I say.

"It's what *he* said to the other one," Jean points at Gaynard. "What he said about the Huguenots. It was foul, Mrs. Sturbridge."

Gaynard says coldly, "You must have misunderstood me. I was telling my friend some of the background behind the exhibit. He speaks little English, so our conversation was in French. I insulted no one present."

"I understand French perfectly," retorts Jean.

Thomas says, "Jean, no matter what he said, it was a private conversation."

"What does that matter?" Jean shouts. "He is not in a private house – he's here, in a place honouring a Huguenot artist."

Gaynard reaches deeper into his coat. Any put-on amusement is dying. In fact, he regards Jean with the same contempt as a man would an insect he'd like to crush beneath his shoe. I rub my forehead. How embarrassing this is, a shouting, jostling outburst in the Foundling Hospital, before an exhibition of paintings. I glance over at Nicolas Carteret. From the far side of the room, he watches us.

It is then that Sam steps forward and says, in a jovial voice, "Hervé, I say it's time to move on. Why don't I buy you and your friend a brandy? I know a fine establishment near here."

Gaynard slowly withdraws his hand from his coat. He's holding his snuff box. With all of us gathered around, he snorts twice.

"That sounds like an excellent idea," Hervé Gaynard finally says. "Who could resist an offer such as this from Sam Baldwin?"

He relays the plan in Italian to the Chevalier de Seingalt, who peers at me strangely before nodding.

Jean takes a deep, ragged breath. Thank heaven he doesn't seem intent on pushing the matter any further. He's got some kind of grip on himself and allows Thomas to pull him further from Gaynard.

Sam says to me, "I'll be in Bloomsbury again on Friday afternoon and will return to finish the exhibition. Good night, Mrs. Sturbridge."

As soon as Sam has led the other two men from the room, I say to Jean, "What did you hear them say that would make you lose your temper?"

"The French one said to the Italian that there has never been a greater hypocrite than the Huguenot. He said the French Protestants weep on English shoulders over Catholic atrocities, but the Huguenots committed much more violence than the Catholics when they still lived in France. 'Next to their Bibles, they keep their knives and their bottles of gin.' And that's not all!"

"But enough for now," I say. "I have to tell you, I'm not all that surprised he'd say something horrible. I formed a poor opinion of Monsieur Gaynard previously."

"I was going to ask you where you'd met this unpleasant man before," Thomas says.

I explain that he was a fellow guest at Joshua Reynolds' house in Leicester Fields, the gathering in honour of Mr. Hogarth.

Jean says, "Mr. Reynolds has a damned funny idea of who's a fit friend. What's a Papist like him even doing, living here, in London?"

"Now that the war is over, there's nothing to stop the French from crossing the channel," I say, thinking of Evelyn Willoughby.

Jean says, "I'm not sorry I challenged him, but I am sorry if I upset you. I didn't come here to put your grandfather's exhibition in jeopardy."

I struggle with how to address this. Issuing public threats is not the sort of behaviour I should let stand. But for Gaynard to insult the Huguenots, and to do so literally in front of my grandfather's paintings? It's an outrage, and if I had been the one to hear Gaynard instead of Jean, I can't swear to being able to hold my temper any better than he had done.

"We'll talk about it tomorrow, Jean," I say.

Thomas and I stay until the last interested members of the public leave. I hate to make him wait with me, he looks so tired. Even riding in as fine a coach as any in London, Thomas is worn down from this

Chiswick-to-Spitalfields travelling. If I were a more attentive wife, I'd have noticed his state by now. But I've been caught up in preparing for the exhibition. And for what? Right now, I feel deflated. Not too many people came.

I'd been looking forward to the evening as a crucial next step, but to what? As has been the case for the last month, each meeting with Joshua Reynolds leads to talk of the next meeting. I hope this dinner will finally make his interest in my art clearer.

"Were any enquiries made about purchasing my grandfather's paintings?" I ask Mrs. Stillington.

"No, none," she says briskly. "I shall let you know if I receive any over the next fortnight."

I thank her, and we take our leave of the Foundling Hospital. Lawrence and the carriage wait outside. The lights are very dim within both of the long wings that house the children. They've all been put to bed.

We are nearly home when Thomas asks me about Sam Baldwin.

"I met him at Joshua Reynolds' as well," I say.

Thomas says, "He showed a cool head. We should all be grateful he extricated those two."

"Yes."

He says nothing more for a minute. I think his thoughts turn to another topic. In that, I am mistaken.

"When this Mr. Baldwin walked in the door and you spoke to him, you looked... different," Thomas says hesitantly. "You were lighter and freer, more so than I've seen for a long while."

"I was relieved," I say. "Apart from Mr. Reynolds, no artists attended."

That's not strictly true, but I don't know how to explain my affinity for Sam Baldwin. There's an ease to our conversations, we take the

158

same avid interest in art and, to be honest, artist gossip. This would seem so shallow to Thomas.

My husband says nothing more until the carriage reaches Fournier Street. We both notice how bright the front parlour room is. The curtains are drawn, but on the other side, the light of at least a half dozen candles shimmers. It is well past time for Pierre to be put to bed. Why on earth is the house so full of light?

"I don't understand this," I say to Thomas.

We scramble out of the carriage and hurry to the front door. I have not finished unlocking it before George pulls it open. He and Sophie haven't left for the day. How surprising.

"You have guests," George tells us. "Your friends have waited a long while for you. We gave them some wine, I hope that's all right, sir."

Guests? Friends? Certainly, no one was expected, and George holds no card to inform us who they are.

My throat dry, I peer down the hallway. Sophie stands there, very still. Her eyes gleam with what seems like excitement. There's no sign of Daphne or my son – he must be with her in her alcove room or put to bed upstairs.

Thomas and I walk into the parlour together. And there, to my astonishment, sit Hervé Gaynard and the Chevalier de Seingalt, surrounded by flickering candles and warmed by a robust fire.

"What are you doing here?" I cry.

Gaynard's eyebrows arch at my rudeness. His words directed not at me but at Thomas, he says, "We wanted to apologise for that unfortunate scene at the Foundling Hospital. The last thing we wanted to do there was cause you distress."

But as they must see by our faces, it's far more distressing that they came here, to our Spitalfields home, uninvited. Somehow Hervé Gaynard has talked his way in. With chagrin, I think how they must have bamboozled George. At least my servant had enough of a brain to stay until we returned. It's deeply chilling to think of the men alone in the house with just Pierre and Daphne.

I can't get over how strange it is. In my grandfather's favourite chair – the stuffing grown lopsided in the seat cushion – lounges the half-Savoyard Hervé Gaynard and his lace sleeves. Next to him perches the glamorous Chevalier de Seingalt, his well-groomed fingers tapping the side of a narrow maple table that on top bears my neglected embroidery.

All I can think of to say is, "I thought you were having a brandy with Sam Baldwin."

"We enjoyed that pleasure and then proceeded here," replies Gaynard.

"But how did you know where we live?" I ask, wonderingly.

Hervé Gaynard just smiles, as if I amuse him.

Thomas says, "Very well, we accept your apology. And now, it's late, and my wife and I need to retire for the night."

"Is it late?" He repeats the question in French to the Chevalier de Seingalt, who shakes his head.

"In Covent Garden, the night is just beginning," says the Venetian.

Thomas, his tone hardening, says, "In case you haven't noticed, this is not Covent Garden. Now I must insist you go, gentlemen."

"Not before we have a conversation," says Hervé Gaynard, still speaking French. "You see, I know a lot about you, Thomas Sturbridge. And I know a great deal about your wife, Genevieve. She and I have a friend in common. He told me how you two met. The real story about how you met."

Next to me, Thomas makes a startled noise. I stand frozen.

"It was a very romantic story." He turns to the chevalier. "You appreciate such things much more than I ever can."

160

"I do," sighs the Venetian.

"It is a touching story. A spy sets out to catch her quarry – and falls in love with him and marries him." He takes a sip of his wine. "However, the story hasn't had too lovely an ending." Gaynard looks around the room. "Living in Spitalfields, a meagre income, a humble workshop up on the third floor of the house. Teaching the younger son of a dim English peer. Doing everything they can to stay in the good graces of King George's government. It's sad, really. Quite a steep descent from working as a master chemist at Sèvres Porcelain under the personal sponsorship of Madame de Pompadour and His Majesty King Louis the Fifteenth, eh, Mr. Sturbridge? You had everything you could wish for then. Money, connections, the friendship of France's finest men of science."

He knows everything about us.

While I am fighting down panic, Thomas says not a single word. He stares at them with fixed concentration.

"What do you want?" I ask, breaking the silence.

Hervé Gaynard leans forward, smiling. "Right to the point, Genevieve. I like that. It makes you a woman I can do business with, as others have before me."

"Monsieur, I have not given you the right to use my Christian name," I spat.

At that, Gaynard laughs, but it's not the nasty chuckle of before. He seems to find this genuinely funny. "What shall you do to punish me for taking such a liberty? Throw a glass of wine in my face too?"

"What?" asks Thomas.

Gaynard's eyes flick between us. "I see I know a little more about your wife's recent behaviour than you do, Mr. Sturbridge. I suspect I know a little more about you than she does as well."

161

Thomas takes a step toward Gaynard. I can see he is angry, truly angry.

"When did Sir Gabriel Courtenay tell you about us?" he demands.

I wince at the sound of my spymaster's name on Thomas' lips. But yes, Sir Gabriel could only be the source of these intimate details of how we met.

"Oh, it's been several years since I spoke to Sir Gabriel," Gaynard says. "Three, perhaps."

"And you are spying for France – as Sir Gabriel did?" asks Thomas.

Hervé Gaynard and the Chevalier de Seingalt look at each other and laugh.

"Sir Gabriel was one of the most important men in King Louis' service, trained by the best there is, protected here for years and entrusted with crucial missions," says the Chevalier de Seingalt, patronisingly.

Gaynard continues in English, "My friend and I are available to help our country's diplomats, we may perform small errands when called upon, but it is of little consequence. I certainly wouldn't give it the name 'espionage'. We cannot pretend to be worthy of selection for le Secret du Roi."

In his switching so frequently between English and French, most likely to inform the Venetian sitting by his side, Gaynard risks betraying how he really feels beneath his offensive banter. In the reverence with which he says le Secret du Roi, he shows his respect for King Louis.

"What exactly is the point of this visit if not to draw me into some spying mission?" asks Thomas. "I am rapidly losing patience."

Hervé Gaynard says, "We want you to join with us, but not as a spy, Mr. Sturbridge. For a man of your gifts, there are glittering fortunes to be had."

Thomas says with disgust, "So this is about money."

Gaynard says, "I implore you, do be seated. Both of you. Only hear me out on a prospective opportunity that is tailored to your skills, Mr. Sturbridge. If you're not interested, we will leave, and I will not be the one to put anything more to you."

"Very well," says Thomas. "I will hear you out, as it is the best way to see the end of you."

I struggle to hide my shock – and my dismay. Why is he giving Gaynard an opening? Since there is no possibility of his being interested in the Frenchman's proposal, Thomas must want to learn what it is. I cannot imagine why that would be so.

Thomas and I sit in the only place left to us, the settee sofa opposite our unwanted guests. It puts me close to the fire, and my arm prickles from the heat.

No doubt to taunt us, Gaynard takes a leisurely sip of wine before beginning. He says, "My friend sitting beside me in your parlour prefers to be addressed in England as the Chevalier de Seingalt, but he has another name, and as a show of good faith, I will share it with you. He is Giacomo Casanova. You may perhaps have heard of him? No? He is a man of the world, shall we say."

"I beg you, I beg you, do not be crude, Hervé," says the man I now know to be named Casanova.

Gaynard reassures him with a wave of his hand. "My friend has enjoyed many amours, but he came to London planning to reunite with one in particular, a dear friend from his past, Mrs. Theresa Cornelys."

"The hostess of Carlisle House?" I ask, startled. Thomas glances at me sideways.

"The very same," says Gaynard, pleased. "They share a daughter, though this is known by few people."

I shouldn't be surprised that Mrs. Cornelys had a love affair with Casanova. I remember her from The Society of Artists evening: tall and proud and pretentious, exactly like the Venetian adventurer. But to say that a daughter is "shared", like a book or a slice of cake, leaves me chilled.

"A sweet girl, nine years old, very pretty eyes, dances and plays the pianoforte," says Casanova with a smile. "But that is not the point of the story."

"Yes, it *is* the point," says Gaynard. "To establish an income in order to secure her. Correct?"

"I suppose it could be argued—"

"Gentlemen, please," Thomas interrupts. "The hour is late and—"

Thomas is interrupted by a coughing fit. Watching him hunch over, wracked by such painful choking spasms, I wish that I could banish our unwanted guests to the grimmest corner of Southwark.

"Excuse me," Thomas gasps. "Be back… in a minute…"

My husband waves away my offer to get him a glass of water and staggers from the parlour.

Gaynard says, "I am sorry to see your husband is not well. I understand he suffered the effects of an explosion in the mines of Saxony."

I look away, stricken. Sir Gabriel has told Gaynard so much about us!

Not caring that he's upset me even more, Gaynard says, "I've heard of other such accidents among his profession. Didn't the real Faust blow himself up in his laboratory while trying to raise the devil?"

"My husband is a chemist, not a necromancer," I say, furious.

"Ah, of course." He is sombre for no more than a few seconds. "I was sorry to miss your assistant – Caroline, is that her name? – at the Foundling Hospital tonight."

"She did not attend," I say curtly.

Gaynard's crooked smile deepens. "Such a shame." He turns to Casanova, says, "A real beauty," and they plunge into Italian.

Thankfully, Thomas reappears, his face chalky pale, but he moves with determination. Sitting forward in my grandfather's chair, Gaynard says, "Well, here is where I must disclose that my friend Casanova has not enjoyed good fortune since he came to London. Mrs. Cornelys is indifferent to him. He is not invited to spend time with their daughter. There have since been some, shall we say, regrettable incidents involving other ladies in London."

Casanova winces and holds up a pleading palm.

"If a means is not found to restore his fortune, my friend will have no choice but to leave England and soon," Gaynard continues. "Yet, we are not despairing. No, because Casanova came very close to acquiring a tremendous fortune when he was still in France. It would require some persuasive arts to restore the trust of the person in question. When I heard about the quest, I knew that Thomas Sturbridge would be just the man to carry it off. That is what I enjoy doing for my friends, making introductions. It was a matter of finding a private moment."

Thomas says slowly, "You honestly expect me to assist you in some sort of theft?"

"Theft?" Hervé Gaynard throws back his head and laughs. "The woman we have in mind is the third wealthiest in all of France, and she longs to give her money to someone – yes, give it! – who can deliver what she wants."

"And what is that?" I ask, my chest tight with anxiety.

His eyes shining, Gaynard says, "An alchemist who can control the Philosopher's Stone."

Thomas jumps to his feet, his face an accusation. "It was you two who sent that man to the Mathematical Society to ask me questions about alchemy, wasn't it?"

"Yes, of course, and your answers to him gave us hope," says Casanova, completely unashamed. "You understand very well that chemistry *is* alchemy. I have some talent in this sphere, but I lack your education and your scientific accomplishments. I'm nothing compared to the man who invented the most beautiful colour blue."

Hervé Gaynard has risen to face Thomas. Now, he throws his arms out as if embracing the entire room. "You can't expect me to believe that you would rather remain here than live as the spiritual leader of the Marquise d'Ufre, a widow worth three hundred thousand francs!"

A gasp escapes me before I can stop it. I had no idea that any one person could possess so much money. Thomas does not hear me, thank God. Neither does Gaynard, whose attention is tightly fixed on my husband.

It is Casanova, the Venetian adventurer, who hears me gasp over the sum. He nods just a fraction as if to confirm the size of the prize and then winks at me with conspiratorial merriment. I look away quickly. I could never ally myself in any way with these two libertines, but I have just gained a bit of understanding of Casanova's appeal to women. He relishes these games, and though the games might be wicked, he takes boyish pleasure in them. That kind of joy can be infectious.

But Thomas is experiencing no joy whatsoever in this company. Pacing across the room, he says with exasperation, "If this widow possesses such wealth, then why is she interested in obtaining the Philosopher's Stone and turning base metals into gold?"

"Ah, I see you have no understanding about the situation that we French find ourselves in," says Gaynard, taking his seat again. He drains his glass of Burgundy. "The cruel loss to England – the years of war, being driven out of America and India – it has stripped us of not just colonies and trade ports but our prestige. We are French! We cannot exist without prestige. Still, we must go on. Some men lose themselves in debaucheries. It is only in revelling in new forms of depravity that they find some purpose to their lives. The seductions and ensnarements. For those who do not care much for women or boys, there are the secret societies. The Freemasons, the Rosicrucians and all the others…"

Gaynard's tone of voice subtly changes. He described debauchery with his usual sneer. But when it comes to secret societies, he is much more serious – and more watchful of Thomas. My husband looks uncomfortable, but I'm not sure why. Thomas would never join a secret society or club, he's never said anything good about them in the past.

I say, "You speak only of men, Monsieur Gaynard. What about Frenchwomen? I know that in England, women are not allowed to join such societies, as they are barred from many other things. It must be the same in France, even for a marquise."

"It is so in France. But when it comes to women, they are willing partners in the debauchery I spoke of. Most importantly, it is the women who become obsessed with mysticism. The Marquise d'Ufre, having the most money, can pursue her occult interests to the greatest extent. She searches for someone who can obtain the Philosopher's Stone."

"But why?" asks Thomas. "You say an awful lot, Gaynard, but you talk in circles. Why does she want the stone?"

It is Casanova who answers.

"You know that turning metals into gold is just the first challenge of the alchemist," says the Venetian. "The ultimate is the Elixir of Life… the quest for immortality."

Immortality?

Hervé Gaynard opens his mouth, but Thomas is already in motion. He leaps to the door and declares, "Leave, both of you. This very minute."

His face is red, the muscles in his neck quiver. Since the day we met six years ago, even while we were at the mercy of Sir Gabriel, I have never seen my husband this angry. Something has pushed him to this point.

"But Mr. Sturbridge, there is a specific course of action we haven't explained yet," protests Casanova. "It is about a soul transfer."

"I swear I will throw you out of this house if you won't leave," cries Thomas.

Thomas is thinner than either of our two guests. But the power of his fury is in no doubt. If they don't go and go now, I cannot answer for what happens to them. I walk over to my husband, to stand by him. I say, "You heard Mr. Sturbridge. We bid you goodnight."

Casanova looks truly crushed, yet he rises to leave. Gaynard hasn't moved. Not yet. He seems to be trying to decide something. Slowly, he removes a packet of papers from his coat.

"Mr. Sturbridge, if you would, with a calmer head, read these papers on the efforts made so far to accommodate the Marquise d'Ufre? From the perspective purely of a chemist, you will find them of great interest."

"Leave nothing behind, not a single shred of paper," says Thomas.

Muttering in Italian, Casanova strides out of the room. Gaynard rises, pulls his sleeves down and straightens the corners of his lace cuff so that each sleeve hangs down prettily. With an air of remote dignity, he walks across the room to the door and out into the hallway, where Casanova waits. The Frenchman pauses and half-turns. He has only

168

one more thing to say to us before departing into the night, and his hard eyes glint as he says it.

"It is very dangerous, Mr. Sturbridge, for a man to try to be virtuous in an age of corruption."

Chapter Thirteen

I assume Thomas to be so deeply exhausted that he'd collapse minutes after Hervé Gaynard and Casanova left, but he says goodnight to George and Sophie, then checks on Pierre and still my husband is too troubled for rest. He sits on the edge of the bed, his head in his hands.

"It seems foolish to think they could persuade a rich marquise that you have the secret of immortality," I say. "And to bring up that business of the soul transfer?"

"People are desperate and gullible," Thomas says. "That is probably the one true aspect of what was said tonight."

"So you think Gaynard was lying?"

"A mix of truth and lies," he answers. "But I am certain of this – that Gaynard is part of a chain of people and that chain is responsible for creating the message mentioning me written in invisible ink, the one in the French ambassador's letter."

I am horrified it has come to this, two reprehensible men sitting in our parlour, spinning out their reprehensible offer.

"If I hadn't met Gaynard at Joshua Reynolds' house, how would he have entered our lives?" I ask.

Thomas shrugs. "Some other way would have been found."

I take my husband by the hand. "But what a dreadful coincidence that this horrible man, who possesses knowledge of us, should be an acquaintance of Joshua Reynolds."

"A coincidence," he repeats and frowns, staring into space.

"It has to be. Mr. Reynolds has no part in this sorry business, you surely agree?"

Thomas says his brain is no longer able to generate theories, and we finally crawl into bed.

"At least it's over," I say. "We wondered what sort of overture would be made, and now we know."

His voice thick with sleep, Thomas says, "I hope… that is… the case."

Dawn arrives far too soon. When I push myself out of bed, I can barely walk down the stairs. My limbs ache with weariness. I splash cold water onto my face to jolt me out of my haze. I can focus now, not that there's much to like about what lies before me.

My grandfather, bless him, was never one to spout empty bits of wisdom like *everything always seems better in the morning*. I can't for the life of me think who told me that. I wish I could because then I'd have someone to blame. Things seem worse this morning than they had last night. Two men were able to talk their way into the house when we weren't here and then subject us to an unpleasant conversation with frightening implications, one that had ended with a threat.

When George and Sophie arrive for work, I will make clear to them that this must never be repeated. I'll take steps to make our home more secure.

Thomas looks ghastly when he awakens. His eyes are bloodshot, and his complexion is grey.

"Please stay home and rest, surely the lessons can be suspended for one day?" I plead.

"No, no," he says. Thomas resists giving in to his bouts of illness. But a moment later, I know that even he realises rest is desperately needed when he makes a suggestion. "I'll stay the night in Chiswick and come home tomorrow for the dinner with Joshua Reynolds."

He forces down a few bites of toast, turning down the tea I can't live without. When Pierre wakes up and hurtles himself at his father, shouting, "Mornin', Papa!" I see Thomas wince from the impact.

Once our son is devouring his own breakfast, Thomas tells Pierre that he won't be home tonight. He takes this news badly. Whining and pleading, he tries to get Thomas to change his mind.

"Pierre, your father needs the rest, enough of this," I say.

But Thomas shakes his head at me and then talks to Pierre, slowly bringing him around. At the door, I slip my arms around him and kiss him. How I hate the toll this takes on Thomas. And how I wish I had the power to make it all disappear.

But perhaps I do.

Minutes after Thomas climbs into the carriage and Lawrence shakes the reins, setting off for Chiswick, Jean and Caroline arrive for work. I tell them to start without me and then sit down to write my letter to Evelyn Willoughby. A scheme to commit a fraud against a gullible French marquise is not what keeps Sir Humphrey Willoughby up at night. But Gaynard saying that he runs errands for French diplomats could be of interest. And I must record the fact that he spoke years ago to Sir Gabriel, Sir Humphrey's nemesis, and knows about me and the colour blue. That, he'll want to know. I describe Gaynard's offer, sparing nothing in my description of his poor character. As I put down the quill, I think – with bitter satisfaction – that Gaynard and Casanova will now enjoy the experience of Sir Humphrey Willoughby chasing them.

I seal the paper, write Evelyn's name on it and then place it in the centre of a larger paper, folded and sealed and labelled "*11 Downing Street*". I am imitating the way Evelyn communicated with me but in reverse. I see no reason why it wouldn't work.

I'd like to dispatch the letter to Westminster immediately. George has not yet appeared, however. So first, I will put in some hours in my workshop.

But it is this day, the day before my dinner at the house of Joshua Reynolds, when I face the fact that something has gone wrong, terribly wrong, with my silk design business.

We've finally settled on an exotic flower to feature in the first set of designs for Carteret under the new fee. It's a lotus, a beautiful flower of India with an intriguing complexity to the circling rows of petals and a sensual contrast to the colours, a dark cream on the outside, intensifying to a golden orange in the centre.

Planning the sketches of the lotus was difficult enough. After much back and forth, we narrowed our choices to five different perspectives.

Now comes time for painting and the moment when it all goes awry.

What must be understood is that watercolour painting is very different from oil painting. With the latter, the paintbrush holder mixes the various oils and the various shades in the strokes that are made on canvas. Colours intensify or weaken as part of the process, a long and detailed process if need be.

But with watercolour, it all must happen quickly. Once an artist plans a design and chooses the colours for it, he or she must paint in a flurry of strokes. The image dries in minutes, seconds actually. This is why skill and confidence are essential. Successful watercolour artists must possess nerve. We must have it completed in our heads, what we plan to paint, before dipping the brush.

Today the lotus' beauty eludes us, time and again.

As tempting as it is to blame Caroline's difficult mood for this failure, Jean fares no better at capturing the lotus in his painting. I try not to alarm either of them when I announce that I'll give it a try.

I've been painting in watercolour since I began training at Ana Maria Garthwaite's workshop fourteen years ago. I've honed my technique over the years, and with this assignment, I have spent considerable time preparing watercolour pigment cakes to match our lotus. But every time I try, the lotus looks either flat or garish. I don't feel the necessary rush of pleasure looking at it any more than I did at Caroline's or Jean's. The sketches lack charm as well as authenticity.

Forcing a smile and a shrug, I say, "It's just not a day for victory with the brush. But we shall prevail."

I excuse myself to see if George has decided to show himself. He has, though he looks nearly as exhausted as Thomas had this morning. Nonetheless, I instruct him to take my letter to 11 Downing Street right away, and off he goes.

He doesn't return until the late afternoon, and when he steps into the house, he carries a different letter, one handed to him right outside the house.

My heart plummets as I take in the sight of the Nicolas Carteret seal. Why a message from him now? The first set of designs aren't due until the end of the following week. We can't take on any more work until that is accomplished.

"Mrs. Sturbridge, I must see your first five designs by twelve o'clock on Thursday if we are to continue our business. Nicolas Carteret."

I read it twice and then a third time. Part of me simply can't accept the fact that Carteret has sent this unreasonable business order. Yet here it is.

My breathing turns shallow.

This means he expects to see finished watercolour designs tomorrow.

Last month, he sent word he needed to see a book of designs a couple of days ahead of what I expected. This is pushing it to a full week ahead of schedule. And the scope of the assignment is more ambitious than anything we've yet completed.

"Why would he do this?" asks Caroline, dumbfounded, when I share the letter with them.

Jean, guilt-stricken, wonders if Carteret is reacting to his loud challenge of Hervé Gaynard at the Foundling Hospital. "He likes everyone quiet and compliant, and if they give him trouble, he has all sorts of ways to punish people," says Jean.

Suddenly, I picture Nicolas Carteret's face, set with anger and resentment, after talking to Thomas.

"Hmmm, I don't think *that* was it," I say.

"There was something else said?" asks Jean.

Caroline presses me to share with them my theory. I finally talk about Monsieur Carteret's request of Thomas, urging him to support the bill before Parliament seeking protection from foreign silk imports by speaking to the Earl of Sandwich, and my husband's response.

I expect to hear their outrage on my behalf, but I don't.

"Carteret probably feels justified to make his case," says Jean, as Caroline nods. "He thinks it's all for the good of the Huguenots."

My head is splitting. I shouldn't have told Jean and Caroline about Thomas' involvement. I am supposed to be their employer, not their older sister. I must not have explained it very well, anyhow, if my artists are taking Carteret's part. As it's near time for them to depart, I insist they leave and tell them we will solve our workshop problems on the morrow.

Staring down at our tentative lotus sketches strewn across the work table, I face the truth – this might not be something that can be solved. After dinner with Pierre, I ask Daphne to brew a pot of very strong tea.

I'll never forget that night in my Fournier Street workshop.

Every moment of effort seems to crawl by. Yet when I glance at the pocket watch that I've brought upstairs, the hours are rapidly passing. Midnight arrives and then slithers away.

I am trying to replace something that is very hard to do without. What's worse, I can't put into words the missing element. I might well wish I were in Thomas' laboratory, the one he meticulously assembled in Derby, stocked with glass vessels and bizarrely shaped apparatuses. In his world, chemicals are identifiable. Scientific procedures do not vary, and outcomes are identical if the steps and the components are the same, while I am left with trying to put a name to this mysterious process and coming up with nothing better than "creative spark". Every painting I produce, whether it's a personal vision or a workshop flower, must spring from it. And the truth is, this beautiful lotus, flourishing in India, should be the source of plenty of inspiration, but it simply hasn't happened, not with me or Jean or Caroline.

It's too late to pick and plan another flower, so I take a deep breath and proceed. This must be made to work. Using every scrap of skill that I've gained over the years, I paint the flower from various angles, adding the meticulous dimensions that Jean is so good at applying. This will be a triumph of technique over inspiration.

Slowly, very slowly, watercolour paintings appear that are good enough to send to Nicolas Carteret. It's almost like I am managing to vanquish some dread medieval curse. The tea's benefits recede, I'm now fighting exhaustion as much as anything else. Strange thoughts dance through my head about wizards and alchemists casting their spells and enacting their cryptic transformations. I could use one of their spells right about now. A hysterical giggle bubbles up inside me as I remember a story we girls whispered in secret at school. Our sombre Calvinist-moulded teachers looked on French magic as the

176

foulest of superstitions, so, of course, we were drawn to those tales. The one I think of now is about Nicolas Flamel's fifteenth-century stone house in Paris and how the stones were supposed to hold clues to his mystical formula. The person who could decipher the clues would live forever.

My eyes burning, I lay down my head in the crook of my folded arms. The intensity of this ordeal leaves me empty and trembling. In this state, I remember Thomas' tense face, his knuckles white on the side of the lecturer's stand, when that blonde man, who we later learned had been sent by Hervé Gaynard, mentioned Dippel's experiments. And then there were his reactions to Gaynard and Casanova and their proposal. It feels like I'm edging toward an idea, but exhaustion claims me, throwing a black cloak over every thought in my head.

The next thing I am aware of is Pierre. Or rather his high voice calling, "Mama? Mama?"

My eyes fly open. The dull grey light of wintry dawn fills the workshop. The candles have burned out – thank God without starting a fire. My neck aches. I hurry to Pierre and take him to Daphne, who is plainly horrified that I have slept in my clothes.

I manage to change into another dress before Jean and Caroline arrive. My designs leave them stunned. "How could you possibly have done all of this?" asks Caroline. Jean, spotting the candle wax heaped around the sticks, looks at me sharply.

Jean takes tremendous pains to organise the design pages into the best possible presentation. George takes them to White Lion Street. I'm grateful that I am at least spared having to meet Monsieur Carteret in person today.

The afternoon passes quickly, and soon enough, there's the sound of Thomas coming through the door. He doesn't look as ill as yesterday morning, to my relief. Spending a night in Chiswick, with its country air, has helped. I don't tell him about working through much of the night on Carteret's order, I've no wish to bring up the master weaver with my husband now, while I'm tingling with expectation of the dinner to come.

As we dress, I do tell Thomas more about our host. "I don't wish to prejudice you against Mr. Reynolds, but I should inform you about a disagreement he has with his sister over her art."

Thomas nods after hearing my story. "Perhaps it's true that a young and beautiful woman would have advantages in some quarters, but I hope you were able to reassure her that it is not a prerequisite for success," he says. "It hasn't presented an obstacle for you."

My hands freeze on the stitch I'm pulling through his breeches.

"So, you're saying I am not young and beautiful?" I say, striving for lightness of tone.

Thomas laughs, depositing a kiss on my shoulder. "Always the most beautiful woman in the world as far as I am concerned!"

I fall silent. The lump in my throat is such that if I speak, I fear my voice will shake.

It's ridiculous to take his comment this badly. I am thirty, a wife and mother. Even ten years ago, no one would have raved about my beauty, with my chestnut hair, light hazel eyes and narrow chin. No, I'm feeling crushed because I fear it's too late for me to have the artist's life I dream of. Just as the attitudes of those who control the training and livelihood of English artists are changing toward females, just as the door opens, I am too old to walk through it. I'm making a fool of myself to think I can try.

A minute later, my rebellious spirit revives, crying out over this injustice. I'm younger than Joshua Reynolds, and I can't be sure, but I believe I'm the same age as George Romney, Sam Baldwin and that swarm of male artists I saw at the Charing Cross exhibition. Nor were they so strikingly handsome. A couple looked downright homely. Why can the men be of any age and any appearance and no one cares?

I don't feel much like talking during our carriage ride to Joshua Reynolds' house. I'm not in a bad mood exactly, but no matter how hard I try, I can't get free of my new pessimism about my future, and Thomas doesn't rouse me from my mood. He is preoccupied. It is something I've grown used to, the long silences. The workings of his mind require them.

When we arrive at Leicester Fields and step into the crisply cold night air, Lawrence has a laugh at the sight of the Reynolds' carriage.

"I recognise that one – it belonged to the Lord Mayor of London seven years ago," he crows. "A painter buying a mayor's carriage? I'd never have expected it!"

Our knock at the front door brings the harried-looking Ralph, and a moment later, the ebullient Frances Reynolds. Glancing over my shoulder at the carriage sitting on the street, she says, "Lord, how I loathe that conveyance."

As she leads us deeper into the house, Frances says, "I don't *ever* want to ride in it, it makes me feel utterly ridiculous. Joshua gets angry with me for refusing. Some days, he's too busy with his subjects to get away from the house. He insists that I take it for my errands and calls. And I know why. He wants people all over London to say, 'Who does that carriage belong to?' and then one of the coachmen can respond, 'It belongs to Joshua Reynolds!'"

It's a question I shouldn't ask, but I feel like she's aching for me to do it, so I say, "Why is it so important that Mr. Reynolds be known to own such a carriage?"

She laughs shortly. "If you but knew our parents, Mrs. Sturbridge, you'd understand."

Frances explains as we proceed down the corridor, "Our father, the Reverend Samuel Reynolds, was a master of a grammar school in Devonshire – Joshua was one of his only pupils! – until the school went bankrupt. Such an amiable father but, I fear, eccentric. Some called him garrulous. More generous with words than his purse. In our household, we had to watch every penny. Father's plan for Joshua was to apprentice him to an apothecary. I don't think my brother ever in his whole life had to do anything as difficult as convince Father to apprentice him to a painter instead."

"Your father had no sympathy toward art?" I ask.

"No, but no one could deny Joshua's calling. When he was a small boy, he drew on the whitewashed wall of our house with a burned stick – it was all he had!"

A moment later, it is that brother who joins us, all affable charm. Suddenly, a picture of Joshua Reynolds leaps into my mind, not as he is now – wearing this embroidered waistcoat and jacket, silver buckles gleaming on his shoes – but clad in a long white apothecary's coat, briskly measuring the powders to be poured into a cordial bottle.

It definitely isn't a cordial on offer now. "You must try this champagne, the case arrived yesterday," he insists. Ralph materialises with glasses that look more like wide, shallow cups poised on crystal stems.

I remember what Madame de Pompadour once said in her high musical voice: "Champagne is the only drink that leaves a woman still beautiful after drinking it." I speculate what she would have made of Joshua Reynolds. Her devotion to talent would have made him an ally.

And so we sip champagne with Joshua Reynolds, emphasis on the word *sip*. Wine goes to my head hard and fast when I haven't had

180

enough sleep, which is precisely what's been lacking these last two nights. What makes this a challenge is I do love the taste.

Joshua launches the conversation with praising the exhibit at the Foundling Hospital as a success. I'm not sure what barometer he uses for success, but I want nothing so much as to agree with him, to feel hopeful that my grandfather's paintings will find admirers beyond his small Spitalfields circle.

Reynolds moves on to theatre, the city's great and consuming passion, and the news he's just heard from his friend, David Garrick, of yet another production being planned of *The Beggar's Opera*.

"If I could share a confidence with you, it's that I'm not as enamoured with that particular play as everyone else in London," says Joshua.

"I feel the same way," announces my husband. They explore this common ground as I reflect that *The Beggar's Opera* courses through the veins of every true Londoner. Neither my host nor husband are creatures of the capital city by birth. I am, and that's why I can't help but exult in the scoundrel Captain Macheath. Perhaps it's because London, rife with danger and disease, swift to grind the unfortunate to dust, is a place to be bested any way one can. The master criminal can be gifted with celebrity just as much as the regal beauty.

During conversation before dinner, Mr. Reynolds drinks two glasses of champagne in the same time that I've sipped a half glass. Frances says little, which seems odd until I realise that each time she's gone on at length with me, her older brother has not been within earshot.

Our dinner is served in a room where the wallpaper seems to shimmer. The creamy tablecloth, I note, is edged with lace. The delicate glasses and translucent porcelain are also of the highest quality to be

181

found. The food, though, is not. We are served a tasteless pea soup, stale bread and a heaping platter of roast venison. I appreciate that the Reynolds choose to serve us such a costly course of game – it's been years since I ate venison – but the redcurrant sauce is far too vinegary. I ache to balance it with sugar.

Still, I'm here for the company, not the cuisine. Joshua proves a superbly attentive dinner host, shifting the conversation from theatre to politics. It turns out that Mr. Reynolds holds distinctly Whiggish views. He and Thomas both support the cause of the colonials in North America, the ones making trouble over taxes. From what I understand, the core of their grievance revolves around lack of representation of these faraway colonists in Parliament. I find it hard to drum up much sympathy. In my workshop, we've done the research on who pays the most for a silk dress with flower designs, and right at the top of the list are those dazzlingly rich planters' wives in Virginia, followed by the prosperous merchant families of Philadelphia and New York. I pay crushing taxes, far more than the Americans do. And of course, as a woman, I lack the right to vote, much less stand for Parliament.

As I brood over these ironies, the conversation has apparently shifted to science and Cambridge. I only become aware of this when Thomas says, "Actually, Mr. Reynolds, I am surprised you are aware that I attended college at Cambridge."

Blinking in the candlelight, Joshua Reynolds says, "I believe your wife told me."

"Did she?" Thomas frowns.

I can't remember ever mentioning his college to Joshua Reynolds or anyone else, it's not something Thomas wants to be emphasised.

Reynolds pushes on with his point. "But you do agree with me, Mr. Sturbridge, that it was Francis Bacon who changed everything for us by saying that anyone can gather knowledge through experimentation and observation, not needing to submit to the texts of any elders?"

"It was a fundamental shift," agrees Thomas. But he fingers his glass while giving our host a sombre, searching look. Something is bothering him.

"My father sent none of his children to university, not a single one," blurts Joshua. I realise he's lost his early gregariousness. I begin to wonder if he'd begun drinking before we arrived.

Frances says, "But Joshua, haven't you always said that, after apprenticing for Mr. Hudson, Italy was like a university for you?"

He nods slowly. "Those months I spent studying Michelangelo and Raphael and Titian and Tintorello, they meant everything to me. I tried, in every way I could think of, to understand the course they charted in a painting, every choice they made."

"It sounds like an invaluable experience," says Thomas politely.

Reynolds, who has often used his ear trumpet to hear what my husband is saying, regards Thomas closely as if he means to continue this thread of conversation. But then he turns to me. "Mrs. Sturbridge, I've been to several meetings in the last month with others who are interested in forming a Royal Academy of the Arts in England. My God, look at France. They created their academy over a century ago. Why should we hesitate?"

"I couldn't agree more," I say. "The time for giving way to Paris is over."

"It is – by God, it is!" Joshua cries. "We shall create a new age in England. Art shall flourish here, as do science and literature. There will be classes for students, lectures, exhibitions. British painting has languished for too long. There's talk of selecting people to be founding members of the royal society. Perhaps you would consider joining the effort, Mrs. Sturbridge?"

The enormity of what he's suggesting, the honour of joining other artists in creating such an academy, leaves me stunned. I cannot say anything except a faint, "I would, Mr. Reynolds."

"Ah, the possibilities that a royal society could create," he muses.

Possibilities? My heart, already beating quickly, is now a hammer in my chest.

This is the moment – he will now speak specifically about my art, my career.

Joshua scowls as he says, "Yet the difficulty with forming a group to guide such a society is that many artists are not, shall we say, of harmonious character."

Yet again he veers away.

Reynolds continues, "They can be so small-minded, bitter and angry, turned half mad by envy. Look at George Romney, for God's sake. But I do not find him half as threatening as Thomas Gainsborough. He sits in Bath, doing nothing but plot my fall from favour. But they all do – I know it. I'm not fooled."

His face is florid, his voice is raised. Neither Thomas nor I know what to say. His sister looks stricken.

Reynolds says, "I am greatly misunderstood by my fellow artists, you see. They think I am driven purely by commercial interests. No, Mrs. Sturbridge, don't debate it, I know it's true. But the thing that drives me is what they can never understand. I want to paint a portrait that captures the very essence of my subject. Each time I begin a new subject, and I mean each and every time, I think this will be the occasion of a breakthrough." Joshua stares into the candlelight flickering on the table as if he were falling into a trance. He continues, very sombrely, "With each duchess, each actress, each admiral, I try to capture the essence of character while paying homage to the deep-toned brilliance of the ancients."

Such a specific and archaic phrase. But this obviously means a great deal to him.

After a minute, Reynolds resumes, "Romney paints portraits for the money they bring, but he really wants to devote himself to forging this new style of history paintings. Gainsborough paints portraits, but he would prefer to concentrate on landscapes. While for me, for me, the portrait is... everything."

Thomas and I exchange a glance across the table. Our host is baring his soul.

With a decisive nod, as if he's answering a question posed to himself, Reynolds says, "Mr. Sturbridge, Mrs. Sturbridge, I would very much like to show you my painting studio."

Thomas draws back in his chair a little. He's reluctant, though I have no idea why. A visit to the studio of Joshua Reynolds, given by the man himself, is too exciting an opportunity to miss. With an imploring glance at Thomas, I say we would be delighted.

"Excellent," says Reynolds, calling for more wine, unfortunately. The four of us rise from the table. I fear that he will stumble on the way because of a surfeit of the grape, but his step is steady. I suspect he is well used to its effect.

Joshua Reynolds says to his sister, "Not you, Frances. You've seen the studio often enough."

She turns and walks away, her skirts rustling in the awkward silence that follows. I perceive now why he has not married and prefers that his sister keep house. Many wives would not tolerate being dismissed in this way.

It gets worse.

When Frances is out of earshot, Reynolds says, "I must thank you, Mrs. Sturbridge, for taking to heart what I said the other night and not encouraging my sister in her lamentable portraits.

They make other people laugh – and they make me cry."

"Oh." It escapes me before I can stop, an exclamation of surprise, of disappointment at his cruel mockery. Next to me comes Thomas' sharp intake of breath.

Joshua Reynolds takes no notice of our reaction. I suspect he didn't hear us. Ralph leading the way with a towering candelabra, we walk the length of the gallery I visited several weeks ago, hung with both Joshua Reynolds' paintings and those of the Great Masters he worships. At the end is a doorway. Ralph opens it, and Joshua holds it for us while his servant lights candles here, there, everywhere and then leaves. It is just us three.

The studio comes to life like the magic cave of the genie's lamp. I happily inhale the warring scents of oil paint, linseed, turpentine, varnish, mahogany, polish, glue and one or two substances I can't readily identify. There's a whiff of pine in the air. It's been a while since I inhabited an oil painter's domain.

The room is at least twenty feet long, shaped like an octagon. I'd expected it to have many windows, but there is only one, high up in the wall. Close to that window is the much-gossiped-about armchair, floating more than a foot from the ground and turning on castors. In front of it rises a large standing easel, a half-finished canvas portrait fixed to it. And interestingly, behind the sitter's chair is a beautiful mirror, framed with polished mahogany. Large canvas stretchers are placed against the far wall. A shelf holds books and other references. Running my fingers along one stretch of readied canvas, I detect it is plain weave.

I'm most curious how Joshua Reynolds handles his colours. I peer around the studio – neat as a pin, no surprise with his large staff – until I spot a square wooden palette with a handle. So, while painting, he holds it in one hand and the brush in the other.

I'm also drawn to the canvas painting mounted on his standing easel. Just above the centre floats a woman's face, painted on layer upon layer of grounding, primer, varnish and various colours. Then come the details of her face. Her generous mouth is half-smiling, her light blue eyes questioning. She has a dimple in her chin with the very slightest layer of fat underneath. It's an incredibly specific face, with the translucence Reynolds is famous for. Untalented artists produce portraits in which there is a sameness to the subjects. But with Reynolds, as he has just so passionately explained, every face is a new challenge to be captured on its own terms.

"I would like to show you something in particular," Reynolds says.

He is already in the corner, moving aside a few large, framed paintings to reach one propped up at the back.

"This is Charles Lennox, the third Duke of Richmond, direct descendant of King Charles the Second," Reynolds announces as he carries the painting toward where Thomas and I stand, square in the middle of the studio and near the strongest source of light, the blazing candelabra.

The three-quarter-length portrait shows a handsome, fit young man, pale of complexion, wearing a deep red coat, waistcoat and breeches. He has a certain modest air to him, despite the obvious expense of his clothes. I suppose royals can afford to be modest.

"It was good of His Grace to write to me first, to bring the matter to my attention that I may handle it discreetly," Reynolds says in a low voice. "But it isn't the first incident reported."

"I don't understand," I say.

Reynolds picks up the portrait and moves it closer to us and tilts it back a couple of inches. In the full candlelight, the Duke of Richmond's face is no longer simply pale. It is ghostly white, so completely bereft of the lifelike luminous skin colour Reynolds is known for, the warm luminescent flesh of the woman's face across the room. This man looks like a corpse, or in some frightening way, inhuman. I can't think why Reynolds would have chosen to paint *anyone* like this, especially not a duke.

"Mr. Reynolds, why exactly have you brought us here?" Thomas' tone is as sharp as when he ordered Hervé Gaynard out of the house.

"Thomas, please," I whisper, appalled. Only the most severe provocation forces rudeness from my husband. Joshua has been gracious and personable.

Instead of answering, Reynolds props the painting of the duke against the opposite wall and beckons for us to follow him to a tall cabinet. He pulls a set of keys from the pocket opposite to the one holding his ear trumpet.

When he unlocks the cabinet, a burst of intense smells escapes. This is definitely the source of the pine. On the shelves sits an assembly of pigment colours for oil painting: reds, blues, browns, yellows. I spot the distinctive Prussian Blue, invented by Dippel. At the cabinet bottom are two deep drawers with their own locks. With a separate key, Joshua Reynolds kneels to open the bottommost drawer. I spot bottles and vials and tubes of all sizes. He carefully removes a board with a series of small dishes glued to it. Inside the dishes sit blobs of various strange substances. I see among them oils, pigments and perhaps, varnishes. He puts the board where we can all see it.

He hasn't stood up yet. Joshua kneels in front of these blobs and oils and concoctions as if it were an altar.

"I use them to help me create a certain colour, a shade that I saw in a painting by Titian or Rembrandt, one that I want to create for myself. Using these substances is the only way to achieve it. But due to the chemical composition of what I apply in a painting, the colour might fade or crack. It happens over time. This face took four years to fade to white. I've only learned about the transformations in the last six months."

He rises to his feet, a trifle unsteadily, and turns to face us. His eyes are both mournful and pleading.

"These are my fugitive colours," says Joshua Reynolds.

I feel lightheaded. A dozen gestures, comments and significant looks, all the invitations and encouragements are coming together and beginning to make terrible sense.

"Mr. Sturbridge," says Joshua Reynolds, "I know you are a master chemist and perhaps the finest colourist in all Europe. I need your help."

Chapter Fourteen

"How did you find out about me?" asks my husband.

Thomas is far calmer than me. I've fallen back, fumbling for the edge of the table holding the candelabra. This hurts, a pain deeper than any slap or shove. So Joshua Reynolds was only interested in me to get to Thomas. I thought that Hogarth's rejection of me as an artist was the worst pain I could suffer. But at least he was straightforward. There was no manipulation.

"A friend told me of your talents," says Joshua Reynolds. "Someone who wishes to remain anonymous."

"Was it Hervé Gaynard who told you what happened in France?" presses Thomas.

Joshua Reynolds whips out his ear trumpet and steps closer to Thomas, "Who?"

Thomas repeats the name, distaste in every syllable.

"Oh, no, I'd hardly tell him about *this*." Reynolds points at the board holding the small cups. "Hervé is such a gossip, he seems to know everyone in Covent Garden. I'd be ruined overnight."

His hands clasped before him, Joshua makes his case directly to Thomas.

"Mr. Sturbridge, I have to say that your gifts are better known to the world than the misfortune of my fugitive colours. There were quite a few people in Sèvres that day when your colour blue was presented to King Louis. Word circulated. Of course, it was in the middle of the war, and afterward, you seemed to disappear. When I realised that I would need a specialist's help, my friend told me that you were back in England and married to Genevieve, who I remembered from William Hogarth's Christmas party. I invited you both to my house in order to meet you and become acquainted, to see if I could possibly trust you."

Now I understand everything. When I showed up at Reynolds' gathering without Thomas, the artist then had to spin out a reason for future meetings. With considerable humiliation, I realise this must be why Reynolds proposed the exhibition of my grandfather's paintings at the Foundling Hospital, why he enquired after my husband's health, why he invited us to dinner.

Now, Reynolds' focus rests entirely on Thomas, and I am cast aside. But my husband cares much more about my feelings than Reynolds' fugitive colours. He reaches over and squeezes my shoulder comfortingly. I must look fairly devastated.

"I do not appreciate the lack of forthrightness you've shown to my wife and to me," says Thomas quietly.

"With so much at stake, I had to be cautious," insists Reynolds.

Thomas sighs. "I fear you've wasted your time. I must inform you, Mr. Reynolds, that I am under strict orders from officials in His Majesty's government. In fact, I have signed certain documents pledging that I will not work in the creation or production of colour in England."

Joshua Reynolds groans. "Why, oh, why would they do that to you? They should give you a laboratory with twenty people, not punish you. The British can be so vindictive – do you think the French would

191

refuse to use your talents under similar circumstances? I thought you were merely being secretive, but your only occupation really is teaching the second son of that idiot, the Earl of Sandwich?"

Thomas nods tightly.

"God, I don't know what I'm going to do," says Reynolds, staggering to a chair in the room and sinking into it.

As angry and disappointed as I feel, I can't deny a curiosity that nags at me too.

"Why did you even use these fugitive colours?" I ask. I have heard the phrase before but in reference to watercolour hues. There are certain paint colours to avoid because over time and with certain weather conditions, they will fade or change. I did not think it possible an oils artist of Reynolds' stature would ever make such mistakes.

Thomas shakes his head, sending me a reproving look. He does not want to be further drawn in.

But our host, slouched in the chair, is already explaining himself.

"It's what I told you at supper – I am always seeking the deep-toned brilliance of the ancients. I became obsessed with colour in Venice when I studied the paintings of Titian, Tintorello and others. The knowledge I gained from apprenticing to Thomas Hudson and from reading every book on colour preparation just didn't suffice. I wanted those colours – God alone knows how much! I even bought a couple of pictures from the Renaissance period and I tried to analyse them, scraping from the canvas. That taught me a little, not much. Those artists are like the damn alchemists, everything a secret, nothing written down. So I began to conduct my own experiments. Is that not the point of the scientific method, Mr. Sturbridge? Didn't Francis Bacon say we must learn from personal observation?"

Thomas regards him with compassion for the first time. "Yes, that's what Bacon believed," he says quietly.

"I used carmine reds, despite everyone's saying I shouldn't. It was the mix of carmine that gave flesh the tone I craved. It was what made my portraits special. But now, I know it's the carmines that fade. It's the same with the bitumen in the blacks. It's cracking. Then there are the pine resins I purchased in Venice. In certain mixes, they give the results I need. But they are at fault too. There are also problems with the mixes using certain oils. Time is the enemy. When the picture is new, everyone is happy, no one more so than me. But four or five years later…"

"I wish I could help you," says Thomas.

"Are you sure that it's really impossible?" asks Reynolds, almost begging. "No one would know. We could arrange total secrecy. I'd pay you very well. I'll not use the defective colours in new portraits. And I'd like to fix my past mistakes. I'm known to be a picture restorer. When I take a painting back, I'd address the problem with the new colours you create with me. They'd be colours just as beautiful, but they'd be stable. I could sleep at night knowing there'd be no fading, cracking or bubbling in my paintings."

"I understand that you have heard of my work with creating blue, but what makes you think I can be helpful with these other colours?" asks Thomas.

Reynolds sits taller in his chair. "But I've seen your work! I knew it had to be you. In your house, your wife displayed a still life showing brilliant shades I'd never ever seen in my life. I knew two things right away, that she is a talented artist in her own right and that you had to have been her colourist."

The gloom and humiliation encircling my heart dissolve. Joshua Reynolds was not pretending to favour my work so he could get hold of my husband? The leading artist in England actually believes I have talent.

But then I realise Thomas is looking at me.

His eyes are afire with accusation, his lips tremble with anger.

"If you'd let me explain," I say.

Thomas strides away from me and toward the door of the studio, saying, "Mr. Reynolds, I cannot be of assistance to you."

"Mr. Sturbridge, please don't make a decision tonight," says Joshua Reynolds, running after him. "Send me your reply in one week, after thinking about it. Mrs. Sturbridge, can you not discuss this with your husband? Use your influence?"

My cheeks burning, I say nothing.

"It's not just fear of my rivals' glee that is behind my asking this," says Reynolds. "My portrait business supports my sister and other family members, loyal servants and many students. I don't know what would happen to all of them."

Thomas tells him, with reluctance, that a final answer will be forthcoming in one week, and he pulls open the door to leave, not even looking in my direction.

The walk through the gallery and house to the street and our waiting carriage is the longest imaginable.

Once Lawrence has slammed the carriage door and we are alone, I say, "I did not display the painting from The Hague for Mr. Reynolds to see. You must allow me to explain."

I tell Thomas about being late back from the Tower Menagerie and Caroline taking it upon herself to hang my pictures in the workshop.

"This story strains belief," says Thomas when I've finished.

I feel as if I've been slapped in the face.

"You are accusing me of lying?"

"If it was an honest mistake, an act well intended, why didn't you tell me that Reynolds saw the painting that shows my colours?" he demands.

"I don't know," I stammer. "I didn't think it was important. I certainly didn't think he was looking for someone to correct his colour mistakes."

"Oh, no? There were signs along the way that he had an ulterior motive for forging an acquaintanceship."

"You think I manipulated you for my own gain, Thomas?" I whisper.

"I don't know what to think. Once before you did something immoral – something illegal, to be clear – in order to advance yourself as an artist. That was taking a position as a porcelain artist in Derby to steal my formula. You've sworn that such a thing could never happen again, that it was a mistake. Yet here we are, Genevieve. Here we are. I am being pressured to do something else that would help *you*. Can you deny that you'd very much like me to become Joshua Reynolds' private colourist so that he will assist you in your art ambitions?"

"I would never want you to do anything that would place you in any jeopardy, you must know that," I say, horrified.

"All I know is that if I do it and am discovered, I'm the one who goes to prison, not you."

"Do you not think I am in prison right now?" I cry. "I feel guilty every minute. I work as hard as I can at keeping the design workshop afloat because it was my actions that led to your kidnapping, that deprived you of a proper livelihood."

Thomas laughs. "Ah yes, your workshop, glorifying the conquests of the British in luckless places around the whole world, whether it be the Caribbean or India, with little flowers. You are making pretty something that is very, very ugly."

I fumble for the handle to the carriage door. I have no serious wish to hurl myself onto the street, but this so distresses me, I almost can't bear to sit next to him. The accusations about hurting Thomas' career, as ugly as they are, are no worse than the things I've said to myself. But attacking my silk design business?

I manage to say, "If this is your opinion of me, then why would you live off the money of the business, eat at the table of someone so loathsome?"

"Why indeed," he mutters.

This is not happening, this cannot be happening.

Here, in this carriage, owned by John Montagu, Earl of Sandwich, on the streets leading from Leicester Fields to Spitalfields, my marriage is shattering.

My fingers slip off the handle. Tears streaming down my cheeks, I say, "You know, Thomas, you must know how much I love you."

An agonisingly long silence ensues. When Thomas speaks, his voice is as cold as the North Sea.

"I know what you told me in this carriage a minute ago. You feel guilty. As to whether that is the same as love…"

I say nothing more for the rest of the carriage ride. When we reach Fournier Street and step out of the carriage, Lawrence detects that something terrible has happened.

"Mrs. Sturbridge, are you well?" he asks.

I can only nod, unable to speak. Inside the house, Thomas silently gathers his things to sleep in the parlour. He will not share my bed tonight.

Through everything I have endured in the last six years, I've been able to hold onto one fact that I was supremely sure could never change: my love for Thomas and his love for me. For the first time, I confront the distinct possibility that it *could* change.

After yet another near-sleepless night, I rise to find Thomas gathering clothes. "I'll remain at the Earl of Sandwich's house for the next week," he informs me. "I, unfortunately, said I'd have an answer for Mr. Reynolds in a week's time. I'll keep my word on that. I will be back next Friday to communicate with him."

"Oh, Thomas, no, please don't go away from me," I say.

He holds up a hand to stop me from saying another word. "It's not only what we said last night. I need to do something, finish something, it's very important. I can't say more about it now."

Pierre runs into the room at that moment. As I cannot bear to quarrel in front of our child, I pick him up, planting kisses, embracing him. I hope he doesn't feel my body quivering, for it is impossible to keep from crying when Thomas hurries downstairs as if his desire to distance himself from my physical presence outweighs his love for Pierre.

I do not say goodbye to Thomas. The coldness in his eyes, the disappointment and disillusion freeze my tongue.

Instead, I sit at the workshop table, hands folded, listening to the noises of the street, knowing that among them is the clattering of hooves belonging to Lawrence's carriage, speeding my husband west and away from me.

I fear that Jean and Caroline's arrival for work will strain my nerves to the breaking point, but instead, it is a relief. I thrust everything from my mind that is unrelated to the workshop – Joshua Reynolds' shocking confession, Thomas' anger and distrust – and focus on our designs and the next set of flowers to paint.

We exchange ideas and opinions on the next direction, the atmosphere free of the rancour that usually sours Jean and Caroline's dealings with each other.

But inevitably, Thomas' criticism of the design business creeps into my thoughts. His view of our work has come as a complete shock.

I say, "Do you think that the flowers we choose, their place of origin, says something unpleasant about our business?"

"Whatever do you mean?" asks Jean, dumbfounded.

"Britain might be perceived as taking advantage of these faraway places," I say.

Caroline says, "We're hardly responsible for what armies and navies do."

"Or the British East India Company," chimes in Jean.

Caroline says earnestly, "We are trying to bring beauty to the world. How can that ever possibly be judged unpleasant?"

"Well said!" Jean thumps the table with his hand. I tense, expecting Caroline to recoil from Jean's gusto-fueled admiration. But Caroline bows her head so low that her chin touches her breastbone and then makes a funny little gesture with her right hand as if she were tipping an invisible hat.

I laugh a little – I would probably laugh harder if my marriage weren't threatening to collapse – and wait for Jean to react.

Now it's his turn to do something I've never seen before. Jean blushes.

A knock on the door interrupts this interesting moment. George peeks in, a letter in his hand. It's another message from Nicolas Carteret.

What does the man want from me now?

I break the seal to read it:

"Mrs. Sturbridge, in light of the designs you have sent, it's of the utmost importance that we meet to discuss the changes that will need to be made in our work agreement. Come to my house no later than two o'clock today."

Caroline, who read the letter along with me, breathes, "Oh, no."

Jean insists that it's just Carteret's rude and arrogant style. "Those designs were very fine – no one can doubt it," he says. "I don't think this is necessarily bad news."

I am too drained to feel either fear or hope. Finally, I say, "Well, it seems I should ready myself for a walk to White Lion Street."

Downstairs, George is missing, but only because Daphne sent him to the market. I don't want to wait. Now that I know this new ordeal is before me, I can't bear the thought of sitting in the house. I must be moving.

The air is cold and dry, as dry as Joshua Reynolds' prize champagne. Perhaps that's why the smoke is in retreat, clinging to the roofs and building corners, instead of stretching out to blind and choke me.

I stride toward Brick Lane. How long ago was it that I walked to Monsieur Carteret's with my book of Le Grenade flower designs? I don't think it was even a month.

I turn off Brick Lane, though it is well before the turn to White Lion Street. I'm not going to continue to Nicolas Carteret's house. If I were to knock on the door, follow a servant upstairs, take a seat opposite that gleaming desk, as big as a ship poised to sail off to the West Indies, and face criticism or implicit threats from the master weaver, I'd not be able to hold my tongue.

But what about the workshop? What about my livelihood? What about Pierre, Thomas, Caroline, Jean, Daphne, George and Sophie?

In a rather detached spirit, I wait for the realisation of my many, many responsibilities to take hold and send me back in the right direction, toward Nicolas Carteret's house.

It doesn't happen. My feet take me out of Spitalfields as if I weren't the one controlling my movements. I walk for one hour, then two. For some of it, I keep to The Strand, which is crowded with other Londoners. Yes, it's cold, but my brisk walking has worked me up to a point that I'm comfortable under my cloak. And I'm grateful the temperature has plunged to the point of freezing, for it means my shoes are never stuck in mud. The London streets are flat and hard, some stretches are even newly paved to speed my journey. I pass an endless string of taverns and shops before I pause, take a breath and turn north for Bloomsbury.

The Foundling Hospital is bustling and busy this afternoon. At the gatehouse, they smilingly wave me on to see the exhibit. I don't expect to speak to Mrs. Stillington. I admit to a twinge of disappointment that the exhibition room is empty of people. But then, I tell myself, this is the time when many people drink afternoon tea.

In the exhibition room, I make my way to the portrait of the young silk thrower. By looking at the fine brush strokes used for the subject's long, dark brown hair, the composition chosen in placing the figure within the weaver's room, I feel an echo of Grandfather. Of course, it's not in the same category as a Joshua Reynolds' portrait in colour and expressiveness, nor does it have the satirical bite of a William Hogarth. But I don't care. This is the only way I can think of to spend time with Pierre Billiou.

"Mrs. Sturbridge!"

Mrs. Stillington hurries across the room to greet me. "What a marvellous coincidence, that you should appear just as I'm arranging a purchase."

"Someone has bought a painting?" I barely recognise my own voice, that of an excited young girl.

"Yes," she says, turning to look over her shoulder. "In fact, the patron's coming through now."

Sam Baldwin, a grin lighting up his face, strides through the doorway. "I am so pleased," he says. "I had no idea you were coming."

"It wasn't planned," I say. "Thank you so much for what you've done – the purchase."

With a final few pleasantries, Mrs. Stillington eases away. By that time, Sam's smile fades. "Your face – your eyes – you look as if you've been…" He reaches for my hand. I'm encased in a warm grasp, surprisingly strong. "You're ice-cold, Mrs. Sturbridge. Did you walk a long distance?"

"I walked here from my house in Spitalfields."

"Why on earth?"

I tell Sam I wanted to be in the same room as my grandfather's paintings.

"You were close to him then?"

"He raised me," I say simply. "My father died before I could remember him, my mother, when I was a girl. Grandfather was... my whole world for many, many years."

Sam leads me to the couch in the middle of the room, saying I require rest after such a long walk in the cold. "I envy you," he says, sitting beside me. "My father and I do not get on. My grandparents are long dead."

I say, "I think that I'm drawn here because he would get exasperated with me, sometimes angry, but no matter what happened, Grandfather would always forgive me." I can hear myself babble but don't wish to stop. "How he would worry! He'd talk about me with Daphne, our housekeeper. And sometimes with those canaries of his, those prize birds, I could hear him talking over his problems with me." I laugh a little. "Do you know, both birds died within six months of his passing?"

My voice thickens, and Sam slips a handkerchief into my lap, a snow-white embroidered one.

"I'm so sorry," I say, dabbing my eyes. "You've done something quite wonderful in buying a painting, and your reward is my blubbering on your shoulder."

He is quiet, and though I should feel embarrassed by my outburst, it is quite a relief to be able to talk to someone about my feelings. We sit in silence for a few minutes as he kindly waits for me to gather myself.

"I could see straight away that you were distressed about something," Sam says. "Is it to do with Joshua Reynolds?"

I nod. "Yes. His motives are not what I thought."

"I've been concerned that something like this might happen. I'm very sorry."

We sit in silence for a moment. There's no question but his support is a consolation.

Sam says in a low voice, "I would like to know why you'd ever require forgiveness, Mrs. Sturbridge. You seem to me to be someone very much worthy of admiration."

I clutch his handkerchief, struggling to ward off more tears.

"You're mistaken about that, Mr. Baldwin. I've made some serious mistakes in my life, I've paid for them, and I continue to pay for them."

His voice drops even lower to a husky whisper as he says, "And what of your husband? I am sure he admires you."

I turn away from Sam Baldwin on the couch, for I find myself unable to look him in the eye. "My husband is the one who is admirable. You could ask anyone who knows him. He's brilliant, upstanding and highly, highly ethical."

I feel Sam's hand on my shoulder. His touch is gentle. "Mrs. Sturbridge?"

I turn. His dark eyes are full of longing.

"If your husband does not admire you, he is the very opposite of wise."

Sam pulls me toward him, tipping my face up to his, and kisses me. At his touch, I feel a warm rush of excitement. I've not felt this sort of desire in so long. He is tentative and curious. I touch his face, and his lips press mine with growing ardour.

This is wrong.

"I can't," I gasp, pulling free.

This close, his unmistakable feelings rage across his face: joy over our embrace clashing with frustration that I broke off the kiss.

"I'm sorry," I say. "I'm very sorry."

I jump to my feet. He looks up at me, chest heaving as if he's trying to catch his breath.

Voices from just outside the room remind me this is anything but a private place.

Sam says, "If I could tell you what I feel, what I know that you..."

But I can't hear any more. I pick up my skirts and run from the room and into the corridor leading out of the building. All I want is to get away from Sam Baldwin as quickly as I can.

Chapter Fifteen

When I return to Spitalfields, hiring a hackney carriage because I'm too exhausted – and too distressed – to walk that distance again, night is falling, and Jean and Caroline have left. It's just as well, for I don't know how to explain that in all those hours, I never even met with Nicolas Carteret.

As for Sam Baldwin, no one must ever know about that embrace. I was weary and confused, that's why I allowed him to kiss me. That is what I keep telling myself.

I don't want to think of the feel of his lips on mine. His touch startled me, it frightened me.

The part of me that strives toward honesty asks: Why did I go to Bloomsbury at all today? Sam had said at the exhibit that he'd return on Friday. Had I actually wanted to see him, to turn to him?

This must end immediately. I intend to stay well away from Sam Baldwin and every other painter in London, including Joshua Reynolds. I've no doubt whatsoever that Thomas will refuse to help Reynolds with his fugitive colours. After that, I am equally sure I won't hear anything more from the man from Leicester Fields.

"Don't make any mistakes," Evelyn Willoughby had told me at the

Tower. Since that day, I've made far more than one. But from now on, I will tread the most careful path. I will dedicate myself to my family and to my workshop business. Which is, in a way, a second family to me.

Certainly, they seem as close as family when Caroline and Jean arrive on Saturday, keen to know about my meeting with the master weaver. I tell them only that I was waylaid by important personal business the day before and could not see Carteret. The answer is too vague to satisfy my intelligent artists, but they don't press it. When I find a discreet moment, I send George over to Monsieur Carteret's house saying I will call on him on Monday. By that time, I will have gathered my strength.

I am worried about what the master weaver will have to say when we next meet, so much so that I decide to not attend church on Sunday. Instead, I dedicate the day to Pierre.

"What would you like to do?" I ask.

"Boats! Boats!"

I bundle up Pierre, and with George for company, and of course, protection, we walk down to the Thames and find a spot for my son to watch them all go by. Whether it's a shabby little barge or a magnificent ship boasting a forest of wooden masts, my son is enthralled. He has a chemist for a father and an artist for a mother, but what does he love most? Ships. It makes me smile. No one can predict a person's path.

I only wish that George wasn't so gloomy. I always give George and Sophie Sunday off, and Daphne too, though she goes nowhere but church. Sophie stayed home, but George appeared at the house this morning. He has a strange air about him. I wonder if he feels guilty for so many absences and is trying to make it up to me.

After a delicious dinner, I read a story to Pierre, feeling more relaxed – and more optimistic – than I have for a while. When Thomas returns, I will do everything I can to strengthen our bond of marriage.

My optimism fades when morning comes on Monday. Jean arrives but not Caroline. She's rarely sick, but this must be one of those times. Last spring, when Caroline had a bad episode with her stomach, she was absent for two days. Caroline pays boarding fees for a room in a house owned by a seamstress widow and her two daughters. The seamstress had sent a servant to tell us that Caroline was feeling poorly in the spring.

I start the day's work with Jean, my ear alert to a knock on the door. None comes. No servant arrives with an explanation. Perhaps no one could be spared. By late morning, I decide to send George to Caroline's home to make sure this is nothing but a passing illness.

"And when will you go to see Nicolas Carteret?" asks Jean bluntly.

I don't take offence. Jean's livelihood is tied up with my workshop.

"As soon as George returns and I have a report on Caroline, I'll prepare myself," I tell him.

Time seems to inch along as I wait for news from George. When I venture downstairs to have a moment with Pierre, I hear voices at the back of the house, and to my surprise, one of them is George's.

I find him talking to Sophie in a corner, a worried look on his face.

"George! Why have you not come to talk to me?"

Gulping, George says, "I was just on my way, Mrs. Sturbridge. My apologies."

"And what news of Caroline?" I ask impatiently.

George pushes his hair back from his face and says, "She's gone."

"Do you mean she's left, that she is on her way?"

"No, Mrs. Sturbridge. She left her room sometime yesterday, and she never came back. Her lady – the one who owns the house – is saying she can't believe it, that Miss Mowbray isn't that kind of young lady to step out. She is worried."

A stab of fear rips through me.

"Caroline would never leave her home overnight without something being terribly wrong," I say. "We must go there to make more enquiries and then see the constable."

A pounding on the front door makes me jump.

This could be Caroline now! It's all been a dreadful misunderstanding.

George lopes to the door that opens to the street. But a moment later, he slams it again and returns.

Saying it was dropped off by a boy, George hands me a blank folded paper. It bears no initials or crest, just a hard, dark grey seal that I tear open with my hands. I'm consumed with curiosity, mingled with mounting dread.

"*Mrs Genevieve Sturbridge,*

"*We have Miss Caroline Mowbray in our keeping. If you wish to see her freed, you must come alone tonight to engage in a conversation. Your husband may not accompany you. No other person may accompany you. If you tell anyone in authority of this meeting, you will never see Miss Mowbray again. Should you come in a spirit of willingness and hear the proposal put to you, you will leave unharmed, as will she. The place of meeting is number ten, Spring Gardens at eight o'clock tonight. This is your only opportunity to save her.*"

I read it three times, the strange black scrawl swimming on the parchment.

"My God, Caroline's been kidnapped!" Jean cries.

I have been concentrating so intently that I haven't heard Jean come down the stairs or sidle up to me to read the letter over my shoulder.

"Jean, that was wrong of you," I shout.

"Who cares about matters of privacy when a life is at stake?" he shouts back.

He's right. The threat to Caroline is savagely clear.

"This person wants something from you and wants it pretty badly if he's willing to kidnap Caroline to induce you to come," says Jean.

For a horrifying second, I wonder if Joshua Reynolds has written this. But he knows that Thomas won't be giving his answer until Thursday of this week. Why would he commit a criminal act now? And it's frankly ludicrous to think of the respected artist doing such a thing. Then there's Hervé Gaynard. I find it much more possible that he would do something despicable. But I can't believe that Casanova's desperate idea for fooling a marquise would push him or Gaynard to take such a drastic step. And why exclude Thomas?

"I have no idea who has done this or why," I tell Jean. "Evidently, I am going to find out at eight o'clock tonight."

"But you can't be serious," says Jean, taking a step back. "This is a very dangerous person. You could be kidnapped as well, or worse."

"If someone wanted to harm me, I think there are far more effective – and straightforward – means to do so than in such a roundabout fashion."

"You should take this to the constable!"

Shaking my head, I tell Jean I have little confidence in the ability of those hired to protect London's citizens to accomplish anything.

Growing desperate, Jean says, "Shouldn't you send a message to Mr. Sturbridge? Talk to him before you decide what to do?"

I glance at my grandfather's clock in the hall. "It's almost two o'clock. I'm not sure it is possible to hire a hackney coach for Chiswick, secure my husband and be back in time." What I do not tell Jean is that I cannot bear the thought of inflicting another compromising drama on Thomas.

Jean says that if I don't intend to enlist the help of my husband or a constable, then he intends to be by my side.

"No, Jean. The letter emphasises I come alone, and so I shall."

We argue about this for some time. Jean becomes overwrought at the thought of my expecting him to sit at home while I undergo this dangerous enterprise. Since he knows nothing about my past as an operative for Sir Gabriel Courtenay, Jean naturally has no idea there is another aspect – a distinctly unladylike side – to his employer. I try to explain that while Caroline's being taken somewhere and held without consent is abhorrent, my instinct tells me that physical harm is not what's intended for her or myself.

But Jean simply refuses to stand aside. We eventually settle on a compromise. He will accompany me in a hackney coach to Threadneedle Street in Soho, where he has Huguenot friends. From there, I will walk alone the remaining few streets to the designated meeting place. When I am finished with the night's business, I will come with Caroline to where he waits.

"The address is the exhibition hall for The Society of Artists," I point out.

"And I find that very interesting, Mrs. Sturbridge. The person who wrote this letter knows you attended this exhibition. It's someone who has intimate knowledge of your doings or has met you in person. It must be."

"I'm inclined to think that too. But I've no idea who."

We settle the time, and Jean hurries away to arrange the hackney coach. I have preparations to make too. I go to my bedroom, reaching to the top shelf of my dresser, a place far from Pierre's curious little hands. I remove a long, flat box tied with thick string. I haven't opened it for years.

Cutting the string, I open the box and withdraw the velvet triangle. The knives' handles gleam. How undiminished they are. Undaunted.

As I take them out, one by one, handling them carefully, I remember the day I purchased them, in a sinister little shop in the Faubourg

209

Saint-Antoine of Paris. After King Louis released Thomas from his obligations at Sèvres Porcelain, Victoire, the man who had guarded me in Sèvres and become a trusted friend, took Thomas and me to a place to stay that he deemed safe. It was a district of butchers, traders, printers, bakers, carpenters and more, all living and working on narrow, winding streets, permanently in shadow. At night, lying in our airless room on the third floor of a sagging building, I listened to men shouting and drunkenly singing below. I didn't mind staying there as much as one would think, for it reminded me of London.

One afternoon, Victoire led Thomas and me to a shop where I could, apparently, turn in my only valuable, the piece of jewellery Madame de Pompadour had given me, in exchange for money. Thomas had not wanted to ask Jean Hellot for money. While I didn't blame him for holding such scruples, an expensive journey to England stretched ahead of us. We hadn't yet gained permission to travel to the Netherlands. Money had to come from somewhere.

"How do we know we can trust him?" I whispered to Victoire as I eyed the man who owned the shop, an elfin creature with white hair and beady eyes.

"He offers a good price under the circumstances," Victoire said. "The earrings must be broken down and the gems removed. We can't have word travel to Versailles that you've taken cash in exchange for a Pompadour gift. Not until you're out of France."

I agreed to the exchange. But before we left, Victoire advised me to buy something from the shop to create some additional goodwill. "It will help deter him from informing the secret police," he whispered.

"I thought you said that in the Faubourg, everyone hates the police," I whispered back.

"Ah, but the streets run thick with police informers. Lieutenant General Sartine is everywhere, even here."

I bought a set of four knives that hot afternoon. I did it because my artisan's eye, my Huguenot instinct, was drawn to the handles' workmanship. "Excellent choice," said the shop owner in his gravelly voice. "Venetian. They make the best assassins."

Suppressing a shudder, I had put down the money. There was a certain irony to it. Sir Gabriel Courtenay had promised me enough money to live in Venice and establish myself as an artist if I obtained the formula for the colour blue. Now, Sir Gabriel was in disgrace, and the closest I ever came to reaching Venice were these knives.

Victoire gave me a few lessons in using them. The stiletto, with its long, slender blade, is the best for stabbing at close quarters. He always worried about the secret police and repercussions from other quarters for our breaking away from Sèvres. But no one threatened or bothered us for the rest of our time in France. It is only now, back in my beloved England, that I feel the need for a weapon.

I slip the stiletto knife up my sleeve, holding it in place with a stitch of my needle that can be torn if need be.

In the carriage with Jean, I feel the same cold rage toward whoever abducted Caroline. But I'm also baffled over what this person could want from me. Not from Thomas… but me. I've thought about it for hours, and it doesn't make sense. Surely, if there were anything of me to ask, it could be done without danger to another party? I think of Caroline, a determined person but not, perhaps, possessing the strongest nerves. What a terrible ordeal for her.

The carriage stops in Soho. I memorise the street name and house number where Jean will await me. It's a handsome brick building with freshly painted window shutters.

"Huguenot silversmiths turned to watchmaking," he says with a shrug. "It's a sure way to make a good living these days."

It's not that much further to Spring Street. The night is cold but the streets throng with people. I pass two smiling couples, fashionably dressed. On their way to the theatre or the opera perhaps, or one of Mrs. Cornelys' ticketed balls. No one would describe me as fashionable, and that is how I've planned it. I'm wearing a dark brown dress and hood to look as inconspicuous as possible.

My destination, the large building halfway down the street, is not drawing a crowd of art admirers as it had the last time I was on this street. The front doors are shut, the windows dark. There's no reason why a respectable woman would stand in front of a closed building, alone at night near Charing Cross. But here I must wait.

No one approaches me. The street is fairly well lit with street lamps, so it would be impossible to miss me. I stand like a lone sentry, trying not to give off visible nervousness. It comforts me to brush my left arm, to feel the presence of the knife, although my mind stops short of picturing the circumstances under which I'd wield it.

A flash of white teeth and a friendly wave set one young man apart. I stiffen as I realise he is waving at me. What an absurdity. He's so carefree, he practically bounces down the street, a tricorne hat perched on his head, long chestnut hair cascading below. He holds a cane in one hand. How could this person be the one who has gone to such lengths to talk to me? I have no idea who he is.

"So very good to see you," he drawls when he reaches me. He peers over my shoulder with studied calmness.

"Did you come alone, Mrs. Sturbridge?" he asks.

"Yes. Now tell me what you want of me."

"What do I want? Why, nothing, Madame, except the pleasure of escorting you to Covent Garden."

"Covent Garden? Why? Is Caroline there? Is she all right?"

He extends his arm, saying smoothly that all my questions will be answered soon.

212

Having no choice, I take the young man's arm. He is merely the means of conveying me onward, to some other person. A deeper dread takes hold. This is all very elaborate.

It doesn't take long to walk to nearby Covent Garden. Our being together wouldn't make sense to anyone giving us a close look. He's younger, a man of fashion. But no one takes a second to scrutinise us. We are heading into the pulsing heart of the most frantic part of town.

Londoners don't like foreigners as a rule. While we may see the value of Italian art, French clothes and furniture and German music, we don't want to obviously mimic anyone who isn't English. That's why you don't see us imitating other cities in our architecture. There's too much native pride for that. But Covent Garden is an exception. A century ago, Inigo Jones designed its square, church and porticoed houses to resemble a grand Italian piazza. Everyone liked his work, admired his style, and yet, so many other things appeared afterward: a fruit, vegetable and flower market on the piazza, with a handful of grand theatres and a hundred taverns and coffee houses surrounding it.

To my surprise, my coxcomb-ish escort leads me right into the piazza. The vegetable sheds are empty now, the people gathered here are loud and mostly drunk. Some are wearing outlandish costumes as if they are part of the theatre world, though they'd probably be lucky to get a part in a Punch & Judy show. Jugglers and card sharps jostle for attention. A bonfire rages.

A great many of the men appear to be looking for love that comes by the coin. Young women wearing gaudy dresses tug on men's sleeves, just as I saw in the alleyway with Sam Baldwin. Here, they find eager takers. Some women seem to be leading customers off the piazza to the same side of the square as St. Paul's Church. When we have walked far enough to be parallel with the church, I glance over. By the light of the moon, anyone can see the couples to the side and in the back, in positions more fitting to the barnyard than the churchyard.

My cheeks grow hot. This is an appalling situation. Am I being deliberately humiliated? A promenade through one of the most dissolute districts of London is not what I expected. I'm about to pull my arm free and demand an explanation when the young man comes to a stop.

He looks around for a few seconds, expectantly. I can't believe this is my destination. Crowds of people are around us. It couldn't be less private.

"Wait here," he says, pointing straight down as if I'm being ordered to stay rooted to this square of the piazza.

I seethe over this ungentlemanly treatment. If it were not for Caroline, I would walk back to Soho.

The young man approaches someone else, showing a certain tentativeness, even respect. The second man looks older. But, most importantly, he is wearing some sort of uniform, a dark blue jacket with matching breeches. A gold slash crosses his lean body. But the lofty hat perched on his head? That does not look like part of a military uniform. It's like part of a costume.

There's no mistaking the sword swinging from his hip.

The soldier walks toward me, bows stiffly and makes a flourish as if I am to follow him. He has dark eyes, sombre eyes.

I know those eyes from somewhere.

My mind works frantically as I struggle to place him, without success. He glances sideways, frowning. He may detect that I am on the point of recognising him. He turns and strides deeper into the piazza. I don't know what else to do but follow. He glances over his shoulder to make sure of it but doesn't want to walk side by side. Is he trying to avoid my scrutiny?

It does not take but five more minutes, at this pace, to leave the piazza entirely. The instant we cross a bordering street, a boy materialises holding a flickering torch. He takes his place in front of the soldier. In a strange procession, we enter the warren of streets beyond the Covent Garden piazza.

These streets may be dark, but they're not quiet. We pass a long coffee house, bursting with candlelight and joyous noise. A group of men join in song, the one currently being roared all over London:

"*Rule, Brittania, Brittania rule the waves.*

Britons never, never, never shall be slaves."

The soldier leading me stops short, staring into the grimy windows of the coffee house. His right hand travels to the head of his sword. Treading carefully, I come up so that I might see his face.

In the light thrown out on the street of the coffee house, his eyes are pools of resentment.

"*Chiens d'anglais,*" he says.

And with that, a click in my brain tells me who this is, though the answer is extraordinary. Yes, I have met the person who just said "English dogs" in French. No wonder it was such a struggle to place him.

"Good evening, Mademoiselle Duvall," I say.

He takes a step toward me. "So you know me," he says in that whispery, cultured French-accented voice I remember from Sir Joshua Reynolds' reception.

His eyes travel up and down my body, not in a lascivious fashion but assessing me for some other reason. With one swift lunge, he seizes my left hand and pulls me toward him. His fingers snake into my sleeve and reach up my forearm, touching the stiletto knife fastened there.

With a tight smile, he shoves me back to where I was.

"My compliments to Sir Gabriel Courtenay," he says.

This is an even greater shock. "You know him?" I say, unnecessarily.

"I have that honour, yes." After a few seconds of silence, during which he seems to be deciding something, he stands taller and says with pride, "My name is Charles Geneviève Louis Auguste André Timothée d'Eon de Beaumont."

So this is the Chevalier d'Eon. The French diplomat who went into hiding, who toyed with blackmailing King Louis XV and who, much more significantly, was a member of the French king's elite spy service.

"Let us go on, Madame," he says and signals to the linkboy with a snap of his fingers to continue.

Our passage takes us past the brightly lit coffee house and down the length of a short street that curves into darkness. Ominously, the linkboy steps into the point of darkness. By his torch, I can see him edging into a narrow alleyway.

"This is madness," I protest.

"Don't you want to help your friend?" asks the Chevalier d'Eon, contempt underlining his question. "Is that not why you came?"

Without waiting for my reply, he follows the linkboy, turning sideways to slide into the opening of the alley. I do the same, shuddering at the touch of the ancient wall, which crumbles slightly as my shoulder scrapes through.

The alley reeks of filth, more so than most of the streets in the city, and that is quite saying something. My stomach churning, I step quickly over the uneven cobblestones. I thank God that the night is cold enough to freeze whatever lies beneath my shoes.

The linkboy stops well before he reaches the end of the alley. A man has stepped out of a door, blocking our path. Metal flashes in his hands. A second later, another man stands with him. The duo's intent could not be more obvious – to rob us and most likely cut our throats.

The chevalier signals to me to stay behind him. With our linkboy flattened against the opposite wall, the Frenchman steps forward, withdrawing his sword with one swift movement. Should I pull out my own knife and fight alongside him?

One of the two criminals charges toward us, the chevalier's sword flashes as swift as a lightning bolt, his other arm aloft in the air. The criminal crumbles, groaning. The other man melts away.

A second later, the chevalier turns, seizes me and pulls me swiftly to the end of the alley. It opens to a far wider street. He whistles for the linkboy.

"Your city is a cesspool," the chevalier informs me, as cool as can be.

My brow is damp with sweat and my knees a bit wobbly, but I force myself forward. I refuse to dissolve into a fearful puddle in front of this man. No matter what his deeds of the past, his undoubted espionage, he just saved my life.

Five minutes later, we stand in front of a townhouse of very light grey brick, three storeys high. Candlelight in the shuttered windows exudes some sort of welcome. It is strange indeed to find a fashionable building in the middle of this dire neighbourhood.

The building boasts an archway instead of a front door. Stepping through, I find a greater surprise: a large courtyard with three handsome carriages waiting and single horses too. On the other side of the courtyard opens an entrance to a wider street than any I have seen in this neighbourhood for a while.

The chevalier beckons for me to follow him through a dark red door off the courtyard. Inside is a marble foyer and a wigged servant wearing livery.

"Before we proceed any further, stand still," says the chevalier. Using a small knife he extracted from his pocket, he snips the thread holding in place my stiletto knife and eases it out. "Superior workmanship," he says. "You obtained this here, in London?"

"If you must know, I purchased it in Paris."

He looks at me assessingly once more. "Sir Gabriel Courtenay was the best of the best," he says. "And because of you, he lost his position in England."

"It wasn't because of me," I counter. "Sir Gabriel always made his own choices."

The chevalier hands the knife to the servant, who disappears with it. He says, very quietly, "There are some who believe that when Sir Gabriel could no longer obtain critical information here for King Louis, France lost a significant advantage in the war. The tide turned against us. The Treaty of Paris signed last year is the worst military defeat for France in a century. So you see, Madame Sturbridge, you have much to answer for."

Or much to be proud of.

If anything I did tilted the balance against France in war, I couldn't be happier.

I stare back defiantly at the Chevalier d'Eon. The seconds tick by as we take each other's measure. But this allows me time for other thoughts. In this foyer, lit by candles, I can see what a smooth complexion he has. And a set of narrow shoulders. I can't help but wonder…

"Until later then, Madame," the chevalier says and strides away.

I assume this means he will lead me out of this dangerous neighbourhood when my business here is completed, later tonight. And I have just alienated him. This was not the most intelligent choice. I must try harder to not let my emotions lead me in Covent Garden.

The servant who took my knife away from me reappears to lead me up a set of winding stairs. The faint sound of women and men talking and laughing pulses on the other side of the wall at the first landing. We keep going to the top of the stairs. The servant pauses, his hand on the doorknob as if waiting for a signal. At least a minute crawls by.

A wave of furious weariness hits me. I fling myself at the door, pushing the servant to the side so I can pound on it.

"Hervé Gaynard, I've had enough of these games," I shout. "I know it is you! I know you sent me the letter. I demand that you let me in at once."

Chapter Sixteen

The room in which Hervé Gaynard has chosen to receive me boasts all the trappings of a man of the most sophisticated taste. The carved wooden furniture gleams, tapestries hang on one wall, a framed portrait of a pretty brunette offering a bold smile on the other. It could very well be a Joshua Reynolds.

An exquisite Sevres vase rises from a table. I instantly recognise its pink-and-gold design and delicate porcelain outline from my stay in France. But the room is dominated by a six-foot-tall folding screen showing, on one panel, a dozen beautiful naked women gathered around a circular bath and a tile roof soaring over their heads. Gaynard sits behind a desk positioned in front of the second panel, but I can see enough of it to say that the visible couples would feel at home in St. Paul's churchyard.

I take this all in during my first seconds in the room, the brief period of time I have for observation before I launch myself at Gaynard, the only person present. The sight of him, sitting utterly relaxed behind his Chippendale desk, fills me with such disgust I could throttle him. I slam my palms on top of the desk.

"I want to see Caroline Mowbray immediately," I thunder. "Why would you kidnap her? Why on earth was that necessary? You should be thrown in Newgate Prison for this! Believe me, I have the contacts to see to it."

Unimpressed by my threats, he says, "When did you know it was me who wrote the letter? I'm just so very curious."

"I wondered all along, but I knew for certain when it was Mademoiselle Duvall who escorted me through Covent Garden."

Gaynard bursts out laughing and leans over to open an enamelled snuffbox on the corner of his desk. "I will admit, I did not think you would recognise him. He considered it a possibility, but I thought he was safe."

"In this matter, it seems the Chevalier d'Eon had the advantage over you," I say.

Laughter vanishes. His fingers freeze amid measuring a pinch of snuff, and a nerve dances in the side of his face. "I would have preferred that he not reveal his true identity to you," says Gaynard.

"Why? Because it confirms that you are part of a ring of French spies operating in England?"

He sighs as if dealing with a stubborn child who won't learn her sums.

"I've told you before and I'll say it again, Mrs. Sturbridge, I'm but a businessman. The chevalier is my friend, nothing more. I asked him for a favour, knowing he is one of the finest swordsmen in all of France."

"Then proceed to the point of our business. What do you want from me, and why would you abduct Miss Mowbray as part of that?"

"You're here, aren't you? And please sit. You achieve nothing from standing there shouting at me."

I don't want to sit, I don't want to behave as if this were an ordinary meeting. But as he's made plain, I can't make him do anything. I've no choice but to listen. I say, sourly, "This entire affair – unsigned letters, kidnapping and escorts taking me back and forth across Covent Garden? Absurd. And then to drag me to a brothel of all places?"

"Mrs. Sturbridge, I beg your pardon," he says and snorts two pinches before continuing. "A brothel? You are mistaken. This is a bagnio, one I have invested some of my money in. A discriminating client may have a bath downstairs and then a fine meal and some agreeable company upstairs. Before this accommodation was built, London bathhouses left much to be desired. This is a well-respected establishment. You'd be surprised to know the names of some of the men who patronise it."

"Well respected? You must think me such a fool."

"Oh, but I don't think that at all," Hervé Gaynard says and picks up the stiletto knife that the Chevalier d'Eon had taken from me. "I make my compliments to Sir Gabriel Courtenay."

How I dislike their assumption that any measures I might take to protect myself are the result of training from Sir Gabriel.

He continues, "However, I do think your husband is a fool. Perhaps that's too strong a word. He is an idealist. That's why I wanted to see you alone and have gone to considerable trouble to make sure of it. My two associates who helped to deliver you here were not taking you on certain routes for their own amusement but to make absolutely sure you were not followed. The matter to be put before you must be presented in a highly secure and safe manner, in the most private setting."

A chill scurries down my spine. This is becoming deadly serious. For the first time, I reflect that no one actually knows I am here. Jean is aware that I planned to meet someone near Charing Cross an hour ago, but that is all. For an instant, I imagine Thomas' anger with me at coming here alone and hastily push the thought away.

Adopting a light and disdainful tone, I say, "If you expect me to persuade my husband to engage in stealing money from that marquise with schemes of alchemy, to become a conspirator with you and Giacomo Casanova, then *you* are the fool, Monsieur Gaynard."

He smiles. "That proposal is dead. My friend, Casanova, has left the country. Russia is his next destination."

I shift uneasily in my chair. Casanova sat in my parlour just four days ago. What sort of men are these? At least I wrote to Sir Humphrey Willoughby, telling him of their uninvited visit. I wonder if Sir Humphrey has already discovered that Gaynard owns this bagnio.

"Left the country?" I say. "Well, that is Casanova's affair. Mine is collecting Miss Mowbray. I assume she is waiting within this building."

"She is."

My fingernails dig into my palms at the thought of shy, prim Caroline held here, doubtless horrified by such surroundings. It would be dangerous to provoke Gaynard, yet this cannot pass without reproof.

"Monsieur Gaynard, by my choosing to entangle myself with Sir Gabriel Courteney years ago, I am forever tainted. I accept that as a result of it, I may cross paths with the likes of you, Casanova, the Chevalier d'Eon and others of your ilk. But Miss Mowbray should never have been drawn in. Not someone like her. That is breaking the rules of the game."

To my astonishment, he laughs, not the sneering chuckles I've grown accustomed to but as if I've said something really funny.

"You think so, Mrs. Sturbridge?"

He presses a tiny bell on the side table. Within seconds, the servant appears.

"Have Miss Caroline Mowbray brought here."

"Yes, sir."

The servant withdraws.

Hervé Gaynard studies me, a strange flicker in his eye, before saying, "Mrs. Sturbridge, what do you think of the work of Joshua Reynolds?"

My stomach somersaults.

I say carefully, "He's a supremely talented artist. Why do you ask?"

Gaynard pulls at a tiny thread on his long, dainty white sleeve. "I think his high status in England is very interesting. It's all so different in France. Versailles is the temple of taste, and King Louis, well, it may be blasphemous, but he is the temple's high priest. Here, there is – how shall I put this? – a royal reluctance to rule the arts as much as there is to rule the country. The Hanovers are such an unimpressive family. So all sorts of people jump in to be leaders. One of them is our mutual friend, Joshua Reynolds. The son of a failed schoolmaster from the West Country. Yes, he is supremely talented, Mrs. Sturbridge." He takes a breath, "However."

My mouth dry, I repeat, "However?"

His eyes locked into mine, Gaynard leans forward and says, "Do you think he knows what he's doing?"

The possibility that Hervé Gaynard somehow knows about Reynolds' plea for help with his colours hits me with the force of a blow. I struggle to control my panic just as the door opens, and two women appear.

The first is hard-faced, with a thick waist and thicker arms who turns and pulls in the second. She is taller, slender, wearing a pale rose dress with a scandalously low neckline, blonde hair loose around her shoulders. The face is Caroline's. But something is very wrong. Her eyes take in the room, settling on me for a few seconds and then moving on as if she fails to recognise me.

"What have you done to her?" I cry.

224

The hard-faced woman steers Caroline to a chair opposite mine, pushing her down with a rude shove. Incredibly, Caroline smiles up at her.

"It seems the reunion with old friends was not to her liking," says Gaynard with a shrug. "She was most distressed at the prospect of your coming here tonight. So we gave her a calming tincture."

"A tincture? You've made her drunk!" I want nothing so much as to seize Caroline and force our way out of this horrible room. But how do I get us both down the stairs and out to the street when she's in such a state? And what will I do if Gaynard tries to stop me?

"No, no. Nothing so crude." He turns to the other woman. "Strong tea for her and for Mrs. Sturbridge as well, I think."

Gaynard rises and walks over to Caroline, bending down to look into her face more closely. "You can best see the effect in her eyes," he comments. "They've gone completely black."

"What you've done here is reprehensible," I say, my voice trembling.

"The tincture is an adaptation of one invented by the Swiss alchemist Paracelsus. I'm sure your husband could tell you all about Paracelsus." Gaynard returns to his chair. "You say she isn't part of the game? I'm afraid you aren't in possession of the facts."

With a taunting smile, he says, "She *is* the game. Caroline was a most promising girl at Mrs. Baird's house. Of course, she wasn't called Caroline then. She was the best of her year – and sold for a very good price to a certain gentleman, eccentric perhaps, and quite old, but with more money than Croesus. After his death, she disappeared, oh, it must have been five years ago. No one knew what had become of her – until she appeared with you at Joshua Reynolds' gathering for William Hogarth."

I want to scream at Gaynard that he is a lying scum. But I know with a terrible certainty that he's telling me the truth, or at least a version of it, for it explains so much that I've never understood about poor Caroline.

I approach her, filled with equal parts concern and dread. Placing my hand on her shoulder, I say, "Caroline, are you all right?"

That same vacant smile plays across her mouth. I'm not sure she knows me.

"I would like to take her home now," I say quietly. "Can she be made ready? She must be changed into proper clothes."

Gaynard studies me, his eyebrows furrowed as if this were not quite the reaction he expected.

"Don't you think that you should hear my proposition first?" he says, a trace of anger underlying his words.

And with that betrayal of his true emotion, I feel a little power flowing back to me for the first time this evening.

"By all means, Monsieur," I say, returning to my chair. "Tell me what you want from me. Do your worst."

"My 'worst', as you put it, is a highly valuable opportunity for you and your husband as well as for myself."

I fold my hands, steeling myself to listen to this sordid scheme.

"First of all, I know about Joshua Reynolds' fugitive colours," he says.

I shake my head. "So he *does* confide in you."

"As a matter of fact, he does not. There's no reason for you to be told how I obtained this information. What is important is that, to try to emulate the Venetian masters, Reynolds has been concocting his own colours, and it's causing him embarrassment. A few years after having his portrait done, the proud owner might see a faded face or a streaked and crumpled sleeve. Am I not correct?"

I stare at him without confirming anything.

Gaynard plunges forward. "Your husband's reputation is such that

Reynolds is willing to put the colour experiments completely in his hands. *That* is where the business opportunity presents itself. What if your husband were to, instead of fixing Joshua Reynolds' colour problems, make them far, far worse? Without letting him realise it, of course. So that within one year, a group of finished Joshua Reynolds portraits were to deteriorate into utter disasters?"

I cannot find the words for several seconds, I am so appalled.

"But that would ruin Mr. Reynolds," I finally say. "Why on earth would Thomas do such a cruel thing?"

"For the sum of eight thousand pounds."

My head swims at the vastness of the amount. It's more than I am likely to earn in my lifetime.

"Who?" I whisper. "Who would pay so much to destroy Joshua Reynolds?"

"Now, that is something I can never ever tell you. A condition is anonymity of the source. Suffice it to say I am satisfied that the person is good for the amount. In fact, you and your husband would receive a portion of it upon our agreement to proceed, and I'll receive half my fee."

Yes, his fee would have to be hefty. Why else would he go to so much trouble? But the question is, what will Gaynard do when I refuse? And as sure as I know anything, this will be refused.

Our tea is served. The woman who's brought it needs to hold the cup to Caroline's lips for her to drink, I'm sorry to see. She is in no fit state to go anywhere. I have to buy myself some more time.

"I don't see how my husband is supposed to explain his actions after the colours deteriorate drastically," I say. "The work he does will be obvious. Mr. Reynolds could take legal action against him. He'd be within his rights to do so."

"And in so doing expose himself to the scorn of all London for hiring a chemist to fix his mistakes? I doubt it. That's the beauty of it. We are all protected."

I can't stop myself from saying, "Beauty? You find beauty in this crime?"

He sneers, "You weren't always so high and mighty about committing a spot of crime if there were something in it for you. Believe me, Sir Gabriel was never going to be able to come up with this much money for you as reward for stealing him the colour blue. It's an opportunity that comes once in a lifetime."

Hervé Gaynard can't manage to conceal his excitement over the fugitive colours scheme. His eyes glitter, a red tinge warms his cheeks. Greed is what drives him more than any other appetite, only its bounty can satiate him. The suffering caused in pursuit of his avarice means nothing, whether it's the humiliation of Caroline or the potential destruction of Joshua Reynolds.

His chosen fragrance, powdered violet, shimmers. I feel the same kind of disgust I would if confronted with a river rat from the Thames. There is no point in postponing the refusal any longer.

"As I've said, I know I am tainted by my past," I say. "But my husband is a different matter. Even if he were tempted by this amount of money – and it is not in his nature to be guided by money – he is forbidden by His Majesty's government to work in any way on the creation of colours, and he intends to follow that dictum."

"His Majesty's government…" Gaynard repeats the phrase with deep contempt.

"If King George and the English fill you with disgust, why don't you go back to Paris?" I demand.

"Because Paris, and all of France, fall under the vigilant eye of the secret police. One must be careful every second of Lieutenant General de Sartine. While in London, anyone may pursue lucrative interests with scarcely any interference at all. When you combine that with the freedom of speech laws and all the merchant money flowing through this country, those Bristol plantation owners..."

With a strange smile, he spreads his hands across his desk before continuing, "That is why, with a few precautions taken, it would be more than possible for Mr. Sturbridge to agree to work for Joshua Reynolds, and no one would be the wiser, certainly not Sir Humphrey Willoughby."

My throat tightens. Thomas and I never mentioned Sir Humphrey's name. How *does* Gaynard know so much about us and Joshua Reynolds?

"So, all that remains is for you to persuade your husband." His eyes run up and down my body. "Your power over him is undisputed. And not just him. I must say, I don't understand it. Your supposed charms are not to my taste. I say this without intending an insult."

Again, I must struggle to hide my revulsion. Even the faintest possibility of Gaynard finding me to his taste makes me want to gag.

"And what, may I ask, if I should be unable to persuade my husband?" I ask.

"Oh, Mrs. Sturbridge, I don't accept that as a possibility. But should you disappoint me, I'd really have no other choice but to inform Nicolas Carteret and any other sanctimonious Huguenot silk weavers you do business with that you employ a harlot once sold to the highest bidder."

He points at Caroline. Her smile has disappeared. It's possible she is emerging from her mist, that she understood him.

Anger rises in me like an unquenchable fire. I don't know how much longer I can control my words and actions.

I take a breath and say, "Well, perhaps I've lost interest in the silk design business."

"Oh, really? You don't think you'd be in dire need of money after your husband is sent to debtors' prison?" Gaynard smiles. "Yes, I'm referring to the Earl of Sandwich. I could very easily convey some select facts to him about Thomas and Genevieve Sturbridge that would make him discharge your husband on the spot. And any future employer would do the same after receiving one of my letters."

He smiles with pleasure at the prospect. I can't speak. For a moment, I am as lost to my surroundings as Caroline. This is the worst future I could ever have. Despised, destitute and most likely alone. Thomas could never forgive me for pulling him into this. My ruin is what delights Gaynard. His glittering eyes, his smile, it's the same glee as when he talked of the silkworms, boiled alive. I want to rush at him, hurt him as he's hurt me.

But I have to get out of this room and with Caroline in my keeping.

"Well," I say. "I will think about this. Now, please have Caroline made ready. She leaves with me."

Hervé Gaynard rises, studying me. He is suspicious.

"By all means think about it. But Reynolds expects his answer by the end of the week. So, I shall have my answer from you no later than Thursday night. I will be expecting you at, say, nine o'clock?"

"In three days? That's not possible."

"You're a resourceful woman when you want to be."

"I deliver to you the news that Thomas will perform sabotage on the colours of Joshua Reynolds – or else your blackmailing punishment begins."

"Exactly," he says.

"Very well."

Servants take Caroline away, and when I see her next, she wears her own clothes. Her eyes are no longer black; confusion spreads across her face.

"Let's go, Caroline," I say very gently.

The manservant leads us both down the spiral staircase. We walk slowly, with my arm around Caroline's waist, guiding her steps.

The dark red door opens, and we step outside. The night air is so cold, it's painful. But it also affords me with mental focus after all that time in Gaynard's nauseatingly warm room. I see four coaches waiting instead of three. A group of servants loiter outside, warming their hands at a small fire set well away from the house.

On the top of the smallest coach, the driver tips his hat to me. To my shock, I realise it's Jean Orgier.

From the corner of my eye, I spot the Chevalier d'Eon walking toward Caroline and me from the largest door off the courtyard, his sword firmly in place. He's no more than twenty feet from us.

Gripping Caroline tight, I turn away from him and run across the courtyard toward Jean's coach. He leaps down from his seat and pulls open the coach door. Caroline runs alongside me, to my relief. I don't have to drag her.

"Get back up, back up," I scream at Jean.

I push Caroline into the coach and whirl around to face the Chevalier d'Eon. He has caught up to us, of course. He could easily draw his sword on me and kill me, all three of us, since Jean hasn't jumped up to the driver's seat but stands protectively by my side.

Breathing heavily, I peer over the chevalier's shoulder. The servants gathered around the fire stare at us. We could not be hurt, or forced to do anything, without their noticing.

"Monsieur, please do not take offence, but we have secured other means to return to Spitalfields," I say, still short of breath.

The chevalier says, "So I see, Madame."

I take a step, then another, up into the carriage, taking a seat beside the quivering Caroline. Jean slams the door. As the carriage jerks forward, I glance outside.

The Chevalier d'Eon holds the handle of his rapier sword close to his forehead and then points it at me, bowing his head.

He maintains his salute position until the carriage turns onto the street, and I can see him no more.

Chapter Seventeen

In the carriage to Spitalfields, Caroline fights the fog of the tincture. This means she feels the force of the pain of what she has endured – and the deep shame of my knowing about her life before she came to Ana Maria Garthwaite's. I hold her as she weeps, her body heaving with sobs.

After returning to my house, I urge her to lie down, but she refuses. "I don't want to close my eyes until I'm sure all the poison is out of me."

Jean lingers to be of service, and I soon learn that late yesterday afternoon, he had hired a boy familiar with the streets to follow me from Charing Cross, posing as a linkboy if necessary. Once I'd entered the bagnio, the boy had raced back to Soho and told Jean its location. The courtyard opened onto Drury Lane. Knowing it to be thick with bordellos, taverns and other places of vice, Jean had brought the carriage there to wait.

"Mrs. Sturbridge, you may be angry with me as long as you wish, but I would not have been able to live with myself if I had done no more than wait like a useless lump in Soho," says Jean.

Caroline, huddled by the fire, says, "After what you and Jean have been through on my behalf, you deserve to know the truth."

"You don't have to talk about it, not if it pains you," Jean insists. But Caroline says she needs to speak, and so she begins.

"My father was not of my mother's station in life, and she was warned by friends and all her family not to marry him. But she was in love with him. That changed after my birth, and my father lost employment time and again. I know that she approached her father, my grandfather, for help, but he refused to do anything for us. When I was twelve, my father disappeared."

"He abandoned you?" I ask.

"Yes. My mother heard a report that he was later taken into the army and forced to fight in Quebec. Perhaps he died there. If he did return to England, he wouldn't have had any way of finding me. I stopped using the name I was born with long ago."

I glance at Jean. His face is as sombre as if he were in church.

"We had come to a small town in Kent. Oh, my mother and I worked hard, but we went to bed hungry many nights. She didn't want us to fall back on the parish poorhouse, so she took me with her to London."

She shakes her head. "Everything was worse in the city, not better. There were so many women vying for every respectable job! And then she began drinking gin…"

Caroline stops again, gathers herself and continues.

"My mother sold me to a bawd named Mrs. Baird when I was fourteen. Mrs Baird put advertisements in the newspaper regularly for serving girls. It was a ruse to find fresh recruits. My mother, in desperation, answered the notice in the newspaper. She was much too old for Mrs. Baird, but unfortunately, Mother had brought me along."

Her lips trembled. I don't know how she finds the strength to push on, but she does.

"I was completely innocent," Caroline says. "That changed, of course. All I will say is that she was no more brutal than she needed to be. The auctioning of the unspoiled in a bawd's house, I don't know if you've heard of the practice. I'd prefer not to describe it."

"There's no need for that," I say quickly. I don't know a thing about such auctions. Just when I think myself inured to the depravity of the London rakes, some new horror emerges.

"A Lincolnshire lord purchased me," says Caroline in a dull, toneless voice. "So, you see, I was sold twice. He was old enough to be my grandfather. I lived with him for three years, it was just the two of us in that ancient house, besides his loyal servants. He gave me books and drawing paper, and had me schooled. It amused him to do that. In drawing and painting, I found the only escape from my existence."

So this is how she found her way to art.

"When he died, the will said a small inheritance would come to me. The solicitor made it plain he expected me to return to Mrs. Baird or someone of her ilk. I took the money and returned to London, but I took this name and was extremely careful about who I spoke to."

"What about your mother?" I ask.

"Gin killed her years ago. I wanted only to be hired by Ana Maria Garthwaite. I owned one of her flowered silk dresses in Lincolnshire. I had found out enough about her to discover she employed artists. A woman employing other women in respectable labour. It was my only goal."

I rub my temple and say, "I am so sorry that in bringing you to Joshua Reynolds' house, I exposed you to people from your past."

But something about this is wrong.

"I don't think that Hervé Gaynard could have been in London when you were in the clutches of this Baird creature because that would have been during the early part of the war," I say. "There were no French Catholics daring to live in London then."

Caroline shakes her head. "Not him. I never met Gaynard until the night in Leicester Fields. It was Kitty Fisher who knew me. We are the same age. She was working in a milliner's shop when an army officer debauched her, and she became known to Mrs. Baird."

I remember with a shudder Kitty Fisher's eyes on us – not me, but Caroline – as she whispered in Gaynard's ear.

"And there's something else you need to know, Mrs. Sturbridge. I overheard that Kitty Fisher tells Gaynard everything that Joshua Reynolds tells her. She is a close confidante. And Mr. Reynolds tells her quite a bit after he's had a large portion of wine."

"What a fool!" explodes Jean.

I finally have some answers. If it were Kitty Fisher who told Hervé Gaynard about the fugitive colours, that solves one mystery for me. Others remain, such as who would be willing to spend a fortune to wreck Joshua Reynolds' life?

But before I can contemplate this any further, the future of the workshop is in question. Caroline declares that she can no longer work for me. I was expecting this, and I insist with all the vehemence I can summon that she remain. "You did nothing wrong at any point, all wrongs were perpetuated against you – many of them when you were still a child as far as I'm concerned."

Jean blurts, "If you leave, then I must go too. And then, whatever will Mrs. Sturbridge do?"

Incredibly, a smile wobbles on her wan and tear-streaked face.

"I'll stay, but only if you permit me to work today," Caroline says.

"That's ridiculous!"

"I must be useful, it's the only way I can think of to begin to compensate you for what you have been through," she says, pleadingly.

Jean, too, shows no sign of desiring sleep rather than work. As the first rays of sun fight their way through the heavy fog and grey smoke to penetrate my front windows, the two of them are sitting at the wooden work table.

I ask Daphne, when she rises, to make breakfast for Jean and Caroline, who are already upstairs, to which she agrees without comment. I suppose she is growing used to odd goings-on in this house.

I'm years older than my artists, and I feel the exhaustion more keenly, especially as I play with Pierre and get him dressed. My eyes flutter, and I can barely speak. I just want to stumble into bed, holding my son close.

Or perhaps it's the growing sense I have, one of suffocating dread over the coming encounter with Hervé Gaynard, that drains my strength. I know I must return to his repulsive bagnio at nine o'clock on Thursday night and tell him that Thomas Sturbridge will not take part in his scheme.

Thomas himself is unaware of Gaynard's despicable offer. Since I know as sure as I'm alive that my husband would never agree, there's no need to pull him in.

But it's more than that. The responsibility must remain mine alone. Six years ago, I entered the ranks of criminals and spies – and I was not sold into it or blackmailed or fooled because of my youth. I walked into this hard, cold, violent world with open eyes. Now, I must leave it forever.

A significant danger exists, there's no point in denying it. Hervé Gaynard has threatened to tell the silk weavers about Caroline, to expose Thomas' past. The only protection I have is that if Gaynard tries to pull me down, I can take him down with me – and I'll reach out for the Chevalier d'Eon and Kitty Fisher too. If Giacomo Casanova were still in England, he'd be joining us. Anything I can think of to hurt them all, I will do it.

This is not a matter for the constable. If Gaynard refuses to take my "no" as the final answer, I shall go to Sir Humphrey directly. He already knows that Gaynard dabbles in spying, thanks to my letter. He could be learning more soon.

I manage to make it through the rest of the day. The next one I try to concentrate on workshop business and enjoy a quiet evening with Pierre. I hope to awaken on Thursday with fresh determination.

I sleep soundly, yes, but I awaken with the fear that this could be my last day alive.

I'm set to defy someone without scruples or pity, who is utterly ruthless. Sir Gabriel Courtenay ordered people to be murdered, I'm aware of that. The Chevalier d'Eon is clearly no stranger to violence. And I believe Hervé Gaynard to be the most ruthless of them all in pursuit of his greed. Although I cannot think how it would benefit him to kill me, I've long sensed that if thwarted, Gaynard would behave viciously.

It's no good to take a knife along. Or any other weapon. I must win this contest with words. If only I could come up with the perfect sentences.

In the early afternoon, a letter arrives from Thomas:

"*Genevieve,*

"*I will not be back in Spitalfields until next week. It seems I need more time to complete something important. Once that is done, I believe many of our difficulties will be at an end. I will write to Joshua Reynolds soon and decline his request, don't worry about that further. I'm truly sorry that we quarrelled. It is entirely my fault that our life together has made us vulnerable to forces beyond our control. When next I see you, I will explain everything.*

"*Thomas.*"

The letter both cheers me and fills me with fresh anxieties. What is he working on – is it something that could land him in prison? Does it violate his agreement with the government? I cannot believe that Thomas would do anything reckless. But then, why keep it hidden from me?

I sit down and write two letters, one addressed to Thomas and one to Sir Humphrey.

I seal them and look for George. I find him going over the inventory of food with Daphne in her kitchen. It's a warm, familiar scene. A box of shiny yellow onions sits on her table. A pot of broth bubbles over the fire. She's crushed a few bulbs of garlic for the broth. I can not only smell it but also spot a frail white garlic skin caught on the edge of her cutting board.

"George, I need you in the parlour for a minute. Can you spare him, Daphne?"

"Of course."

I press the two letters into George's hands and tell him to post them if the following day, I am missing from the house and Daphne doesn't know where I am.

His eyes widen.

"George, can you do this? Without telling Daphne tonight? I don't want her to know. The chances are, I'll be here in the morning when you report for work. If I'm not, you must do this for me."

"Yes, Madame Genevieve."

"Do you have a place to put the letters tonight, safe from Daphne, and where you can find them tomorrow? It's important."

"Yes. I understand you."

My next stop is the workshop. I push open the door as gently as I can. Jean and Caroline are working in companionable silence, sketching some preliminary ideas with chalk. The shouting of the coal man on Fournier Street is the only noise.

Tears prick my eyes. I can't bear the prospect of this workshop coming to an end.

"What's wrong, Mrs. Sturbridge?" Jean has spotted me.

"Nothing."

I walk over to the table and make a show of examining their work. Caroline says, "You're returning to Drury Lane, aren't you? It's not over."

I swallow and say, "It's *almost* over."

Jean and Caroline immediately become alarmed, pleading to know why I must see Hervé Gaynard again, what he wants from me. When I won't divulge the information, they demand that one or both of them accompany me.

Caroline must never go anywhere near Gaynard again. On that point, I cannot be swayed. As for Jean, I'd considered asking him to escort me but then discarded the idea. He is too much of a hothead. At the Foundling Hospital, he'd almost come to blows with Hervé Gaynard. And Jean disobeyed me the night I went to Drury Lane. I did not ask him to wait for me outside the bagnio. And really, after the benefit of some contemplation, it would have been better if he had not intervened. We would have found our way to Spitalfields without Jean. In his swooping in with a carriage, I was made to look a liar. I'd said repeatedly I had come alone and had not been followed. While it may sound ludicrous to try to appear like a woman of my word in front of criminals, Jean's actions weaken my position tonight.

"The matter that concerns me, which forced me to meet with Monsieur Gaynard on Monday night, is a private one and has nothing to do with our workshop," I say. "I don't want either of you involved. He proposed something to me, and tonight at nine o'clock, I'll see him and make it plain that my husband and I cannot agree to what he proposes."

"And what happens when you tell him that – a man such as Gaynard?" presses Jean.

"What do you mean, what happens? What can he do to me?" I say with a shrug. I even manage to produce a smile.

Caroline has a strained, faraway look. I fear that she might remember Gaynard saying he would tell the master weavers of Spitalfields that I employ *a harlot sold to the highest bidder*. But she still bore that horrible empty smile when he said it. I pray she didn't understand.

There must be a way to prevent Gaynard from unleashing his blackmail.

I tell Daphne once more that I have an evening engagement and to put Pierre to bed with her.

I change my son into his nightclothes myself. Running a comb through his silky red hair, I want nothing more than to put on my nightdress afterward and climb into bed. Gaynard could be bluffing.

I put my son to bed and back away. I've been in the presence of Hervé Gaynard four times. He is capable of the darkest acts – there isn't any way to talk myself into believing he isn't. I take out my shawl, lined gloves and other winter garments to shield myself from the freezing night air. Walking to the door, I hear a voice.

"Madame Genevieve?"

A sombre Daphne wishes to speak.

"Your grandfather confided his thoughts with me. I am not asking you to do that. But I see you have many, many troubles, and I wish that I could help."

"It's because of the troubles that I have to go out at night like this, Daphne. Believe me, I wish it were otherwise."

"If I could offer just one piece of advice? I think that you feel the weight of many burdens. But it is the love for your husband and son – that is what matters. What I mean is, their love for you. It is not many women who have such love in their lives."

241

I value her loyalty and hard-earned wisdom. But what if it is love for my family that necessitates my stepping out into the night? Protecting them is hard. It is dangerous.

"Daphne, I thank you."

I press her hand and open the door.

The hackney carriage to Covent Garden smells of the food that the last person inside it ate. I'm not usually sensitive to such odours, but this one fills me with queasiness. Or perhaps, my nerves make short work of my belly. In any case, it's almost a relief when the carriage reaches the bagnio courtyard on Drury Lane.

I instruct the driver to wait, and I step out, taking my measure of the place. Hardly recognisable. It seems strange that only one carriage waits, and it is absent its driver. Nor do I see any of the bagnio servants clustered at the main entrance. It seems that the place is unpopular tonight.

I try the dark red door. It's unlocked. The tension running down my shoulders and arms eases a little bit. I prefer this way into the house over the main door. I would hate to encounter any of the bagnio's customers or the poor women forced to entertain them. I anticipate that the servant I saw before will be somewhere about the small marble lobby, and he will again lead me to Gaynard's study.

But the lobby is empty too. I don't hear a footfall or a voice.

Now I'm not sure what to do. This is the time that Gaynard set down. I edge over to the spiral staircase and look up toward the top. For the first time, I hear a faint human voice. Gaynard must be in his office.

Seeing no other choice, I walk up the spiral staircase, still wearing my winter outer garments. The voices coming from the other side of the door on the top floor grow a little louder.

By the time I've reached the upper landing, I can tell there are at least two men talking in the study, maybe three. The language is English, and I do not hear Hervé Gaynard's among them.

Why did he invite a swarm of Englishmen into his study to coincide with the precise time I am supposed to meet with him?

Yet again, I feel a surge of rage at Gaynard. But it doesn't send me flying against the door to bang on it with my fists. The situation is too precarious.

One voice stands out with more authority than the others. A firm tone. Serious. None of these strike me as gentlemen interested in a bath and female entertainment.

But there's something more. The voice of the most serious man is familiar. My mind races as I try to place him. With a twist in my belly, I sense he comes from a very different time and place. And not a place that makes me happy.

"Those letters have nothing to do with it."

For the first time, I can make out the words clearly enough to understand. And with that, I know who the man is.

His identity inspires equal parts fear and relief.

I turn the knob and open the door. The second I step into the room, four men stop what they are doing or saying and stare at me, astonished.

Their faces are a blur to me. I see only the piece of expensive furniture in the centre of the room, the Chippendale desk. Behind it sits Hervé Gaynard, looking as if he were sleeping, his head tilted down, except for the knife buried in his chest. Blood soaks his finely embroidered matching blue jacket and waistcoat, spilling onto the surface of the desk in a grotesque crimson pool that would have left the dead man himself highly annoyed.

I step close enough to the body to recognise the knife handle stuck in Gaynard. Yes, it is my stiletto knife, the one the Chevalier d'Eon pulled from my sleeve and handed to Gaynard.

"Genevieve, oh, Genevieve," says Sir Humphrey Willoughby, catcher of spies for His Majesty's government. "You have a knack for turning up in the most interesting places."

Chapter Eighteen

"Should we hold her downstairs with the others?" asks a man with a sharp nose.

Sir Humphrey says, "Ah, but Mrs. Sturbridge is not like the others," and as if to prove his point, he waves a piece of letter paper in the air. I recognise my own handwriting. Relief courses through me. Sir Humphrey has brought last week's letter with him. They can't suspect me of being in league with Gaynard – I wrote to Sir Humphrey alerting him to the Frenchman's crimes.

"Who killed Monsieur Gaynard?" I ask.

I should be weeping and cowering at the sight of a murdered corpse. I can tell by the looks on some of their faces that I'm not behaving as other females might. But I can't summon up horror or regret over his death. All I feel is curiosity.

"Someone who really, really did not like him," says Sir Humphrey. He is an even sleeker, stronger version of the man I last saw nearly four years ago, just after Thomas and I returned to England. As with his wife, Eleanor, time has burnished him, not frayed him. His tightly coiled white wig gleams atop his patrician head.

The sharp-nosed man chuckles at Sir Humphrey's remark as he

sorts through some papers stacked on a side table. A stout older man grunts with laughter too.

All the men are caught up in reading papers and documents, holding them close to candles or the fire to better examine them. There is one exception, a young, plain and very tall man with lank brown hair. He wears a red vest under his rather shabby coat. He is the one paying attention to the body of Gaynard and says, "Sir Humphrey, after the coroner's finished with him, we should be able to progress to identifying the killer through this murder weapon. It's a pretty unusual knife."

"It was made in Venice," I say.

For the second time, the men in the room stare at me in astonishment.

"How do you know that?" Sir Humphrey's voice carries an accusatory lash.

Why did I say it?

As I stand there, frozen, one of the men makes an impatient clicking sound with his teeth. I've no choice but to answer. And how much worse it would be for me if I didn't tell them the truth now and they discovered it?

"The knife is mine," I say.

"My God," says Sir Humphrey.

The sharp-nosed man pushes his way around the desk to get closer. They're all taking steps toward me. The stout man looks apprehensive as if faced with a possibly violent woman. Sir Humphrey has a resolute expression as if the next thing that happens may be unpleasant.

"No, no, you don't understand – listen!" I cry. "I purchased the knife in Paris. But I never used it on anyone – certainly not Gaynard. I carried it with me the first night I came here, I tried to hide it in my dress, and the Chevalier d'Eon discovered it and took it away from me. Monsieur Gaynard kept it."

Something I've said is a lightning bolt thrown into the room. They begin shouting at one another. Sir Humphrey leaps over and grabs my left arm.

"How are you mixed up with the Chevalier d'Eon?" he says, shaking me.

I explain it was the chevalier who escorted me through the piazza of Covent Garden to the bagnio. "Monsieur Gaynard said it was a favour to him, that the chevalier is a friend. Was a friend."

The stout man says, "But this is absurd. A highly trained spy comes out of hiding to perform this bit of theatre for scum like Gaynard?"

"Hiding?" I repeat.

Sir Humphrey said, "The Chevalier d'Eon has been on bad terms with his fellow diplomats for a year. Very bad terms. At an embassy dinner, they poisoned his wine. D'Eon survived and went into hiding in London, trying to keep from being kidnapped. He assumes disguises, changes his address, issues blackmail threats through intermediaries. He knows many things about his government and about King Louis that we would like to know. But we haven't been able to catch up with him. I admit I did not think he would stoop to associating with a man like Hervé Gaynard."

The other men murmur agreement.

"And Genevieve, I am at a loss, after all the warnings you've been given, that you would consort with such a despicable man. Blackmailer, pimp, forger, thief – we first heard about Gaynard last year."

"So you knew of his criminal nature before receiving my letter?" I ask.

"Yes, I did, and since I only began to read your letter ten minutes before you slithered through the door to his study, I'd say it's just as well."

"But I posted it to you last week," I say. "It went to Downing Street."

"Posted it? When the hue and cry went out of a murder here, I happened to be at Bow Street in a meeting and came to the scene of the crime, having an interest in Gaynard. I found this letter on his desk along with a second letter addressed to your husband. To my knowledge, I've never in my life received any correspondence from your hand."

With every bit of strength I possess, I fight my way out of this crippling confusion.

"No. This is wrong. Those two letters should be in my house, in the keeping of my servant, George," I say. "Should I not return to the house tomorrow, should something terrible happen to me, they were to be posted. Only then. I told George that. He understood. This is all wrong."

"Yet, here the letters are," says Sir Humphrey.

Stubbornly, I say, "But why didn't you get the first one? I wrote it the day after Gaynard and Casanova pushed their way into my house and—"

"Casanova?" interrupts Sir Humphrey. "Giacomo Casanova?"

Someone laughs. It's the young man with the lank brown hair and red vest. "Oh, Sir John is going to love this," he says.

Sir Humphrey beckons for him. "Mr. Oliver, I need you to take Mrs. Sturbridge to number four, Bow Street. She'll have to be interviewed in depth, but I can't attend to it this minute. We must look through all the papers in this room, and I have to speak to the coroner whenever he deigns to join us. Then I will come to Bow Street and interview Mrs. Sturbridge."

Mr. Oliver reacts quite badly to this.

"I am Sir John Fielding's householder," he sputters. "I represent him in this room – a murder's been committed. I am investigating, and the corpse is in front of me. I've no wish to shuffle a disreputable woman back to Bow Street and guard her for you."

"And I've no wish for your company," I snap.

"I am not interested in either of your wishes," says Sir Humphrey, his voice rising. "This man is linked to crimes of import to the entire country. Clearly, Genevieve has information to contribute. Mr. Oliver, you are part of a team that specialises in theft. I see no sign that Gaynard's murderer stole anything. For now, I need someone to put Mrs. Sturbridge in a secure place and keep her there until I'm ready for her."

"Then, by God, why not arrest her?" says Oliver. "It's her knife. Even if she didn't kill him, she is obviously involved with the group, how willingly is to be determined. There is cause. And then you will know where to find her."

I can feel a trickle of sweat roll down my back under all these heavy clothes. At the same time, my blood runs ice cold. It's a sickening combination.

Pierre. Thomas. Never to see them again, never to pick up another paintbrush…

Sir Humphrey says, "Creating cause is Genevieve's gift. But we shall not arrest her. Not at this point in the evening anyway. Please take her to number four, Bow Street, as ordered."

Fuming over his expulsion, Oliver grabs my arm and leads me out of the bagnio. Drury Lane itself is crowded with finely dressed Londoners. The theatre has just let out, and patrons now proceed to their late suppers and parties. Mr. Oliver and I, wearing dark and ordinary clothes, are invisible to the beau monde. Some of them may have known Hervé Gaynard, I suspect. Discussed with the Frenchman the talent of the new crop of actors over champagne. What would this same society make of his being stabbed to death in a bagnio?

Bow Street is a short distance. It is crowded too, with people pouring out of the Opera House on the far end. They mill about, rather than hurry to their carriages, looking highly agitated.

"Long live the knife!" someone shouts.

"Giovanni Manzouli is a genius. We won't give him back to the King's Theatre!"

When did I last hear that name? With a shudder, I remember. It was Gaynard, telling the Earl of Sandwich about the famed Italian castrato touring London.

Long live the knife.

We steer clear of these ecstatic opera worshippers. With a rattle of his keys, Oliver opens the front door to a narrow, grim stone building set among the townhouses. A single man sits next to a smouldering fire in an entranceway lined with benches and chairs. Oliver converses with the man, who trots off gratefully, relieved for the night.

I'm told to be seated on a bench near the fire. Oliver feeds its flames.

"You can take off your cloak and winter things," he says after a few minutes. "It's warm enough now."

"I'd rather not."

He shrugs. "Suit yourself."

"What is this place?"

"The Westminster Court of the Magistrate, Sir John Fielding presiding."

I stare at the fire, dazed, unable to make sense of what's happening. The confusion of my letters torments me.

Oliver's voice pierces my haze. "Do you want something to drink? We have ale."

"No, thank you."

"Mrs. Sturbridge, you look bad. I won't be blamed for you taking sick."

He presses a mug of warm ale in my hands. I don't have the strength to resist. It's flat and sour, I manage a few mouthfuls.

Next, he pushes two coarse blankets on me. "You can make one into a pillow," says Oliver. "Put the other on top of you."

I sit there, silent, the blanket around my shoulders. I must find the words to explain myself to Sir Humphrey, but the best course of action eludes me. There are so many secrets. An overpowering exhaustion takes hold as if my brain can't continue the struggle.

I hadn't thought it possible to find rest on a hard bench in the middle of the night in a magistrate's court. Yet the blanket does make for a fine pillow, and when I turn on my side, the position is bearable. It's surprising Oliver would be so attuned to the needs of someone in my desperate circumstances. But the last thing I think before losing consciousness is that this is a courthouse, and he may be well versed in caring for prisoners.

"Genevieve."

It's Sir Humphrey. I push myself up, rubbing my eyes. "Forgive me," I say, my voice hoarse.

"Not at all. There was much to do at the scene of the crime. I'm afraid it's four in the morning."

I stumble to my feet, wringing my hands. "But my son! I need to be home before he wakes up. My housekeeper must be terribly worried."

Sir Humphrey lays a steadying hand on my shoulder and pushes me back to sit down. "Everything will be all right. It will be dawn soon. I'll have more men at my disposal. Everything will be attended to. Give me the address on Fournier Street and your servant George's house too."

After I've done so, Sir Humphrey tells me to splash water on my face in the retiring room for ladies. "We will have some tea. And then you'll make your statement for the official record."

I throw the water in my eyes with vigour, and not just to please Sir Humphrey. What I say and do next is very important. No missteps.

The tea is hot, strong and very sweet. Who knows where it came from.

"Now, Genevieve, I've spent hours poring over the papers in Hervé Gaynard's study. I've talked to those who worked in the bagnio. They knew little, or they're pretending to. I don't yet have an understanding of how much he spied for the French – who his contacts were or the nature of his assignments. I will know these things, be assured."

I say, "I accused him of being a spy, and he laughed at me. He said he was a businessman who may have run a few errands, but his only real interest was money."

"That he was a greedy man, there can be no doubt," says Sir Humphrey. "But it's not quite that simple. I'm not at liberty to disclose the facts obtained thus far, except I will tell you one thing we found in a letter, an edict that it seems was issued by King Louis: '*It is the duty of every Frenchman to thwart the ambition and arrogance of England.*'"

"Bloody hell!"

Sir Humphrey winces at Oliver's curse, but his attention is on me. And despite the roaring fire and piping hot tea, I feel chilled to the bone.

"Doesn't surprise you at all, does it, Genevieve? Nor me. What's to be expected after seven years of war? The vindictiveness of Louis is as beyond question as his depravity. The question is, how many of the French people who have flooded London since the surrender follow this royal edict? Of course, it's even more worrying if the French should try to make trouble for us in our colonies, now that we are flung far and wide and, it must be acknowledged, pretty damn thin. But my charge is to determine if Gaynard was an active spy for France and if that is in any way the cause of his murder."

Sir Humphrey drains his tea. He's had not a wink of sleep, but his entire body radiates determination. I know that Sir Gabriel Courtenay feared few people. The man across from me was the exception.

"You must tell me everything from the first moment you met Monsieur Hervé Gaynard," he says. "If you leave anything out or lie to me in any way, it will go badly for you, Genevieve. Oliver here will write down everything you say. I'm told he has a fast hand with a quill. We shall see, eh, Oliver?"

"Do my best, sir."

Oliver's attitude toward Sir Humphrey has changed. I wonder if they talked for long before waking me up.

"Start at the beginning," Sir Humphrey repeats.

I make my decision. I will tell him everything, beginning with the invitation to Joshua Reynolds' house. I hesitate twice. The first time is on the tragic background of poor Caroline. How devastated she would be to know that these two men have heard it. And also I hate to disclose the secret of Sir Joshua Reynolds' fugitive colours. I have no choice, though, but to tell it all. There is no other reason to give for Gaynard's drawing me into his sordid scheme, and it is only Caroline's abduction that made me go to Covent Garden a few nights ago.

Sir Humphrey is amazed at the Chevalier d'Eon's versatility and his appearing as a woman one evening and a male swordsman on another. "I begin to see how he eludes the French ambassador," he says.

Mr. Oliver asks, "What were you planning to do when you met with Gaynard last night?"

"Tell him to go to the devil. I calculated that Gaynard could not ruin me or Thomas without ruining himself."

"Zounds," says Oliver.

"And where was your husband in all this?" Sir Humphrey demands.

"I didn't want him to know about Gaynard's offer," I say. "I wanted to deal with him myself."

Oliver says, "He'd be a dangerous man to try to push that way – and with a fortune in his sights!"

"Yes, and that's one of the key questions," says Sir Humphrey. "Who would be so ill disposed toward Joshua Reynolds that he – or she – would pay that amount of money to muck with his paint? I suspect Gaynard's fee was two thousand pounds, on top of the eight thousand Thomas Sturbridge was set to receive, rounding it up to ten thousand."

"Sir, does that mean you believe this scheme of the fugitive colours was the reason for the murder?" asks Oliver.

"It's possible," says Sir Humphrey. "I know damnably little about portrait painters. I've no time for art."

"Does anything about the fugitive colours have to be made public?" I ask. "It will be so injurious to Sir Joshua Reynolds."

Sir Humphrey rubs his temple with the knuckles of his right hand. For the first time, he lets his fatigue show.

"Perhaps something can be done to conceal it," he says. "When

I speak to Mr. Reynolds, if he is fully cooperative, I can offer some protection. It depends on what he can bring to my investigation."

The door to the street opens, and two men walk in, greatly surprised to find the three of us inside. Dawn has come and with it, my distress over what will happen on Fournier Street after I'm discovered absent.

But when I ask Sir Humphrey Willoughby if I can leave, he says no. "Just a little longer," he informs me.

"I *must* go home now."

"You'll be made comfortable here."

"I have told you everything as you demanded, but I'm imprisoned," I say bitterly. "This is not right."

Over my protests, I am more or less pushed into a small room filled with boxes of ledgers and other recording books. It is cold and windowless, with a single stool set out for me. It feels like a jail cell after the key turns in the lock. Certainly, it is anything but comfortable.

After about an hour, a sour-faced woman appears with a tray of breakfast. She has no answers to any of my questions, saying she's just an employee of the Brown Bear Tavern across the way on Bow Street. She's gone in a minute.

I'm tempted to throw the breakfast at the locked door, but eventually, I force myself to nibble the stale bread and drink the flavourless tea. I'll need my strength for whatever comes. With mounting dread, I contemplate my next confrontation with Sir Humphrey Willoughby. In our first one, I told him everything, he told me very little, and my requests were met with unenthusiastic perhapses or flatly denied.

I have no idea what time it is when the door opens again. Sir Humphrey himself stands there, wearing a change of clothes and a fresh wig. How nice that must be!

To my dismay, rather than freeing me, he steps inside the room, closing the door behind him.

"I'm sorry, but this confinement couldn't be helped," he says, a genuine note of regret in his voice. "I had to be sure of your innocence first. And there was no place to keep you besides this room once the business of the court began. When we want to keep a man in custody, we use the rooms kept for that purpose in the Brown Bear. Obviously, that wouldn't be fitting for you."

He takes a breath. "I want you to know that we questioned your housekeeper, Daphne. Her statement, taken with that of your hackney driver, establishes beyond doubt that you were in Spitalfields when Hervé Gaynard was being murdered."

My throat dry, I say, "Did you really think I could drive a knife into someone?"

"You had far and away the best motive for murder. Everything to lose if Gaynard made good on his blackmail threats."

"But now, I am cleared of suspicion?"

He nods uncomfortably, his eyes flicker.

"What more do you have to tell me, Sir Humphrey?"

"Genevieve, I have bad news."

A dozen terrible possibilities flash through my mind. I shouldn't have gone out last night at all. What a reckless fool I am.

Sir Humphrey says, "George and Sophie Harris have been arrested. He confessed that they took money from Hervé Gaynard in exchange for personal information about you and your workers, and they subverted certain of your letters."

I try to say something, but the words don't come out. I close my mouth and open it again like some sort of gasping fish. Sir Humphrey steps toward me, asking, "Are you all right, Genevieve?"

I would very much like to speak. My throat closes. Strange black

256

splotches dance in front of my eyes. A few seconds later I see nothing at all, just a spreading darkness. All that remains is the sound of Sir Humphrey Willoughby's voice, growing ever fainter.

"Genevieve? Genevieve? Genevieve?"

Chapter Nineteen

I wake to a room filled with light, though this being London in winter, the light is mottled grey. My head throbs. I reach up to touch my temple; the tips of my fingers burn ever so slightly, a strange tingling I've never felt before. I am stretched out on a rather lumpy couch.

"Mrs. Sturbridge, are you awake?"

The voice is unfamiliar but belongs to a gentleman, I'd guess one of older years.

I turn my head and start at the sight of my companion, sitting in profile in an armchair three feet away. He is somewhere between forty and fifty years of age and dressed entirely in black, topped by a formal white wig. But most unusually, he has a two-inch-wide black ribbon tied around his head, covering his eyes.

"Yes, I am awake," I reply.

"My name is Sir John Fielding, and I cannot see you, Mrs. Sturbridge, for I've been blind since the age of nineteen. I can, however, hear you."

But then how did he know it the minute I woke? Was it from my reaching for my forehead? That is phenomenal hearing. I remember the name from last night – sitting beside me is the magistrate of the court. A blind magistrate. This seems impossible, but I know little of courts.

"Can you tell me how long I've been here in this room, Sir John?"

I learn that about an hour ago I was carried, unconscious, to the couch in Sir John's inner chamber. A doctor has been sent for. This is turning into an all-night-and-all-day ordeal in Covent Garden when I am desperately needed in Spitalfields. Daphne's distress is almost beyond my comprehending. Will she even be able to take care of Pierre?

I push myself to sit up, saying, "I apologise for this inconvenience to you and your office." The room spins a little. Nonetheless, I say, "I don't require a physician. I must return to my home as soon as possible."

Sir John says warningly, "You've had quite a shock, Mrs. Sturbridge. We could have revived you with swooning salts, but I counselled rest. You've been exposed to the sight of a deceased person. That in itself is an assault on the delicate sensibilities of a woman, especially that of a wife and mother. My worthy colleague, Sir Humphrey Willoughby, told me you have been manipulated and tormented by men mired in vice. They turned your own servants against you."

I wonder just how hard they were to turn.

I picture Sophie's secretive smirks and George's compliant nods, pretending he would follow my instructions. I should be beside myself with rage at the couple, but at this moment, all I can feel is pain. I didn't deserve this.

Sir Humphrey strides into the room, complaining of the scarcity of proper doctors in Covent Garden.

"Excellent, you're awake," he says, relieved.

"Please, if I may just go to my home, I'm more than strong enough now," I say firmly.

Sir Humphrey is now the one to oppose it, insisting that I should take a nip of brandy for shock. After that, one of the men at Bow

Street will escort me to Spitalfields. He shows a new anxiety for my welfare. I am not a woman given to vapours, but I have to admit I prefer this attitude to the suspicion I've faced up to now.

As I sip brandy, Sir John Fielding expands on the pervasiveness of vice. "It is the pursuit of luxuries that corrupts the men and women of London," he informs me. "That is why they lose themselves to drink, gambling and harlotry. They shun a life of honest work. It's what my brother, Henry, believed, God rest his soul."

Despite the purr of brandy warming my body, I feel a surge of impatience. What a Puritanical view! There are many businesses in London, including my own, that pride themselves on catering to a taste for luxury among those who can afford it. I long to leave Bow Street, not listen to a general lecture on bad morals. But then Sir John Fielding becomes more specific.

"Oh, there is Mrs. Cornelys with her infamous masquerade balls. How many have been led astray at Carlisle House? I did not know about her shameful association with Giacomo Casanova until I heard your report from Sir Humphrey – yet it does not surprise me. Casanova's life of debauchery and dishonesty is beyond the pale, Mrs. Sturbridge. I hold myself personally responsible for the criminal proposal made to your husband by Casanova and the dead Frenchman, Hervé Gaynard."

Startled, I say, "But how could you be at fault, sir?"

He takes a deep shuddering breath and says, "Because he fooled me. We had Casanova in Newgate a year ago, and I let him go. I was fooled by his voice. And he a foreigner!"

Sir Humphrey explains, "Sir John has a well-deserved reputation for being able to sort criminals only by their voices. He knows who is lying."

"Well deserved? Well deserved? I did not know Casanova was

lying," he says, so anguished that the black ribbon around his eyes quivers. "He was accused of violence against a French-Swiss courtesan of sixteen living in Soho. In his Italian, Casanova assured me it was a mistake. I released him after men came forward with bail and signed sureties. Why do they pollute England, these rogues and harlots and criminals? Why leave France or Italy or Switzerland?"

I say, "Monsieur Gaynard told me he was keen to leave Paris because of the diligence of its secret police and Lieutenant General de Sartine. He found it much easier to manoeuvre about here."

Too late, I realise the offence I've given. Sir Humphrey rolls his eyes at me while Sir John Fielding presses his lips and tightens the large hands resting in his broad lap into two fists.

Sir Humphrey clears his throat and says, "It's been confirmed that Casanova departed England. And I don't think he is at the centre of whatever led to Gaynard's murder."

With all that I've endured, the murder itself hasn't even been uppermost in my thoughts. I ask Sir Humphrey his belief on who killed Hervé Gaynard.

"It could have nothing to do with your fugitive colours. That seems to be his most recent scheme, but Gaynard was a man with a finger in many crimes – I believe he described them to you and to others as 'business interests'? – and there could be various motives for someone to want to remove him from this earth. I do believe it to be a crime of spontaneous action rather than one carefully planned."

"Why is that?" I ask, curious.

"Because of you, Genevieve."

I recoil, horrified.

"Well, because of your knife. He had it on his desk. No one brought a weapon into the room, in other words."

Sir Humphrey says to the magistrate, "I need to know if espionage was involved. If so, I will continue to lead the investigation, using the offices of Bow Street as a base if I may?"

Sir John nods.

"We may have a breakthrough with the snatching of a young rogue who sometimes worked for Gaynard. Just nabbed him in Covent Garden. I believe he was the one who met you and escorted you halfway through Covent Garden, Genevieve."

"Ah, yes," I say.

"He's quite a macaroni. Takes an absurd amount of pride in his wardrobe. He shouldn't be hard to crack."

"You see?" mutters Sir John. "It's all about luxuries."

A few minutes later, I am finally freed from Bow Street with Mr. Oliver as my escort. I require no companion for a daylight carriage ride, but I don't wish to argue. At least he remains silent for most of the time. It isn't until we cross the eastern boundary of London and roll into Spitalfields that he speaks.

"I'm sorry I held a low opinion of you, Mrs. Sturbridge," he blurts. "Sir Humphrey called you by a French name, and I thought you had to be one of Gaynard's French harlots. I was put straight later that no, you're one of these Huguenots." He peers out the window. "You're God-fearing people without a doubt, but your weavers do get fiery when they believe themselves wronged."

"They do indeed," I say, thinking of Guillaume and the Bold Defiance.

But the people first in my thoughts are not disgruntled weavers but my family, my servants and my artists.

My heart pounding, I unlock the front door and am immediately greeted with unfamiliar voices. I rush into the parlour and there see Evelyn Willoughby and her nursemaid on chairs, clapping their encouragement at Pierre and Diana, happily playing together on the threadbare carpet.

Did Sir Humphrey send them to spy on me?

"Genevieve, how good to see you," says Evelyn with perfect calm, though her eyes brim with worry.

"Are my workers here, Caroline Mowbray and Jean Orgier?"

"Not since I've been here, about a half of an hour," she says.

"What about Daphne?"

"In her kitchen."

To my astonishment, the scent of warm dough with butter and cloves meets me on the way to the kitchen.

I'm not sure what I expected, but it wasn't the sight of Daphne behaving as if nothing has happened. She looks just as she did yesterday when issuing her warning at the door. The only thing out of place is a dish of butter, gleaming around the edges as it softens. That should go back to the cellar, but of course, Daphne has trouble with the stairs.

"Will the two ladies want chocolates or do they prefer tea?" she asks. "The chocolates will be ready soon for the children."

"Oh, Daphne," I say softly. "Did you see George? Have you spoken to him?"

"No, and I don't want to," she snaps. "The constable told me when he came to the house. They arrested George and Sophie at their home early this morning. What they did was unforgivable."

"Yes," I say. "I was shocked. And now, when I try to picture George in jail…"

Daphne knows even better than I that George, with all of his fears and superstitions, would suffer in a place like Newgate. Her reaction, again, is not what I expected. She shakes her head and says harshly, "I was in a French prison for years, and I committed no crime at all. It was purely because of my Huguenot faith, while George and Sophie have behaved like criminals. They must accept their punishment."

She bows her head for a minute, clearly struggling to compose herself, before saying in a low voice, "Do you think the ladies will want chocolates or tea?"

"Chocolates will be fine," I say, picking up the butter dish to walk it down to the cellar myself.

I rejoin our uninvited guests. Pierre is having a wonderful time, I have to admit.

"He plays well, he will do splendidly in school," Evelyn comments.

When the pastries and chocolates are served, Evelyn picks up her cup and walks to the window overlooking Fournier Street. I follow her. Evidently, this is when the real conversation begins.

"Did you spend the morning locked in Sir John Fielding's records room?" she asks quietly.

"Is that what it is?" I ask.

"Yes, it was Sir John's idea to keep a record of every criminal who has been arrested. Or was it his brother's idea? Sir Henry Fielding may have been the one who started it before he died. He wrote the novel, *Tom Jones*. Funny, isn't it? But in any case, nothing like it has existed before. And Sir John has six householders working for him, investigating crimes. In London, they call them the Bow Street Runners. Humphrey is very impressed."

"Hmmmmm."

Arching an eyebrow, she says, "I take it you, however, are not impressed?"

"On the one side, you have half a million people in the city of London, a significant portion of that number relishing their crimes. On the other are Sir John Fielding and his six men, a tiny records room and a few holding cells in the Brown Bear Tavern across the street."

Evelyn laughs.

"What's funny, Mama?" calls out Diana.

"Nothing, nothing, go on with your playing." She puts down the chocolate and says, "I've so missed you, Genevieve. There's no one else like you."

I'm taken aback to see Evelyn's eyes brim with tears. Hastily, I tell her that my ordeal on Bow Street wasn't all that terrible.

"It's not that," she says. "I feel strongly about it, that what happened when you returned to England, it wasn't right."

"What are you talking about?"

"Remember, we were still at war when you wanted to leave France? Englishmen had died in battle. That's why it was so difficult for you and Thomas to come back. But something less harsh could have been negotiated. Thomas agreed to the first set of demands he was sent. I think they were a little surprised. But Thomas was pushing very hard, he was frantic to get you back to Spitalfields."

To me, it's as if Evelyn is speaking a language I've never heard.

"Please, explain this," I beg.

"All these restrictions on what he can do in England in the government's demands? They went too far. But you were pregnant, and Thomas would have agreed to anything to make sure you were back with your grandfather before the birth and getting the best care."

I'm overcome with a flood of warring emotions.

"If Thomas hadn't been put in such an impossible corner, you wouldn't have been exposed to the Gaynards of the world," Evelyn says. Her dark eyes snap with anger. I realise what an admission this is for Evelyn, and I'm moved. I doubt now that her husband sent her. She must have heard about my being detained and rushed here to help me.

"Well, at least it's over," I say. "I can resume my design business and try to put this all behind me."

Evelyn winces, and to my astonishment, her eyes overflow again. She takes out a handkerchief.

Struggling to remain calm, I say, "Why are you upset now? Your husband said I'm cleared of suspicion. No one thinks I was the one who murdered Hervé Gaynard."

"But Genevieve, it was your knife buried in his chest. The coroner's inquest is on Monday. All the evidence gathered so far will have to be made public. The name of the owner of the murder weapon has to be entered into the public record. And the newspaper writers are already clamouring for the facts at Bow Street. Sir John Fielding loves to be in the newspapers. This could be the crime of the year. You are going to have to prepare yourself for the fact that you may soon be one of the most famous women in London."

Chapter Twenty

Among the streets of London, I'd have to place Bow Street at the top of the list of my least favourites. But here I stand, at just past eight in the morning. I asked the hackney coach driver to let me out on the south end of the street to allow a few minutes to work up my courage. I have a plan, hatched last night after Evelyn told me her fears and predictions. There is only a slender hope of staving off disaster, but I have to try it.

On the way through Covent Garden, I passed many bright-faced sellers of flowers, vegetables, fruit, fish, bread and other food, their booths raised on the same ground where men negotiated with prostitutes at night. But Bow Street shows no such radical transformation. The tendrils of morning mist can't disguise its ugliness. On my way to number four, I pass a townhouse with its front door hanging open. A young man appears, suddenly he swings around and grabs a woman, smacking her on the bottom. She laughs and pushes him away. I watch, stunned, as he saunters down the steps, fiddling with his breeches.

Sir John Fielding's court is on the same street as a brothel?

The man doesn't notice me because he's too occupied with

entertaining the three men who are standing outside a building that I realise is number four. He makes obscene thrusting motions as he walks.

I study the ground as I approach the building behind him, hoping they will be so caught up in their lewd jovialities, they'll overlook me.

But of course, that's not what happens.

"Madame, over here," one of them shouts eagerly. "Why so bright and early? Anything to do with the murder of Hervé Gaynard?"

I shake my head, avoiding eye contact, and hurry to the front door.

"If you have a story to tell, it could be made worth your while," says another man, his voice wheedling.

The door opens a crack in answer to my knocking. "I need to speak to Sir John Fielding or Sir Humphrey Willoughby," I say. "Please let me in."

The door opens wider.

"We want the facts about the Covent Garden killer!" shouts someone behind me. "The Beak of Bow Street can't bar us forever."

At first, I think it's Mr. Oliver who admitted me because of the bright red vest before me, but this man has blonde hair. The red vest must be a uniform for all Sir John's men.

"Genevieve, why are you here – do you have additional information?" asks Sir Humphrey Willoughby, standing by the fire.

With all the confidence I can muster, I say, "I can assist in your investigation into the murder."

"You can assist?"

The sceptical question comes from Mr. Oliver, who is coming up behind me. But Sir Humphrey is studying me, curious. My plan depends on his determination to solve the crime outweighing his disdain for women's abilities as well as our personal history marked by mutual distrust.

"What did you have in mind?" Sir Humphrey says.

Instead of answering, I counter with a question: "Have you spoken to Joshua Reynolds yet?"

"We were just deciding who would go to Leicester Fields this morning."

"You've said yourself that art is not one of your interests. But art is at the heart of this investigation, and I am an artist. Let me come with you."

Sir Humphrey frowns. "That's not necessary."

I anticipated a refusal. At least he didn't laugh or act insulted. Which means there might still be a chance. What I need to do is show him my insight into the world of art and particularly the world of Joshua Reynolds, not just state I possess it.

"You're planning to go to Leicester Fields? I think it would be more effective to interview him at Bow Street. At his house in Leicester Fields, Mr. Reynolds is master of his domain. Here, he would be slightly intimidated. And I think he would come quickly if someone with a title, an earl's son, summons him. He likes to be near men with titles. He enjoys moving in those circles, and of course, ideally, he would like to paint them."

Sir Humphrey's eyes widen.

"Well, Genevieve, that is… interesting. I certainly don't have the time to sit for a portrait though. I'm in the middle of a murder inquiry."

"Not now. You'd be a new social connection for the future – that prospect would bring him running to Bow Street, and these official surroundings would make him more cooperative."

At that moment, two men burst through the door. Sir Humphrey confers with them briefly then says, "At last! That macaroni of Gaynard's was good for something. He supplied an address for

269

the Chevalier d'Eon, and it looks as if our master spy is there right now." Glancing at me, he says, "Joshua Reynolds will just have to wait."

Inspiration strikes.

"Is it possible for Sir John Fielding to interview him with me present?" I ask. "He is a magistrate, and the brother of a famous author should have an effect on Joshua Reynolds. He prefers novelists and playwrights to other painters. And this way, you will get more accomplished in the same period of time."

Sir Humphrey smiles and then says, "Genevieve, a moment in private?"

"Of course."

We retreat to the far corner of the room, where I can feel the eyes of all upon us, though they can't hear what we say.

"What is the reason for this new surge of helpfulness?" he asks.

"I want to bring a murderer to justice," I say.

He raises an eyebrow.

"But there is also a request I have to make."

"Ah. I thought so."

"At the coroner's inquest, please see to it that my name is not mentioned in connection with the knife."

Sir Humphrey grimaces in distaste. But I've come this far, I must push on. "If I become a public part of this murder investigation, my business in Spitalfields will be finished. It will ruin Thomas as well. The Earl of Sandwich won't want a tutor who is mixed up in a murder inquiry."

"That would be regrettable, but it's unethical to hide important facts in a public proceeding."

His pomposity sets my teeth on edge. *Regrettable?* Does he have the least idea of what it's like to survive without the resources of a noble family to fall back on, such as an older brother with a big brick house on Grosvenor Square?

Forcing myself to not sound aggrieved, I say, "We've tried our best at every turn, Sir Humphrey. Your restrictions have made things very hard, but Thomas and I have always followed them. You know we have. We've been drawn into hearing offers that we have turned down, whether it came from Joshua Reynolds or Gaynard. It's cruel to keep punishing us."

Directly criticising Sir Humphrey carries risks. I've never seen him admit even the possibility of making a mistake. Evelyn's regret over what happened to Thomas and me is not shared by her husband.

Or is it?

Sir Humphrey purses his lips as if weighing something before he says, "We'll see, Genevieve. If you can help extract something from Joshua Reynolds that is of use? Then I may be able to fashion a partial omission. But only for the coroner's inquest, which establishes whether the death is of a suspicious nature. I can't make any promises about the trial – if there is to be a trial. We need to make an arrest first."

"And you haven't yet settled on who killed Gaynard, or why, I assume?"

"Our investigation is wide ranging – and we are interviewing many people, some of them multiple times," says Sir Humphrey evasively.

There is that same flicker in his eyes as just before he told me about George and Sophie. My belly clenches, but before I can decipher his meaning, Sir Humphrey goes off to find Sir John Fielding. The magistrate shows more enthusiasm than I expected for a joint interview of Sir Joshua Reynolds, with Oliver attending and taking notes.

Sir John dictates a note requesting the presence of Joshua Reynolds at number four, Bow Street as soon as possible to assist in the inquiry into the death of Hervé Gaynard. A young employee rushes it the short distance to Leicester Fields. Now, all that's left is to wait. If Reynolds puts us off, my announced insights into his behaviour will look flawed. And any hope of my name disappearing from tomorrow's coroner's inquest fades.

Sir John attends to matters of the court while I sit alone in his inner chamber, not on his lumpy couch but on an equally uncomfortable armchair next to the window. It provides a view of the activity on Bow Street. Sir John's householders are hurrying here and there, waving off the newspapermen gathered outside, whose numbers, I note, have doubled.

Hervé Gaynard was a heartless criminal, but his murder will be much written about and his funeral well attended, no doubt. I can picture the elaborate grave marker.

My brooding comes to a halt when Oliver sticks his head into the room to tell me that Joshua Reynolds has just arrived. I jump to my feet, eager to play out my role.

Oliver leads me to the court chambers, where the only occupant is Sir John Fielding, sitting high above us in his magistrate's station. I take a seat at a small table on the far side of Oliver.

"These official surroundings should assist us, don't you think, Mrs. Sturbridge?" says Sir John. I swear I can detect a smile tightening the corners of his mouth. Investigating crime isn't purely a duty of conscience. He enjoys this.

The door opens with a loud click. A red-vested man leads Joshua Reynolds in, who I note is wearing a coat and waistcoat in matching patterned material and a fine wig for the occasion. His cravat, though, is crooked. Ralph must have been rushed.

Reynolds does not see me or Oliver. He looks only at Sir John Fielding, openly fascinated by the magistrate.

"Mr. Reynolds?" says Sir John in an authoritative boom. "Thank you for coming so quickly. I cannot see you, for I have been blind since the age of nineteen. I can, however, hear you."

Reynolds says, "I have long wanted to make your acquaintance, Sir John. I'm a supporter of your reforms here on Bow Street. And may I say that the novels written by your late brother are some of my favourites. I was at supper only last week with a few friends, and we were extolling the quality of *Tom Jones*."

"Why, I thank you. Henry would be quite pleased to know this." Sir John's voice is softening. I know what it's like when Reynolds exerts his personality. Even now, after he's brought so much trouble to my life, I find it hard to dislike him. Why? Part of it is simple to understand – he is open and friendly, enthusiastic in his many artistic and literary interests. There is no denying his ambition drives him to try to befriend the titled and powerful, the beautiful and seductive, but he's straightforward about it. There is no pretentiousness. And part of it is his West Country accent that he's done nothing to shed. That reminds me of Sam Baldwin, who I suspect has made efforts to get rid of his accent. I hastily push him out of my mind.

"I knew Mr. Gaynard, though not terribly well," Reynolds is saying. "He had an interest in the Drury Lane Theatre, and I have a number of good friends in the theatre. But of course, I will do anything to assist Bow Street in your inquiry."

Sir John Fielding says, "That is good news, Mr. Reynolds. I'm afraid that the Hervé Gaynard investigation does concern you, and Mrs. Sturbridge as well." He gestures in the direction of my table. Only then does Joshua look over and see me, and he visibly recoils. Now he's worried.

Sir John moves straight to it.

"Mr. Gaynard made an offer to Mrs. Sturbridge several days before he was killed. He said he represented someone who would pay her husband, Thomas Sturbridge, eight thousand pounds to work with you in the business of your fugitive colours, but instead of helping you solve the problem of the colours in your paintings, he would create colours that would deteriorate faster and do greater damage."

"What?" Reynolds shouts, his face turning bright red. "But that would destroy me – I'd be humiliated before all of England." He whips around to point a finger at me. "Why in the name of heaven did you tell Gaynard about the fugitive colours?"

"I didn't," I say heatedly, trying not to shout back. "I told no one. My husband didn't even want to help you with the colours, he was going to refuse you."

The artist makes a scornful sound. "Oh, how could Gaynard find out if not from you?" Reynolds then glares at Oliver. "And what the hell is this man writing down? I won't have anything about this made public."

Sir John Fielding says in a thunderous voice, "Sir, there will be no profanity in my court and especially not in the presence of a lady. As to Mr. Oliver, he is my householder, performing a legal duty. You shall calm yourself. We require your assistance in this murder investigation. There is a belief that the murder of Hervé Gaynard could be connected to his scheme to recruit Thomas Sturbridge to ruin you. I have no intention at this point of informing the newspaper writers of your involvement, but I could change my mind."

Chastened, Joshua Reynolds stumbles into a chair, mopping his face with a handkerchief. But he does not apologise to Sir John for his outburst or to me for his insults, and with that, I am freed from my lingering admiration for the man. And I can speak out.

I say, slowly and clearly, "Mr. Reynolds, it was Miss Kitty Fisher who told Hervé Gaynard about you asking my husband to help you with the fugitive colours. It is she who shared your secret with a criminal and a blackmailer."

As he stares at me, the colour drains from his face.

"Is this true, Mr. Reynolds?" demands Sir John Fielding. "A known courtesan is your confidante?"

Joshua takes at least a minute to gather himself. "Not any longer," he says, his voice thick.

Sir John presses him, asking for his theories on who could have approached Hervé Gaynard with the idea to turn the fugitive colours into a weapon against him.

"There is absolutely no one I can think of who would do such a terrible thing," he says, sounding offended, if not pained.

Sir John Fielding turns his head in my direction. It's my turn. I have to prove my usefulness in this investigation or else there's no reason for Sir Humphrey to protect me.

I say, "But Mr. Reynolds, haven't you said that there are rival artists who would like to take your place?"

"I don't know what you mean," he says through gritted teeth.

Sir John Fielding says, "So you do not intend to offer my office any assistance in this matter, am I correct?"

Joshua Reynolds sits up straighter in his chair, peering anxiously at Sir John as if he doubts the man's blindness.

"I will endeavour to assist you, Sir John," he says.

"Then please answer Mrs. Sturbridge's question."

Looking at Sir John, not me, Reynolds says, "Portrait painting is a competitive business. There are other artists who may wish to receive more commissions. But I can't imagine any of them taking such an extreme step. No, I can't think of a single one."

I clear my throat. "Perhaps if I mention some of the names of the other artists? Others whom you have brought up to me?"

"I really don't think—"

I interrupt, saying, "Mr. Allan Ramsay, court painter to King George and his family."

Reynolds snorts. "The man is more than fifty years old! He has become quite selective about his portrait commissions. Why would someone who is choosing to slow down his output wish to replace a painter whose studio is overwhelmed with subjects?"

Reynolds makes a convincing case. I push on to the next name.

"George Romney," I say.

He shakes his head. "The thought of that fragile soul executing such an audacious attack? Ridiculous. Even if I thought he had the strength of nerve – which I assure you he does not – he's nearly penniless from what I hear. He can barely pay for a London studio. Eight thousand pounds? Even more ridiculous."

Another theory demolished. But now I come to the name of the man I anticipate Joshua Reynolds will most hate to hear: Thomas Gainsborough.

Sure enough, Joshua Reynolds flinches slightly. "The man from Bath would no doubt like to rise in everyone's estimation, although I really can't see him going to these lengths," he says. "And once again, where would that sort of money come from? I'm not privy to his finances, but I believe he is largely dependent on his wife's income of two hundred pounds a year, as she is the natural daughter of the Duke of Beaufort."

Oliver speaks for the first time. "Excuse me, sir? Bath, you said?"

"Yes, Gainsborough lives there through every season. He has no London residence."

Oliver shakes his head. "Bath is a hundred miles from here. For someone to travel there with word of Mr. Reynolds' offer to Mr. Sturbridge, tell this Gainsborough fellow, then have to send someone hotfoot to London to cook the deal with Gaynard and try to force Mrs. Sturbridge to agree? There's not enough time. It's not possible, not even by fast post."

Impressed, I nudge Mr. Oliver and nod. He's made a convincing case. He ducks his head, embarrassed. I suppose praise is rarely ladled out at number four, Bow Street.

"Are there no other artists who come to mind?" asks Sir John Fielding. The magistrate may think we've a great many more to consider, but I fear we have reached the end of the list of plausible candidates.

"None of the other artists in England have the talent to hope to ever replace me," says Joshua Reynolds dismissively. Once more, Sam Baldwin leaps to mind before I can squash the thought. He has never ever boasted about his talent. But he wouldn't relish hearing this. Still, Reynolds is right. Sam would never think he could replace Reynolds; he has no motive.

"Perhaps it's not a matter of trying to replace you as a successful artist but wishing to see you ruined," says Sir John Fielding as if he were trying to decide on cake or crumpets to be served with tea today.

Again, Joshua Reynolds sits up taller in his chair and says, "I don't see why your first order of business is to try to determine who would wish to see me ruined. I believe that whoever murdered Hervé Gaynard might have been trying to stop his plan from going forward. That is the motivation of the man you seek."

Reynolds' comment leaves me feeling unsettled, an emotion that only intensifies after our questioning of Joshua Reynolds ends and Sir Humphrey returns to Bow Street. I'd thought that confronting the Chevalier d'Eon, the infamous missing diplomat and perhaps secret spy of King Louis, would leave him exultant. But such is not the case.

"His countrymen are trying to poison him, kidnap him, defame him, and yet he made it clear that the lowliest Frenchman, even scum like Hervé Gaynard, are preferred to representatives of King George's government," he says, disgusted.

"Didn't he tell you anything useful?" I ask.

"He did."

Sir Humphrey stares at me as if he thought he'd been talking to someone else. "Any information I gain must be kept in strict confidence," he says severely.

"I do not pry for the sake of gossip! I am endeavouring to assist you, Sir Humphrey."

"If only we could say the same for your husband."

I feel a rush of protective fear.

"What do you mean by that?"

"This morning, one of Sir John's senior men went to Chiswick to talk to your husband and confirm what you've told us and find out his whereabouts the night of the murder, and he was refused permission. First by some officious carriage driver and then by John Montagu, Earl of Sandwich, himself. 'Mr. Sturbridge is too busy with his work to be disturbed,' Montagu says. The earl himself vouched for his tutor, said Sturbridge never left the house the day or night of the murder."

Stunned, I repeat, "The Earl of Sandwich spoke to Sir John's man, but Thomas did not?"

Sir Humphrey takes a step closer and says, "If this is some plot between you and your husband, I'll show not a fleck of mercy."

"It isn't! I swear before God!"

He sighs. "Then go home, Genevieve. You were of use today to Sir John Fielding, that will be taken into account."

"And my name won't be mentioned or put into public record at the coroner's inquest?"

"Everything you've done will be taken into account," he repeats.

"That's not a promise, Sir Humphrey."

His temper flares. "I don't owe you a promise, Genevieve. If you hadn't been stashing French knives up your sleeve like some kind of assassin, you wouldn't be in this fix." He points at me, though we're but inches away from each other. "If I were you, I'd be more worried about your husband. Something's not right there. I can smell it. A murder's been committed, he's involved in the scheme leading to it, the whole affair put his wife through a dangerous ordeal – and he does not bother to come home?"

My face flushing, I say, "I don't think the death has been written about in the better newspapers, and I haven't had a moment to send word. There are always good reasons for what Thomas does."

"You can tell yourself that if you want to. I know from experience that Thomas Sturbridge does not always display the best judgement."

I open my mouth to launch into a passionate defence of my husband, but Sir Humphrey Willoughby waves his hand rudely.

"Enough. I am busy with what is turning into a devilishly complicated investigation. Moreover, you of all people shouldn't be privy to these conversations. I don't wish to offend, but I need you out of here."

"Very well," I say, straining to hold onto my dignity as I go to search for my long cloak.

Before stepping out of the building, Sir Humphrey has one last thing to say.

"Now that he has, without question, been informed of Hervé Gaynard's murder, your husband's place is by your side. I hope he returns to Spitalfields soon for your sake – and his."

As I march out of number four, Bow Street, ignoring the shouts of the newspaper writers, I ponder Sir Humphrey's admonishments and threats. The most ominous was, "You of all people shouldn't be privy

279

to these conversations." Who has given Sir Humphrey and the Bow Street investigators information that needs to be concealed from me?

I reach Fournier Street before sunset. There's no sign of the Montagu carriage outside, but it's still fairly early, I tell myself. The carriage traffic in London on a Saturday would make the eastward drive slow going. Inside, I find only Pierre and Daphne. Apparently, Jean came to work this morning but left after two hours because I hadn't returned. Caroline never appeared at all. There seems little doubt that my silk design business is in danger of collapse. If my name is not mentioned in the coroner's inquest – and that's an enormous "if" – I must work hard to rehabilitate it.

The experience of the next two hours, taking care of Pierre on top of many necessary chores, puts this future to the question, though. Without Sophie or George in the house and Daphne unable to cope with stairs, the household responsibilities must fall to me. I will have to hire at least one other servant, even though I can't face that right now. I'm also uneasy about money. After meeting with Nicolas Carteret and confirming the work contract, I will need to prepare a plan.

"Lay a third place at supper for Mr. Sturbridge," I tell Daphne.

I know my husband better than anyone else in the world. It's impossible that Thomas would not come to me tonight.

Pierre is delighted to hear Papa will be back. I play a game with him in the parlour before supper, but both of us are distracted, listening for the turn of the key in the door, followed by Thomas' cheerful shout and quick, light step. The street is noisy tonight, even more than usual, and several times I turn, thinking, "Here he is at last," as a surge of relief courses through me.

But it's never him.

With reluctance, Pierre and I start supper. I've hardly eaten today, and Daphne's meat pie is delicious, yet I possess little appetite. After doing my best to force some down, I give up.

When it's past ten o'clock, I change into my nightclothes with heavy limbs, forced to accept the fact that all my excuses for his being late to Spitalfields are just that – excuses.

My husband has abandoned me.

Chapter Twenty-One

After a fitful night, I wake to a Sunday morning of freezing rain rattling the windows. If it were a bit colder, snowflakes would silently caress the glass, a much-preferred experience. My nerves are so strained, it feels like someone is attacking my house.

Mercifully, Caroline comes to work. She looks as if she's lost weight and slept not at all since I last saw her, but I suspect I am her mirror image. Jean does not appear at his usual time. I know he was in the workshop briefly yesterday. I expect him to show himself soon. He knows we must work through the weekend to make the schedule.

In the meantime, Caroline and I lay out sketching paper, dishes of water, brushes and watercolour cakes. I'm deeply grateful for her silence. I don't know what's going to happen with the investigation into Hervé Gaynard's murder. My husband doesn't seem to wish to live with me anymore. Two of my servants are in jail. Any hope of developing a painting career under the sponsorship of Joshua Reynolds has vanished. All that I have is my son, my house and my silk design business.

The rain subsides as we settle into the work. Just as it does so, a group of people on Fournier Street make loud noises. Not eager tradesmen hawking wares, no, it's much more chaotic, even angry.

"It's Sunday and too early for public drunkenness, or is it?" I say with a sigh.

Caroline shrugs uneasily.

Bang. Bang. Bang.

Someone pounds on my front door. I hurry to the staircase and call down to Daphne, "What's happening? Do they declare themselves?"

"No, Madame Genevieve," she shouts up the stairs. "But they're calling for you."

"Is it the constable? Someone from Bow Street?"

"I don't think so."

I fight to think clearly. This could not be Londoners outraged by my role in Gaynard's murder. Mr. Oliver told me the coroner's inquest was scheduled for one o'clock in the afternoon the following day. Nor could it be a reaction to newspapers. Unless something has gone horribly wrong, no one on Grub Street knows about me.

George would have been useful just about now. He was foolish and fearful, but that was rarely obvious from looking at him. He was a young, fit man, and just his standing in the doorway would make troublemakers think twice. Three women and a small boy are not able to launch a defence against a group of angry men. The only course of action is to keep the door closed and locked.

I know there is no possibility of this mob forcing the door open, but nonetheless, I make my way to the ground floor, my palms moist with fear.

"We want to talk to you, Genevieve Planché!" shouts someone from outside.

Pierre starts to cry, and I soothe him, saying it's only a silly game.

After a few more minutes go by and the people haven't dispersed, I give Pierre to Daphne and edge toward the window onto Fournier Street. I need to know who I'm dealing with.

Peering past the curtain, I see five men of various ages and a woman. They look upset and angry, but they don't resemble ruffians. They look like Huguenots. In fact, I recognise the oldest man. He's Francois Orgier, the father of Jean.

I rush to the door to unlock it.

Daphne shouts from the end of the hallway, "Madame Genevieve, what are you doing? Please, we will none of us be safe."

"Something has happened to Jean; his family is outside. I need to speak to them!"

I do not bother to put on a coat or even a shawl. The cold, damp, foul-smelling air envelops me as I step outside and immediately begin shivering. I say, "I am sorry to keep you waiting. Is there something wrong with Jean?"

All their faces are twisted with anger. I'm not sure what my fiery young artist has done to make them so furious with me.

"She doesn't even know," says one of the men, perhaps Jean's brother, with disgust.

Confused, I turn to the one woman among them, dark haired and in her forties, respectably dressed. I am fairly sure she is Jean's mother.

"What's happened, Madame?" I ask.

She takes one step, then two and finally three, so we are face to face. Her eyes are red and puffed, her lips trembling, though not from the cold.

She raises her right hand and slaps me across the face with such force that I fly back against my own door. My shoulder hits the door jamb. I'm in such pain that I cry out, but it sounds more like the bleat of a sheep.

"My son is in Newgate because of you," she says, her voice hoarse.

"He confessed to murdering the Frenchman, Hervé Gaynard," says one of the young men.

"No!" I cry.

"The Bow Street Runners kept coming back to talk to him because they found out he had a fight with Gaynard at the Foundling Hospital. Last night, Jean said he went to Covent Garden and stabbed Gaynard because the man was blackmailing *you*."

These words hit me and seem to bounce off and dissolve. I can't take this in, I simply don't believe it.

"Jean would never kill anyone," I say, picturing the knife driven deep into Gaynard's chest.

"He *confessed* it – are you deaf?" the young man bellows, shoving my shoulder with the heel of his hand. "There was the first article about the murder in the newspaper last night. What will they write when they learn of Jean's confession?"

Now, it's the turn of Francois Orgier, who takes a step closer. "You have destroyed my son," he says, raw with a father's agony. "I should never have asked you to employ him."

"They hang murderers, that will be on your conscience," says the young man, lifting his hand as if he intends to push me again.

"Women should never run businesses," shouts someone. "Look what it leads to!"

The door swings open behind me, nearly knocking me into the Orgiers. Daphne flies out into the street, her apron flapping behind her in the stiff, cold wind.

"*Comment osez-vous vous comporter de cette manière?*"

Daphne stands not even five feet tall, but she is like a statue of righteous fury. The Orgier family is struck dumb.

"How dare you do this?" she repeats in English. "Madame Genevieve is a fellow Huguenot. You do not act like followers of Calvin but like dragonnades from the army of Louis! Hitting someone on the street? Shame, shame, shame. She did not send Jean Orgier to do violence. She has been nothing but good to him. If he learned violence from anyone, it was from his family. Everyone on Fournier Street can see that today!"

Daphne grabs me by the arm and pulls me back into the house, slamming the door behind us and locking and latching it.

"Look at your face," she says. "Why did they behave like animals?"

"Because Jean's in Newgate, and it's all my fault," I say. My knees are shaking so badly that I can barely walk.

Daphne calls out, "Pierre, I want to make a special treat for you – can you help me in the kitchen? I just have to help your mama with something first."

Her arm around my waist, Daphne helps me to the water closet. She combs my hair and dampens a cloth with cold water, pressing it to my cheek. "I may need to secure some ice."

"What happened to you on the street?"

It's Caroline, standing in the doorway.

"We need our privacy, Mademoiselle," snaps Daphne.

"No, I want to tell her," I say. "Caroline, it's just terrible. Jean is in Newgate. He confessed to the investigators to the murder of Hervé Gaynard. He must have gone there right from this house. It's unbelievable, I know, but—"

"No."

Caroline's face is ashen, her eyes wild with an emotion I can't identify. She opens her mouth, closes it, opens again as if panting for breath.

"No, no, no," she says.

Daphne insists that Caroline return to the workshop to calm herself. "Madame Genevieve was attacked by the Orgier family, I must tend to her."

Caroline turns and flees upstairs. "I'll come and talk to you shortly," I say weakly. I doubt she has heard me.

Daphne, after finishing with my face, leads me to the kitchen. "You've had a shock," she says. "I'll make you some tea, then you will rest."

"No, I have to go to Newgate at once to try to see Jean," I protest.

"Do you think you have any chance of being let in there for a visit?" asks Daphne, appalled.

"Then I will go to Bow Street, there may be someone there today. I will—"

A sharp knocking on the front door withers the words in my throat.

"Lord, give us strength, who is that?" Daphne says. She marches off to see, murmuring that no one with bad intent will be allowed over this threshold, only to return with the news that Nicolas Carteret is here.

After one more splash of cold water in my face and wrapping myself in my favourite shawl, I meet Monsieur Carteret in the sitting room, where Daphne has brought him to await me. I sit across from him and immediately feel I'm not welcome – and this is my home.

"Mrs. Sturbridge, at last, you have found a moment for me," he says. His tone is cold, but at least he's not physically attacking me. My dealings with my fellow Huguenots are improving.

Carteret continues, "I've been wanting to tell you how much I like the new designs, the flowers of the Mughal, and to increase the order further."

A surge of pleasure, the first I've felt in many days, fills me.

Catching my pleased reaction, Carteret leans forward and says deliberately, "But that's all changed."

My throat tightens.

"It has?"

"Jean Orgier's confession to murder and arrest is going to bring great scandal to Spitalfields and particularly to you. I was always unhappy with his presence in your workshop, but I never imagined Orgier capable of *this*. I can't be associated with you from now on, Madame Sturbridge. Our business connection is severed. It was a risk to come here in person today, but it would be a nightmare for you to be seen at my door."

To my horror, tears gather in my eyes. I cannot trust myself to speak.

"How could it be a nightmare to have my wife at your door?"

I whip around in my chair to see Thomas, his face red from the cold. He holds a stuffed satchel in each hand.

"I have a business to think of, Monsieur," says Carteret, stiffly rising.

"Then please think of it elsewhere," says Thomas. "I would ask you to leave."

"If you understood how many people depend on me, you would—"

Thomas drops his satchels and, his face darkening, walks toward the master weaver.

"Leave this house *now*," he orders.

Carteret stalks out, Thomas slams the door behind him and rushes back to me. "I came as soon as I could. My darling, what you have been through…"

Still unable to speak, I hold out my arms, and Thomas falls to

288

his knees, burying his head in my lap. His red hair is damp with the rain.

"I love you, Gen, I am so sorry," he says.

The tears come then, my chest heaves with sobs.

"I thought you hated me," I gasp. "You didn't come home."

"I didn't know about Gaynard until this morning."

"But they talked to you yesterday morning. Sir Humphrey Willoughby told me that someone went to Chiswick."

"Their visit was hidden from me!" He pulls back, his eyes blaze with anger. "The Earl of Sandwich did not want me disturbed, even if it was something that directly affected me and my family. Lawrence had an attack of conscience about it, he told me what he knew. I learned about Bow Street, that Gaynard had tried to draw you into a terrible plot. I have left his employment, Genevieve. I've had enough of this absurd work, this secret quest of his!"

"Quest? So you have not been working as the family's science tutor?"

"Oh, I've given lessons to young Montagu when he is inclined to listen. But the Earl of Sandwich offered me a sizable sum to get answers to questions that have no answers, that are best not even attempted by sane men."

Now I begin to understand.

"Was it the Philosopher's Stone?" I ask.

He looks stunned. "So you suspected… But no, it wasn't that, not exactly. The earl and his circle wanted the spark of life. That's right, I was charged with identifying the life force for all living things. The hubris of it! For them to ask – and for me to agree to it. I was mad. The alchemists have been searching for the Philosopher's Stone that produces the Elixir of Life for a thousand years. But of course, no one can unlock the secret to immortality. In the last twenty years, the search has taken a new turn, with all the experiments into electricity. There are those who believe that electricity is the spark of life – some fools believe it could reanimate dead flesh."

Thomas throws himself into a chair and runs his hand through his hair.

"The Earl of Sandwich thinks electricity possesses the power of life and death?" I ask.

"Well, it was not his idea alone. He belongs to a secret society, led by his good friend Sir Francis Dashwood. They call themselves the Monks of Medmenham, and they even wear monks' habits during their secret meetings in a ruined abbey."

I remember the Hogarth portrait of Dashwood exhibited at the Society of Artists.

"People think their society is just about drunkenness and fornication," Thomas says. "Of course, that goes on. But it serves their purpose for outsiders to believe there's nothing but debauchery, while they do discuss God, religion and the secrets to life. Dashwood began correspondence with Benjamin Franklin, the Philadelphia printer who conducted electricity experiments. The Dashwood group wants to take it a step further, drawing conclusions to the spark of life."

"They dress up as monks and think they can solve the mysteries of human existence?" I ask, dumbfounded. "They sound like naughty children."

"Whether it's Joshua Reynolds with his fugitive colours or Dashwood's secret society, yes, everyone believes they can conduct their own experiments into just about anything, Gen. But just as with Reynolds' colours, the electricity experiments didn't go as planned. So they decided to pay a natural philosopher, as they call me, to get them the answers they needed – and expected. And, finally, they demanded."

"Why didn't you tell me this before?" I ask.

"I had to sign a document swearing utter secrecy. At first, I hoped it would give us enough money that it would all be worth it. Later, Genevieve, when my work foundered, I was ashamed. Am I any better than Casanova with his plan to extract money from a rich woman with gibberish about immortality? I have run electricity experiments, and it can't bring any spark of life to animal or man. These are dangerous experiments too."

"That burn on your arm," I whisper.

He nods.

"Gen, I feel terrible that I shut you away," Thomas says. "These have been the darkest days of my life. When Courtenay forced us to France, when he stowed us in boxes for the ship across the channel, it wasn't as bad as the last three months. I can't believe you're not furious with me."

It's so hard to explain my feelings. His admission is frightening, his deceptions have been many, but it's as if we are drawn closer than we've been for some time. Marriage to a wronged genius has been... hard. As much as I haven't wanted to admit it, I've been a little lonely. Thomas' mistakes make him a fallible man, one for whom I feel the tenderest affection. The gulf between us is shrinking.

"Could you not reason with the Earl of Sandwich?" I ask.

"Oh, he never wanted to hear the truth. I was forced to run experiments on eels, frogs, even mice. It was a nightmare. He kept me practically a prisoner during the last week, with Lawrence acting as guard." He explained that the earl had demanded that Thomas finish his work and have answers for the Medmenham Monks before Christmas and his planned festivities at the Montagu country house, when Sandwich's young mistress would sing, showing off her beautiful voice for his friends.

"My entire life was subordinate to his Christmas party! When I left his service this morning, he told me he'd not pay me a penny beyond tutoring fees. Lord, I've failed you, Genevieve."

"No, you haven't," I insist. "We will find solutions together."

"With all the restrictions on my work, here in England, I thought if I could fulfil this commission for the Earl of Sandwich, we'd have enough money to leave London," he says. "I could publish a paper, find a serious teaching position. But I was fooling myself to believe that I could find the secret to the spark of life. I could never produce something to satisfy Dashwood and Sandwich's circle – and I refuse to abandon my family when they need me."

Just as he finishes his sentence, Pierre runs into the parlour and flings himself into his father's arms.

"My boy, my boy," says Thomas, holding him tight.

After I've drunk deep of the pleasure of our reunion, I tell Thomas I must see Caroline in the workshop. Perhaps I've gained enough strength to at least help her through the shock of Jean's arrest.

I climb the stairs to the third floor and find Caroline sitting at the work table, her hands folded. She has regained her calm if not her colour, being deathly pale.

"Jean will be freed, Mrs. Sturbridge," Caroline says.

"I pray he will be, Caroline, but it is difficult. He has confessed."

"The confession is false," she says flatly.

"But why would he do that?"

I take a closer look at my artist, the fierce tension in her eyes. "Tell me, how do you know that the confession is false?"

Caroline says, "Because Jean did not kill Hervé Gaynard. It was me. I murdered him."

Chapter Twenty-Two

I did not discover the details of Caroline's murder of Hervé Gaynard until Thomas and I delivered her sealed letter to Bow Street, and we learned its contents. What she said to me in the workshop was, "I understand why Jean did it, but I will not allow him to pay for the crime. And the world should know it was a woman who struck the blow."

I stood there, shaken and speechless, as Caroline rose from the table to leave. At the door to the stairs, she said, "It must be in two days, Mrs. Sturbridge. They will not find me before the appointed place and time."

I heard her determined steps on the stairs leading down, the door shut on the street. It was as if this were any other day at the workshop.

Thomas and I took her letter straight away to Bow Street. Sir Humphrey Willoughby was there, even though it was Sunday, discussing with Sir John Fielding the coroner's inquest to be held the next day.

"Another confession?" cries Sir John when I explain why we've come. "This is absurd."

But Sir Humphrey has a different opinion after he reads her letter carefully. It turns out that Jean's story has always struck Sir Humphrey as vague, while Caroline's letter contains the more convincing details. It was she who went directly from my house to Covent Garden to talk to Hervé Gaynard. She managed to slip inside and climb the winding staircase. Listening through the door, she was surprised to hear my servant, George, talking to Gaynard. After George left, someone else had business to discuss with the Frenchman. She waited a little longer. When she found an opportunity to speak to him alone, she attempted to plead and finally, threaten him, but all he did was laugh. The stiletto knife was lying on Gaynard's desk, and she was so enraged, she seized it.

In her letter, she wrote, "*It was not merely to protect Mrs. Sturbridge, the only person who has shown me true kindness, that I killed Hervé Gaynard, but to avenge myself on him for exposing my past life of degradation. The world is a safer and better place with his death.*"

Silence reigns in Sir John's inner chamber after Sir Humphrey finishes reading aloud. I feel moved and incredibly sorry, not to mention responsible. Thomas puts his arm around me while I fight back tears. Sir Humphrey misses none of it.

Her letter is confirmed by another source. After they question Jean that very day, he admits to making the confession in order to protect Caroline. The Bow Street men's questioning had made him fear that they would soon identify Caroline as the killer. He was convinced from the minute he first heard of Gaynard's murder that she had committed it. But because of the suffering Caroline has already endured, Jean decided to take her place.

When it comes to the terms of Caroline's surrendering herself, Sir Humphrey is greatly displeased.

In her letter, Caroline specifies that Jean must be released and brought at a certain time to a certain place in Spitalfields. That's what her "two days" meant. When she sees with her own eyes that he is at liberty, she wrote, she will step forward and submit to the authorities.

"A murderess has no right to dictate the sequence of events," agrees Sir John Fielding. "Does this woman not trust us to behave properly?"

I bite my lip hard to keep from speaking out. Few Londoners trust those in authority.

Just as Caroline had said, she turned out to be impossible to find before her set time for surrender. She'd left her home. The Bow Street men's search of Spitalfields turned up no clues as to her whereabouts. With resentment, Sir Humphrey said they would bring Jean Orgier to the corner of Brick Lane and White Lion Street at noon, as she stipulated.

The night before the exchange, I find myself tormented over what has happened ever since I received Joshua Reynolds' letter inviting me to Leicester Fields.

"My first instinct was to say no," I tell Thomas. "Why did I agree to go? Part of the reason was so that Caroline could have a glimpse of the art world of London. But Kitty Fisher and Hervé Gaynard were waiting for me – and they saw her. It's entirely my fault she was exposed to them."

"Your motives were nothing but good," says Thomas comfortingly.

"Were they? I don't know. Deep down, I still longed for the approval of someone like Joshua Reynolds. Without his support, it's nearly impossible for a woman to be taken seriously as a painter in England. That support comes with a price, I have learned."

Thomas says, "But don't you think that's the same sort of reasoning that led me to take the position with the Earl of Sandwich? It's the successful painters that anoint new artists and the nobility that funds research into the sciences. There's really no other way."

My throat aching, I say, "So does this mean an end to both of our dreams?"

"No," Thomas says, kissing me as I hold him. "It doesn't. I promise."

The next morning brings a feeling of security I've not known for a long time. The distance between us is gone at last. I have my husband back. But as we ready ourselves for the day, dread takes hold. I am glad that Jean shall be released but heartbroken about Caroline's imprisonment. If only there were a way for both of them to be free.

"It's quite dark today," Thomas says, peering out the window.

When we step out onto Fournier Street, the coal smoke smothers us like a filthy black blanket thrown over us. Within seconds, the stinging, itching air sets my throat afire, and I cough as hard as Thomas. A greyish-yellowish tinge to the clouds suggests something foul and rotting, like the underside of a five-day-old fish. A fine drizzle descends, but it's so cold that I wonder if today the rain will tip to snow.

There, at the corner on Brick Lane, stands Sir Humphrey. When he spots us, he scowls. "There's no reason for you two to be here."

"No reason for *you* to be here," I retort. "The murder of Hervé Gaynard was not motivated by espionage."

"It doesn't seem so," says Sir Humphrey. He walks over to us, so we can converse without any passer-by hearing. "But Gaynard himself was enmeshed in suspicious ventures that have no obvious financial gain. He was a blackmailer, a fraudster and a pimp, that is established. Why then, would he send an underling to report on the defences of the southern coast of England?"

"You believe that someone must have been paying Gaynard for the facts, or he'd never have done it," says Thomas.

Sir Humphrey nods grimly. But before he can expand, I spot two bright red vests across the street. Mr. Oliver and a second Bow Street man are standing in front of two other men. Squinting through the smoky, drizzly air, I make out Jean Orgier. Next to him looms a third man, tall and hatchet-faced and wearing a dark uniform. I suspect he was sent by Newgate.

My heart beats faster at the sight of Jean. He's slouching strangely, staring at the ground. Has he been mistreated? I take a step toward him, and Thomas grabs my arm. "Wait," he says.

But Jean is my worker. I feel so responsible for him, I want to protect him.

Two things happen in the next minute. A faint white cloud descends from the sky. This flurry of snowflakes settles on the heads and shoulders of the group standing rather awkwardly across from us. And the second thing is a young man comes up our side of Brick Lane and shouts, "Jean? Jean Orgier? Is that you?"

"Damn, this is why I didn't want a public exchange in a place where Orgier is well known," fumes Sir Humphrey.

Jean half-waves at the man who recognised him. That man is now excitedly alerting everyone around him to Jean's miraculous appearance in Spitalfields. Everyone in our neighbourhood has heard about his confession, though he was not named at the coroner's inquest on Monday. Sir John thought it best to hold back from the public who was believed responsible until Caroline was safely in jail. Nor was my name mentioned. Sir Humphrey had kept his word.

From the shadow of the towering Christ Church emerges Caroline, neatly dressed, her blonde hair concealed by a white cap. She crosses the street to reach Jean's group.

"She came out of nowhere," marvels Thomas.

As difficult as it is not to rush to Jean, it's agony to stand by as Caroline, my loyal artist, my companion of the workshop, the person who has looked up to me more than anyone in the world, walks up to her jailers to submit herself to Newgate and possibly the hangman.

Sir Humphrey is the one to dart across Brick Lane. He reaches Jean's group just as Caroline does. She doesn't even glance at the wigged, finely dressed man making his official presence known. Caroline seems aware of only one person. Even through the coal smoke, the snow and the crowds of people streaming past, I can feel the strength of feeling that passes between my two artists, Jean Orgier and Caroline Mowbray. They stand no more than six feet from each other.

The red-vested men, the Newgate guard and Sir Humphrey move forward as one so that they are no longer surrounding Jean but Caroline. They then turn around, to go back the way they came, south on Brick Lane, with Caroline as their prisoner.

When I hear the first shouts, I think it is Jean's friends, celebrating his liberation. But there are far, far more people than that, and all of them shouting, chanting and cheering. It doesn't seem possible that what I see pouring down from Brick Lane can be real, which is perhaps a hundred people. Some are holding objects aloft, but I can't make out what. Marching in front, leading the mob, is the giant with a patch over one eye, Guillaume of the Bold Defiance. Next to him, someone holds high a long cloth doll hanging from sticks. It is a figure in effigy.

We are about to be engulfed by a riot. To my shock, the Bold Defiance and their followers picked the same day and place to demonstrate against the master weavers as Caroline did for the trade with Jean. There's no sign of the warden or any constable.

"Genevieve, come," says Thomas, seizing my hand to pull me out of their path.

But I cannot move from this spot for a man runs past us, screaming, "How dare you defame me!" and it is Nicolas Carteret, pointing at the doll, which has the same frizzy blonde hair as the master weaver. They're mocking him as their chief enemy.

"You had some fine silks on the loom, Carteret," taunts a member of the mob who waves a white and blue fabric from a stick I realise is part of a weaving loom. "We'll enjoy them!"

I gasp, grabbing Thomas. Carteret's workshop is but two streets away. I say, "They've broken into his warehouse and cut up his silks, destroyed his looms."

Carteret flies across the street, his fists raised. I can't believe what I am seeing, one man going up against hundreds. Laughing and cheering, the rioters race to meet him.

But suddenly, part of the mob breaks away from the encounter with Carteret. Instead, they run toward the men surrounding Caroline. "See the Bow Street Runners!" one shouts. "Let's show the red vests what happens to them in Spitalfields!"

"And then we'll go to Covent Garden and burn all the arrest records!" shouts another.

"Burn them, burn them! Get the Bow Street Runners!"

The gleeful cheer is so loud, it feels as if the street shakes.

Before my eyes, a half-dozen men assault the group surrounding Caroline. Arms fly in the air. Oliver lands a punch and then leaps onto his attacker. Through it all, Sir Humphrey has his arm around Caroline, whose face is strangely blank.

In the chaos, someone throws Jean to the ground. He had run back to help Caroline. A man who must have thought him with Bow Street kicks Jean in the ribs, and he rolls over in agony, right into Brick Lane.

"No!" I scream, and with Thomas by my side, we run to save Jean. Thomas pushes Jean's attacker off him, and I throw myself on top of my limp artist.

Bang!

An explosion in my ears makes me shudder. Looking up, I see Sir Humphrey has just fired a pistol into the air. I had no idea he carried one. It makes everyone freeze for a few seconds, but as if the mob has one mind, they resume their violence. Twenty feet away, Nicolas Carteret is suffering kicks and punches.

"Sir Humphrey, they'll kill him – you must save the master weaver," I scream.

Sir Humphrey grabs the Newgate guard, who is retreating from the blows of the rioters, and orders him, "Don't let the girl go."

He steps into the melee and roars, "In the name of His Majesty's government, desist, or I will shoot you."

Guillaume is the first to back away, followed by others who cease the assault of Carteret, now sprawled, bloodied on the ground. Sir Humphrey has no one to support him. If they wanted to, they could swarm him too. But some instinct holds them back. No one expected an armed Westminster official to be on Brick Lane while they ran wild. Some of the rioters flee in various directions. Carteret may be saved, but the chaos in the street has just worsened.

I pull Jean up. He's dazed but conscious. As soon as he's on his feet, he whips around to see what's happened to Caroline. The Newgate guard is on all fours, blood pouring from his nose as a rioter hits him with a board. The Bow Street men fight off their attackers.

And Caroline has disappeared.

Chapter Twenty-Three

Nearly a month after the riot on Brick Lane, between Christmas and New Year's Day, Jean Orgier comes to Fournier Street. He moves a trifle stiffly, but other than that, he seems to have recovered. "No more wounds to my face, at least," he says, smiling.

It's hard for me to avoid thinking that Jean relishes his newfound fame. In the newspapers, he is the Spitalfields hero who confessed to murder in order to save Caroline Mowbray from arrest. The same writers have fashioned Caroline into a heroine like no other. She reformed herself from sin and worked hard at a respectable profession until a despicable Frenchman tried to drag her back into debauchery. Hervé Gaynard's murder was justified, all of London seems to agree. As their employer, my name ended up in the newspapers too. Even Sir Humphrey couldn't stop that.

As for the rioters, even though they inadvertently set Caroline free, there's no sympathy for them. A dozen were arrested. There's even talk of hanging the guilty on gibbets erected in Spitalfields.

"Do you think the Bow Street Runners will ever find Caroline?" asks Jean.

I shake my head. I've not seen her since that violent day in

Spitalfields. Sir John Fielding's men have come to question me several times. Was it possible, they asked, that she arranged for the trade with Jean to come at the same time as the riot? I told them that Caroline knew none of the Bold Defiance. It could only have been an accident of fate.

Sir John Fielding's men then watched my house for a couple of weeks, to see if Caroline appeared. She never did.

"I do worry about how she will survive," I tell Jean.

"I don't," he says. "She's the most intelligent woman in the world." He grins again. "Apart from you, of course, Mrs. Sturbridge."

Jean then comes to the point. He will no longer be able to work for me. I thank him for telling me, but my design business is no more. Even if Nicolas Carteret should recover from his serious injuries, I doubt he will wish to see me again.

It's not just the mutual antipathy between myself and Carteret. I could possibly secure other clients, given time. But within the next month, I shall bid farewell to Spitalfields. Thomas, Pierre and I are moving out of London, taking Daphne with us, of course. Thomas was approached by an acquaintance who had heard of a good teaching position at a boys' school in Nottinghamshire and offered to recommend him. The man, a young doctor, is unconcerned by my notoriety, for I have made appearances in the newspapers too, though only as the employer of Jean Orgier and Caroline Mowbray. This doctor's chief interest is sharing thoughts and ideas with Thomas on scientific matters, and I am deeply grateful to Dr. Erasmus Darwin for his generous action.

My own ambitions, whether to find acceptance as an artist or to run a silk design business, seem dead. Sadness closes around my heart whenever I think of it, but I am determined to conceal that from Jean during his visit.

"So what will you do to make a living?" I ask Jean and say, teasingly, "Every Huguenot must have a profession!"

"I will follow my parents' wishes and work for our cousin in Soho, who is seeing such success with pocket watches," he says. "I've caused my family grief, it's time to make amends. And they expect me to make a fortune. Only the wealthiest men in England can afford these watches. The silk business, well, I think it's in decline."

I can't disagree. The competition from France and other countries is driving down prices further, just as Nicolas Carteret feared. Also, tastes change. The delicate silk dresses with original floral designs aren't as popular as they were. One senses that rigorous times are coming, an era when many of us could be tested.

Before Jean leaves, I insist on taking him up to the workshop to select a sketch as a personal memento. To my surprise, he selects one by Caroline, the red flower of Grenada – the new English name for Le Grenade – that he criticised for being too bright.

I cannot hold back the question that has rolled around in my mind for weeks.

"Why did you make the false confession saying it was you and not Caroline?"

Jean stares at me as if astounded I would need to ask.

"I love her," he says.

He follows his declaration with a sad little shrug. "I doubt I will ever see Caroline Mowbray again, but I know for the rest of my life, I'll never feel for anyone what I feel for her."

I tell Thomas later what Jean said, that it was the shrug that dealt me the most powerful blow. "They fought every day," I point out. "I simply didn't see it."

My husband doesn't seem surprised. "For such a talented and

intelligent woman, you sometimes miss some obvious truths about the human heart," Thomas says lightly, with a kiss.

And with that, I fumble my way toward another truth, something that has so far taken the form of a fear dwelling in the shadows of my thoughts.

Some of the questions surrounding what happened to Thomas and me have found answers. Sir Humphrey came to our house to tell us that, after two more tense conversations with the Chevalier d'Eon, he believed that the chain of events was this: The French ambassador had months ago requested from aides and hangers-on in London a list of the whereabouts to all people living in England who could possibly be useful to France, following the treaty that ended the war. It was Hervé Gaynard who, with his society contacts, reported the whereabouts of Thomas. No doubt, he was paid something for the information. But Gaynard also told Miss Kitty Fisher, devoted to London gossip, and she passed on the knowledge of Thomas Sturbridge's talent with colours to her artist admirer, Joshua Reynolds. Kitty Fisher and Gaynard knew that we were invited to Reynolds' house in November and made sure to wangle invitations in order to see us for themselves. The chevalier donned his disguise so that he could observe as well. From then on, Kitty Fisher was the conduit between Gaynard and Reynolds concerning Thomas and myself, though he didn't realise it until I told the artist at Bow Street. I doubt there will be another Joshua Reynolds portrait of the infamous Kitty Fisher.

As for the final answer to the mystery, I have decided to secure it alone.

The following morning, saying I need to attend to some shopping, I slip out and hire a hackney carriage to Leicester Fields. I tell the driver to wait a short time, for there will be another destination to give him afterward, though I cannot give it to him at present.

I don't intend to leave the house of Joshua Reynolds without this address.

Ralph tells me that Mr. Reynolds can see me but only for five minutes. I'm taken to wait in the gallery, surrounded by paintings done in the grand manner, whether by his hand or that of the long-dead Italian masters he worships.

"What brings you here?" says Reynolds when he appears, still wearing his painting smock, his expression wary. "I can only give you a few minutes. I have an appointment with the Duchess of Grafton. She thinks a portrait might persuade her husband to stop divorce proceedings."

"I have a question that will take no time at all. Where can I find Sam Baldwin?"

"What makes you think I know his address?" he counters.

"Aren't you both from the West Country originally?" I ask. "Isn't that the basis of your friendship?"

He laughs shortly. "Bristol is a different world to Plympton."

"So, he is from a Bristol family?"

"You could say that."

I am not a gambling woman, but I throw the dice.

"Their wealth in sugar is no secret to me," I say.

He relaxes slightly. "Yes, the Baldwin fortune is the envy of kings. I never knew Sam before I came to London. But one fact he made clear to me, he does not want people to know his family background. He wants to be accepted on his own merits, such as they are."

I say nothing. I wait for Joshua Reynolds, knowing he won't dare to refuse me. Reynolds negotiated hard with Sir John Fielding and other important people to have his name kept out of the Drury Lane murder. It became purely the story of Caroline Mowbray, not of the fugitive colours. I could have spoken out and altered that. I never did.

"The Baldwin family owns a house on Berkeley Square for the London season," he finally says. "It's on the opposite end from Lansdowne House. Pale pink stone. You'll know it at once."

When I step outside the house, I see a dejected Frances Reynolds disembarking from the grand carriage she hates so much. Her face lights up when she sees me.

"Mrs. Sturbridge, I've not heard a word about you from my brother, only Angelika Kauffmann! She's even written him a personal letter, if you can believe the forwardness. Some of his friends tease him that she wants to become Mrs. Joshua Reynolds. It's been difficult, he has been so short-tempered of late. I fear he prefers I desist my painting completely. Are you still intending to paint?"

"I am," I say, and in that instant, I know that it is not even a question. I have my path, no matter the obstacles. "By heaven, you should too, Miss Reynolds," I say with a ferocity that startles but pleases her. "Never ever stop painting. Do you hear me? *Never stop painting.*"

Berkeley Square is but a short distance for my carriage. And Reynolds is right. One corner house, built in light pink limestone and marble in the latest fashion, dominates the other homes in this wealthy square. The sun sparkles on its brick surface.

A gleaming carriage is pulled up to the side, with liveried servants loading two large trunks on top and tying them down. A man, warmly dressed, strides toward the carriage but stops short when he sees me. A delighted smile lights up Sam's face, only to collapse into a worried frown. He peers behind me as if trying to see if I've brought anyone else.

His reaction confirms everything I suspected.

I cross the street and ask, as calmly as I can manage, "Am I saying goodbye?"

"Just ten minutes more and you'd have missed me forever," says

Sam. His gaze sweeps me head to toe. "Although you being here means I might be in serious trouble, I am glad to see you again, Mrs. Sturbridge."

The most confusing part of it is, my heart quickens, and I must force myself not to smile. I thought I would tremble with rage at this moment. But I find I am glad to see Sam again too, even while the truth tears at my heart.

"I've brought no one else," I say. "I just want to ask why you did it."

"Ah, I see."

A movement catches my eye. A dark-haired woman stands at a second-storey window, watching us. Mother or sister?

He turns around and spots the same person. His face darkens. A silent moment crawls by.

I take a step closer to Sam Baldwin. "Tell me, please. You were someone I always felt I could talk to."

"It's ironic, isn't it? I don't think I've ever felt as at ease with a woman as with you, Mrs. Sturbridge. And now I'm struck dumb. I suppose it's because I'm ashamed."

His brown eyes shine with misery as he says, "The most dreadful part is, it was an impulse, an idea that I didn't even think Hervé Gaynard would take seriously. It's important for you to know that I never dreamed he would try to force you to take the money, that he would kidnap your artist, Miss Mowbray, or threaten to blackmail you. He was to suggest it to you and your husband on behalf of an anonymous benefactor. That's all. He went far beyond what we discussed."

"You didn't account for his greed," I say.

"Apparently not."

"But still, you know everything that happened afterward," I say. "Few people do, it's been kept quiet."

"Some I pieced together through the newspaper accounts, some

307

I was able to discover through paying a man at Bow Street. They're not as incorruptible as Sir John Fielding likes to boast."

I'm not interested in Bow Street's vulnerability.

"You still haven't told me *why*, Mr. Baldwin."

He reaches up to push his black hair out of his eyes, blown there by the winter breeze, and then takes his watch out of his vest pocket and, after a quick check, slips it in again. That's it, the pocket watch that made me wonder about his discreet wealth, the watch that brought me here.

Speaking haltingly, he says, "That afternoon at the Foundling Hospital, you seemed so unhappy. I thought you were tied to this genius husband, this paragon of virtue. I saw Hervé Gaynard that night, and... well, he disliked your husband very much. He made him sound like an insufferable prig, to be honest. After a bottle of port, he told me how Joshua Reynolds was trying to persuade your husband to correct all his mistakes with the fugitive colours. It came to me: What if your husband *could* be corrupted? A large sum of money just might do it."

So in a drunken interlude, in a moment of jealous pique, he set loose Gaynard.

"You thought if my husband suddenly became corrupt, I'd leave him?" I asked.

"I wanted you to be free of him, yes." He takes a deep breath. "My motives were base and selfish. I know this must make me sound contemptible."

"I'm confused as to why you'd want to destroy Joshua Reynolds."

Sam Baldwin says, "With Reynolds put out of the way, George Romney might have had a chance to become the most successful artist in London. It's a chance he deserves."

"So this was done for a friend and not for yourself?" I ask sceptically.

"Reynolds hurt you as well. I knew that he would."

I shake my head. I think I'm very close to the truth but have not yet found it.

"I believe there is something else. You owe me nothing, Mr. Baldwin, but I wish you would tell me. I'll share it with no one."

Not meeting my eyes, he says, "I have no true talent for art, Mrs. Sturbridge. I know I will never create work that leaves a legacy. But creation comes in many forms. I thought by removing Reynolds, I could create a new landscape of artists, so to speak. It would be my way of shaping England's artistic future."

As bizarre and twisted as his reasoning is, I sense that this is much of what drove him.

"Of course, *you* could never do such a thing," he says. "That's why I'm so drawn to you. You're bursting with talent and ambition and passion but in its purest, finest form. I had a fantasy that with you by my side, I could at least be a better person."

I cover my eyes for a minute. Yes, the sun is bright. But it's the pain of this reality that blinds me. For whatever reason, Gaynard never told him about my past. He had such a mistaken idea of who I am.

"Mr. Baldwin, you really don't know me at all," I say.

"No, I suppose not. And now, we will never know each other. This carriage is headed for Bristol. From there, I will set sail for Jamaica and our plantations. I hate everything about Jamaica. The brutality, the conditions under which we harvest the sugar, it all sickens me. But I fear I will be spending the rest of my life there."

"I've already said I don't intend to tell anyone about your actions."

"Even if that's true, I deserve a punishment. You don't agree?"

I think about the people in my life who have suffered some form of punishment already, all because of what Sam Baldwin initiated.

Caroline will spend the rest of her days in hiding. Jean will have to live without her. And then there are Sophie and George. She pleaded her belly to the jailers and was released. George is the one who remains in Newgate, even though he was following the wishes of his wife. And of course, Hervé Gaynard is dead.

I take a last look at the man I thought a friend. Perhaps I had felt more than friendship for him, as he did for me. I took such pleasure in his company. Something happened when he kissed me. We are two people who could not be more different in background, yet a bond took form. I can't insult him by denying it.

"Goodbye, Mr. Baldwin," I whisper.

"Goodbye, Mrs. Sturbridge."

By the time I've crossed the square to find my hackney waiting, Sam's carriage has departed, moving smoothly on the road to Bristol.

It's a cold day, but I'm warmly dressed, the sun glows, the coal smoke has shrivelled and the streets carved through London are dry and hard. I dismiss the hackney driver, paying him what I owe so far.

This is a good time to walk. And if I know one thing, it's that I can make it all the way to Spitalfields.

The End

Author's Note and Acknowledgements

In this novel, I plunged into four overlapping worlds that existed in 1760s London: the ambitious painters making their mark; the spies moving in the city's shadows at the end of the Seven Years War; the remarkable Huguenot silk-weaving community in Spitalfields; and the chemists – "natural philosophers", as the word *scientist* was not yet in use – who were attracting widespread interest. The main characters of Genevieve Planché and Thomas Sturbridge, Hervé Gaynard, Caroline Mowbray, Jean Orgier, Sam Baldwin and Nicolas Carteret are fictional. But Joshua Reynolds, Frances Reynolds, George Romney, Sir John Fielding, the Chevalier d'Eon, Edmund and Jane Burke, John Montagu, Earl of Sandwich, Sir Francis Dashwood and Kitty Fisher are real people from history. The Mozart family, Giacomo Casanova, Theresa Cornelys and Giovanni Manzouli are some of London's best-known visitors from the Continent in 1764.

If London was the "it" city of mid-eighteenth-century Europe, Joshua Reynolds was its star artist. The founder, and first president of the Royal Academy of Arts, is believed to have painted the most subjects and charged the highest fees. Some believe he created the modern concept of celebrity. His use of "fugitive colours" in his paintings is also well documented and was commented on during his lifetime. A 1792 obituary lamented the "*chemic experiments, which, whatever brilliancy they may lend his colours for the present day, certainly will add to the fading powers of time upon the finest tints.*" His most complimentary biographer insisted, "*We do not love Reynolds less for his experiments – they sprang naturally from an eager nature that never tired of experimenting.*"

During this time, espionage simmered in London. Louis XV did issue an edict encouraging his diplomats in London, such as the Chevalier d'Eon, to interfere with the ambitions of the English. There were victims to the policy. Francois Henri de la Motte, a French army officer, was convicted of spying after he was caught sending information about the British fleet to France. He was sentenced to be hung, drawn and quartered at Tyburn in 1781. Another Frenchman who was busy spying on the English during this period was Charles-Claude Theveneau de Morande, whom I used as an inspiration for the character of Hervé Gaynard. De Morande was, in addition to a spy, a blackmailer, pimp and publisher. The Chevalier d'Eon challenged him to a duel when it was revealed that de Morande was running a wager on whether d'Eon was a man or a woman. De Morande managed to fend off the duel, which he almost surely would have lost, and later returned to France.

I am deeply grateful to James Faktor, publishing director of Lume Books, for his support of the novel and acquiring it for publication, and I also wish to thank Rebecca Souster, Aubrie Artiano, Imogen Streater and Miranda Summers-Pritchard, as well as Alice Rees for her editing of *The Blue*.

Special thanks are due to Emilya Naymark and Harriet Sharrard for their insightful notes on my novel. Without their generous assistance and the input of Rhonda Riche, Hans van Felius and Sophie Lechner, my book would have suffered.

I agree with author Walter Mosley who has said, "*A novel is bigger than your head*," and without the encouragement of these people, I couldn't have finished the book: Amy Bilyeau, Erica Obey, Kate Conroy, Kris Waldherr, Donna Bulseco, Adam Rathe, Laura K. Curtis, Annamaria Alfieri, Sophie Perinot, Elizabeth Kerri Mahon, Libbie Hawker, Judith Starkston, Susan Elia MacNeal, Dawn Ius, Ricardo Martinez, Evelyn Nunlee, Stephanie Renee Dos Santos, Daniela Thome, Theresa Defino, Max Adams, Michele Koop, Christie LeBlanc, Timothy Miller, Peter Andrews, Mariah Fredericks, Triss Stein, Laura Joh Rowland, Jen Kitses, Radha Vatsal and Shizuka Otake.

And finally, I'm grateful to Max, Nora and Alex for putting up with my historical obsessions.